ISLAND IN THE MIST

J V Briggs

Hadrian's Wall
Trust

ISLAND IN THE MIST

Hadrian's Wall Trust
East Peterel Field
Dipton Mill Road
Hexham
NE46 2JT

Cover design and typesetting by Raspberry Creative Type.

Printed and bound in Great Britain by Martins The Printers.

ISBN: 978-0-9927484-0-1

to
DUNCAN
for support and advice

REVIEWS FROM *THE FLAME OF BORGIAS*

SUNDAY TIMES
The Flame of the Borgias by Jean Briggs. Impressive first historical novel which sympathetically portrays Lucrezia Borgia's love affair with Venetian nobleman and future Cardinal. Restrained writing and deep research capture vividly the sense of evil, courtly intrigue, social fabric and romance and brutality of Renaissance Italy.

BARBARA BOURKE, *IRISH TIMES*
Heart sank at the thought of reading 'Flame of the Borgias.' In fact, I had nothing to fear. Miss Briggs is a specialist in Enlgish and Italian medieval literature and her extensive research for the novel has led her to portray Lucrezia Borgia not as an incestuous, scheming murdress but as the only attractive and normal member of an admittedly monstrous family. That was the first surprise. The second was that Jean Briggs has proved herself by her first book to be a novelist of very considerable ability.

The trade and bustle and wealth of sixteenth-century Venice almost assaults one's senses, as do the delicate, but no less richly described pleasures of the Tuscan countryside: the politics and intrigues of the courts of Ferrara and the Vatican vie with Venetian democracy, and Miss Briggs consummate understanding of this period in Italian history makes the plots and counterplots as clear and bright to the reader as the paints on Raphael's palette. Raphael, in fact, does figure in the narrative; he is seen in the two Pietro Bembo's idyllis garden near Padua, where he is feverishly sketching plans for a Cardinal's bathroom in the Vatican. It is touches such as this that make Jean Briggs' achievement of a fine first novel as deeply satisfying for the reader as it must surely be for herself.

VALERIE WEBSTER, *SCOTSMAN*
Italy seems to be enjoying a sudden vogue.[..]The obvious choice is the first novel by Jean Briggs set at the time of the Renaissance, Miss Briggs who has specialised academically in medieval lyric verse writes a lyrical love story.

Top Choice
This impressive first novel[...]has a splendid ring of authority.

ELIZABETH GREY
I particularly enjoyed Jean Brigg's remarkable first novel: The Flame of the Borgias a surprisingly tender love-story based on the still extant correspondence of Lucrezia Borgia (the Duchess of Ferrera) and Pietro Bembo, Venetian poet and nobleman. The author spent four years on research and translating the letters from Italian. The book rings with authority. It is crammed with authentic detail with the glowing colour, and brutality, of Renaissance Italy. The lovers' mutual passion was, of course, hopeless and hazardous-but very, very romantic.

CONTENTS

MAJOR CHARACTERS

FLAVIUS VALENTINUS PAULUS, commandant of the Roman
auxiliary fort of Alauna

His family and household:
LUCILLA, his wife
CRISPUS, his father
AELIUS, his steward
ALIS, wife of Aelius, maid to Lucilla
ARTEMON, a Sicilain Greek slave, secretary to Crispus,
father of Aelius

Military personnel inside Alana:
RUFUS LUGO, the senior centurion
QUINTUS, the adjutant
NORICUS, a section leader
LUPUS, a stone-carver
THE CHIEF CLERK
THE DOCTOR

MARCELLUS FABIUS GALLUS, commandant of the
fort of Ravenglass
CELIA, his wife
THE COMMANDANT of the fort at Hardknott
THE LEGATE, Sixth Legion, York
ELPHIN, a native of the island of Manannàn

THE EMPEROR HADRIAN

NOTE

This story centres round Alauna, a Roman auxiliary fort on the Solway Firth, in the time of the emperor Hadrian in the second century CE.

The site of Alauna is now part of the northern edge of the Cumbrian coastal town of Maryport – built in the mid-eighteenth century from stone taken from still existing walls of the fort.

The names of some of the second century commandants of Alauna are known to us from the altars which are exhibited in the Senhouse Roman Museum on the site. With the exception of the first commandant, Agrippa, who was the friend of Hadrian, we know nothing more about them than their names and places of origin.

The commandant, Flavius Valentinus Paulus is a fictional character, but many of his experiences reflect incidents which happened, mainly in the north-west of Britain.

Towns and places that were in existence before the Roman invasion are given their current English names. The Roman name is used only where no previous settlement is known to have existed, as in the case of Alauna. It is hoped that this will help the reader to identify distances and locations with ease. The Isle of Man is referred to as Manannàn, the ancient native name of which the present one is an abbreviation.

Excavation on the site is on-going.

Part One

FLAVIUS

I

In the coastal fort of Alauna, in the north-west of Britain, the prefect Flavius Valerius Paulus was preparing for his first Saturnalia as camp commandant. No holiday across the Roman Empire was more exuberant than the midwinter festival of Saturnalia, when for five riotous days the world stood on its head. Lights blazed until dawn. Strangers shouted the Saturnalian greetings of goodwill to each other. Dancing and music spilled out across the streets. Senators disported themselves in public like unruly schoolboys, and slaves, granted freedom for the holiday, strutted about, loaded with glittering finery.

Even in the Roman Army discipline was relaxed, daily weapon practice was suspended, and the men were served at the festive table by their officers. The Prefect was not a man who cared for over-eating or drinking himself into a torpor, nor did he greatly enjoy being with people who did, but with good grace he was willing to play his part in the traditional rites. In the absence of his own household of servants and slaves, who appeared to be starting their holiday with a long sleep, he found himself an old faded tunic that had once served him well at times of grape-harvesting. Wearing it unbelted as a servant did, he joined the other officers outside the granary where the quartermaster had stored the festival supplies (for which, Flavius had been somewhat startled to discover, the men had been required to contribute a monthly sum from their pay over the past year).

Rufus Lugo, the senior centurion, was standing at the top of the granary steps. Draped in a bedcover arranged like a general's cloak and with a wreath of ivy on his head in lieu of a conqueror's laurels, he appeared to have appropriated to himself the role of master of the feast. With a cheerful expression rarely witnessed on his face at any other time of the year, he was briskly distributing menial tasks to his superiors.

The commandant was required to deal with the extra wine rations. Flavius and the senior centurion not infrequently failed to see eye-to-eye on fort matters, and there was no denying the touch of malicious satisfaction in Lugo's manner as he handed over the keys to the wine store. It must be known in the camp that the wealth of Flavius's family came from their business in the wine trade, though it was a generation or two since any of them had humped barrels about on their own backs.

Flavius gave the senior centurion a long look and then bobbed his head like a good servant. 'As you please, general,' he murmured.

It was a long day. Flavius diligently shifted wine to the various barracks. The feasting began in the early afternoon; towards midnight, he was still filling empty beakers. He started collecting broken fragments of pottery in empty baskets – the shards were useful for scratching notes or for messages that could be thrown away. As he looked round for a place to leave the baskets, he saw the senior centurion padding towards him. The wreath was askew over one ear and he was wiping his mouth with the edge of the bedcover. In one hand he carried, somewhat unsteadily, a dish of local oysters.

'Prefect,' he called out, 'wait!'

The senior centurion may have been having his difficulties with Flavius, but he was not a man to deny praise when it was deserved.

'You have done very well, sir, very well, especially for your first Saturnalia in camp.'

Flavius thanked him, feeling rather like a schoolchild having an exercise assessed. He started to drag one of his baskets out of the way.

'No, prefect, you have done enough ... quite enough. Leave that.'

Twice Flavius had been addressed by his title as commandant of a provincial corps five hundred strong. He was not sure if Lugo had discarded the Saturnalian role-play, or was too confused to remember it.

Flavius said cautiously, 'My orders for tomorrow, general?'

'Oh, nothing more, sir, nothing more.' They were evidently back in the normal world. Flavius raised his hands. 'No privileges, please, senior centurion.'

'None given, I assure you, sir, none given.'

They were standing in the main street of the fort. At one end stood the principal gate facing the sea, at the other the headquarters building. Barracks lined the street on either side. From one block came the noise of rowdy singing, from the other angry shouts.

'Tomorrow, sir, half of that lot won't know what's happening to them and the other half won't care. They can look after themselves. Go home, sir, and enjoy what's left of the holiday, with your lady.'

The shouting had turned into a brawl, which had overflowed on to the veranda which ran the length of the barracks.

Flavius looked round in alarm. 'Can't do anything about that now, sir,' said Lugo, shaking his head. 'No rules, no discipline, during Saturnalia.' He lowered his voice confidentially. 'Still, I'm thinking we shall be able to find a few little items for up there.' He waved his dish towards the headquarters building.

Now that he had stopped working, Flavius was beginning to realise how cold the night air was. He was shivering. He was also exhausted, and the sight of the oysters was making him think that he never wanted to see food again. His mind was a blank. He couldn't grasp what the senior centurion was talking about.

'The headquarters building?' he murmured, turning his head towards it.

It was flanked on one side by the quartermaster's granary, and on the other by the commandant's villa. Affixed to the walls of all three buildings were a row of brackets holding torches. In the black night these burned with steady, clear flames, lighting the stones of the street beneath and casting a long, pale glow between the barracks. Flavius wished he could scoop up a handful of that bright warmth and clasp it in his fingers.

Lugo, offended by his lack of attention, said curtly, 'After Saturnalia, first thing.'

Immediately after the celebration, thought Flavius, was the day of the winter solstice, which by Roman calculation fell on the twenty-fifth day of December, also the date of his birthday. But the senior centurion wouldn't know that, and he had probably never heard of the winter solstice either.

'Headquarters?' Flavius said again.

'Prefect's court-martial,' snapped Lugo. The cordial nature of their encounter a few moments ago was rapidly fading.

Flavius nodded without enthusiasm. 'Ah, yes. You, Senior Centurion, have responsibility for drawing up the list of charges.' He paused, listening to the sounds of revelry around them. 'Tell me, if army rules are suspended during Saturnalia, how can a man be charged with breaking one of them?'

Rufus Lugo had too deeply ingrained a respect for the army ever to offer an argument to his commanding officer, but nevertheless, when he considered him to be in error, he had a habit of sucking in breath through his teeth and then slowly releasing it.

Flavius heard a small hissing sound now. 'It may not, sir, be a matter of army rules, but there could be conduct which offends military decency.' Gratified by the phrase, which was of his own devising, he repeated it: 'Military decency.'

What on earth, Flavius asked himself, did that mean? But he stopped short of asking the question aloud. The senior centurion's long service deserved some degree of courtesy.

They stood together in silence. Flavius remembered the keys to the wine store. Earlier in the day, he had slipped them on to a piece of cord and tied them round his waist for safe-keeping. He started fumbling with the knot.

Perhaps Lugo was reminded that the other officers had disappeared some time ago, and only the commandant was still on his feet. Flavius heard him make another noise but it wasn't the irritating hissing sound. This time it was a low clearing of the throat, as if he was finding difficulty in choosing his words.

Finally he said, 'Would the prefect allow me to send Saturnalian greetings to his lady?'

Flavius, still worrying the knot with his cold fingers, didn't lift his head. 'Of course, yes,' he said briefly. 'Thank you.'

Flavius suddenly felt ashamed. He had loosened the knot, but went on pretending to be occupied with it. The senior centurion, who certainly had no cause to feel any warmth towards him, had gone out of his way to offer the goodwill that Flavius felt was the most precious part of Saturnalia, and he had been barely civil in return. He made a show of releasing the keys and handed them to the senior centurion with what he hoped would be a convincing smile of gratitude. . 'Lucilla, my wife, will be delighted' he said, struggling with the lie. 'Thank you again. I know she would wish me to send you her kindest thoughts at this season.'

Lugo gave one of his rare smiles. 'Get some sleep now, sir – though you'll be lucky to have much chance of it for the next few nights.' They both nodded and shrugged their shoulders ruefully.

For a minute the true spirit of the midwinter festival seemed to hang in the air between them like a golden chain. It was not in the nature of their relationship that this connection could last, but they had shared it briefly and been touched by it. 'Good night, general,' said Flavius gently. As he walked back under the torchlight towards his own door, he suspected that in the senior centurion's eyes he seemed to be a happy man returning to a warm and elegant house where a devoted wife sat waiting up for him. Nothing is as it seems during Saturnalia, so everyone said. Flavius sometimes privately wondered if the same might not be said of life itself: nothing was ever as it seemed.

Lucilla was not waiting for him when he opened his door.

II

The gaudy hours of Saturnalia were at last over, and with them the spell of crisp, dry weather. In the early hours of the winter solstice Flavius was woken by the rattling of a loose shutter in a fierce wind spiked with sleet. The lamp that usually burned all night was out. He lay surrounded by the thick darkness, listening to the onslaught of the wind. Tomorrow a white, clinging mist would be hanging low over the sea, and the damp air would creep everywhere.

This was the kind of day that the men under his command hated; black-eyed and olive-skinned, they had been raised in the blazing sunlight and dry, dusty air of Spain.

They were part of the provincial force that made up the auxiliary corps which, in forts along the empire's borders, supported the elite companies of Roman citizens serving in the strategically based legions.

It was not the policy of the Roman Army to deploy provincials on their home territory. Flavius's Spaniards had thus found themselves in the north of Britain.

They had been recruited as his First Cohort of Spaniards by the emperor Hadrian himself who, when it suited him, was pleased to declare himself a Spaniard. 'I am a Spaniard among Spaniards,' he would cry, throwing out both arms as if to embrace every one of his recruits.

That was not entirely true, of course. His family did own vast olive-producing estates in Spain, which they had acquired when it became a province of the Roman Empire, but they came originally from a town in the Po Valley. Hadrian himself had been born in Rome, and brought up to follow his father and grandfather into the Roman Senate. There were times when, towering above everyone else in his imperial gold and purple, he liked to murmur that he was 'but a senator among senators'. This – delivered to a Senate with a cynical core that laughed at his rustic accent and did not wish him well – failed to elicit the acclaim he could expect to receive on the recruiting field.

On Hadrian's orders, and supervised by engineers of the Sixth Legion from York and the Twentieth from Chester, the First Cohort of Spaniards built the fort of Alauna on a green bluff overlooking the Solway estuary. While working on his plans for the western end of the defensive wall he was erecting across the north of Britain, Hadrian used as his base the house intended for future commandants. He could happily eat a soldier's rations on campaign (a soldier among soldiers), but his tastes were not simple. He had an obsessive passion for Greek art and Egyptian luxury, and the villa at Alauna was finished in a style that reflected these preferences.

He stayed there from spring to late summer then departed for Judea, leaving his Spaniards to cope with their first winter in one of the most desolate parts of his empire. Flavius suspected that few of them, if any, had ever been further away from their farm or village than a local market, and it would never have occurred to them that anywhere in Hadrian's empire might not be the same as Spain. Even now, after eight years, it seemed as if the annual coming of winter was a shock to them.

When his circle of acquaintances had learned that Flavius was planning to leave for Britain, they expressed amazement and dismay. People who had never been nearer Britain than the shores of the Tiber described to him the country's bitter cold, the incessant rain, the thick woods full of ravenous bears. Flavius was touched by their concern, but in no way persuaded to change his mind.

For Flavius was not a Spaniard. He was not even a native of Rome. He was a northern Italian, born on the edge of a lake which lay among the foothills of the Alps, and his light-coloured hair suggested somewhere in the past a strain of Celtic Alpine blood. He was used to cold weather and to rainstorms so fierce that as they swept the lake they wrecked boats. He loved mountains and beaches, snow and sand.

When he first rode rode towards Alauna, tired and not a little apprehensive, and then saw the settlement itself, he felt a moment of excitement. The stretch of water in front of the fort was much, much wider than the lake at Stresa, the mountains beyond not so high ... but he would be living beside water again and in sight of mountains.

As he settled into his life there, he watched with wonder the changing colours of the sea. On some summer evenings, in a golden sunset, the water reflected the rose and apricot colours of the clouds. Driven by strong winds, choppy green and brown waves broke in drenching white spume below the fort, and if a weak ray of sunlight could slip through the ragged edges of storm clouds it left briefly shining pool of silver. Then on cloudless, windless days, azure-blue silk lay across the estuary.

Lucilla liked colour, and Flavius had hoped she might derive as much pleasure as he did from walking along the shore or standing on the bluff outside the fort. He took her there one sunny afternoon when he was sure that they would be able to see the mountains on the opposite side of the estuary, and perhaps, if they were lucky, the island to the south that was only visible on clear days.

Against his advice, she'd insisted on wearing a pair of the currently fashionable sandals known, Flavius had been told, as Persian slippers. Lucilla's were made of purple leather with decorative gilding, and she kept glancing down at them in delight as they walked towards the coastal gate.

They passed through the gate-house and crossed the road which served the fort on its way to Carlisle. On the other side was the grass verge leading to the edge of the bluff.

Lucilla was not happy. 'The grass is damp!'

Flavius prodded a tuft with the toe of his boot. 'Hardly.'

He took a stride forward. The view was perfect. 'Lucilla, look how blue the water is. And, see – on the horizon.' Even the island was there for them today, a long, low shape under a string of white clouds.

She was lagging behind. He stepped back and eagerly caught hold of her elbow. 'Lucilla, can you see it?'

One of the purple shoes slipped. She screamed and pulled her arm free. 'My shoes! You've ruined them.'

Flavius was beginning to realise that Lucilla's declared interest in colour was limited only to what she chose to wear. The sea stood no chance by comparison.

'Look at my shoes, look at them!' she was shouting. 'Take me back. Now.'

Flavius felt a strong urge to shake her and ask why she had to be so wilfully foolish as to wear sandals that were meant for marble pavements in Rome, but what good would that do? He lifted her up and carried her back to the gate-house. The guards on duty, who had heard her shouting, gazed fixedly at the road in front of them, at least until the commandant was out of sight.

Flavius then felt guilty for being angry with her. He knew she was wilful, and he was the foolish one for thinking she would ever be interested in sharing something that mattered to anyone else. Later in the day, when the tears of temper had subsided into sulking, he offered to have a pair of ankle-boots made for her to use around the fort. He was sure he had seen the centurions' wives wearing something of the kind, so one of the leather-workers in the camp had probably made them. They would draw him a diagram.

Lucilla looked at him in disgust.

His next suggestion was even more unfortunate. His mother, he remembered, had little boots made for the country. They could order a pair from her shoemaker in Rome.

Lucilla's temper flared again. 'I don't choose to dress like your mother. Who would?'

From then on, Flavius walked alone on the shore. When winter approached he acquired one of the hooded, knee-length goatskin capes that the local men wore. In the growing settlement that clustered against the northern wall of the fort, he found a shop that provided him with long, thick, native-style boots. Dressed like this he could keep warm and dry in any weather, and this was how he saw the first fall of snow on the mountains.

He was surprised that he met so few of the other men from the fort on his walks. Occasionally he saw one of them in a boat with a local fisherman or looking for oysters. At times army wagons passed him delivering supplies to nearby fortlets or milecastles, but they were certainly not particularly interested in the beauty of their surroundings.

This was evidently the last thought in the minds of his men when they argued in the fort bath-house and in the settlement taverns about their commandant's preoccupation with the shoreline. It was eventually concluded, after the suggestion that he had been searching for sea-monsters or mermaids had been rejected, that he was expecting a sea-borne invasion from the uncharted stretches of the western sea. But was there any habitable land out there? There was reputedly Ireland, but where was that exactly? And what about that island that came and went? Wasn't that Ireland?

Flavius, in bed in his dark room listening to the wind, drowsily letting thoughts of the sea and the island wander through his mind, was almost surprised that his men had actually noticed the existence of the island, given their usual indifference to things around them. But then he too, he admitted to himself as he drifted back into sleep, felt interested in the elusive island.

When he opened his eyes again, he wasn't sure if he had slept for a few minutes or much longer. He could no longer hear the broken shutter, so someone had presumably dealt with it. Perhaps the household was already stirring. Yet the room was no lighter.

People at home had been anxious to warn him about the cold, damp weather of north Britain, but nothing had prepared him for the amazing length of the hours of darkness at the turn of the year. By the time that the first fragile grey streaks of dawn appeared, the camp had already been following its routine duties for two hours. After noon, it was barely three hours before the light faded. The sun, if it did come out, was little more than a blurred disc of pallid silver on its shallow orbit.

Flavius hated having to leave his bed in what seemed to be the middle of the night; but that was not yet, he hoped, not just yet. Then he realised that he could feel the room getting warmer, which meant that his household was not only stirring, but had already been busy for quite a while.

It was morning. It was his birthday. He was thirty-one.

If he had any doubts about the time, they were dispelled by the faint sound of a trumpet. It was the end of the night, it was the end of the holiday. Army routine had been resumed, and that meant for him, as commandant, presiding over the morning's court-martial. He buried his head in his pillow.

Sometime during the night the sleet had turned to rain. Large drops were hitting the plants in the inner courtyard outside his room and even pattering on to the paving of the portico which surrounded it.

Flavius began to face the prospect of the cheerless birthday morning ahead of him in cold, dripping, remote, pitch-black Alauna. Before long he would be perched on the dais in the headquarters' gloomy, torchlit assembly hall, with an aggrieved Lugo hissing at his back, passing judgement on so-called 'offensive acts', which were in reality too trivial for any reasonable man to take action against; and before that everyone – officers, guards, men on charges – would have to go through all the saluting and elaborate manoeuvring that was required before anything else could proceed. By then, they would all be drenched.

Early in life, Flavius had realised that the worst day in the whole year on which to have a birthday was the twenty-fifth of December. It was one of those forlorn, lacklustre days that follow a glorious, hectic public holiday: when the world was struggling to adjust to the sober habits of everyday life, when the days of over-indulgence were taking their toll, when the jolly pranks of Saturnalia were an embarrassing memory. Flavius's parents, nevertheless, feeling that their son deserved his special day like other children, settled on the fancy of giving lavish parties for him on the day of the summer solstice instead, with picnics on the lake, clowns to entertain everybody and races along the beach.

Yet on his actual birthday morning there were always little treats and surprises, and as he grew older there were trips with a few close friends through the snow to a quiet meal in a lodge owned by his father, among the foothills on the far side of the lake.

Flavius had grown to love these modest celebrations. All the people who had shared them with him were now a thousand miles away, though he had hoped to arrange something similar inside Alauna with Lucilla and perhaps some three or four new friends that they might have made. But his wife had been difficult about finding new friends here, and anyway she had forgotten his birthday. With the present friction between them he had no intention of reminding her – especially as he was not quite sure that she hadn't in fact remembered all along and was merely pretending to have forgotten.

The irony of all this was that the trouble between them had arisen from his trying to do something special to please her.

He came from a family that always kept the old winter festival custom of giving gifts. At home, Flavius would ride out to deliver gifts to relations and old friends he would probably not see again until the next Saturnalia. Likewise he gave gifts to all his servants and slaves. For Lucilla that year he'd planned a gift that he hoped would be a lasting pleasure to her, and perhaps compensate her a little for the life in Britain she detested. He was so delighted with his choice that he was foolish enough to tell her that there would be a surprise for her at Saturnalia, though not what it was.

It should have arrived by the end of November, but now in late-December it still had not come.

Lucilla, her disappointment turned to spite, accused him of forgetting to buy it, of never meaning to buy it in the first place, of caring more about presents for his slaves than for her.

He heard footsteps approaching his door. It was gently pushed open. A slice of light released at last from darkness the bronze corner of a chair and half the painted panel of a chest.

Flavius sat up in bed. 'Lucilla?' he whispered.

A man's voice said, 'Push it harder, boy. Look, like this.' The door swung open under a heavy thrust, and Aelius, the Greek steward of Flavius's household, appeared on the threshold.

III

Aelius peered into the room. 'And what,' he demanded of the world in general, 'has happened to the lamp in here?' His tone suggested bewilderment that any article acquired for a household under his control should have had the temerity to fail in its function.

Flavius slid back under his covers. Aelius removed the lamp from the boy who was lighting his way for him and advanced towards the bed. He was followed into the room by two more of the house slaves, one carrying a bowl of steaming water and the other a tray with freshly baked rolls, fruit and honey.

Flavius put a hand above his eyes to shield them from the lamplight.

'Ah,' said Aelius, 'the prefect is awake.' He inclined his head. 'May I offer the prefect my felicitations on the occasion of his birthday?'

Flavius nodded his thanks.

Aelius made a signal to the two slaves. 'Good morning, prefect. Our felicitations on your birthday,' they said, more or less in unison.

Flavius withdrew a hand from under the covers and waved it at them. 'The bread,' he murmured, 'lovely smell.'

'May I remind the prefect,' said Aelius, 'that he is expected shortly in the headquarters building?'

'I know that,' said Flavius.

Aelius glanced at the boys. 'You can put those things down now and go. Take that lamp with you, there's good lads, and see if you can find out what's wrong with it.'

He waited until they had closed the door behind them, and then he kicked the bed. 'Flavius, get up. Now!'

Flavius groaned. 'It's so dark.'

'It's dark for everyone. It's the shortest day of the year. Now, hurry up.' The steward turned his head. 'That was the second trumpet. When the third one goes, we want you inside the headquarters building.'

'They can't start without me.'

'True, they can't,' said Aelius, 'but imagine the satisfaction it will give your friend ...' he rolled his eyes '... the senior centurion if you fail to arrive on time. You will be seen as lacking in self-discipline, indifferent to army ways.'

Flavius felt obliged to admit, 'Aelius, he went out of his way to offer seasonal greetings to Lucilla and myself.'

Aelius dismissed the interruption. 'That was only Saturnalia. Nothing to do with anything that really matters.' He continued, 'You are supposed to care so much about the welfare of the men, but think nothing of keeping them standing in the pouring rain until you choose to make an appearance.'

Flavius pushed back the covers and reached for one of the rolls.

He and Aelius had been born in the same house, in the same year: Flavius the privileged son of an affluent father, Aelius a slave, born to a Sicilian-Greek scholar forced to seek employment by selling himself and his wife into slavery. Aelius was the elder by five months. They had been brought up together: eating together, playing together, learning their first letters together under the tutorship of Aelius's father. As they grew older and began to understand their difference in status, Aelius gradually slipped into the role of Flavius's personal slave. He carried his master's things for him, brushed his hair and made sure his tunic was clean when his parents sent for him; but at the same time, being senior by birth, he regarded Flavius as his charge, to be protected, guided, and, if necessary, instructed. In time, when Flavius embarked on the course of education which his position demanded, Aelius walked behind him in the street carrying his cloak and writing materials, but sat beside him in his classes where they laboured over the work together.

At eight years old Flavius had decided that Aelius was his best friend. He had never found any reason to change his mind.

When he married, it went without question that Aelius should take charge of the new household. He gradually took over from Lucilla the chaotic household accounts, which he managed with an impeccable honesty that was rare in slaves. Staff discipline and rotas, which were a mystery to her, were soon his responsibility also. Whenever other people were present Aelius behaved to Flavius with deferential courtesy, but when they were alone together they talked as freely to each other as the boys they once were.

Flavius needed Aelius to be formally accepted from the beginning as the steward of the commandant's household when they arrived in Alauna. Then he began to realise how unfair it was that Aelius, because he was a slave, had no choice about the way his life was to be spent for the next two years. He knew for a fact, said Flavius, taking the problem to his father, that Aelius hated cold weather. His father provided a solution: buy Aelius his freedom. Then he could be offered the position together with a suitable income and make his own decision whether to stay in Stresa or go to Britain.

Aelius seemed at first startled, then affronted, that anyone could ever imagine he wouldn't follow Flavius as a matter of course. Finally his mood changed to one of almost wild delight. It transpired that he had suddenly realised that, no longer a slave, he was now able to marry; he could admit to himself and to everyone else that for some time he had loved in a hopeless way one of the slave-girls whom Lucilla had brought with her on her marriage. While Aelius was struggling to collect the money to buy her freedom, Flavius bought it as his wedding present.

Aelius and Alis, his new wife, with most of the rest of the household and the baggage wagons, set out for Britain ahead of Flavius and Lucilla. By the time the commandant and his wife arrived, Aelius had the house in meticulous order, had sorted out the peculiarities of the heating system, and was on cordial terms with the best of the camp bakers and the chief clerk in the headquarters building. Within a few weeks he had acquired enough of the local dialect to find himself at home in the settlement, and enough Spanish to be invited to use the soldiers' bath-house just outside the fort walls.

Yet whatever the weight of his other responsibilities, Aelius refused to let anyone else act as body servant to Flavius. With the commandant washed and shaved and starting on his second bread roll, Aelius opened the chest that held Flavius's military dress and laid out the various items on the bed.

'One tunic or two?'

'Two? Why should I want two?'

'It's a cold morning, that's why. I'm wearing two.' He lifted the sleeve of his tunic and showed a second one beneath.

Flavius looked scornful. 'Why should you need two? You spend most of your time inside this house where you can walk from one warm room to another.'

'*You* can walk from one warm room to the other. *I'm* working. I have to rush round that courtyard out there, and the wind chases me, and the rain chases me.' Aelius brushed one shoulder as if it had recently been splashed by cold drops of rain. It looked dry enough to Flavius.

It was understood in the households of both Flavius and his father that Aelius disliked cold weather, but his repeated insistence that this was due to his sensitive Greek blood was a long-standing source of amusement. Even Aelius himself had been known on occasion to say it with a wry smile.

Not on this occasion, however. 'I am Greek. My blood is more sensitive than yours.'

'I had heard,' said Flavius.

Aelius was folding the rejected second tunic in a somewhat aggressive manner. 'Your emperor Augustus used to wear four tunics in the winter, and that was a Roman winter, not one of these up here.'

'He wasn't Greek, so what's that got to do with anything?'

Aelius ignored this. 'Flavius, when we left the ship and rode up through the south of Britain, we saw quite a scattering of villas like this. Perhaps not as large but Roman-type houses. Here in the north there are none. The natives all live in round stone houses with thatched roofs ... even the better-off people. And do you know why?' He was walking round Flavius, threading laces, tightening straps and fastening buckles. 'You have to come to a place to know why the people do what they do.'

Flavius, not quite sure what to say to all this at this hour in the morning, commented, 'The south is more affluent, they have more resources, they've known us longer.'

Aelius shook his head. 'No,' he said, and then hesitated for a moment. 'Perhaps what you say could be true,' he conceded, 'I don't know. But what I *do* know is that those stone houses keep them warm in the winter. You can't feel the wind through such thick walls, and the thatch holds out the rain. Why should anyone want to build a house like this with an open courtyard up here?'

Flavius, running his finger under a strap that Aelius had pulled too tight, said impatiently, 'You know as well as I do why this house was built as it is. All Roman forts are designed to the same plan. It's an excellent idea because ...'

'Yes, yes, I know,' said Aelius, reaching out to adjust the strap. 'That's fine if your fort is in Syria, or Egypt, or Spain, or anywhere else where you need to be cool in summer ... and that applies to nearly all of them ... but not this one.'

'What do you want me to do? Pull this down and put up a stone one in its place?'

'Don't be ridiculous, Flavius.' Aelius lifted a long, red military cloak from the chest and shook out its folds. 'I was going to say that in those stone houses they have a central hearth for the fire. Why couldn't this courtyard here be roofed, and then instead of plants, which we can barely keep alive in winter, we could have a hearth?'

Flavius concentrated on fastening his sword-belt. Aelius had a wily imagination which Flavius thought probably derived from his Greek background, although this never seemed to have occurred to Aelius himself. He was given to throwing out wild ideas – or ideas that appeared wild in a Roman world that revered conformity –but from time to time were eminently sensible ideas that no-one else in the household had ever thought of.

Flavius was not quite sure which one this was, and there was no time then to consider it. Instead he said mildly, 'I believe the emperor himself took an interest in the building of this house. I don't think we can change anything. Aelius, if the cold makes you so miserable, why not wear the kind of clothes the local people choose? I wouldn't be without my goatskin cape. What about the long woollen trousers most of them wear? I would have no objection to you or anyone else wearing them around the house if it made life more comfortable for you in the winter.'

Flavius smiled, expecting a grateful response. There was nothing of the kind. 'And what about the lady?' Aelius always referred to Lucilla in a grave, polite voice as 'the lady'.

The lady,' he went on in the same careful tone, 'unfortunately believes that anyone in outlandish dress must be a barbarian, only marginally less savage than the wild bears hunted in the woods round here.'

Flavius frowned. Lucilla had never so much as seen a bear, and the 'barbarians' in the settlement were not of the class to hunt. All their time was spent in trying to scratch a living from fishing or brewing or baking. Aelius, even given his rather colourful way of expressing himself, was right; Lucilla was convinced that if the local people had given up their unwholesome savage ways they would now dress like Romans. Flavius wondered what interfering fool in Rome had planted that idea in her head. If someone had truthfully told her that some of the most savage acts in living memory had been committed by men in Roman dress, she would most probably not have troubled herself to listen.

He said, 'It was not a good idea, was it? Lucilla would never have accepted it.' But why, he thought, do I so often turn away from a sensible course of action because it might upset one of Lucilla's whims? Why do I behave as if I have to placate her for some past transgression, and then, when I do, feel aggrieved with her? She is my wife and subject to me in law. She owed him obedience.

Flavius had grown up with parents who lived pleasantly and easily within the Roman structure of marriage. Like his Spaniards, who had assumed that the whole world would be like Spain, he had taken it for granted that all marriages were the same. He, too, had been wrong. Lucilla had made it clear on many occasions that she had no intention of behaving like his mother.

Aelius, waiting with the cloak in his hands, thought that Flavius, splendid in the burnished leather and metal of his military dress, looked for a moment as if all the strength had drained out of him.

Then the door opened, a head appeared and nodded at Aelius. As the door closed again, he said gently, 'The escort has arrived. Are you ready, Flavius?'

Recovering, he nodded. 'Ready.'

Aelius stood behind him and fastened the cloak to his right shoulder.

'Arm.'

Flavius stretched out his left arm sideways. Aelius gathered up the cloak's heavy folds and laid them over his arm.

'Ready.'

Flavius bent his arm and slipped his thumb into the sword-belt at his waist. 'In this rain I would have been better wrapping it round me.'

'Did you want to scuttle up to the senior centurion like a rabbit of a recruit?'

'No.'

'No,' agreed Aelius. 'Anyway, it's no more than a drizzle now.' He smiled encouragingly. 'Commandant.'

He opened the door and they both felt the rush of cold air from the courtyard. Aelius made a point of shivering.

'It seems to me,' said Flavius, 'that where your delicate Greek blood is concerned, the only thing left to do is to pray for an early spring.'

'And which, may I ask, of the gods in your Roman pantheon deals with improbabilities?'

They left the courtyard and walked through the house to the atrium. A slave sitting beside the main door left his stool and stood ready to open it. . Another slave was waiting with the commandant's plumed helmet under one arm. Flavius paused while he and Aelius were still out of earshot.

'There's something I've always meant to ask you,' he said. 'Your father has Greek blood, which must be as delicate as yours, but I've never heard him even mention it.'

Aelius was unfazed, 'You know him, Flavius, long-suffering to a fault.' He made a sign for the door to be unfastened. 'When you get into the street, make it a brisk march,' he muttered.

'Because of the rain?'

'No! Why all this fuss about the rain? Remember, you haven't long before the third trumpet.'

The heavy door had been swung open. The two armed guards waiting in the dark street outside saluted their commandant as he appeared. Aelius accompanied him to the threshold.

As Flavius stepped out into the rain, followed by the slave carrying his helmet, Aelius inclined his head. 'May I wish the prefect a fruitful morning.'

He watched the departure of the escort party. The guards had positioned themselves in front of the commandant, armed as though to clear a way for him among a crowd although the street ahead of them that morning was empty. They were moving at a fair pace, the young slave having to make bold strides to keep up. Flavius walked as though every stone in Alauna was his, and the rain a blessing to him. The wind fluttered the red hem of his cloak, and the torches against the walls shone one by one on his light-coloured hair as the procession approached the headquarters building.

IV

Flavius was halfway across the elegantly porticoed courtyard of the headquarters building when he heard the third morning trumpet.

His escort had faded away in the darkness after an elaborate exchange of weapons drill with the men on guard at the entrance, which meant, Flavius supposed, that they had thereby relinquished responsibility for his safety to others. There was more chinking of metal as a line of men in the chain-mail tunics of the auxiliary cohorts – presumably those on charges – acknowledged his presence and he stepped gratefully out of the rain into the assembly hall.

An orderly relieved his slave of the helmet. Flavius thanked the boy with a nod and sent him scampering off with orders to get dry. This was a task that all the younger slaves liked doing because it gave them a chance to learn what was going on among the soldiers.

In daylight the hall was well lit by windows set high in the roof, but this morning it was still dark and lamps mounted on tall bronze standards cast circles of light hardly adequate for the size of the room. In the long wall facing Flavius were the doors leading to the most important administrative offices in the fort – his own, for example, and those of the senior clerks dealing with the unit's records and finances. The doors were ranged to either side of a deep alcove, which glowed with amazing brilliance in the surrounding gloom. This was the shrine, the sacred core of the camp.

Against walls panelled with crimson were ranged the gilded standards and the flags which represented the honours of the First Cohort of Spaniards. Beside them was an altar dedicated in the name of the commandant, on behalf of the whole company, to their chosen god, Jupiter. A fresh altar was ceremoniously dedicated every year on the third of January. The one now before Flavius bore the name of his predecessor, the man who had been in command of the fort during the previous winter. In a few days' time, in what was usually the coldest and bleakest period of the winter in this northern outpost, Flavius himself, arrayed not in military dress but in a white toga with a fold covering his head in his role as priest of the cohort, would unveil a new altar bearing his name and on it would offer a sacrifice to the god to ensure his protection and favour during the coming year. The new altar would then be placed in the shrine, and the old one buried along the border of the parade ground.

But dominating the shrine, overwhelming even the standards and the altar, was a larger-than-life gilded statue of the emperor Hadrian in the dress of a victorious Roman general, baton in his left hand, his right stretched out in command.

A fine grille protected the shrine. Two armed guards watched over it night and day, for in a cellar beneath the emperor's golden boots was a bank vault containing taxes collected in the district, the soldiers' pay and their personal savings.

Flavius crossed the floor to the shrine and briefly went down on one knee before the emperor's image. Then he moved towards the dais that occupied one end of the hall. His adjutant and Lugo, the senior centurion, were waiting for him. There were more salutes to acknowledge as he mounted the steps. The dais had been prepared with a high-backed chair and a table covered with a fringed red cloth.

Lugo started laying copies of the charge sheets on the table. The adjutant, seeing Flavius about to remove his wet cloak, hurried forward to help him. He was a very young officer, had been at Alauna only a few weeks as the first step on the ladder that his distinguished senatorial family, which included the wife of the influential legate in York, hoped would lead him to military honours. Flavius liked him; he was unassuming, eager to please and engagingly clumsy. He took the cloak, tried to fold it and tripped over the hem as he passed it to the orderly. He flushed with embarrassment as he felt Lugo's cold gaze on him.

Flavius tried to reassure him by smiling his thanks. He sat down in the chair. In the dismal light he could barely read the lists in front of him. 'I need a lamp here.'

The senior centurion was impatient. 'I can read the charges out loud, sir.'

Flavius observed Lugo already had one of the lighted standards conveniently placed on the dais next to him. 'I need to read them myself,' Flavius insisted.

He leaned back in his chair, indicating that nothing further could happen until his orders had been carried out.

In the absence of the orderly who had disappeared with the cloak, the adjutant precipitated himself down the steps of the dais and through the door to the commandant's office. 'Assemble the men in here,' ordered Flavius.

Lugo stared at him. 'The men outside, on charge? Sir, the usual procedure requires—'

'It is raining,' Flavius interrupted. 'I don't propose to allow any man to stand all the morning in the rain, waiting to be called by us.'

'All the morning, sir?' The senior centurion almost laughed. 'For Saturnalian misdemeanours? It shouldn't take us more than an hour.'

'The men in here at once, if you please, Senior Centurion.' Matters then proceeded with the commendable despatch customary in the army. The orderly appeared on the dais again and a lamp was set down on the table. The adjutant was back, sorting out the waxed wooden tablets on which he would record the commandant's decisions and testing the tip of his stylus for sharpness. The men were forming their new line at the far end of the hall and Lugo was returning to his place.

Flavius turned his attention to the charge lists. A moment later, he could hear the senior centurion breathing heavily behind him.

The man had entered the army as an orphan of sixteen. The usual recruiting age was eighteen, but a kindly soul had made an exception in his case. The army had become his mother and father: feeding him regularly, keeping a roof over his head, teaching him to read and write. He felt safe inside a world governed by strict discipline and tradition; one where, if he worked at his tasks, steady promotion followed. In return, he gave unquestioning loyalty and devotion to the only family he had known. When Flavius interfered with one of the camp's established routines, the centurion regarded it as an affront to both himself and the army.

Flavius, sensing something of this, would have liked to suggest to him that at times there was wisdom in flexibility. Instead he gave a brief smile and signalled for the session to begin.

The first charge, he noted, was for 'offensive behaviour resulting in unseemly brawling'. He seemed to remember the senior centurion telling him that during Saturnalia brawling was to be expected and ignored. Flavius lifted his head and was surprised to see eight men advancing towards the dais. 'Eight men on one charge?'

'Eight men on eight similar charges, sir.'

'Are they from the same section?' The six long barracks inside the fort were divided into ten sections, in each of which eight men lived, ate and slept.

Lugo nodded. 'Barracks B, section five. A close-knit group, sir.'

'And all eight are accused ...' Flavius checked his list '... of offensive behaviour, which is described here as dancing in women's dress?'

He frowned. 'You can't charge anyone with role-reversal during Saturnalia. I did it. You did it.'

'We did it in ways that are acceptable in an army camp. Theirs were not.' Lugo was getting impatient.

So was Flavius. 'There *is* no army during Saturnalia. The men are free to dress up as they please, like everyone else. In Rome you see men in women's dress everywhere.'

The senior centurion remarked that he had never visited Rome during Saturnalia, and from his expression it was clear that he hoped never to experience such a misfortune.

Flavius wondered why he had let himself make such a stupid remark. Lugo seemed to admit to himself at the same time that he could be more helpful. 'Perhaps, sir,' he said, 'the dress, though it was crudely done, could have been permitted. But what was wrong was what they wanted it for. I mean the dance, sir.'

'Ah, the dance. Yes.'

'They were trying to perform an old Spanish dance in which only women take part. It is a solemn dance and performed to mark sacred festivals. What they did was a travesty. They were drunk, and not all of them could remember the steps. There were lewd comments from their audience, and that was what started the fighting.'

'Ah,' said Flavius again. He had suddenly realised that during his wine rounds on the first night of Saturnalia he had come across these eight men and their attempts at dancing. They had been using one of the empty stables, and what had made him investigate was the sound of laughter. He had gone inside. Everyone there, it had seemed to Flavius, was happily and companionably drunk. The dancers were stumbling about in their trailing skirts and shaking with laughter when they bumped into each other. Their audience was certainly provoked to crude comment, but it was given and received in good humour. When they took to hitting out at each other no one was sober enough to aim a straight fist, which made them collapse into more helpless laughter.

Flavius found himself having to hide a guilty smile as he remembered it all. He controlled himself and addressed the senior centurion. 'I can't understand why this outbreak of brawling is being treated differently from all the other brawls which we agreed to ignore. Was it particularly vicious? Were weapons involved?'

Lugo drew in one of his deep breaths. 'No. Not weapons,' he said, almost grudgingly. 'That section, they cause a lot of trouble—'

'Trouble?'

'Well, nuisance. They get away with things they shouldn't get away with. This gives us a chance to even matters up a bit. I trust the prefect's verdict will reflect this.'

Flavius wondered what mischief had been going on. He said solemnly, 'If there are other issues to resolve, they must be dealt with elsewhere. I can pronounce a verdict only on the evidence before me today.'

He reached for the adjutant's wax tablets and stylus. He began to ask questions. The men at first looked uncomfortably towards the senior centurion, whose expression remained grim. As Flavius persisted, however, gently probing for answers, they turned their attention in his direction. When he had finished he sat back in his chair, re-reading the rapid notes he had made in the soft wax.

The dawn had come and light was entering the hall through its roof windows. The flames from the tall lamps were being extinguished.

Flavius waited until the task was completed, then erased what he had written with the flat end of the stylus before returning the tablets to the adjutant.

He looked at the men. 'You have been charged,' he said crisply, 'with performing a dance which, because of its sacred origins, caused offence in some quarters.' He paused. 'I am, however, persuaded that the clumsy and haphazard nature of the performance was in no way intended to mock or show disrespect. If you are prepared to give me an undertaking that you will in future avoid displays of this kind ...' he waited for the leader of the section to indicate assent '... then I am prepared to dismiss the charge.'

Before Lugo could release his breath, Flavius continued quickly, 'You are also charged with brawling. I understand that no damage was done to the stables and no one was injured. I will therefore regard this as nothing more than a brief skirmish, and have no choice but to dismiss the second charge also.'

He nodded to the adjutant to record these decisions. 'Next one, if you please, Senior Centurion.'

The parade continued. A few other charges Flavius also dismissed. On some he imposed penalties, but mindful of Saturnalia, these remained negligible. He felt the senior centurion's displeasure mounting against him.

Lugo was staring fixedly at his commandant's strange-coloured light hair. It offended him; it was odd, unnatural, as the prefect's behaviour sometimes also seemed. Lugo believed that an army court should be brief, sharp and predictable: in – charge read; penalty given – out. If occasionally a man was wrongly charged, where was the soldier who hadn't got away with something scot-free? It was, as he had tried to explain to the commandant earlier that morning, the kind of quid pro quo that everyone could live with. He had trained other commandants – less engaged than Flavius, to be fair to him – to follow the regular army way, but not this one. Flavius was disturbingly unpredictable in his judgements: sometimes unnecessarily lenient but at others severe, uncompromisingly severe, especially if the conduct of his officers was called into question.

The senior centurion soon became aware that when he had said the process would be over within an hour he had been gravely mistaken. He was ever the optimist, but with Flavius asking questions, encouraging the men to defend themselves, winkling out careless mistakes in the wording of the charges, he ought by now to have known better. With the final charge yet to be heard, he could already smell food being prepared for the noonday break in the nearby barracks. He dreaded to think how long the commandant would take over this last case; it was a serious one, the most difficult on the list. Lugo thought bitterly of the waste of army time, which could have been better spent elsewhere.

But what seemed a waste of time to the senior centurion had been far from that to his commandant.

The prefect Flavius Valerius Paulus was not a soldier. He was, by training and experience, a lawyer.

The Roman world held the view, peculiar to itself, that if a man showed administrative ability in the chief magisterial office of a provincial city, he would have equal success as the commandant of an auxiliary fort on the outskirts of the empire, even when he had had no previous military experience. In time, this had become accepted as a necessary step on the career ladder for anyone hoping to achieve high imperial office.

Flavius, in his late-twenties already known for his legal acumen, had been elected to the post of chief magistrate in his native town of Stresa. In theory the post was open to any citizen, but in fact it was only possible for men of wealth to stand as candidates; the post carried no remuneration and the elected magistrate was expected to provide benefits for the town at his own expense. It was not uncommon for the new man in office to curry favour with his electorate by means of flashy festivals and entertainments. Flavius, disturbed to see a growing number of orphans in the poorer parts of Stresa, had preferred to spend his money on building and staffing an orphanage, and had also devised a financial scheme which would support it when his year in office was over. The success of his work had attracted the attention of the governor of his province, who had mentioned it in passing to the emperor. Hadrian had committed the name of Flavius Valerius Paulus to his memory, which he always boasted was prodigious and, in fact, was.

Hadrian was always on the alert for able men to govern his empire. The ancient aristocratic land-owning class that had once provided members for the ruling Senate was now no longer able to supply, in Hadrian's view, enough men of quality to serve in the forty-three provinces that stretched across Europe and North Africa. Hadrian thus looked increasingly for support from the curiously entitled equestrian group.

When Rome had been a small state on the edge of the Tiber, its only defence against attack had been its citizen militia. The senators had provided leadership as officers, and if anyone among their men could afford to ride to battle on a horse, he was known as an equestrian. This group, generations later, now consisted of powerful merchants or ruling provincial families, who were required to have a certain verifiable income before admission. None of them had any connection with the keeping of horses. They were a kind of junior aristocracy, entitled exclusively with the senatorial class to wear on formal occasions the purple-edged white toga of rank – with the difference, however, that the senatorial band of purple was wider than that permitted to the equestrians.

Among them were well-educated men, intelligent, enterprising and energetic. They knew how to work, they understood money. For this the senatorial class, living complacently on the income from inherited land, despised them; to acquire money as payment was forbidden among their ancient families. New members were admitted to the Senate only by internal election. The emperor Claudius, being of like mind to Hadrian, had over fifty years earlier created a furore in Rome by demanding a place in the Senate for the leader of a Gallic tribe who had won his admiration. With no small difficulty he eventually succeeded, though by what bribes or pressures no one ever knew. The empire of Hadrian was larger, and he was more ruthless than Claudius. He wanted Flavius Valerius Paulus in his service, and in due course in his Senate.

There was the trifling matter, of course, that entry to the Senate demanded a level of income more than twice that required for the equestrian group, but Hadrian was not unaware that the Paulus family could have proposed a dozen entrants to the Senate without suffering any financial hardship.

The small vineyard which his great-grandfather had planted on his patch of land in Stresa had, by the time Flavius was born, developed into a large industry harvesting grapes in several parts of Italy, in Sicily, along the Rhine, and in south and central Gaul. The family had agents across the empire from Syria to Britain. They had acquired a factory to make their own amphorae for transporting wine, and were experimenting in the use of wooden barrels. They owned a ship, which travelled between Bordeaux and York.

So Flavius belonged to a family that was not only wealthy, but had a working knowledge of many areas of Hadrian's empire outside the walls of Rome. Flavius himself, the emperor had learned from another of his casual contacts with the governor of the Alpine province, was widely travelled. He handled all his father's legal matters, moving from vineyard to vineyard, agent to agent, arranging contracts, settling disputes, hiring staff. Before that he had studied law, not only in Rome but in Bordeaux and Antioch. 'Antioch?' the emperor had murmured on hearing this, something stirring in his remarkable memory. 'Antioch?'

When a vacancy occurred in an auxiliary fort in north Britain, he offered Flavius Valerius Paulus the post of commandant, to give him the required military experience.

An imperial courier delivered into Flavius's hands a document signed by the emperor. This he presented to his father, Crispus Valerius Paulus. Crispus, accompanied by his son, then set out for the villa of his own father. Though he was one of the most powerful merchants in the empire, he was still bound by the Roman code which required him to submit to the authority of his father for as long as that father lived, just as Flavius must submit to him.

He found his father sitting in his favourite room overlooking the lake, enjoying the warmth of the early-spring sunshine that came through long windows and fell in bright panels across the floor. Crispus unrolled the emperor's document and laid it in his father's lap. He had no doubt about the pleasure it would give him, but he was unprepared for the excitement the old man showed, uttering little cries of almost childlike glee.

Crispus sat down beside him. 'Father, the emperor has not offered Flavius half his kingdom. He is merely sending him to serve in the bleakest part of the empire.' He added without enthusiasm, 'Among provincial Spaniards.'

His father said nothing. He seemed to have forgotten that he was no longer alone, possessed by thoughts that made him smile and chuckle aloud to himself. During his working life, when he had first qualified to join the equestrian group and had grown to understand the power that money brought, a tentative notion had flickered in and out of his mind that in retirement had become a cherished dream: one of his blood might perhaps some day wear the broad purple band on his white toga. Now, suddenly, it was no longer a dream. He turned his head and looked at his grandson, standing politely out of earshot just inside the doorway.

'Father,' said Crispus sharply, 'Flavius seeks my approval to accept the emperor's commission, so first I seek yours.'

His father smiled blissfully at him. 'The emperor sees what I see.'

'Father!'

Crispus, who was reaching out a hand for the document, was given a fast slap on the wrist. 'Crispus, I'm not yet an idiot. An emperor's so-called invitation is a command. Of course I approve. What choice have I? Or you?'

Crispus beckoned his son to join them. He rolled up the document, tied its ribbons and handed it to Flavius. 'Your grandfather supports your acceptance, and so, then, can I.'

Flavius bent over his grandfather and kissed his cheek. He heard the old man's hoarse whisper, 'The emperor has chosen you for the Senate. I saw it had to be you.'

Crispus overheard this. 'Father, there are more than twenty commandants round that northern wall of the emperor's, and I don't know how many more in the south of Britain, to say nothing of those on every other border of the empire. The Senate house wouldn't hold them all.'

The old man beat against the arms of his chair. 'It's Flavius he wants, not the others. And shall I tell you why? This place he's going to – it's not very pleasant, perhaps, cold and wet. But that doesn't matter. It's the place where the Spaniards are. The emperor is very well-intentioned towards Spaniards. He calls himself one of them.' His grandfather patted Flavius's cheek. 'It's a sign – for those who have the wit to see.' He nodded his head towards his son.

Crispus, who could hardly fail to overhear this jibe, rose from his seat and walked across to the window. He pointed to a nearby hill terraced with vines. 'Look over there, Father. Ours, yes? What would happen to all that if Flavius sat in the Senate?'

'Happen, Crispus? Everything can only get better for us.'

He looked at his father in desperation. 'You know as well as I do that no senator can accept money made in trade.'

'That's what they all say! But you can get anything done with money.'

'No, grandfather,' said Flavius, as gently as possible. 'That is corruption, and one of the functions of the law is to expose corruption. I believe in the law, and must uphold its principles. I learned enough from my year as magistrate here to be sure of that.'

'The law?' said his grandfather, with a kind of contempt. 'It interferes.'

Crispus reminded him that he had been delighted when Flavius sought permission to study law.

'He was a boy then. I didn't know – how could I? – that he would be the man who could take our family into the senatorial class.' Then, with one of those leaps of thought that were becoming more and more frequent in his conversation of late, Flavius's grandfather added, 'When I was a young man, Flavius, it was said that if a senator was selected to govern a province, he needed three years in office; in the first year he settled the bribes that had secured him the position, in the second he paid the lawyers who defended him against the charges of bribery, and in the third he amassed enough money to live the rest of his life in comfort.'

'That was fifty years ago, Flavius,' said Crispus. 'Times are different now, especially under Hadrian.'

Crispus walked back with his son to the landing stage where Flavius had moored his boat. 'You may find Britain a strange, disturbing place, but if you keep an open mind you never know what you might come across that you will never find anywhere else.'

Flavius let his gaze roam across the gardens at the familiar sights he had always loved- the curving colonnades, the pergolas dripping with blossom, the espaliered tress with fruit ripening in the sun, his mother's cherished white roses, the walkway of cypresses, the stone mask of a lion that poured water into a pool. He laughed, 'How could I find anything in Britain that I haven't already got here?'

V

So now Flavius Valerius Paulus found himself sitting in the chilly, echoing hall of a Roman fort, making judgements which accorded with the legal code to which he had committed himself. It was not proving to be a very satisfying experience. The men were bewildered, and the senior centurion outraged – and that probably meant the other centurions would be of the same mind.

With only one man left waiting to be charged, the hall was quiet enough for Flavius to hear the noise in the streets outside caused by sections returning to eat in the barracks – armourers, leatherworkers, stone masons, carpenters, brewers, clerks. The break in winter was short. Then they would all be marching on to the parade ground for the afternoon's weapons drill.

Understanding something of the Lugo's impatience, Flavius raised a hand. 'Senior centurion, you will request your deputy to lead the drill today.'

Flavius was unable to tell whether the other man was relieved or annoyed as he raised his own hand to summon an orderly. He heard a sharp 'Sir!' cast in his direction as the soldier departed.

Flavius turned his attention to the last entry on the charge sheet. He read it once and then, startled, read it again. This was nothing like all the other trivial Saturnalian disputes inside the fort. This had happened outside its walls, in the settlement. A Roman soldier had broken down a shopkeeper's door.

'This is disgraceful,' he said quietly.

'And dangerous, too, sir.'

Flavius glanced at the glimmering statue of the emperor. 'Yes,' he acknowledged.

Any show of hostility between an army unit and the local settlement incurred a blazing outburst of rage from Hadrian. It was part of his military policy that once a territory had been subdued and brought within the boundaries of the empire, efforts should be made to cultivate and retain good relations. Roman taxation was not, of course, welcome, but it soon became evident that with it came the benefits of water supplies, sewage disposal and roads – not only the great military marching roads, but secondary tracks which linked villages and hamlets. Above all, there was the chance of making money by building shops outside a fort, from which supplies could be provided to the men inside. Local families were free to worship their old deities and to preserve old customs. They could even keep their own chieftains and kings, so long as they understood the emperor's over-riding power.

However, the emperor knew, the army knew, and the officers inside Alauna knew, that resentment simmered below the surface and could flare up suddenly under provocation – the kind of provocation that was roused when a brutal Roman soldier smashed his way through the door of a defenceless shopkeeper's premises. Unrest at such an action could spread quickly from place to place until it became a riot, and riots could explode into a full-scale revolt across the north of Britain. An entire legion had once been destroyed without trace in the north-east.

'Go through the details with me,' ordered Flavius.

Lugo identified for him the man waiting at the back of the hall. 'Decimus Noricus, sir, section three, barracks C.'

Flavius interrupted him. 'One of our usual trouble-makers?'

'No, sir, no previous charges.' The centurion cleared his throat. 'Two nights ago, he was in one of the local taverns with other men from his section. They were gambling.' He broke off to remind Flavius that, being Saturnalia, it was not illegal.

Flavius closed his eyes. 'I had not forgotten. Go on.'

'A child running round between the tables snatched a handful of his coins. Noricus shouted and tried to catch him, but the child got away from him, ran out of the tavern and down the street to his father's house – a bakery. He managed to get through the door and slammed it shut in Noricus's face. Noricus banged on the door, smashed one of its panels, and was trying to open it when two of his section turned up, dragged him off and got him back into camp.'

Flavius groaned. 'He was drunk, I suppose, like everyone else.'

The senior centurion hesitated. 'I doubt that, sir. Noricus rarely drinks. He's very careful with his money.'

'Careful with his money? He was gambling.'

'Only with a few coins, I would think, sir. He's the sort of man who would go to the tavern at Saturnalia just to be companionable with the others, not to make them feel he was being critical of them. He's the section leader. I can understand that.'

'Section leader!' This was a switch, thought Flavius. For once the senior centurion seemed to be acting for the defence.

Lugo was offering him another document. 'This is the man's record. I took the liberty of drawing it from the files. If the prefect would be good enough to look at it?'

Flavius said formally, 'Thank you, senior centurion. That is in order.' He unrolled the scroll and dutifully began to read it. Several minutes passed before he lifted his head again. He turned in his chair to face the senior centurion, hovering anxiously behind him. 'I understand now,' Flavius said gently, 'the nature of your concern.' He held the report in one hand and the charge sheet in the other. 'These do not appear to describe the same man.'

Lugo nodded eagerly and one of his very rare smiles flickered across his face. 'Exactly so, sir. Yes.'

Flavius was looking again at the report. 'For the past eight years, his centurion has noted Noricus's military conduct as "exemplary". For the past five years, he has been elected annually as section leader. You yourself have placed him on a promotion list that could eventually result in his posting as centurion.'

Lugo nodded again. 'I have come across very few candidates as good as Noricus.'

They looked at each other. For most of the morning their loyalty to different professional codes had left a division between them. Now they were in sympathy, and it was an almost humbling experience.

'Who prepared the charge against Noricus?' asked Flavius.

'A decent man. He manages the post-house.' A post-house was found close to any established fort. It was a well-appointed house, designed to provide excellent accommodation and stabling for imperial officials and travellers of means. 'He acts as a link between the locals and the fort. He's a veteran but British by blood, so he can understand both sides. He did most of his twenty-five years' service along the Rhine, but came back as a centurion on the wall. The legate in York asked him to give a month or two to setting up the post-house here. That was seven years ago.'

'So his statement is without prejudice?'

The senior centurion nodded. 'He's outside now, with the boy's father – the baker.' He paused. 'Sir, I sent an officer to escort them, instead of an orderly. I thought it would impress on everyone how seriously we were taking the matter.'

It was Flavius's turn to permit himself a brief smile. 'Excellent,' he murmured. 'You couldn't have done better.'

He looked at Noricus, as he waited to be summoned. He seemed undisturbed by his surroundings, standing with an easy dignity, a man content in his own thoughts.

'You read him the charge? What explanation does he give?'

Lugo shook his head. 'None. He agrees with it. He has nothing more to say.'

Flavius swung round to face him. 'What! That can't be true. Do you think it is?'

'No, I don't. Perhaps he will have something different to say to you. But I don't think he will. Look at him. He's made up his mind to say nothing.'

'Doesn't he realise,' said Flavius in desperation, 'that if he offers no mitigating facts, I shall have to make a judgement based on the only evidence I have – the child's father's? And that will mean penalising Noricus. His promotion will have to go ...'

'Worse than that.' Lugo looked grim. 'The legate will plead the danger of Noricus's behaviour. He'll expect a deterrent punishment, like a public flogging.'

'No, no,' said Flavius vehemently. 'All we need do here, surely, is assure the local people that we will never condone attacks on them or their property. There is no possibility, is there, of stirring up trouble? This fort has been here for eight years, and there has never been any threat either in the settlement or the district around here, whatever the legate thinks.' Seeing from the senior centurion's expression that he was not in agreement with this, Flavius grew more heated. 'This fort was originally built to house a thousand men—'

'And over two hundred cavalry,' murmured the senior centurion.

Flavius glared at him. 'When Hadrian needed reinforcements in Judea, where did he find them? He left you with only half your complement because he knew it would be safe to do so. Five hundred men and, yes, all the cavalry went from Alauna to Judea, from one side of the empire to the other, because, apparently, no other fort anywhere nearer Judea was thought to be as safe as Alauna.'

Lugo waited a moment to be sure that Flavius had finished and then said, 'I don't think the legate would agree, sir, about exempting this fort from the punishments common elsewhere. The emperor demands that even if no attack is expected, a unit must prepare as if it were coming tomorrow. That's why we practise weapons drill every day.'

'Yes, I know that,' said Flavius irritably, feeling like a rebuked schoolboy. 'It's not quite the same thing, though, is it?'

Lugo chose that moment to give the signal for Noricus to be brought forward. Flavius, watching him, had another thought. 'What on earth was a child doing, wandering around a tavern at that time of night?' he muttered.

The adjutant made one of his rare remarks. 'It's that child who needs a deterrent punishment, not Noricus.' Then he swallowed hard, flushed, and became very busy with his wax tablets.

The outer door opened and they heard from outside a shrill, belligerent voice speaking in the local dialect. 'That's the child's father,' Flavius whispered to the adjutant.

A man appeared in the doorway, still shouting and waving clenched fists, obviously seeking a confrontation with somebody. The adjutant hoped it wasn't him.

The squat, menacing figure of the irate baker, fastened into a thick goatskin cape, crossed the threshold into the hall and found himself face to face with the towering golden image of the emperor. His words dried up, his hands were frozen in mid-air and his bulky shape seemed to shrink inside its black covering.

He was followed, at a more measured pace, by a man of unmistakably military bearing. He took the baker gently by the elbow and steered him towards the shrine, where he bowed to the emperor's statue and nudged the baker to do the same, then turned him to face the dais.

'He is the veteran officer from the post-house,' Flavius murmured to the adjutant. 'He acts as a kind of warden there.'

The veteran was wearing not one of the goatskin capes favoured in the area but a shorter version of a military cloak, pinned on one shoulder. As he came in from the cold air, he had thrown the two edges back over his shoulders and Flavius could see that he had one of the thick leather belts worn only by serving soldiers and which, after an honourable discharge, they were allowed to keep. A provincial recruit, as he once was, who had completed his twenty-five years' service, received not only the belt and a grant of land anywhere he chose in the empire, but also Roman citizenship.

It was the emperor's wish that all Roman citizens should acknowledge each other in public. Flavius duly rose to his feet and moved to the edge of the dais to offer the veteran his hand. The adjutant, whose patrician lineage boasted generation after generation of Roman citizens, joined Flavius after a moment's hesitation and extended his own hand. Despite the emperor's wish, it was not a courtesy that all men of rank were prepared to share with those of humbler origin, and the veteran officer grasped both hands in turn with obvious gratitude.

Flavius resumed his seat. The baker and Noricus faced each other from opposite ends of the space in front of the dais.

Lugo cleared his throat and began to read out the charge against Noricus – namely, that he had broken down the door of a settlement bakery in pursuit of the baker's child who had taken refuge there. The family had been terrified and alarm had spread throughout the neighbourhood.

Lugo spoke slowly to allow time for a translation to be made to the baker. He also spoke very loudly as if an ignorance of Latin implied defective hearing.

Flavius addressed the veteran. 'Councillor ...' he said, using the term which looked ahead to a time when the settlement would have become a small town in the Roman style with annually elected officers, and implying that the baker's present companion would certainly be the first of these '... you were a witness to this incident?'

The man acknowledged the commandant's courtesy with a slight bow, at the same time modestly disclaiming it. 'I am here, sir, merely to translate for my good friend. I was not a witness.'

Flavius turned to Noricus. 'Section leader Noricus, you have heard the charge. It is now your right to refute it, or to give your own explanation of what happened.'

'Thank you, sir. I accept the charge.' When Flavius stayed silent, staring at him, Noricus added, 'I did not intend to break down the door, sir, but a panel splintered when I struck it with my hand. I accept responsibility for the damage.'

Flavius was growing more and more puzzled by the man's behaviour. 'Why were you following the child?'

'I have nothing more to add, sir.' He spoke quietly, politely, as though the matter were already resolved and of little further concern to him. What, thought Flavius, did concern him?

'Noricus,' he said sharply, 'if you have nothing to say in your own defence, then my judgement will have to rest on the evidence as laid down in the charge. That makes you guilty of an act of mindless brutality. Your punishment will have to reflect that. The army will not tolerate behaviour that could threaten the peaceful accord between this fort and its settlement.'

He had failed to move Noricus. 'I understand, sir,' he said.

The baker, no longer under the golden eye of the emperor, had recovered his power of speech and was demanding in his shrill voice to know what was being said.

Flavius cut across him. 'Councillor, is your good friend aware that his child stole money from section leader Noricus? Two of the men in his section saw it happen, and would have spoken for him if he'd called them.'

'If he didn't know, he wouldn't believe it; if he did, he would deny it.'

'What was he doing,' Flavius demanded, 'allowing his child to be wandering about in a tavern at an hour when he should never have been let out of the house?'

'The father is a baker,' the veteran reminded him. 'He works unusual hours.'

Flavius failed to see the relevance of this. He caught a warning glance from the senior centurion. Yes, he was behaving more like an attorney for the defence than a judge, but someone had to try to save Noricus from the effects of his own stupidity. He needed to speak to Noricus on his own, but how was he to do this? How could he get rid of everybody else?

The baker was growing impatient again. 'Would the prefect like me to translate this conversation?' the veteran murmured.

'No, not at this time,' said Flavius, 'but I would appreciate it if before long he could be persuaded to take some responsibility for his child's unacceptable conduct.'

The veteran said quietly, with courtesy, 'The prefect will know that he has no authority over civilian behaviour here.'

With the same gravity, Flavius replied, 'As a former centurion, the councillor will understand that I have an obligation to ensure that when my men visit the settlement taverns they will have no cause to regret it. Let us not forget that Section-leader Noricus was robbed.' He gave a brief smile. 'You will appreciate, Councillor, I am sure, that I do no more than offer a request for your help.'

He took a deep breath and then said briskly, 'Let us now deal with the matter of the door. You will translate, if you please, councillor. Section leader Noricus accepts liability for damaging the door of the bakery. The army extends its apologies to the owner and takes responsibility for restoring his property.'

On hearing this in his own tongue, the baker's face took on a look of smug satisfaction. So it should, thought Flavius; he was getting a brand new door, crafted in good wood, in place of a cheap, flimsy thing. 'One of our carpenters will go back with you to the bakery now to take measurements, and the replacement door will be fitted as soon as possible.'

The baker had a question. Flavius reassured him. 'The army will bear the initial cost. The sum will then be deducted from the section leader's pay over a period of six months.' He glanced unhappily at Noricus, still searching for a way of seeing him alone.

It was, surprisingly, the baker who provided the opportunity. He had suddenly become very agitated gripping his hands together as he threw out more questions. He had wanted to know how long it would be before the new door was finished. Flavius was unable to answer that, he explained, before the carpenter had assessed the damage. The baker had then begun bemoaning the fact that until the work was done his house and bakery were open to anyone who wanted to walk in, and that his wife was terrified of being alone there. She had not even wanted him to leave her for the fort that morning, and he had already been gone much longer than he had promised.

Flavius was out of his chair and moving towards the baker with a swiftness that startled the senior centurion. 'I understand your distress, sir,' he said to the fretful man, and then turned back to Lugo. 'This is a most urgent matter.'

He talked, thought Lugo, as though they were both seriously remiss for not having realised that themselves. He stared at the commandant in surprise, at a loss to follow the sudden change in his manner.

'The carpenter will be instructed,' Flavius was saying, 'to erect some temporary cover over the opening. If this is not possible, a guard will be posted on the house. The senior centurion will take you to the carpenter now and go back with you to your wife.'

'Me?' Now there was indignation as well as surprise on Lugo's face.

Flavius whispered, 'You yourself decided – very wisely – to send your deputy to escort them up here. It will be all the more reassuring to the settlement if the senior centurion himself shows concern.'

The idea of parading through the settlement in style held its appeal. 'But what about Noricus?'

'I shall go on with the questioning. Have him moved into my office.' Before Lugo could wonder about this, Flavius added, 'A word before you go. This has been an exhausting morning. I have received a new wine from Sicily. I wonder if you would share it with me? I would welcome your opinion.'

The senior centurion was shaken by yet another surprise. But he had a palate for wine and could not afford a Sicilian import. 'Honoured, sir. Half an hour, sir?'

There was a short burst of movement in the hall. Relieved that the baker was now pacified, the veteran paused to thank Flavius. Then he added in his gracious way, 'I think my good friend may wonder what penalty you decide to impose on section leader Noricus.'

'I can promise you,' Flavius answered softly, 'that when I have explored his conduct further, my judgement will be the appropriate one. I suggest we all leave the matter there.' He smiled and offered his hand again to a fellow Roman citizen. 'Advise him, councillor, that if he raises the matter again, facts about the shabby timber of his door and the activities of his child might sadly come to light.'

Their eyes met. Flavius's hand was grasped.

He and his adjutant were left alone on the dais. The only other men in the hall were the guards on duty at the shrine, and they were out of earshot.

Flavius walked to the end of the table where the adjutant was writing notes on his wax tablets. 'Quintus,' he said, using his given name to warn him that he had something personal to say, 'would you be good enough to do something for me?'

The adjutant looked up at him, pleased to hear his name, pleased that the commandant was asking for his help. He would have done anything for Flavius who was exactly the sort of officer the younger man wanted to become.

'It's not something I ought to ask my adjutant to do,' added Flavius with a gesture of apology.

Quintus smiled. 'I don't mind.'

He came from one of the oldest and most respected of senatorial families, yet there was no trace in him of any arrogant patrician manner. Flavius thought of Lucilla, who was obsessed with her senatorial rank.

'I need you, if you will, to go across to my house and send my steward here.'

If the request was an odd one, it didn't bother Quintus. 'At once, sir,' he said, getting out of his chair and looking towards the main doors of the hall.

'Not that way. Use the other door.' Flavius pointed to a small door at the far end of the hall. It opened on to a narrow alley that ran between the headquarters building and the commandant's villa. Facing it, on the other side of the alley, was the gate to the commandant's kitchen courtyard.

'Ah, yes, of course, sir, ' said Quintus cheerfully. 'That will be best for your lady.'

'Best for my wife?'

'We all understand that your lady doesn't choose to see any of the cohort in her house.' He nodded amiably.

Flavius, for one, didn't know that. However, he laughed and said, 'You can see then that I am sending you on a perilous mission. I needed a good man for it.'

Quintus hesitated for a moment. 'The wax tablets, sir. I can't hand them over to the clerks until I have a judgement on the Noricus charge.'

'I'll see to it,' said Flavius, reaching out for them. 'I shan't need you any more this afternoon. Take a boat out or borrow one of my horses for what's left of the daylight.'

Quintus hurried off down the hall, pausing only to salute the emperor in passing.

Flavius was beginning to feel like a juggler. The senior centurion and his flock were in the carpentry sheds, his adjutant was disappearing through the door, Noricus was shut in his office. It needed only Aelius now. He paced up and down along the length of the dais. He had barely covered the ground twice when the steward appeared.

He was dressed in the calf-length russet tunic that he had favoured earlier that morning, but round his neck now was the thick scarf he always wore when stepping out of the villa into the open air.

He ignored the shrine and its statue. 'Are you ill, Flavius?'

'Do I look ill?'

Aelius gave one of his shivers. 'It's cold in here.'

'Well, at least you were wrapped up warmly for your long journey across the alley.'

'What do you want?'

'In half an hour I want someone to bring across a large flagon of my father's best Sicilian red with two glasses – not beakers – glass goblets. I want the tray in my office.'

'Who's coming? The governor?'

'No.'

'You know I'm always busy at this time of day. Couldn't you have mentioned it this morning?'

' No.'

Flavius picked up the wax tablets and stylus. He looked for Noricus's record. 'By the way, as you leave, remember that it is required you acknowledge the emperor.' He waited for the answer he knew would come. It did.

'I am Greek.' Then Aelius added, 'We don't worship our emperors as gods.' He tightened his scarf and reached the door again without a sideways glance.

Flavius, with relief, hurriedly left the dais and opened the door into his office. Noricus and his two guards were drawn up in a row, all looking slightly uneasy to find themselves in the commandant's private quarters.

Flavius dismissed the guards and then faced the section leader across his desk. 'Noricus, we have a few moments alone together, and I want to spend them finding out precisely what did happen in that tavern.'

'I told you the truth, sir.'

'I don't doubt that, but it wasn't the whole truth, was it?'

Noricus studied his boots, avoiding Flavius's gaze. 'I don't quite understand, sir.'

Flavius asked suddenly, 'What were you using for wagers? Gold? Silver?'

The question startled Noricus and put him off guard. He almost laughed. 'Sir, never in all my life have I held a piece of gold in my hand. As for silver ...' He shook his head. 'I don't like to gamble, sir, and if I have to, it's only with a few small coppers, a negligible amount.'

'So, a child steals – in your own words – a few negligible coins, and a man with your solid reputation in this cohort turns into a wild animal. Your actions could have threatened the peace up here. I have explained to you before, and I think the centurion has done the same, that unless you can persuade me otherwise, I shall be forced to impose appropriate penalties. I do not believe you deserve these, and I do not wish to use them. Help me, Noricus.'

The other man looked back at him. He was trembling.

Flavius banged the flat of his hand on the desk. The ink-well shook, the stylus fell off the pile of wax tablets. The section leader flinched.

'Noricus,' declared Flavius, 'I have taken a great deal of trouble to arrange time for us to speak alone. If there is something that you wish to keep confidential, then I promise you that it will remain so.' He waited a moment and then added in a gentler tone, 'What else did that child do?'

Noricus closed his eyes and took a deep breath. 'He made offensive remarks about a person I respect.'

'One of your section?'

'No, sir.'

'A member of your family?' As soon as he had spoken, Flavius realised how unlikely this was. 'No, of course not. The child would know nothing about them.'

'No, they are in Spain, sir, but then I would never be surprised at the mischievous things that child might say about anyone, whether he knew them or not.' Flavius's patience was loosening Noricus's tongue. 'Sir, I have never heard a child use the kind of language he used. He probably didn't understand what it meant, but he knew if he used it that it would attract attention. People laughed – sniggered – and encouraged him. I wanted to stop him talking like that ...'

'About the person you respect?'

'Yes, sir. I didn't want him repeating it at other tables, or out in the street. I wanted to try and talk to him. When I caught up with him at the door to his house, he smashed it shut against my elbow and It broke. It was an accident, sir.'

While he was speaking, a thought flashed into Flavius's mind. It was a memory of something he had seen on one of his barracks inspections – not one of the formal inspections that took place on alternate Fridays, when he would be accompanied by centurions, clerks and assorted others, and would see nothing that hadn't been scrubbed, scoured, repainted or polished; not on one of those, but on one of the unobtrusive inspections he carried out on his own on a quiet afternoon when everyone else was engaged in shouting and banging weapons on the parade ground. What he had seen, more than once, was the figure of a woman drawn on a section-room wall, her long hair brushing bare feet. She was not unlike an image of Venus or one of the water nymphs worshipped by the local tribes. He had no doubt, however, that the remarks scribbled around her in various hands were not expressions of votive piety.

'Is it a woman in the settlement?' he asked.

Noricus sensed the direction of his thinking. 'Yes, sir, but a decent woman, well thought of.' Flavius could hear the reproach in his voice, but also a gentleness.

'Is she special to you?' Flavius murmured.

'She is my wife, sir.'

'Noricus! What?' Flavius was lost for words for a moment, then his temper snapped. 'You have been in the army for ... what ... eight years? I have been here for a few months, but even I know that marriage is forbidden during a man's period of service, unless he is the one out of eighty or so who achieves the rank of centurion – and the way you are going, breaking the law, you aren't likely to be one of them.'

Noricus said politely, 'Sir, I have broken no Roman law. I would never do that. I have been married by my wife's tribal law. I wanted to be sure that in the eyes of her friends and neighbours here, she would be held in the same respect she has always been. I wanted it understood, too, that she was under my protection.'

Flavius, confused, foundered among the legal niceties that were familiar to him. 'The Celts have no written language, so there can be no written contract of marriage.'

'It will be in the mind of the wise man who witnessed it, and it will pass from him to his successor.'

Flavius nodded. Yes, he knew that happened in the great Celtic universities of Gaul, but in the wastes of northern Britain?

Noricus, feeling at ease now with Flavius, tried to help. 'When you married, it was probably an affair of consequence, sir, with banquets, processions, wedding finery. But people like me have nothing like that. If a bride comes to live under her husband's roof and stays for a year, then that is regarded as a legal marriage.'

'True.'

'There is no written document.'

'Not at the beginning, no,' Flavius agreed. 'Are you trying to tell me that you feel as committed to your wife by her Celtic law as you would if both of you were in Rome?'

'That, sir,' said Noricus, 'is what I guessed you might be wondering.'

Flavius nodded, realising that that was, in fact, what was in his mind. 'You are a soldier under my command. Your wife has a right to my concern.'

'In some ways, sir, I feel more committed by her law than I would by mine. Divorce is easy for us Romans, but not among the Celts.'

'Does your wife realise that it might be fifteen years before you could offer her Roman marriage? And even if you were to become a centurion with your own married quarters, it could be eight or nine.' Flavius felt obliged to put the question.

'She understands, sir.' Noricus smiled at him.

'Tell me about her.'

Noricus looked at him with a flash of gratitude. 'She is the widow of the weaver who came from Carlisle when he thought there could be enough work here to provide a living for him. He died three years ago. She decided to stay here. She was becoming known for her cloth at all the local fairs. She makes shawls for the centurions' wives ... beautiful shawls they are, sir, warm for the winter, with bright strands of colour.' He smiled. 'Do you remember those trousers the baker wore under his goatskin – brown with little checks? They were made from a fabric she wove.'

'Is she living alone?'

'No, sir. She has a son of eight years. He can help her now with dyeing the wool, and goes out collecting the plants she uses in the dyes. That was how I came to meet her. I saw the boy caught up in a tree in the woods one morning. I got him down and carried him back home. She was making a green dye that day, and she let me watch. My section does the painting and the plastering for the fort, and I like to see how other people mix their colours, although there's a lot of difference, of course, between making dyes for wool and paint for plaster ...' He broke off suddenly, embarrassed by his own flood of words. 'I'm sorry, sir.'

'No,' said Flavius. 'You were answering my question. Just wait a moment, if you please, Noricus.'

He reached for the wax pads and took up the stylus to erase the notes which Quintus had made earlier during the hearing. He thought for a moment and then began to write on the freshly smoothed wax. Noricus watched him in silence. Eventually Flavius put down the stylus.

'Noricus, time is passing and I need to talk to you about the charge against you.' He paused and the soldier stiffened to attention. 'I cannot entirely condone your conduct that night, although I now understand that it was prompted by an obligation of loyalty, and loyalty is a commendable quality. Nevertheless, such an incident must never happen again. There are other ways to express loyalty, and you must look for them.' Flavius paused again. 'However, I am also aware of two other circumstances: if a badly behaved child had not been unwisely allowed to run loose that night, and if a certain door had been properly maintained, no charge against you would have existed. I therefore dismiss the charge on the grounds of unjustifiable provocation. You will retain your present rank, and will remain on the promotions list.'

Noricus, looking startled, saluted smartly.

'I think, section leader, that you will find weapons drill still in progress. Join your group now, and then continue with your normal duties.' Flavius indicated his private door into the hall. 'Go that way. It should be quicker.'

Flavius wasn't sure that it was, but he didn't want Noricus running into the senior centurion before there was time to think how best to explain what had been happening during his brief absence.

Noricus marched with a brisk, military step towards the door. With his hand on the latch he hesitated for a moment, and then turned his head to give Flavius one of his gentle smiles. 'Thank you, sir.' Then the door snapped shut behind him.

Flavius looked down at the wax tablets in front of him. He tried to think about the meeting with Lugo, but what was filling his mind was the memory of the brightness that seemed to light the room when Noricus was speaking about his Celtic-law wife. He loved her. It was not a kind of love that Flavius himself had ever experienced. In earlier years, of course, there had been young girls in other wealthy villas around the lake who had pleased him, and the enchanted summer days had drifted past; but in the winter they had been married off, or taken back to the city, and now he could barely remember their names.

The wind was rising again, and Flavius glimpsed a line of trees beyond the window shifting against a pallid afternoon sky. He thought of Noricus again, finding the boy in a tree, and wondered if he could have had any idea then of what the rest of the day might bring. Something stirred inside Flavius and he realised it was a feeling of envy.

He was disturbed by a knock on the door. He drew a breath and braced himself to meet Lugo. 'Yes.'

It was not the senior centurion but Aelius who stepped past the clerk into the room. He carried a tray with a flagon and glasses arranged on it.

'What do you want, Aelius? We have a houseful of servants and slaves to carry things for you.'

'This is a delicate wine. It needs careful handling.'

'It's come all the way from Sicily without you to nurse it.'

'Haven't you noticed how rough that alley is in winter?' His steward set down the tray on the desk. 'Your guest isn't here yet?'

Flavius peered round the room and under the desk. 'No.'

Aelius produced a cloth from his sleeve and began to polish with meticulous care the already spotless glasses, trying to prolong his stay until the unknown guest should arrive.

His effort was rewarded. He had barely started on the second glass when Lugo was announced. Aelius was standing at that moment with his back to the door, facing Flavius across the desk. 'The senior centurion?' he mouthed silently, contorting his face into a comic mask of amazement. These antic performances were the despair of Flavius who had to fight to keep a straight face. Yet when the senior centurion had rattled across the threshold, Aelius, grave-faced, was ushering him to the chair that had already been set in place for him.

VI

Lugo appeared to be in an agreeable mood as he sat down at Flavius's invitation. His glance rested with satisfaction on the wine tray. Aelius ingratiatingly enquired if the prefect was now ready for him to pour the wine. He stretched out a hand, but Flavius had his fingers on the neck of the flagon before Aelius could reach it.

'Thank you, but no. I realise how busy you are at this time of day. I shall manage.'

Aelius departed, and Flavius, with the flagon in his hand, smiled at the senior centurion. 'I assume your business went well.'

'Indeed, sir.' Lugo actually returned the smile. 'The carpentry detail was very welcome, and you were right – my presence there was much appreciated.'

Flavius started to pour the wine into a goblet. 'I have a confession to make ... I was not entirely frank with you earlier.'

Lugo's face dropped a little, as if, after all, he was about to be fobbed off with an inferior vintage.

'Today happens to be my birthday, and my father has sent this to mark the occasion. It comes from one of his most cherished vineyards.'

The senior centurion's expression brightened again, and he watched appreciatively as the glass was filled.

Flavius placed it in front of him. 'I think it is an insult to a wine of this quality to drink it alone. I am grateful to you for sparing the time to share it with me.'

Lugo lifted his glass. 'May I offer you, sir, my felicitations on your birthday?' He spoke a trifle awkwardly as if unused to exchanging such greetings. Then he waited until Flavius had filled his own glass before taking the first sip. He savoured it on his tongue, closed his eyes and swallowed. When he opened them again, he looked at Flavius with one of his rare smiles. 'Very, very fine, sir.'

Flavius smiled back. 'This was something,' he said gently, 'that I was sure we would never disagree about.'

Lugo gave an amused grunt. He returned to his glass, again with his eyes closed. This time when he opened them he seemed to be reluctantly recalling that there were duties to be discharged. 'Noricus,' he said.

'Noricus, yes?' Flavius braced himself.

'I didn't see him in the hall, and he isn't in here. Did you decide to confine him?'

Flavius reached for the wax tablet and pushed it across his desk. Lugo picked it up and squinted at it.

Flavius took a sip from his own glass, waiting uneasily for a reaction: amazement, anger, outrage that the decision had been made in his absence. Whatever it was, Flavius trusted that the wine might soften the edges.

'Ah, I see. So you dismissed the charges,' said the senior centurion. 'That accounts for this.' He emptied his glass, and cast a glance at the flagon. Flavius refilled the glass. 'So something happened, did it, sir?' Lugo enquired amiably.

Flavius nodded.

Lugo looked gratified. 'It's all down to that brat in the tavern, isn't it?'

'Yes,' said Flavius carefully. 'It seems that when the child realised that Noricus had seen him stealing the money, he started shouting damaging remarks about someone well known to Noricus, which he knew were untrue.' He paused. 'Forgive me, senior centurion, but that is as much as I can say. Other information was entrusted to me in confidence.'

'I accept that, sir, I accept that.'

Lugo's good-humoured lack of curiosity was still troubling Flavius, but he was grateful for it. 'I appreciate your forbearance in not pressing the matter further,' he said.

'Well, sir,' Lugo responded, 'it wasn't difficult for me to guess what Noricus was anxious about, was it? The brat was going for me, and Noricus was too respectful to repeat his words in front of me, especially in court.' Lugo held up his hands, 'No need for you to say anything, sir. 'You gave your word. May I enquire what your verdict was?'

Flavius pushed towards hum the wax tablet on which he had written his decision.

'Unjustified provocation,' Lugo read aloud. 'That's good, sir, very good.'

Lugo's unexpected but delicious solution to the Noricus problem left Flavius barely able to speak. He felt as if he had drifted into calm waters, instead of an expected storm. 'Yes,' he murmured after a moment, 'it doesn't deny his actions, but exonerates him from blame. He is no longer responsible for the cost of the door, and his promotion is not affected.'

'That is gratifying, sir,' said Lugo. He hesitated. 'There is just one thing. What about the door?'

'I thought we'd dealt with that.'

'Yes, putting it up, sir, but how are we to report it?'

Flavius stared at him. 'Report it?' he repeated blankly.

Lugo said impatiently, 'Yes, sir, in the monthly lists for Rome. The quartermaster will have noted the allocation of wood and paint in his own file. Its use has to be explained.'

Flavius realised that his refreshing mood of relaxation was going to be short-lived. 'Where,' he demanded, 'do we report new doors? I presume there's some kind of note kept of building maintenance?'

'Yes, sir; fabric repair and replacement within the fort, with costs. There is no authorization for the army to spend money or work outside the fort. And that, you see, sir, is what we've done.'

'Does it matter what you write down?' said Flavius with mounting exasperation. 'Do you imagine anyone reads it?' He reminded Lugo of the number of forts in Britain that were sending a batch of monthly reports to Rome, and then of the forty or so other provinces across the empire doing the same.

Lugo felt obliged to protest against what he plainly considered a slur on army organisation. 'Why would we be required to provide this information if it was not read?' he asked stiffly.

'Well perhaps,' Flavius conceded, 'if Rome wants to know about a shortage of grain supplies or tribal insurrections, they do, but surely not lists of rusty locks and chipped pavings.'

The afternoon light was already fading. Lugo began to rise from his chair. 'It's getting late. I should be going, sir, with your permission.'

'Listen a minute, senior centurion. You are right if you are thinking that, legally, the baker should pay for his door because he lost his case; the cost is not the responsibility of the army. But if we insisted on that judgement we should probably have to deal with a riot in the settlement.'

Flavius reached again for his wax tablet and scribbled rapidly across it.

Reluctantly, Lugo sat down again and picked up the tablet. He frowned. 'You've headed it – replacement of bakery door?'

'Yes. Read on.'

'Funded by the cohort as the wisest – and most economical – way of maintaining the goodwill of the local people; commandant's order.'

Lugo seemed for a moment to be struggling with conflicting emotions. Then he raised his head and looked at Flavius with surprise and yet what appeared to be an attempt at a small smile.

'It is not, sir,' he said, 'what one is accustomed to see among the rusty locks and chipped pavings. It is – he collected his thoughts with an effort – 'a statement of cohort policy as well as a repair completed.'

Flavius nodded. 'Just so. And now, senior centurion, you will remain in this room until this flagon of wine is empty. That is an order.'

Lugo held out his glass. After settling himself comfortably in his chair again, he said, 'There's something I think I ought to tell you about, sir.'

Flavius shook his head which was beginning to throb. 'No, nothing else, please.'

'It's nothing to do with any reports,' Lugo assured him. In fact, far from it. I went down to the bakery to make sure that all was going well with the carpentry and there was the brat, making a nuisance of himself. I grabbed him and took him round the back of the house, out of sight, and told him what I thought of his behaviour.'

'I didn't know you spoke his language.'

'I don't, except for one or two of his choicer words. Actually, I just counted from one to twenty in Latin, but very fiercely with a lot of threatening gestures, whipping my cane through the air once or twice. He understood well enough what I was telling him.'

'Will it have any effect?'

'I don't know, but at least his expression, before he scampered off, was very gratifying.'

After Lugo had made his way with careful, deliberate steps from the room, Flavius lay back in his chair with a groan and closed his eyes. Despite the aching in his temples, he must have drifted into a sleep. The next thing he was aware of was lamplight flickering across his eyelids.

He opened his eyes. Aelius was standing in front of him, holding a lamp.

'What do you want, Aelius. Go away.' He put a hand across his eyes to shield them from the light.

'That's a nice kind of greeting when I've come all the way over here to tell you that while you were conferring with your senior centurion, a crate arrived for you.'

'What crate?'

'How many crates have you got trundling across Britain? What crate? The crate from Gaul, the lady's Saturnalia gift?'

Flavius sat up. 'Lucilla's pottery?'

'Yes. She's already unpacking it, couldn't wait for you, coo-ing like a dove. All your crimes are forgiven. Not that it was your fault the thing was late. I gather there was ferocious weather across Gaul. Still, it's made a nice birthday present for you.'

'It's not my present. It's hers.'

'No, but she might thank you for it. That would be an unexpected birthday treat for you. But don't get your hopes up too much. Anyway, I thought you'd want to unpack the crate with her.'

Flavius clutched his head. The sound of an excited Lucilla, jumping up and down with squeals of delight was not something he wished to face at the moment. 'Not just yet, Aelius' he gestured vaguely at his desk 'I have work to finish.'

Aelius observed the empty flagon. 'No. I have a better idea. An hour in the bath-house?'

VII

Half an hour later, Flavius emerged from the cold water of the plunge pool in the elegant bath-house that formed part of the commandant's villa.

The two slaves who had charge of the building were waiting to wrap him in thick, warm towels. In the adjoining dressing-room, one of them, a Greek who understood such matters, gently massaged the tense muscles in his neck and shoulders. Then, swathed in fresh towels, he lay down on a padded bench, cushions beneath his head, and allowed himself to enjoy the painted walls that surrounded him. It was a pretty room. On one wall was a grove of lemon trees, heavy with fruit. On another, peacocks walked in a garden where water from twin fountains glistened against the deep vivid blue sky of a hot summer's evening.

Feeling relaxed and drowsy, he could almost smell the lemons and hear the splashing of the drops of water. The cold, dark stretches of north Britain seemed far away. Flavius stretched comfortably in his warm towels and gave a little sigh of contentment.

'Better?' said Aelius, coming into the room with Flavius's clothes for dinner neatly folded over his arm.

'Mmm.'

'Your dinner will be served in the library tonight,' said Aelius, shaking out the clothes and hanging them on hooks. 'I'm having a table moved in there. You can have a few more minutes in here.' He turned and waved a warning finger as he left. 'But not too long.'

Flavius nodded. Nothing had been said about a special meal for his birthday, but he knew Aelius and he knew that he and the household would have spent most of the day quietly preparing it. It did not occur to Flavius at that moment to ask why he wouldn't be eating it in his beautiful dining-room. Roman furniture of quality, with its decorations of bronze and ivory, was nevertheless light and easy to move so changing the function of any room was not difficult. Aelius no doubt had his own good reasons for choosing the library.

A tall lamp burning near the row of hooks cast its light on the finely woven woollen fabric of the tunic and mantle Aelius had left hanging there. It reminded Flavius of the weaver's widow who was now, by her own law, the wife of a Roman soldier, but who would still spend most of the long winter hours of darkness alone with her son. He had never really thought before – and was ashamed that he hadn't – about what life was like for someone dependant on the work of her own hands. She would need daylight to be able

60

to mix her dyes, and what little light she could afford to use after dusk would hardly be enough to let her work at her loom. She would have to work every possible hour through the long northern summer and carefully husband the money she earned to keep herself and her son through the coming winter.

The Celtic attitude towards women was something that Flavius found puzzling. They actually allowed women to rule over them as queens. Within living memory, the tribe of the Brigantes, which occupied a vast area of northern Britain, had been governed by a queen. To Flavius, a woman magistrate elected to lead a provincial city ... a woman consul in the Senate ... a woman at the head of the empire ... was incomprehensible, even ludicrous..

As a man brought up in the Roman world, he had always subscribed to the Ciceronian view that women were fragile creatures who lacked the judgement to take charge of their own lives and must therefore, by law, be subject to the authority of a male relative. Wasn't that what all women wanted, Flavius asked himself, security and protection?

Had the weaver's widow been part of a Roman family, she would not have been allowed to go on working alone as she was now doing. A brother, perhaps, would have arrived to take her and her son back to live in his household. Her husband's funeral, the disposal of his goods, her son's future, would all have been arranged without her involvement. But that, sadly for her, thought Flavius, was not the Celtic way.

Vague sounds reached him from somewhere in the villa complex. The service of dinner was probably beginning. This was the first year he would not be dining on his birthday at his parents' table. Instead he would be sharing the occasion with Lucilla alone, happy because her present had at last arrived and perhaps even a little contrite – graciously so – because she had been wrong to believe that it had never existed. She might even be delighted by the extravagance of it.

He suspected that in Stresa his mother was marking the occasion too, arranging a small but very special meal to please his grandfather, who had always hated the inanities of Saturnalia and had looked forward to Flavius's birthday as the time when he could emerge again into the world of reason. She would also invite, perhaps, one or two of their neighbours who had been children with Flavius, and his father would have the pleasure of opening one of his best wines – it could even be the Sicilian red – and drinking his son's health with them.

His mother lived the life of the respectable Roman matron, devoted to following her husband's interests. Much of her time was spent developing and tending the garden at Stresa, a skill she had begun to acquire when as a young bride she had noticed how much her husband loved walking there and sharing it with like-minded friends. If he had enjoyed reading a new essay or poem or play, she would read it afterwards so that they could talk about it together if he chose, and guide her understanding of it. She ate the food he liked, and wore the simple, pale-coloured dresses he preferred. She loved him so this was no constraint but a source of contentment and pleasure to her.

Lucilla was not a Roman wife made in the same mould. What he wanted or liked, Flavius knew, was of little concern to her. She could be wilful and stubborn about doing the trivial, frivolous things that amused her, but taking responsibility for anything else in her life was not something that troubled her. In this respect, at least, she was the true helpless Roman woman – all that could be left to Flavius. He must surround her with people who would arrange for her days to pass smoothly and agreeably. She would not have understood or admired, any more than his mother would, the kind of sturdy independence that was natural to women like Noricus's wife.

He would like, Flavius decided, to go the next day to the weaving shed, taking Lucilla with him, to help her choose one of the bright shawls Noricus had described. To walk among the stalls of 'the barbarians' in her delicate slippers was not, as Flavius knew only too well, in Lucilla's scheme of things, but in her cooing-dove mood of the moment might she not be persuaded, over the excellent dinner that Aelius would have waiting for them, to change her mind?

They had been married now for five years. She was not the woman he would have chosen had the choice been his, and he was sure he would not have been her choice either. The union had been arranged by their respective fathers, for the mutual benefit of their two families. As was expected of them, both Flavius and Lucilla accepted the arrangement without question.

It was an unusual marriage. Lucilla belonged to an aristocratic senatorial family and she would have hoped for a bridegroom from the same class, but an indolent, dissipated life had left her father with little more than his name and rank and no way of providing the necessary dowry for a patrician marriage. Flavius's merchant father, belonging only to the lower-ranking equestrian group, was nevertheless one of the richest men in Rome. He was willing to forgo a dowry in order to introduce his son into the senatorial network, in the hope of fulfilling his own father's ambition that he might one day see his grandson invited to enter the Senate.

At the time of their betrothal Flavius was twenty-six, Lucilla seventeen. An age difference of something like ten years was considered propitious. They first met on this occasion, when Flavius placed the customary metal ring – in this case, a gold one – on the fourth finger of Lucilla's left hand. In his first fleeting glimpse of her, Flavius found her pretty, decorative and appealingly demure. He later discovered that she was shallow, self-centred and obsessed with her rank. The demure manner was put on and taken off like a piece of clothing.

Marriage in Rome had no religious context. No priest was required to preside over the exchange of sacred vows. At its simplest, if a woman lived in her husband's house for a year, it was a legal marriage. At its most extravagant, a lavish feast was given that lasted long into the night, the guests paraded in their finery through the streets and the old wedding rituals were observed.

Lucilla wanted the most sumptuous wedding her father-in-law was willing to provide. Flavius's grandfather wanted the same. Crispus Paulus therefore agreed, but made it a condition that his son's wedding should not become a vulgar display in the noisy, crowded streets of Rome, but should take place in his villa in Stresa.

A party of Lucilla's senatorial family, surprisingly perhaps, agreed to make the journey to Stresa. It was not so much to support the bride, Crispus suspected, as to take the opportunity of seeing the Paulus lakeside villas and estates. For him, too, it meant the quiet satisfaction of watching his father chuckling with glee as he glimpsed a clutch of white togas with the broad senatorial purple band moving across his lawns.

Lucilla appeared in the traditional dress of the patrician bride: a flame-coloured gown, with a wreath of white flowers on her elaborately plaited hair under a flame-coloured veil. She also wore a demure expression, touched with an appealing – and, to those who knew her, insincere – modesty.

Flavius's mother, wearing a magnificent collar of jewels that he didn't even know she possessed, entertained the bride, her bevy of young bridesmaids and the other ladies inside the villa. The men, together with Flavius, dined in pavilions in the garden.

Later that *night, in the warm summer darkness, a* string of gold lights flickered on the black water as a torchlit procession, led by musicians, escorted the bridal couple along the lake to the bridegroom's home. His groomsmen lifted Lucilla across the threshold, where she was handed a phial of water and a lighted wand: water and fire to represent the needs of the home. The water she offered to Flavius, the flame she applied to a hearth. When the fire burned, she blew out the flame and tossed the wand, which was decorated with ribbons and flowers, into the group of young unmarried girls who were gathered around the open door.

If Lucilla resented marriage to a man of lesser rank than herself, she was certainly not dissatisfied at being able to lead a life of the kind of luxury which she believed she deserved; nor could she be ungrateful for the benefits her father received from his generous son-in-law.

She had no interest in the legal work that took up most of Flavius's time, but when the family was in Rome she loved attracting attention as she was carried in a silk-curtained litter to the expensive shops near the Forum. In Stresa she was happy being rowed about the lake to visit the villas of other idle young wives.

When she was having her own way, Lucilla could be charming and even amusing, but her father had spoiled her and when she couldn't have what she wanted, or was required to do something she would never have chosen to do herself, she lapsed into disagreeable silences or, if she was alone with Flavius, childish tantrums.

Flavius soon learnt that if he talked about something that didn't interest her, she stopped listening and played with her fan.

She collected fans and nearly always carried one with her, or was followed by a slave who carried it for her. His mother, confronted with a poised fan, was sure she could engage Lucilla's interest by discussing possible plans for the garden of Flavius's new villa. Lucilla, fingering the tips of the feathers, said she thought that was what servants were for.

When he became chief magistrate of Stresa, Flavius hoped he might involve her in his work for the town, but she wasn't interested even in his scheme for an orphanage, and retreated in distaste from the sight of the sick, half-starved and homeless children he was collecting from the streets. However, the family had to admit that when the town hosted a visitor of distinction she was always willing to play the chief magistrate's gracious lady.

When Flavius's appointment as commandant of the Spanish cohort at Alauna in north Britain was confirmed, he approached her uneasily with the news and his decision that it would be wiser for her to stay in Stresa. But before he embarked very far into his carefully thought out description of the hardships of life in the remote north, she had seized with squeals of pleasure on the prospect of being a commandant's lady. It appeared that a distant cousin of her mother's had married a senator who had been appointed the legate in charge of a legionary fort. Lucilla had always envied the style of living she had enjoyed during his stay of office.

Flavius told her, 'Lucilla, Alauna is not a legionary fort. It is an auxiliary fort, staffed by provincial recruits not Roman citizens. It is not at the centre of a large town. It stands isolated, apart from a small settlement of local people against one of its walls. Lucilla, are you listening to me?'

'Mmm,' she murmured, remembering what her cousin had told her of her glittering life as the legate's wife.

'Lucilla, I do not qualify for a legate's appointment because I am not of senatorial rank.'

That seized her attention. 'But you will be one day?'

Flavius hesitated. 'That's what my grandfather hopes. That is why he is so anxious for me to take the posting. For myself, I don't—'

'But of course we must go. I am of senatorial rank. I can introduce you to all the legates.'

Flavius sighed. 'Not very easily. There are only three legions in Britain, Lucilla, none of them near enough to Alauna for you to arrange dinner engagements.'

He took one of her hands in his. 'It is very cold and wet in the country round there.' He gripped her hand more tightly to stop her attention from wandering again. 'It will be very lonely. I shall be very busy. I do not think I have any right to ask you to come with me. My commission will only last for a couple of years. I will understand if you would prefer to stay here – in fact, I think it would please me to think of you safe and warm in Rome or Stresa, near your father and your friends, doing all the things you like doing. You can write to me all about them and that will be something I can look forward to, don't you think?'

She was hesitating. He was almost there ... and then he made his mistake.

'You can live with my parents. My mother will be pleased to look after you.'

Lucilla snatched her hand away from his. 'I don't want to be looked after by your mother! She never *does* anything.'

Flavius stared at her in amazement. 'That's nonsense, Lucilla, and you know it. She's always busy. There's the garden, her sewing, helping in the school, visiting the tenants, caring for my grandfather ...'

'Nothing worth doing,' snapped Lucilla.

They had left Stresa together in early spring. With them went their servants, their slaves and a vast amount of baggage.

When they landed in the south of Britain, Aelius went ahead to the north-west with most of the household and the baggage. Flavius, with Lucilla and two of their servants, took the opportunity to discuss business with his father's agent in Colchester.

To placate her for the delay, Flavius walked with Lucilla through the streets that surrounded the market-place. They were part of the splendid rebuilding of the city that had taken place after its brutal sacking by Boudicca's army. The finer shops displayed luxuries that delighted Lucilla.

'Some of these things you would be pleased to find in Rome,' she explained excitedly as she darted about after items that had taken her fancy.

He bought her a little glass swan and a garnet bracelet. Then she gave one of her little cooing noises and pointed to a green silk parasol with a green silk fringe. He said he doubted she would have any use for it where they were going, but still he bought it for her.

They wandered then into a street selling nothing but pottery: cheap kitchen dishes at one end, and at the other dinner services of the finest quality imported from a distinguished factory in Gaul. Lucilla stood entranced before a display of cream-coloured ware, decorated with trailing summer leaves. There were leaves round the rims of the plates, on the handles of serving dishes, even hidden at the bottom of bowls.

'No,' said Flavius, laughing and holding up his hands. He turned to the maid who was standing behind them, holding their parcels. 'We're not asking Elpis here to carry a crate of pottery as well.'

The girl laughed, and even Lucilla was laughing as he took her arm to lead her away.

Flavius had always hoped that he might one day come to love his wife, as men sometimes did after an arranged marriage. That day in Colchester he thought it might happen. Yet it never did. He had then supposed, more realistically, that with the passing of the years they might expect to develop an affectionate regard for each other. But at times he doubted even that.

From Colchester they travelled north to York, where Flavius was required to report to the legate of the Sixth Legion before taking command at Alauna.

As they entered York, Lucilla was no longer in the happy mood she had enjoyed in Colchester. The white Mediterranean-type villas which Romanised Britons built in the south made her feel safe and at home, but the further away from the south they went, the fewer of these they saw. Near York, there were none at all. There were only the native round stone houses with conical roofs of straw through which smoke seeped. She had seen stone houses as they passed through Gaul but they were square, not menacing like these round ones.

She pointed to a cluster of them. 'Look, Flavius. They don't want us here. They don't like us.'

He noticed a woman in a doorway, playing with a child.

'Because they don't want houses like ours? I doubt it.' He waved at the baby, and the woman picked up the infant's wrist and waved back at him. 'The weather is different here, and the land is harsher. I think that's all it is. The houses do look grim, but there's no need to feel frightened by them.'

Lucilla shook her head, unconvinced. She was also furious with him for waving at the barbarian woman. There was more to upset her when they were in York. She had been sure the legate and his wife would invite a woman of her rank – with her husband – to stay in the official residence.

'We are here, Lucilla,' said Flavius, keeping his patience with difficulty, 'because I have received an army summons to wait on my superior officer. It is no concern of the legate's wife or of yours, and I am sorry that you mistook it for an invitation to a senatorial reception.'

They stayed instead with another of his father's agents, where Lucilla was somewhat mollified by the extreme courtesy she was shown. However, it was not what she had wanted, and in an outburst of temper she told Flavius that she was sick of all the talk about wine wherever they went. He then decided that it was only right to remind her gently that, if it were not for the work of his father's agents in the wine trade, a lot of her boxes of finery then being unpacked in Alauna might be empty.

From York they took the road to the north-west, Lucilla and her maid in their light two-seater carriage, Flavius and his man on horseback. They spoke only when necessary. Flavius felt ashamed; he knew he was married to a silly woman, and it was unreasonable to expect her to be able to act sensibly.

Although Lucilla usually failed to exert even a modicum of common sense, it amazed Flavius how shrewdly she could manipulate him when it suited her. She knew how disturbed he felt when there were unresolved disagreements between them. She knew how to cherish her grudges, when to sulk in silence, when to make little sobbing noises. His own bursts of temper passed quickly, leaving a lingering sense of guilt and then a need to placate her. He ought to despise her, but it was himself he despised for what he knew she saw as his weakness.

Three days later they reached the Roman auxiliary fort of Papcastle, which stood at the crossroads of four military highways. They spent the last night of their thousand-mile journey from northern Italy as guests of the commandant there. Alauna was only five miles away.

The commandant's wife, pitying Lucilla's mournful air, tried to cheer her up by showing her the items she had bought in the local markets. Lucilla looked without enthusiasm at the trinkets and carved wooden animals which her hostess seemed to treasure. 'That woman,' she muttered to Flavius, as though he were responsible for this waste of her time, 'has never seen Rome, or she would have understood the kind of quality I require in anything I choose to buy.'

Flavius seized on a chance to please his wife. 'I believe in parts of Britain the goldsmiths produce work of exceptional skill. When we are settled here, we will find one of them and I'm sure you will see something then that you would be pleased to take home.'

It had sounded, he thought, like rather a lame attempt at reconciliation. Lucilla apparently felt the same. 'Here?' she said. 'No, I don't think so.'

Flavius wanted to turn round and leave her, but instead he tried again. 'It seems they are best known for their gold torcs and collars, and necklaces that look like several very fine lengths of cord twisted together into a thick rope, all of gold with – '.'

'Oh!' Lucilla was looking at him with one of her pretty smiles. 'You will buy me a gold necklace?'

'Yes,' said Flavius, startled by her sudden change of mood. He smiled back at her. 'Yes, as I said, as soon as—'

'Not here. When we get home, take me to Rome and buy me one like your mother wore at our wedding, a gold collar with pearls – I know your mother's had emeralds, but I would rather have pearls – or perhaps emeralds as well, and amethysts? No, perhaps just pearls, very large drop pearls.'

She was getting further and further away from the British goldsmiths' work that had intrigued him when he had heard talk of it in his agent's office in Colchester.

'You will have plenty of time to think of it,' he told her gently. 'But two years is a long time. Why not look at the gold work here?

Just take a look at it and see what it's like.'

Lucilla shook her head. 'No, I'll wait.'

She could be obstinate, too. Flavius had no need to be reminded of that. 'As you please, my dear.'

She nodded happily. With the sparkle of excitement about her, she looked, Flavius thought, as she had when he first saw her on the day of their betrothal – appealing, demure and lovely.

The commandant's kindly wife was gratified to see the overnight change in Lucilla's spirits. 'I thought,' she murmured to Flavius, 'that it would reassure her to know that it's not only in towns you can find markets. We have them in all the settlements and villages around here. She'll soon get to know them all. If you haven't time to take her, I would be happy to help, if you can spare her for the odd day from Alauna?'

'I'm sure I could,' whispered Flavius, and they nodded together like conspirators as he mounted his horse.

The road to Alauna lay across thickly wooded country. Their first glimpse of the fort came as the road crested a hill before dropping down towards the coast. All Flavius could see through the trees at that point was the stark southern wall rising from a bare stretch of open land. They could see nothing of the life on the fort's northern flank: the thriving settlement, the harbour beyond, the metal works, the busy coastal road linking the fort to the nearest mile fortlet.

'So that's Alauna,' said Flavius.

Lucilla happened at that moment to be blissfully engaged in reviewing her encyclopaedic knowledge of Roman jewellers, debating which would be the best to consult about her gold necklace, but the unfamiliar note of despondency in his voice made her look up to see what was disturbing him.

'What is?'

Flavius pointed.

'That's where we're going?' Lucilla looked up at him in dismay. For once they were agreed. 'Oh,' she said. 'Oh, no.'

As they descended towards the sea, the tree cover became less dense, and Flavius could see tracks leading to clearings with four or five low, wooden-framed dwellings in them. These must belong, he guessed, to trackers or wood-cutters – perhaps the men who carved the little wooden toys that the lady at Papcastle collected. As they reached open ground, he caught a quick glimpse of the tops of masts and sails showing above the line of buildings on the edge of the settlement. In front of them the road now rose towards the landward gate of the fort on its eastern wall, and with the whole fort now visible he realised that what he had thought was a desolate patch of dry land was, in fact, the parade ground.

A trumpet sounded from the fort. The commandant at Papcastle had warned Alauna to expect them. The noise roused Lucilla who had dropped off to sleep. A centurion with an escort was taking up position. Lucilla slid back the hood of her travelling cloak and put her hands to her hair to twist up the loose strands. A mounted officer trotted out to greet them. By the time Flavius heard himself addressed for the first time by his military title of prefect, Lucilla had assumed the air of gracious dignity which had stood her so well when she made her appearances as the lady of the chief magistrate of Stresa.

But dignity was forgotten when she saw the house that was to be her home for the next two years. She clapped her hands like a child and laughed with relief and pleasure. Flavius had repeatedly told her that in all Roman forts the commandant's residence was built in the style of a Roman villa, spacious enough to hold his family and household, and with the same degree of luxury to which, as a man of established wealth and position, he was accustomed in his own home.

Yes, yes, Lucilla knew that, but this villa was so much more enchanting than she had ever imagined it could be.

Aelius, who was trying to guide her as she ran in and out of various rooms, reminded her that the first occupant had, after all, been the emperor.

'But the emperor likes living in campaign tents,' Lucilla informed him.

'So he says,' said Flavius, catching them up, 'but he has also built himself an extravagant palace the size of a small town outside Rome. So it's not surprising that he left traces of his preferred style of living here.'

Aelius led them to another door. 'There is a mural in here which is said to have been painted by the emperor himself.'

'Does that mean all of it or just the odd brushstroke?' asked Flavius.

Lucilla and Aelius glared at him. 'The emperor,' said Aelius reprovingly, 'is not, I understand, a man to do things by half. This, I am told, was his favourite room.' He opened the door. 'This was the emperor's dining-room.'

It was, Flavius thought, probably the most beautiful room in the house. As he walked in it seemed to be filled with a clear blue light. The walls were panelled with the warm azure colour of a Mediterranean summer sky. The mural at one end of a long room showed a summer garden; a heron stalked among tall, flowering shrubs, and speckled thrushes perched on the branches of young trees. The colours were muted; pale petals almost transparent against grey- green and blue-green leaves – as though seen through a shimmering heat haze, which melted them into the blueness of the sky glimpsed beyond. Flavius was enchanted by it, even though it had not been painted in the sharp, vivid colours that he would have expected from the hand of Hadrian, although admittedly the beady eye of the heron that stared out at him from the wall did have something of the emperor's sharp curiosity about it.

He turned back to look at the rest of the room. Aelius was trying to interest Lucilla in the tessellated floor. An exquisite pattern of dolphins and long-haired mermaids circled a shell-borne Venus skimming the waves, designed in honour of the villa's position by the water. Lucilla was not interested.

'I don't like this room,' she announced.

'What is there to dislike?' asked Flavius, amazed.

She was pointing at the table which ran down the centre of the room with a dozen high-backed chairs arranged around it.

'The emperor would never eat in a way only fit for ...' she hesitated, searching for a derogatory term '... a shop-keeper! He would have dined in the Roman manner, with couches.' She darted about the room. 'One here, and the other two facing each other ... there and there.'

'Yes, madam,' said Aelius, 'the emperor may well have dined in that way. There are, in fact, three such dining couches in one of the store-rooms upstairs, but the emperor himself or, if not the emperor, then one of the earlier commandants, changed it to this arrangement. Most of the northern forts now have a preference for dining at tables.'

'How do you know? You've only been here a few days.'

'Madam,' said Aelius loftily, 'I converse.'

Flavius intervened hastily. 'Lucilla, the legate in York uses this style himself, because in the military world there is a need always to be on the alert.'

She stamped her foot. 'I won't eat in what is now supposed to be my own house, in a room like this! Aelius, you will remove this table and bring back the dining couches.'

Flavius then gave his first command as prefect of Alauna. 'No, Aelius, you will not.'

He turned to his wife. 'Lucilla, you are the wife of the commandant, living on an army site.' He spoke gently and slowly in the hope of holding her attention. 'You are bound, like everyone else on this site, to observe certain conventions that have been devised to protect the survival of the unit.'

Lucilla stared at him in bewilderment, caused partly by his assumption of authority but more because he had said something that had never occurred to her before: that as the prefect's lady she could be in danger.

'Survival!' she cried. 'You never told me there was fighting up here.'

'I think it highly unlikely that there ever will be,' said Flavius, trying to calm her with a smile. 'But, Lucilla, if everyone here behaved as if they believed that to be the fact, we would be inviting trouble. You will soon get used to seeing the men practising with weapons every afternoon, as if they were preparing for an attack. That is our protection. And I, as the commanding officer, must appear to conduct myself in the same state of readiness – which doesn't mean spending two or three hours every evening dining in the lavish style of the leisured Roman classes.'

Lucilla pouted. 'My father—'

'Your father,' said Flavius, 'is not a serving soldier.' He didn't add that her father was lazy, self-indulgent, and usually ate extravagantly at someone else's expense.

Aelius intervened smoothly, 'Might I suggest to the prefect that if madam is not at ease using this room, I can arrange for her to dine in another. I can bring one of the couches down.'

Lucilla grew even more agitated. 'Then if there were to be an attack, you would all be running about and would forget I was even there!'

Flavius reached for her hand. 'No, I don't think so. Of course you can do what Aelius suggests if you like, but I would much rather we ate together. It's a pity not to enjoy this beautiful room while we have it.'

'It's spoiled like this.'

'Lucilla, when we are at home in Stresa, like most people who live in country towns, we live more simply than we do in Rome. It doesn't seem to upset you there.'

She snatched her hand away from his. 'I don't have much choice, do I? Our house belongs to your father. We live as your mother chooses, and she has never moved in fashionable Roman circles, has she?

'This was once the emperor's dining-room and I wanted it to look as it was designed to look.' Lucilla added, almost in a whisper, 'Then it would really be a beautiful room.'

Flavius took back her hand. 'And I won't let you change it because I come from what I suppose could well be called a "family of shopkeepers".'

Lucilla flushed, then gave a small, quick smile when she saw that he was amused, not offended.

'I want this room left as it is,' Flavius said. Then he smiled back at her. 'But you can rearrange all the others as you please.'

And rearrange them she did.

VIII

During the days when he was preparing for the arrival of Flavius and Lucilla, Aelius had given considerable thought to the allocation of the generous number of rooms in the commandant's villa. As the couple were childless, and he had no need to find space either for nurseries or schoolrooms or tutors' quarters, he had an agreeable range of options. His initial wish was to find a large, pleasing room to house Flavius's library. Aelius was a great reader himself, and trusted no-one else to care for the ever-growing collection of texts – for which there was never enough space for him to arrange them as well as he wished. The room selected, a beaker or two of wine with the quartermaster ensured that an army carpenter was supplied to fit shelving to Aelius's directions.

He then decided that he could afford to offer Lucilla a suite of adjoining rooms for her private use. This, he felt, would not only flatter her sense of what was due to a lady of senatorial rank, but might with luck keep her out of the way of those who had work to do.

For himself and his wife, Alis, he secured a pair of rooms on the upper floor with windows overlooking the street. From there he could see who was entering or leaving the main entrance to the villa, and what was happening outside the headquarters building next door. A small service area attached to the kitchen he had fitted with a door to make an office for himself where he could keep his accounts and make out his rotas in comparative peace.

When the rest of the rooms had been sorted out, he searched among the items of furniture scattered about the villa for pieces he liked and combined them with favourite things brought from Stresa.

Everything was at last ordered to his satisfaction, and there was only one last task to complete. He carefully unwrapped the two little bronze figurines of the gods who protected the buildings of the household and the family who lived in them. He set them in a niche that could be seen by anyone entering the atrium of the villa. Then he lit a lamp before them.

The servants and slaves who had been working with him had gathered to watch him perform the small ceremony.

Aelius turned and nodded to them. 'Now I think we are ready to receive the prefect and his lady.'

Lucilla, unfortunately, did not see the villa as anything like ready for her occupation. She spent a blissful week upsetting Aelius's arrangements to make the villa look as she thought she wanted it to look.

Yes, she liked her suite of rooms, but they would have been better on the other side of the courtyard. It took a whole morning to clear rooms on the other side and settle the contents of her suite in their new place.

Lucilla looked at them when they were finished, and frowned. 'It looks different here. I don't like it.'

Aelius said, in a voice spiked with displeasure, 'That, madam, is because the sizes of the rooms are not the same and the light is different.'

She was indifferent to his problems. 'It'll all have to go back then.'

Flavius got caught up in the return furniture trail as it wound round the courtyard. Aelius, wearing his long-suffering face, halted the march to allow him to pass.

'Aelius,' murmured Flavius, 'I'm so sorry you're having to put up with all this.'

The steward inclined his head. 'The prefect has no need to concern himself, I am a servant. That's what servants are for. To put up with things.' He indicated that Flavius should move out of the way.

Flavius thought it wisest to depart without comment.

Lucilla, coming out of a room that already had been stripped twice that day, thought she glimpsed her husband moving briskly in the direction of his new library.

'Aelius!'

Aelius, who had just restarted the furniture trail, motioned it to another halt in case Lucilla was about to change her mind again.

'Aelius, another thing – that library. That room's much too large to waste on books. You can put the shelving somewhere else.'

No, thought Aelius savagely, never. As he walked back towards her, having put the trail back into motion, he replaced his long-suffering face with his amused-amazement-at-the-simple-mindedness-of-others face.

'Madam,' he said, 'the prefect will require a room large enough to use for meetings with his officers.'

Lucilla nodded in the direction of the headquarters building. 'That's what that place is for, isn't it?'

'Madam,' said Aelius, 'there will be times when the prefect will not wish to discuss the cohort's affairs in front of clerks and orderlies.' Assuming – correctly – that Lucilla would never visit the headquarters building, he refrained from mentioning that, like every other fort in the Roman Empire, it was equipped with a perfectly good private office for its commandant.

From her expression, Aelius could see that she had not yet been persuaded to change her mind. He pressed on. 'We are all, madam, whether we like it or not, part of the army here, but I can well understand that a lady of madam's standing would prefer to have as little contact as possible in the villa with serving members of the unit.'

Lucilla inclined her head. Aelius wasn't sure whether she was agreeing with him, or acknowledging what appeared to be the appropriate deference on his part, which she considered her rank entitled her to receive.

He made a slight gesture which he hoped would cover either possibility. 'Then madam will have realised why I had to choose that room for the prefect's office. It opens off the atrium, close to the entrance, well away from madam's quarters in the private courtyard.' He paused, giving her time, and then added humbly, 'I thought that madam's complete seclusion was worth the loss of space?'

'Yes,' said Lucilla. She sounded, Aelius thought, as if she had no other choice, but wasn't quite sure how she had arrived there. She waved him away. 'Get on with your work, Aelius. Don't waste time.'

Some hours later he slipped into the library, leaned against the door, closed his eyes, banged his head and let out a howl of fury. Only then did he realise that Flavius was also in the room, leaning over a long table, unrolling maps.

Flavius knew from long experience that when Aelius was bristling with temper a few words of praise could sometimes help to calm him down. 'Isn't this a splendid room?' he said. 'I love it.'

Aelius refused to look at him. He stared at the desk as though Flavius was sitting there and not leaning over the map table. 'I had hoped,' he snapped, 'that the whole villa would have given pleasure to the prefect.'

Flavius realised that this was no quick spat of annoyance but that Aelius was very angry indeed. He tried to keep a note of brightness in his voice. 'It did. Of course it did. What you've achieved in so short a time is remarkable. You had a home ready for us – an elegant, gracious home.'

Aelius spun round. 'Then why,' he demanded, 'did you tell that – that lady of yours she could rearrange everything as she pleased?' He added bitterly, 'Except, of course, for the emperor's dining-room that had taken your fancy.'

Flavius said after a minute, 'Cowardice, I suppose. I needed to find something that would occupy her for a few days while I steered my way around this alarming new world I have to learn how to control. I, too, have things to put up with.'

Aelius was somewhat taken aback by Flavius's reaction. He murmured, 'I shouldn't have said that about the changes to the house, should I?'

'Perhaps not, but I can understand why you did. I keep trying to placate Lucilla, and it's wrong to do it at someone else's expense. I'm sorry, Aelius.'

They looked at each other. 'Shall I help you with those maps?' asked the steward, striding across the room.

Two maps lay unrolled across the table; one showed the major imperial roads across Roman Britain, the other sea routes between Britain and western europe.

'Yes, those I know,' said Flavius, pushing them aside.

Knowing how much Aelius liked to instruct him, he picked out two others. 'What about these?'

Aelius spread out the larger one. 'This gives us the territory up here in the north that comes under the authority of the Sixth Legion in York. Look – here are the auxiliary forts.' He ran a finger to and fro across the map. 'Can you see Alauna?'

Flavius peered at the outline of the coast and then pointed. Aelius nodded. 'You've also got the milefortlets, the military marching roads and the slower secondary ones.'

He reached for the smaller map. 'This shows the area for about ten miles round Alauna. You get the same roads, but it also marks some of the wider tracks through the forest and the clearings where you find little clusters of huts. That's where you'd look for pockets of trouble if there was unrest brewing.'

'How did you get these?'

'They're copies of army maps in the headquarters vault. I spent two hours listening to the chief clerk's complaints about your predecessor. I don't think you'll find him difficult to follow.'

Flavius protested, 'He was a good man. He went out to Judea.'

Aelius shrugged his shoulders. 'He was from North Africa. Perhaps he wanted the heat.'

Flavius gave him a reproachful look and Aelius laughed. 'I wonder what they'll say about you when you leave?' He rolled up all the maps and carefully replaced them in their rack.

'Whatever they say,' said Flavius, 'they will have to admit that I had a fine library.'

Aelius's gaze travelled round the room. 'It is good, isn't it?'

They had brought a generous, indeed extravagant, number of texts with them for their two-year stay in Alauna, arguing that they would be spending long, dark winters on an isolated site and would need both diversion and information.

The army carpenters had fitted polished wood shelving along two facing walls. One carried texts in Latin, the other in Greek. On the floor beneath the shelves were leather tubs which housed the rolls of papyrus too large or heavy on their ivory or wooden mounts to lie on the shelves: works mainly of history and philosophy, or poetry of epic length. On the shelves themselves were stored the easily handled scrolls suitable for essays, lyric verses, satires, orations in law, light novels and small one-off pieces, mostly humorous, that Aelius was fond of collecting from minor back-street publishers.

Pale northern light came through a window and lay on the desk beneath it. It was Flavius's desk from Stresa, and Aelius had brought it without telling him to give him a pleasing surprise.

Aelius had found a couch in an upstairs store-room of the villa and had squirreled it away for the library before Lucilla saw it. He had also furnished the room with two cushioned basket chairs which Lucilla had seen but rejected as provincial.

Flavius sat down on the couch with his feet up. He noticed then, on a top shelf, a gold disc shaped like a palm frond. It had been awarded to him after a period of study in the Greek university of

Antioch. He hadn't seen it for years, and had even forgotten about it. But Aelius had looked after it.

Flavius smiled at Aelius. 'I think we shall be very content here in the winter.'

'That's what I was hoping,' said Aelius. He lifted Flavius's feet from the couch and sat beside him. 'I think it might be a good idea if you invited your officers in here, just once or twice.'

'Why should I want to do that?'

Aelius sighed. 'The lady objects strongly to using this room as your library.'

'Why should she want it?'

'She didn't say. She just feels that it's a waste of good space. Don't forget you told her she could do anything she liked with any room except the emperor's dining-room. The last excuse I could think of was to say you needed a large room to discuss confidential matters with your staff, and that this room would be out of her way.'

'Do all Greeks have wily tongues?'

'Silver tongues? Yes, I suppose we do. That's why you like to have us scattered around your households. Roman tongues can at times be a trifle base metal, don't you think?'

'Yes, thank you, Aelius.' Flavius stared at him absently, his mind on something else. After a moment, he said, 'Do you know, I think it's a good idea to bring my officers together here one day.'

'Ah!' said Aelius triumphantly. 'So everything I said to the lady was flawless truth. How many will there be?'

'Six centurions, the senior centurion, my adjutant ...'

'That's nine including you. I shall need to get some more chairs ...'

'No, Aelius, not in here. I shall invite them to dinner in the emperor's dining-room. It's a courtesy that I think I should offer, and it will be a way of getting to know each other. We could manage it, couldn't we?'

'If you mean the kitchen, of course.'

Flavius's mind was leaping ahead. 'Something else occurs to me. Three of the centurions have wives living here. We could invite them with their husbands, and they could be entertained by Lucilla.'

'The lady eat with centurions' wives?'

'But isn't it expected that the wives in a fort should be company for each other?'

'Not,' said Aelius, 'when one of them is of senatorial rank and thinks that that is the only thing in life that matters.'

'Aelius, I must try to help her find friends here – or perhaps not friends, but people she can talk to, or be pleased to spend time with.'

'There's nothing to stop you from trying,' said Aelius, patting him on the shoulder, 'but choose your moment well.'

Flavius nodded. 'What is she doing now, do you know? Is the furniture still on the move?'

'The furniture was exhausted, even though the lady was not. She is now upstairs, rummaging through cupboards which Alis took days to put into order. She is searching for things she forgot to ask to bring, and throwing out things that she says are not needed but which no-one would have dreamed of packing if Madam hadn't asked for them. Her continual complaints about one item in particular have reduced Alis to tears.'

Flavius, who had a high regard for Alis, frowned. 'What item?'

'I would rather you heard about it from the lady herself. And you will hear about it, believe me – as soon as you sit down to dinner most probably.'

When Flavius took his place at the table later that afternoon he sat facing the mural, which never failed to give him pleasure. Lucilla, who rarely showed any interest in it, sat with her back towards it. The long table was covered with a white fringed damascene cloth, and laid with glowing red Rhenish pottery. There was still some time before dusk, but the room faced north and the sky had clouded over, so bronze and ivory candelabra had been lit. The flames cast flickering splashes of pale gold on the shining tableware. Aelius, thought Flavius, had always had a way with table settings.

He was busy preparing plates of salad, which two slaves set down in front of Flavius and Lucilla. Flavius murmured his thanks, but Lucilla stared at her plate and then pushed it away untouched. Her slave motioned to Aelius, who left his serving table in concern. Flavius looked up. 'Lucilla?'

'Why,' she demanded, 'do I have to eat from such dismal, ugly plates?'

Flavius stared at her in amazement. His father had brought the service home from one of his trips to a vineyard in south Germany. He and Aelius had known it since their childhood. The rims of the pieces were decorated with beautifully incised figures of running hares and dogs and deer, all outlined in black. They used to spin the plates on the table to make the animals look as if they were really moving. His mother had always liked Rhenish pottery, and Flavius had been touched that she was willing to let him bring the service with them to Alauna. It had been part of his life for as long as he could remember, and it was a comfort to him still to be using it in Hadrian's elegant dining-room.

Aelius felt obliged to answer Lucilla as the matter seemed to reflect on his competence as steward of her household. He was also aware that Flavius seemed at a loss for words.

'If you remember, Madam,' he said in his most deferential manner, 'the prefect's mother suggested we choose the Rhenish service because it was sturdy enough to travel well, and she was assured that the prefect would be happy with it.'

'Yes, the prefect would be happy with it,' Lucilla wailed, 'but what about me? *I'm* not happy with it. I should have been asked!'

Aelius said softly, his eyes on the ground, 'You were asked, madam, and you agreed. Perhaps you misunderstood the question?'

He turned to Flavius, as if apologising to him on her behalf. 'Madam was very busy at that time. She was preoccupied with deciding which of her fans to pack.'

'Thank you, Aelius, that's enough,' said Flavius. He exchanged glances with the beady, appraising eye of the plump heron in the mural, strolling through his lapis lazuli-tinted paradise.

Lucilla realised that he was not looking at her.

'Flavius,' she snapped, 'we saw nasty, cheap stuff like this in that pottery street in Colchester ... the wrong end of the street.'

'My dear, I'm afraid I don't remember it.'

'If the prefect would allow me to speak again?' said Aelius. Without waiting for an answer, he went on, 'I think the pottery that Madam saw in Colchester was a British imitation of the pottery here. It is serviceable enough ware, but with nothing of the quality that the prefect's father would choose to buy, or the prefect's mother take pleasure in using.'

'The prefect's mother would love anything her husband gave her,' said Lucilla, beginning to sound like a spiteful child.

Aelius behaved as though he had not heard the remark, and Flavius took refuge again in studying the mural.

Eventually he said quietly, aware of the slaves moving about the room, 'Aelius is right, Lucilla. If I had a piece of the British pottery here, I could show you that the colour is lighter and there is no gloss on the surface ...'

She interrupted him. 'But you said you didn't see it in Colchester, so how do you know that? It was just like this plate here, with animals all round the edge.'

Flavius forced himself to be patient. 'The animals on that plate in front of you were incised; the ones on the imitation ware were drawn in the clay while it was still wet, so they are not so exact. And, yes, Lucilla, I do not remember seeing it with you in the Colchester street, but I saw it elsewhere in Colchester – in my agent's house, as it happens.'

'I don't see how you know so much about pottery.'

'My family makes a living from selling wine.' Flavius knew she hated any reference to this, and it showed in her expression. 'We have to know not only the character of the wines we handle but also the vessels from which we pour them.'

The slaves removed the salad plates. They placed dishes of vegetables on the table, cheese and fresh bread, then plates of ham baked in a pastry crust.

'I don't care what you say, I can't bear to eat from these plates! How can I entertain anyone of distinction if this is how we serve the food?'

Flavius was on the point of enquiring if people of distinction included anyone other than those of her own senatorial rank, when she answered the question for him.

'What if the legate came or the governor?'

She gave the plate a contemptuous tap with her finger. Flavius motioned to the slave to take it away.

'My impression of the legate,' said Flavius, 'is that as long as the food is good, the nature of the tableware would be a matter of complete indifference to him. As for the governor, I can hardly imagine he would travel three hundred miles to dine with us and then three hundred more back again.'

Aelius, who was pouring wine for Flavius, added, 'At least madam would have no worries if the emperor were to visit. I understand he always travels with his own gold plate.'

Lucilla, who had been looking rather hungrily at the cheese, glanced sullenly at Aelius. She suspected that this was one of his jokes, though she was never sure when he was making one, or quite why.

Aelius leaned over Flavius. 'Another plate for madam?' he whispered.

'No,' said Flavius. He took a mouthful of ham. Cooked with honey and spices, it was a dish he'd always enjoyed, but at that moment it had no flavour for him. He was upset and angry with Lucilla. Yet, as ever, the whispers of guilt were beginning. Was it all her fault? She had been brought up by a doting father, who denied her nothing. Should he stop Aelius taunting her, though heaven knows he had to bear much more than he deserved from her?

Flavius tasted the wine Aelius had poured, added water to it and then sipped it slowly. Lucilla, he recalled, didn't like cheese. She was trying to crumble a piece of bread.

'Talking about entertaining,' said Flavius, sipping his wine again, as though nothing had happened, 'I've decided to invite my officers to dinner once the house is finished to your satisfaction.'

Flavius was aware that Aelius was trying to convey a warning that this was not the time to bring up such a prickly matter. Lucilla, too, was bewildered by this change in the conversation.

'Your officers?' she said. 'Eating in your library?'

'No,' Flavius answered carefully, 'my officers might work with me in my library, but I would not entertain them there. We shall dine in here.'

Lucilla shook her head vehemently. 'No! I won't—'

Flavius was gracious. 'My dear, of course I wouldn't expect you to join us. Three of my centurions have wives living in the fort. I thought it might give you pleasure to invite them to eat with you.'

'Why,' demanded Lucilla, 'should I want to spend time with women like that?'

'Like what, Lucilla? They are not tribal barbarians. They are the wives of officers in the imperial army. I imagine they come from Romanised provinces anywhere across the empire, like their husbands – or like me. You would be in a separate room where you could enjoy yourselves in a gentler, more delicate way. Isn't that what the empress does? '

Lucilla, about to say something else, stopped. 'The empress?' she murmured.

Flavius could have sworn that an eyelid flickered across the bright eye of the heron. Certainly Aelius, holding in one hand a covered plate which a slave had just brought into the room, held up the thumb of the other.

'Yes,' said Flavius. 'When the emperor dines with his generals, isn't that what the empress does? Receives their wives?'

Aelius passed quietly down the room and laid the plate beside Lucilla. It was another Rhenish plate, but under the cover were small sweet hot cakes of a kind that Lucilla loved. As he moved silently back to his serving table, he raised an eyebrow at Flavius.

Flavius, rinsing his fingers and holding them out for his slave to dry them, gave a small smile and nodded.

Lucilla, in another world, bit into one of her cakes. She was still behaving like a child, Flavius thought, but a child with the touching charm of cheeks pink with excitement at the promise of a special treat.

She chose another cake. 'The empress always receives guests while recumbent on a couch,' she said, casting one of her pleading looks at Flavius.

'Well, why not? Aelius?'

He rolled his eyes in horror at Flavius, but then turned a deferential smile on Lucilla. 'As madam wishes. For four ladies, we shall need to bring down only two of the couches ...'

'Only one,' said Lucilla. 'For me. The others can sit on chairs. Aelius, didn't we see some basket chairs upstairs?'

Without hesitating he said, 'Indeed, we did, madam, but if you remember, you decided that they were not worth using so I disposed of them. But I can assure madam that I will be able to find suitable chairs for her guests.'

'Good,' said Flavius, watching the last of the cakes disappear. 'Lucilla, I want you to enjoy it.'

IX

It was a bright day in late spring when the officers and their wives, escorted by the prefect's adjutant, arrived to dine at the villa. Flavius was in the atrium, ready to greet them. Alis came forward to collect the ladies and lead them to the room where Lucilla was waiting.

The officers appeared gratified by their new commandant's courtesy and by the fine wines he was able to offer them. These were the very early days of his prefecture before he had discovered that some of them were guilty of behaviour he found impossible to condone, but on that spring evening all was goodwill and good humour round his table.

Aelius, despatched to see how the ladies were faring, reported that although the hostess had slightly overawed her guests with her Roman finery, they were now all talking away happily. Flavius felt a wave of relief.

It was an hour or so later that he became aware that his dining-room seemed uncomfortably hot. He then noticed that Lugo's face was unnaturally flushed and one of the younger men had loosened the small scarf knotted round his neck.

He beckoned Aelius. 'Something is wrong with the heating,' he muttered.

Aelius bent down. 'The heating is in perfect order, and doing what I required it to do, or rather what I was instructed to do.'

'I asked you for warmth for a chilly spring evening, not a winter snowstorm,' hissed Flavius.

'The lady was feeling cold, and instructed me otherwise. She is wearing a dress that might be considered thin for an August evening in Rome.' Aelius was trying with difficulty to keep his voice low. 'I might add that it is not exactly convenient with eleven guests dining in the house. Two of my kitchen lads have had to help out in the furnace.'

'Right,' said Flavius, brisk with annoyance. 'You will put them back in the kitchen. Tell the two who understand the heating system to reduce the heat as soon as they possibly can. Ask Alis to find a wrap for my wife. Then get the windows in here open.'

Flavius cast a sharp look round the table. 'Don't worry about them,' Aelius whispered. 'Most of them are Spaniards.'

Aelius was right. With the wine flowing and the jokes circulating to louder and louder laughter, no-one else seemed to have any other concerns.

At the end of a long evening, Flavius and Lucilla stood together in the atrium, wishing their guests farewell. As the door opened on to the street, a keen wind surprised them. Lucilla was now wearing a wrap over her shoulders, but it was made of the same thin silk as her dress. Flavius caught Alis's eye and frowned. She shook her head and shrugged her shoulders.

One of the wives shivered and laughed as she stepped out of the door. Her husband caught up the edge of his cloak and held it round her. Flavius saw the look of tenderness that passed between them. He was conscious of Lucilla standing beside him in her dress glistening with gold thread and her jewels flashing in the lamplight as she moved. He would never, he thought, be allowed to put a cloak round her like that; and, perhaps, sadly he might never want to try.

The porter closed the door after the Lugo who, like a good shepherd seeing his flock safely on their way, was the last to leave. As Aelius stepped forward to turn the keys in the lock, Flavius saw the smile on Lucilla's face disappear. He braced himself for one of her outbursts of temper, but was unprepared for the look of fury she turned on him.

'How dare you do that to me? How *dare* you?' she sobbed. Aelius hastily withdrew the keys and motioned the slaves who had been helping with the cloaks to leave the atrium. Head averted, he followed them.

'Lucilla, I'm sorry, but the heat was intolerable. You cannot dress here as you would in Rome and make everyone else suffer for it.'

She frowned. 'Heat?' She seemed to have forgotten about that. But having been reminded, she said nastily, 'Oh, yes, there is that, too. That was cruel enough, but nothing to the other ... nothing, nothing!'

Flavius grasped her arm and pulled her through the nearest doorway. He kicked the door shut with his foot. She pulled her arm free with a great sobbing wail. 'You made me do it! You made me have her here ...'

Flavius forced himself to speak calmly. 'I don't know what you are talking about. Tell me.'

'You made me eat with a slave. She sat beside me. We shared the same dish.' His wife shuddered.

Flavius was lost. 'She?'

'That woman in the green dress!'

The only woman in a green dress whom Flavius had seen that evening was the one whose husband had wrapped her in his cloak. He sighed. 'Lucilla, you spent the evening with the wives of three army officers.'

Lucilla clenched her fists and shook them at him. 'She was a slave! That centurion bought her in the slave market at Colchester. Colchester!' She repeated the name as if it were unthinkable that a town she had been disposed to like could bring her such distress. Flavius waited.

'He bought that *slave* her freedom, then he married her.'

'How do you know this?'

'They were all talking about how they came to be living here.'

'So the other two wives already knew and treated her as one of them?'

Lucilla scowled. 'Yes.'

'I am relieved to hear it,' said Flavius briskly, 'but it is only what I would expect. All three ladies now share the same rank, and will receive the same respect. That is the law, Lucilla, whether you like it or not.'

'I don't care about your silly law. A slave will always be a slave.'

'No, my dear. You can't pick and choose laws as you please.'

'No?' she demanded. 'Do your family keep the law about slaves?'

'Of course they do.'

'What about Aelius's family?'

'Alis is Aelius's wife, yes, but it is a legal marriage because they were both freed.'

'I don't mean Alis and Aelius,' said Lucilla impatiently, 'though I never understood why you bought them their freedom. They were well enough off as slaves, weren't they? But what about Aelius's parents? They are both your father's slaves, though from the way they are treated anyone would think them part of your family.'

'They are like family to me,' said Flavius gently.

'They are both slaves,' Lucilla repeated, 'yet your father let them marry, and when they had a son he let them bring the child up under his own roof instead of selling him off as bastard slaves are supposed to be. I suppose, because he's so rich, he thinks he can ignore your precious laws and nobody dares to do anything about it.'

She had one of her fans clutched in her hand and was waving it about so angrily it was like a vicious bird fluttering between them.

Lying in the warm bath-house, Flavius recalled how disturbed he had been that she could speak about his parents with such little respect or kindness. He had snatched the fan from her hand, wanting to break it; but she had whimpered, and instead he threw it on to a chair.

'My father is not a man to abuse the law. I would have thought you might have realised that by now. Did it never occur to you that there might be some acceptable explanation for the marriage between Aelius's mother and father?'

Lucilla turned her back on him and busied herself retrieving the fan.

'Lucilla, answer me.'

Without turning round, she snapped, 'No, it didn't occur to me, because there isn't one.'

'Listen to me, Lucilla. Listen!'

The unusual sharpness in his voice startled her. She sank on to a chair with a resentful look.

'Aelius's parents were married before they joined my father's household as slaves. They had both been born free but sold themselves into slavery because they saw no other way of surviving.'

'Sold themselves into slavery?' Lucilla made a scornful noise as if someone had told a stupid joke.

'Let me explain it to you, Lucilla. Aelius's father is a Greek, born in Sicily. He is a man of great scholarship, and was employed as tutor to the family of a prominent political family there. He was still a young man with a pregnant wife when fighting broke out on the island and his employer was disgraced and banished, leaving behind a houseful of homeless and destitute servants. No-one else dared to offer them work.'

From the loud sigh which Flavius heard, it was evident, not surprisingly, that Lucilla was not interested and her attention had wandered to the embroidery on the trailing ends of her belt.

Flavius continued speaking. 'It happened, Lucilla, that about that time fashionable Roman houses started looking for Greek tutors ... '

This was something that touched on the world as Lucilla knew it. She looked up from the belt. 'Oh, yes. My cousins had Greek tutors. It was to please the emperor, because he loves anything Greek.'

Flavius sighed and added patiently, 'There was another reason. More than half our empire was by then Greek-speaking. For families like yours, looking for government appointments in these provinces, a knowledge of Greek was an advantage; for merchant families like mine, it was essential to have agents who could conduct business in the local tongue. Do you understand now, Lucilla, why Artemon, Aelius's father, decided that slavery in a prosperous Roman household was the safest way of being able to make use of his skills?'

Lucilla behaved as if she hadn't even heard the question.

'My father was in Sicily to negotiate the purchase of a vineyard. By chance, he wandered into the auction market where Artemon was submitting himself for sale. Father was in Sicily merely to buy a vineyard, but as he watched Artemon and listened to the way he answered questions, he became convinced that a Greek scholar would be an asset to his family's business. He entered the bidding, which was fierce, and went on bidding until Artemon was his. Artemon then insisted, before he signed away his own freedom, that his pregnant wife should accompany him. My father agreed, and Artemon signed away her freedom as well. My mother was also pregnant at the time and I think my father felt that he had found a companion for her. Certainly, if his future child was a boy, he need look no further for a tutor. And, do you know, Lucilla? The first thing that Artemon did on my father's behalf was to arrange a very satisfactory price for the vineyard. My grandfather was delighted when he heard, but then his face, so they tell me, went white with horror when he learned that Artemon had cost more than the vineyard!'

Flavius smiled, recalling how his father and Artemon would grin at each other whenever the matter cropped up in family conversations.

'Aelius was born in the villa at Stresa not long after they arrived, and I was born a few months later. Artemon became my father's secretary, his librarian, tutor to us two boys, and my father's most trusted friend. Even my grandfather has been known to admit that he was worth all the money my father paid for him and more, though my grandfather tends to add: especially as the family got three slaves for the price of one.'

Lucilla clutched her thin silk shawl round her shoulders. 'Why should I have to listen to all this? It's nothing to do with me.'

'You accused my father of breaking the law. You needed to know that you were wrong. He is not here to listen to your apology, but you can make it to me.'

Lucilla uttered another of her irritating scornful grunts.

'And it occurs to me,' persisted Flavius, 'that since you declare that anyone born a slave remains a slave, shouldn't you agree that anyone born free remains free? In which case, shouldn't you treat Artemon and his wife rather more graciously than you usually do?'

Lucilla easily became confused whenever Flavius started arguing like a lawyer. She struck out at him. 'If your father is so fond of Artemon, why doesn't he give him back his freedom? He doesn't, does he?'

'He has offered to do so more than once, but Artemon always says that if he were a free man, earning his own living, he would never be able to afford a library like the one he can use in my father's house, and his wife could never have a garden like the one she has helped my mother create.'

Lucilla glared at him. 'Is this another of your clever arguments?'

Flavius chose to ignore the retort. He said more gently, 'I also wanted you to know Artemon's story because the lady in the green dress ...'

'The slave woman?'

'One of my officers' wives might have a similar background. Colchester has not always been an easy city to live in. You could ask her about it next time you meet her. She seems quite happy to talk about her life with the other wives.'

'The next time?' Lucilla stamped her foot. 'I shall never speak to her again. She will never be allowed in this house again,' she shouted.

'Lucilla, be sensible. You need to find whatever companions you can here. I know nothing about soldiers, but I have to learn to live with them for the next two years.'

His wife was silent for a moment. Then she said, as though the words were being dragged out of her, 'I suppose I might tolerate the other two.'

'No. The three ladies seem to me to be close friends. You can't ignore one of them. I don't think the other two would accept it. I wouldn't respect them if they did.'

'As you please. Then I'll ignore all of them. I'll find my own company in Carlisle. Aelius can get a litter ready for me.'

'But it is thirty miles from here, not round the next corner.'

'Thirty miles?' murmured Lucilla in bewilderment.

Flavius was certain she had little idea what thirty miles represented in terms of distance, but she did realise that it was not something to be covered in a few minutes by two slaves carrying a litter.

'Then I could go in one of those little carriages with Alis,' she declared.

'The road runs through heavily wooded territory, full of thieves. It is too dangerous, especially for two women alone.'

'Then couldn't I have an escort of soldiers? There's no war on, they've nothing to do.'

'Not,' said Flavius, 'while I am commandant of this cohort.'

Lucilla was tired, cold, angry and not getting her own way. She resorted to one of her outbursts of sobbing.

It was at that moment Flavius heard a quiet tapping on the door. 'Yes?'

Alis appeared, carrying what looked to Flavius like one of his red military cloaks. Aelius followed her. The timing of the interruption was so apt that Flavius was in no doubt that they had both been listening anxiously at the door.

'I beg the prefect to excuse me,' said Alis in her soft way, 'but I was thinking that if madam is wanting to retire after her busy evening, she might be uneasy about stepping into the cold night air to reach her rooms. She has only a very delicate wrap with her, so I hope this might help.'

Aelius took the cloak from her, shook out the folds and very carefully settled it on Lucilla's shoulders.

Outraged, she put up a hand to pull it off. 'Aelius, what do you think you are doing?'

He was magnificently contrite. 'Madam, I beg you to forgive me but I assumed you had heard about the empress.'

Lucilla froze.

'Surely Madam remembers the empress's cloak?' said Aelius, lowering his voice yet speaking loudly enough for Flavius to hear. 'She ordered her dressmaker to cut her a cloak like a general's, which, of course, is very much like those worn by the prefect. She felt that the heavy folds were most becoming. It was quite the rage for a season in Rome.' He stepped back. 'Looking at madam now, one can see she was right.'

Lucilla turned her head to judge how the cloak trailed behind her as she moved. She looked at Alis, who smiled and nodded. 'Yes, I want to go to bed now.' Like a child, Lucilla let Alis put an arm round her and lead her out of the room.

Flavius faced Aelius. 'Are you going to tell me that that was a true story?'

'Of course it was.' He paused. 'However – '

'However, what?'

'The lady assumed that I was talking about our current Empress, but I didn't say that. The empress with the general's cloak was Agrippina.'

'But she died about seventy years ago!'

Aelius shrugged his shoulders and grinned. 'There was one other thing. Her cloak was made of cloth-of-gold.'

'And what's going to happen when Lucilla finds out?' Flavius cried.

'Who is there up here to tell her? Anyway, don't worry. We can think of something in the morning. At least we can all get a good night's sleep first, which we need.'

It was Flavius's turn to grin. 'Lucilla and Alis and I are going to get a good night's sleep, but not you. My wife wants you to provide her with a litter to take her into Carlisle tomorrow.'

Aelius kept a straight face. 'Would that be with red or purple hangings? If she wants gold fringing that might take a little longer. Two years, shall we say?'

The next afternoon, Flavius had set out on the first of what were to become his routine private inspections of the fort. As he walked along the veranda outside one of the barracks, he saw a woman come out of the centurion's house attached to the end of the block. She was leading a small child by one hand and in the other carrying a small posy of spring flowers. Although she was now wearing a darker colour, he recognised the lady of the green dress. They met as Flavius reached the steps at the end of the veranda.

She smiled and made him a small curtsey. Flavius bade her good afternoon. 'Sir, I was just on my way to the villa to offer your wife these flowers to thank her for her kind hospitality.'

'There are not many flowers in a Roman fort, especially in the north of Britain,' he said.

'My husband has made me a little garden behind the house, out of the wind. I like growing things. I hope she will accept these from all three of us.' The woman seemed suddenly to feel shy. 'They are not very much, I know.'

'They are a great deal,' said Flavius. 'Forgive me, my wife must have told me your name, but ...'

'Aemilia.'

'Aemilia, perhaps I could take them to her for you. It is quite a long walk for your little one. May I?'

She handed him the posy gratefully. 'We all hope we shall have the pleasure of seeing your lady again soon. We like to take short walks together. Perhaps she would join us.'

Flavius unhappily prepared himself to lie. 'I am sure she would enjoy that, but I'm afraid she suffers from rather fragile health. She is unable to go out as much as she would wish. The long journey here was very tiring for her.'

Aemilia looked concerned. 'I am so sorry. Then it was all the kinder of her to invite us yesterday. Please give her our good wishes.'

She made another of her curtseys, lifted the child in her arms and turned back towards her house.

Flavius went back into his own home through the kitchen court. Aelius was sitting in his minute office, dealing with a list of figures. Holding the posy with care, Flavius squeezed himself into the remaining space. 'These flowers were for Lucilla,' he explained. 'I've no doubt what she would do with them, but they were given in kindness and Alis would understand that. Do you think she could find a space for them?'

Aelius shouted out for a mug filled with water. 'I'm sure. She likes pretty things like this. Thank you.' Flavius waited while a mug was thrust through the door and Aelius put the posy in it. 'Alis will find something nicer for them.' He bent over his figures again.

Flavius asked, 'What's happened about my cloak?'

Aelius patiently laid down his pen for the second time. 'It's safely back in its chest in your room.'

Flavius looked uneasy. 'How?'

'When the lady asked where it was this morning, Alis told her that in the daylight she'd found the hem was stained, and it would have to be cleaned before it could be worn again. Or, she suggested, possibly the lady might like to instruct her dressmaker to fashion her another, in one of her favourite colours instead of military red?'

Aelius smiled, but Flavius did not. 'Yes, it's a good idea,' he conceded, 'but we're all deceiving her.'

'We're trying to make her see the sense of wearing suitable clothes. Alis has tried persuading her, you tried reasoning with her – useless. Something had to be done, if only to stop her moaning at Alis and having the heating raised outrageously high every time your back was turned.

'After all, it's what she herself does to get what she wants: all those deceptive little temper tantrums and sobs and smiles. Let's say she has a butterfly mind – delicate and fragile, with not much substance behind it. And when there's nothing else left, all you'll find is obstinacy.'

Flavius was already leaving.

X

Several months had passed since that spring dinner party and the bitter quarrel that had arisen from it. Lying in the bath-house, calling for a slave to help release him from the cocoon of towels, Flavius recalled Aelius's words.

Lucilla might be shallow-minded, but she clung to her prejudices with a will of iron. She had never again spoken to any of the centurions' wives, and always ignored their little courtesies. Flavius tried to persuade her to show some common sense or at least civic good manners, but her attitude remained intractable. He found himself telling lie after lie about her supposed delicate health, and was not happy to realise how adept he had become at it.

Aelius pointed out that he had spent years in law schools and had proved to be a good pupil.

As the summer progressed, Lucilla grew more and more lonely and bored with her own company. Flavius offered to let his adjutant escort her on the short five-mile journey to Papcastle to take up the invitation of the commandant's wife, but she told him in a spurt of temper that she didn't want to spend time with that woman.

As the shorter days of autumn approached, Flavius became increasingly worried about his wife. It was true that she had only herself to blame for her discontentment, and he was angered by her and the way she took out her resentment on their household staff. Yet he was unable to escape from the sense that he was partly to blame.

In the five years of their marriage they had spent little time together until they left for Alauna. His legal commitments often took him away from home, and as chief magistrate back in Stresa he had been greatly preoccupied with work in which his wife took little interest. He knew that she was happy to pass her time in frivolous amusements, but had never quite realised before how much they dominated her life. From the beginning, he had had doubts about taking her with him to Alauna, but had felt it proper to leave the decision to her. He had tried to make her understand what life in the north of Britain might be like, but she probably listened, as usual, to about half of what he said. When she'd surprised him by choosing to accompany him, he assumed – stupidly – that she was unwilling to be separated from him, whatever the difficulties.

He now knew that if he had taken the trouble to understand her more, he would have realised how totally unfitted she was to be the commandant's wife in an isolated corner of the empire.

He should have grasped how limited her interests were, and how much her reverence for rank dominated her life. Whenever her behaviour, whether from ignorance or perversity, offended him, once his temper had cooled, he could only reproach himself for thoughtlessly depriving her of the things, however silly, that made her happy.

Dreading the short winter days ahead when she would grow even more sullen and despondent, he felt he must do something to console her, to give her pleasure, to show her that he wasn't without sympathy for her plight. An idea of what he might do came to him one evening as they were about to eat, and the dishes of hated Rhenish pottery were being placed on the table. He was suddenly reminded of Lucilla's excitement in the elegant shop in Colchester where they had shared one of their rare moments of happiness together. He decided that as a gift to celebrate Saturnalia he would order a dinner service in the design that had so delighted her then.

That same evening, Aelius was instructed to prepare a list of the required items. Then Flavius shut himself in his library and wrote to his family's agent in Colchester, describing the pottery he had seen during his visit earlier in the year and giving him the location of the shop. He requested the man to enquire if the shopkeeper could identify the design and its factory of origin. He needed an estimate of the time it would take to complete the work and ship it to Britain. Delivery, he stipulated, must allow for transport to reach Alauna in the first week of December.

Replies reached him in a steady stream; from the agent in Colchester, who had visited the shop; from the shopkeeper, who recognised the design described and placed an order with the factory in Gaul; from the factory on receipt of the order; again from the factory when the work had been completed on time and had been despatched to Bordeaux; from the family's agent in Bordeaux, who had supervised the loading of the crate on to one of the company's vessels bound for York. It was by then early November. Flavius had been greatly pleased. The agent in York had been advised of the crate's arrival and would arrange for the final part of its journey to Alauna. It should be there well before Saturnalia. It would be difficult to hide the arrival and storage of his gift, so Flavius decided to tell Lucilla that a special treat was on its way to her, although she mustn't ask what it was.

She was at first unresponsive to this news. 'What treat can you find for me up here?'

'It doesn't come from up here.'

She stared at him, and then, as he had hoped, her weary expression changed and she gave one of her pretty smiles. 'Will it come from across the water then?'

'Yes,' said Flavius. 'Now, no more questions. You must wait until the first day of Saturnalia.'

She laughed and spun round on her toes. 'Perhaps I can guess what it is?'

Flavius laughed with her and shook his head.

For a while, excitement made her amiable and sweet-tempered, but when the first week of December had passed without any delivery, her mood began to change. By the end of the second week and the arrival of the first morning of Saturnalia, she was sullen and petulant with everyone in the household, and barely speaking to Flavius.

But now, he thought gratefully, all that was over. The dinner service, delayed by a week of bad weather at sea and then by the problem of arranging fresh transport during the holiday, was at last here for her. In a few moments they would be sharing a special dinner together and she should be in one of her pretty, child-like moods.

XI

The slave had pulled Flavius's tunic over his head and was handing him his belt when Aelius came hurrying back into the bath-house.

He waved the slave away. 'What are you smiling about?' He spoke as if Flavius was doing something without permission.

'Food,' said Flavius. 'I'm hungry.'

'Well, it's waiting for you. What have you been doing all this time?'

What had he been doing? 'Just thinking about things,' said Flavius vaguely. 'Admiring the paintings.'

Aelius shook his head, reached for Flavius's mantle and arranged it round his shoulders. The fashion for wearing a tunic and mantle in a matching colour was known in stylish Roman circles as a dinner-set. It had been devised as informal dress for the late-afternoon dinner hour at home or among intimate friends, and replaced the heavy, uncomfortable toga required in public places.

Flavius had pointed out that meals in army camps were not always eaten at the accepted hour, and that he himself was not, at the present time, a toga-wearing lawyer. Aelius, however, insisted that for a man of his standing a change of circumstances should not affect his dress code. Flavius, who had grown up tending to do as Aelius told him, gave in and every night dressed as if he were still living in Rome or Stresa. Aelius also disapproved of the more flamboyant members of Roman society whose dinner-sets were 'in colours like a summer garden'. The only dinner-sets in Flavius's chests were in dark jewel-like colours; for the celebration of his birthday, Aelius had chosen one in sapphire blue which he particularly liked with Flavius's fair colouring.

Flavius had started fiddling with his belt again. 'Hurry up,' said Aelius. Flavius stepped briskly out of the warm bath-house into the cold air and made for the villa. Aelius followed, ahead of a handful of slaves carrying parts of Flavius's military dress for immediate attention: his cloak for brushing, his tunic for washing, his cuirasse for polishing.

A covered way led into the kitchen courtyard. The slaves disappeared in various directions. Flavius looked round in surprise.

'Where is everyone else?'

'Where do you think they are on a cold, dark winter's evening?'

'You said the crate was being unpacked.'

'Not here,' said Aelius impatiently. 'The lady took charge. Can you imagine her ever doing anything in a kitchen? They're in the dining-room.'

'The emperor's dining-room?' Flavius was appalled. 'Why couldn't you have put her in some other room to make her mess?'

'Because that's where she wanted to go. It's not for me to say what she can and can't do, when ...'

' ...when I can't either,' Flavius interrupted.

'I was going to say, when I am as much her servant as you are.'

'Couldn't you at least have tried to dissuade her?'

'No, I couldn't. I'd already had one unpleasant brush with her today, and I've reached the age when two in one day is more than I can bear.'

'You're the same age as I am.'

'Some months older. It all tells.' They had passed through the kitchen quarters and had reached the open courtyard. Flavius stopped. 'What unpleasant brush?'

'As a matter of fact, it was all your fault. You sent that young adjutant of yours over here. I was walking him across to the stables to get him a mount when the lady fluttered by from somewhere or other, like a great stinging wasp. "I was bringing soldiers into the house behind her back. I knew she didn't allow that." She couldn't have made more of a fuss if I'd brought in a troop of a dozen men with mud on their boots up to their knees. And there stood this young lad with his courteous manner, exquisitely polished from head to toe, turning pink in the face from embarrassment, with absolutely no idea what he had done wrong. Then he whispered to me that he had changed his mind about riding, and would go back to his quarters to write letters.'

Flavius groaned. 'Doesn't she know who he is?'

'How would she know what an adjutant is? She might recognise a general if he was leading a triumph in a gold chariot, but the rest of them all look the same to her.'

Flavius shook his head. 'The wife of the legate in York is his aunt. I believe her family has some connection with Hadrian's.'

Aelius gave a gleeful laugh and cast his eyes upwards. 'May the gods grant that I am present when madam finds out!'

'Yes, and that I am not,' muttered Flavius.

He glanced across the gardens towards the doors of the dining-room. 'Perhaps I ought to ...'

Aelius said firmly, 'Food first. I'll get the mess cleaned up while you're both eating. Don't worry about it.'

'But that room,' Flavius protested, 'why there?'

'Flavius, she's not as enamoured of that room as you are.' Aelius, despite his feelings about Lucilla, always tried to be fair to her. 'She probably thought a dining-room was the place to unpack a dinner service, especially this new one you chose for her. Don't let it spoil your dinner together.'

'No, no,' said Flavius, 'not this dinner.' He smiled gratefully at Aelius. 'This is a special one.'

Aelius had transformed the library into an agreeable small dining-room. In the centre stood a table laid with two places. The map table had been adapted for serving.

Flavius glanced around. Lucilla was not there.

'My wife?'

'Probably waiting to hear when the prefect is ready,' said Aelius, trying to hide his own uneasiness. He despatched one of the slaves busy arranging the food to find out. Flavius, meanwhile, was looking at the dishes that had been prepared for his birthday dinner, and his little cries of pleasure at the sight of so many of his favourite treats brought smiles to the faces of the remaining slaves. He wandered to the far end of the map table, which was doing duty as the so-called second table at Roman dinner parties where the delicacies which followed the main course were set out.

Flavius turned to Aelius. 'Dates?' he whispered.

Aelius removed the cover from a small dish and nodded.

'Stuffed with nuts?'

Aelius smiled and nodded again.

Flavius was delighted. 'My mother always used to make them for us on our birthdays. How ...?'

'She taught Alis.' Aelius deftly replaced the lid as Flavius stretched out a hand. 'Not now.' He indicated the dining table. 'If the prefect would be good enough to seat himself?'

Flavius sat down as the slave came hurrying back into the library. He murmured in the steward's ear. Aelius frowned and appeared to be asking a number of questions to which the slave was shaking his head.

Aelius crossed the floor and stood facing Flavius. 'I regret, sir, that the lady is unable to join you for dinner.'

Flavius was surprised to realise how disappointed he felt. He half rose from his chair. 'Is she ill?'

'No, sir, it appears that she is still unpacking the crate. She likes to take out each piece herself, examine it and then watch while it is dusted. I gather that she did observe that if you had come as soon as she asked for you, the work would probably have been finished by now.' He paused delicately. 'Would the prefect wish me to remind her that it is your birthday?'

'No,' said Flavius, throwing himself back into the chair. 'If she didn't care to remember this morning, I doubt if it would be of any interest to her now.' He tried to laugh. 'I thought she might at least want to celebrate the last evening she would have to use the Rhenish plates. Sit down, Aelius. You will have to share this meal with me tonight.'

Aelius leaned across the table. 'Have you forgotten who you are?' he hissed. 'We're not eight years old any longer.'

Flavius bent towards him. 'I have never yet eaten alone on my birthday. I am not disposed to change the habit now. Since there is no-one else around with whom I choose to eat, it will have to be you.' He tapped the table. 'I am the master in this house and I require obedience. You can start by clearing the room.'

He placed the tips of his thumb and first finger together to form a circle. It was a secret sign they had used as boys whenever they were about to embark on some act of mischief. Aelius, wearing his solemn face, responded with the same sign.

He motioned the slaves to approach him. 'The prefect,' he announced, 'is concerned about the lateness of the hour and that you have not yet eaten. Since he is dining alone I can serve him myself and you may all go now.'

The slaves filed out of the room, nodding their thanks to Flavius. Aelius put the catch on the door, and then sat down opposite him.

'Are the master's instructions carried out to his satisfaction?'

'Eminently,' said Flavius, grinning. 'Eight years old again, eh?'

They raced to the serving table and, plates in hand, filled them at random with a mound of food as they might have done years ago, at picnics on the lake shore. They put wine and water and large goblets on the table between them.

After a while, Flavius loosened his belt.

Aelius shook his head. 'You can't do that. Only servants are allowed to go without belts.'

Flavius, with his mouth full, said, 'I'm only eight. I haven't got any servants, I don't know anything about belts.' He stuck his knife into a tasty-looking titbit on Aelius's plate. Aelius started on the stuffed dates.

'What's this?' asked Flavius. 'It's delicious.' He peered at Aelius's plate to see if he could find any more of the same.

Aelius pulled himself out of his chair to see if there were any oysters left in the bowl. He caught his foot in Flavius's discarded belt on the floor and gave a deep sigh. 'Put on your belt, Flavius. I think perhaps its time we should think about going.'

Flavius, too, sighed; but, as children, Aelius always knew when an escapade had to end, so Flavius nodded his acceptance. 'Lucilla and the pottery for me. I wonder what sort of mood I'll find her in now.'

Aelius picked up the belt and handed it to him. 'Finish up your dates. There's no doubt that she likes the pottery, but did you know it wasn't the gift she was expecting?'

'How could she know what to expect?'

'She told Alis that you had promised her a gold necklace.'

Aelius unlatched the library door and they walked together across the atrium towards the courtyard. 'Did you promise her a gold necklace?'

'No! Well, yes, but not as a Saturnalia gift.'

'Then why was she expecting a gold necklace?'

Flavius sighed. 'When we left Papcastle, she wasn't in a very happy state so I tried to please her ...'

'There are times when I think you still are eight years old.'

'... by telling her of the quality of the goldsmiths' work you can find in parts of Britain. She always likes talking about jewellery.'

Aelius rolled his eyes.

'I heard about it from our agent in Colchester. It's very fine indeed and of a style found nowhere else in Europe. I remember my father saying that when you visit a strange land, look for things that are like nothing you have ever seen before. So I suggested to Lucilla that when we could, we would find one of these goldsmiths and I would buy her a necklace, but she said she didn't want ...'

'... anything made by a barbarian,' said Aelius.

'Yes, and then I found myself promising to buy her instead a gold necklace from a jeweller in Rome.'

'Six years old, not eight.'

'Aelius!' Flavius glared at him.

He folded his arms. 'So?'

'She agreed that if she wanted this necklace made in Rome, she would be willing to wait until we were back home in two years' time. So how could she have told Alis she was expecting it now?'

They stopped outside the emperor's dining- room. Aelius put his hand on the door. 'Either,' he muttered, 'because she is stupid, or because you are.' He pushed open the door and stepped back to allow Flavius to enter.

The sight that met him drove everything else from Flavius's mind. The exquisite floor was littered with straw, packing and splintered wood. There was dust everywhere. Pieces of pottery lay on every available flat surface, even the seats of chairs. In the middle of all this stood Lucilla, sobbing noisily.

Flavius made his way through the debris. 'Lucilla, what is it? What's happened?'

She answered him with a wail of despair. Flavius took hold of her and shook her gently. 'Lucilla, please.'

'It's broken. I had to wait all this time for it, and it's broken. And you wouldn't come.' The tears poured out again.

Flavius looked round the room. All he could see were shining, undamaged pieces. He couldn't help noticing that the new pottery, with its green leaves trailing over a cream ground, was more pleasing even than he remembered.

He turned to Aelius who was standing behind him, watching with a cold eye. 'She must be very tired. Perhaps some food?'

Aelius bent towards him, 'She is not hungry. While all this was going on, she somehow found time to eat dinner in her sitting-room.'

Flavius sighed and tried again with his wife. 'What do you mean? I can't see anything broken. Why not have a rest? We'll find Alis.'

'I don't need Alis. Alis can't mend plates, can she?'

'Ah,' said Aelius. He walked over to the remains of the crate and looked inside. He noticed that behind it were two piles of the largest-sized plates. Beside them was something covered with a strip of the cheap papyrus used for wrapping. He beckoned to the senior slave on duty.

'It struck me as odd that there were no large plates anywhere. The crate was empty, and then I find them lying on the floor, where any of us could trip over them. Have you an explanation for this?'

The slave hesitated. 'It was madam's order, sir.'

Aelius looked at Flavius. He nodded. 'Pick them up,' he said. 'Find space for them on the table.'

'It doesn't matter if someone does trip over them!' cried Lucilla. 'They're no use.'

There was a shifting of the pieces already laid on the table and eventually the two piles were safely settled among them. The wrapped packet was handed to Aelius. 'It was madam's wish that these should be kept out of her sight,' he was told.

Aelius removed the strip of papyrus. He was faced with two more plates, both broken in half.

'Is anything else broken?' he enquired.

He was assured that nothing else was. It was explained to him that the plates were the last pieces lifted out. The broken ones were at the bottom of the crate..

'What does it matter where they were?' Lucilla shouted across the room to Aelius. 'I can't serve dinner to guests with two plates missing. And if there are no plates, what good is the rest of the service?'

To avoid shouting back at her, Aelius made his way across the littered floor. He held out the broken pieces to Lucilla. 'These can, of course, be destroyed, madam. But even without them madam will still have the full service which the prefect authorised me to acquire. I made extra purchases to cover possible breakages, on the journey and in daily use. I am sure the prefect will agree that it is quite remarkable that, given the size of the order and the hazards of the journey, there has been such a very small loss.'

Aelius paused to give Lucilla the opportunity to express relief or even thanks. He was not, however, surprised or disappointed when she made no response. As usual, when some of her wildest misconceptions were dispersed by reasonable argument, she was resentful rather than grateful.

'If the prefect wishes,' he went on, 'we can re-order, but you have eighteen plates here in the largest size.'

'But I should have twenty,' she snapped. 'What if more than eighteen people come?'

Flavius, who to Aelius looked exhausted and perhaps on the brink of sending for a gold necklace, said crisply, 'Lucilla, you should be aware by now that this dining-room allows for only twelve people if they are to be seated comfortably and the slaves able to move about quickly; using the three couches, which you say you prefer, there is room only for nine. Eighteen plates should do well enough. And perhaps I could point out to you that in the seven months we have been here, the largest number to have dined together was eleven, and only eight of them were in this room.'

Lucilla was furious at being reminded of the night she had eaten with the centurions' wives. She started to cry again, this time tears of temper. She noticed after a minute or two that Flavius was not as affected as he usually was by one of her outbursts. Instead he spoke to Aelius.

Through her sniffs and sobs, Licilla said pettishly, 'We're not going to be here for ever. Back in Stresa, I shall want receptions in the summer by the lake. Eighteen plates will never be enough, will it?'

Aelius murmured, 'For the kind of occasions that madam is considering, I would hardly have thought this kind of service was suitable, but if that is what madam wishes, even twenty would not be enough. However, by then, there will have been ample time to order as many additional plates as madam wishes – '

Flavius interrupted. 'Only, Aelius, if my wife still chooses to use all this.' He waved a hand at the pottery all round them. He looked at Lucilla. 'So far, my dear, you have shown no pleasure at all in it. Aelius, if it proves not to be to her liking, have it re-packed for removal.'

Lucilla's tears dried abruptly. Her mouth fell open in astonishment.

Aelius bowed, not certain that he could hide a look of satisfaction. 'Where,' he enquired, 'would the prefect wish me to send it?'

Flavius's attention had been caught by the activity going on at the door. The slave on duty as porter at the main entrance to the villa had come in, evidently in a hurry, and a couple of the others were crowding round him.

Later, Aelius,' said Flavius. 'What's all this?'

The porter, hearing his voice, moved towards him, picking his way across the litter. Flavius took a quick step to meet him.

'Flavius!' cried Lucilla, in a voice that suggested both anger and bewilderment. Aelius wasn't sure which, and perhaps she wasn't either.

'Not now, Lucilla.' Flavius nodded at the porter.

One of his officers, the man explained breathlessly, had arrived with an important message for the prefect, and was waiting outside.

At that moment, evidently too impatient to wait any longer, Flavius's adjutant pushed his way into the room. He was in a state, Flavius saw, of considerable agitation, and hating the need to break into his commandant's privacy.

Lucilla gave one of her irritating squeals. 'How dare he come back here? Didn't he hear what I said this morning? Aelius, didn't he? Make him go.'

The young adjutant looked as if he would rather be anywhere else in the world than where he was.

'Quintus?' said Flavius, ignoring Lucilla.

'I beg the prefect's pardon for disturbing him,' he said, stumbling over his words in his haste to get them out, 'but a courier has just arrived with urgent information.'

'It will have to wait till morning,' Lucilla waved him away. 'The prefect is busy.'

Quintus avoided looking at Lucilla and kept his eyes fixed on Flavius. 'He requires you to see him in the headquarters building at once.'

'Requires?' repeated Flavius quietly. 'In this fort, I am the commandant. Are you sure that was the word he used?'

Quintus swallowed. 'No, sir. In fact, he commands you to come – in the name of the emperor. He comes from the emperor himself.'

A silence fell on the room. Flavius felt a frisson of alarm,

'What is the nature of this message?' he asked.

'The bearer will share that only with you, sir,' Quintus stole a sideways glance at Lucilla, glowering at him, 'Please, sir, I beg you – '

Flavius nodded. 'Yes, I'm coming.'

'No,' said Lucilla in a shrill voice. 'Flavius, no!'

'Lucilla, I have no choice.'

She gave him a savage look. From the pile of undamaged plates in front of her, she snatched the top one and hurled it at the emperor's mural.

The plate shattered against the wall. A long, jagged sliver pierced its painted surface, trembled and then fell, taking with it a lump of plaster.

Flavius saw with despair that the plaster carried most of the heron's head. The bright beady eye lay somewhere on the floor. Ahead of him, Quintus was already out of the door. 'Aelius,' he said, 'get this room cleared,'

At the moment when the heron's head fell, something happened inside Flavius, It happened as quickly as if the flame of a lamp had been extinguished by a puff of breath. Because of his concern about the emperor's message, he was not, in that instant, aware of what it was, but later, in a quiet hour, he recognised the change in himself. As Lucilla's husband, he knew he would always protect her, help her, and try to provide her with whatever he could to make her happy. But that was where his responsibilities ended. He would no longer feel guilty when she showed her resentment at having to share his way of life, no longer wonder if he was partly to blame when she had her outbursts of tears and temper, no longer feel obliged to appease or placate her. He need no longer deceive himself with the hope that they could at least move towards some degree of affectionate companionship.

The sound of his quick footsteps as he followed Quintus towards the street entrance of the villa had hardly faded in the dining room before, in response to various hand gestures from Aelius, the slaves had started stacking the pottery for removal, first out of the way of Lucilla's hands, and then from the room.

'What are they doing?' cried Lucilla.

'Madam,' said Aelius, looking up at her from the floor where he was searching for any fragments of plaster that still carried traces of paint. 'I have been instructed to clear this room.'

'But I don't want it to be sent away. He wouldn't wait for me to tell him.' She ran towards the doorway. 'Where are they putting it now?'

'I had already placed a cupboard for it inside my office. It will remain locked in there until the prefect decides what is to be done with it.'

'Don't take it away, Aelius.' Lucilla tried to sound in command, but her voice shook.

'Madam, it was to be kept in that same cupboard even if you had wanted it.'

'But I do. I do.'

'Then it is a pity, madam, that he didn't hear you when you thanked him for his gift.' Aelius looked at her with a mournful expression. 'Naturally, he didn't want to burden you with something you didn't like. Might I presume, madam, to suggest that you thank him again, only much more loudly so that he will hear it.'

Aelius stood up and laid a handful of crumbling plaster on the table.

'Aelius, if – ' said Lucilla, hesitating, 'if he decided to send it away, where would he send it?'

'You mean where would the prefect send that pretty service of pottery that he took so much trouble to procure? I have yet to be instructed on that. I could perhaps hazard a guess, if madam wishes?'

Lucilla nodded her head up and down.

'It would have to be to someone who knew how to appreciate it. Perhaps to his mother, as a gift to thank her for letting the prefect and yourself bring her favourite tableware out here.'

Aelius bent down again to retrieve the broken pieces of plate. Lucilla, not pleased by Aelius's last remark, gave him a sour look. 'That plate has made a big hole in the wall.'

Aelius studied the broken pieces in his hands as if this was a suggestion that had never occurred to him. 'The plate?' he murmured. With a raised eyebrow, he looked back at Lucilla and then at the decapitated heron.

He handed the pieces to a passing slave. 'There are now seventeen of the large plates. Carry them carefully. I shall be counting them.'

He returned his gaze to the mural. Lucilla poked the fragments of plaster on the table. 'You can get some more of this stuff to patch it up.'

'Plaster, yes, madam, but it needs rather more than that, wouldn't you think?'

'It can be covered with a length of drapery. Tell Alis.'

Aelius passed a weary hand over his eyes. 'Even in this northern fortress on the edge of the empire, madam, a piece of cloth hanging down the middle of a large mural is hardly going to escape attention. People will be curious to know what we are ashamed of.'

'Then we will cover the whole wall,' said Lucilla defiantly.

'And what will the prefect say to that? He takes great pleasure in the emperor's mural.'

'I knew that.' The note of triumph in her voice made Aelius turn his back on her and walk away.

XII

'I could have wrung' her neck,' muttered Aelius. He was sitting hunched on the edge of his bed, watching Alis unfasten the little brooch she liked to wear. It was only a cheap trinket which Aelius had bought for her from a stall when the settlement had one of its markets – but it was not cheap to Alis.

'You've said that before, and I'd be surprised if you didn't say it again,' she said.

'This,' grunted Aelius, 'was special.'

Alis had a box, saved from Lucilla's rubbish, for her brooch. She laid it carefully inside and closed the lid.

'You aren't afraid someone is going to steal it, are you?'

'Be heart-broken if someone did,' said Alis lightly. Although she laughed, Aelius knew, to his abiding amazement, that she meant it, and that gave pleasure to him, too.

It was an experience he wished Flavius could have known. He thought angrily of Lucilla's jewellery caskets filled with the fine pieces he knew she liked, yet Aelius had no doubt she never wore them with any thought of Flavius in her mind. All that concerned her was the delight of displaying herself in ornaments that were more expensive than anyone else's.

He said out loud, as Alis put her little box away, 'Just think of the stuff she's got. Has she ever thanked him, ever thought of his generosity to her?'

Alis bent over to kiss the top of his head. 'I'm the lucky one, not her.' She sat down beside him. 'What has upset you so much tonight? What was special?'

Aelius gave a great sigh. 'When she threw the plate at the wall, you could see the spite in her. She wanted to hurt Flavius, and, believe me, I wanted to hurt her.'

He was silent for a moment, breathing heavily. Then he turned to Alis with a sheepish look of apology. When she smiled back, he took hold of her hands. 'You know, Alis, we poor ones do have some advantages in life. We can remember what marriage is really about. The wealthy ones and the powerful ones think it's only a counter in their games of acquiring more wealth and more power.

'That stupid old man in Stresa has more money than he could ever need, so he fancies seeing one of his family in the senate. When he finds he has a personable and intelligent grandson, he puts him up for auction in what's no better than a gilded slave market – '

'Be fair, Aelius, so was she.'

'Yes, true, but look what she got, and look what he got. He thought he was lucky – a pretty, demure little thing. He believed, or tried to believe, that her indifference to him in the early days was due to a youthful shyness – quite appealing in its way – and if he wooed her gently and patiently, she would grow at least into an affectionate companion, and perhaps more. Ha!'

'Perhaps,' said Alis, in her soothing way, 'when he is in the senate, as I suppose he will be one day, and she is a senator's lady, living among all the other senators' ladies, she might behave differently.'

'If you think that, Alis, you're as foolish as Flavius can be. The thing is, he doesn't want to go into the senate. Left alone, he'd be happy enough with his law, working for his father, and helping with matters in the town. He's not ambitious. What he really wants is what we have. Have you watched him when he sees a couple who care for each other? Look what he did for us.'

'But, perhaps sadly for him, he isn't one of us poor ones, Aelius, and you can't change that.'

'I could wring her neck, couldn't I? He ought to know her by now, but he never seems to learn.'

'Perhaps he doesn't want to admit, even to himself, that he does know her by now.'

Aelius shrugged his shoulders. 'Even today, Alis, he was lying for ages in the bath-house, trying to convince himself that now her present had arrived she would be in a delighted, receptive mood, she would remember Colchester – that means something or other to him – and she might also admit to remembering his birthday. They would enjoy their special meal alone together and, who knows, she might open her door to him tonight. '

'Aelius,' said Alis reproachfully.

'And what happened? Whatever Colchester means to him, it's certainly in the past for her. The present that was meant to enchant her was nothing but a disappointment to her, because she wanted a gold necklace. You should have heard her whining.'

'But she made him angry, and it was not one of his quick spurts of anger. It was different, a kind of hard, crisp, sustained anger. When the plate struck the wall, he looked for a moment as if it had struck him.'

'Still, it's no use hoping anything will have changed, is it? I don't know how important this message is. It'll occupy his mind for the time being, but when he's done whatever has to be done, you'll see, he'll start feeling guilty again. She'll seize her moment, and be sweet, simpering Lucilla until she gets what she wants from him.'

'The gold necklace?'

Aelius nodded. He smiled. 'I could always garrotte her with it.'

'Aelius!'

Part Two

HADRIAN

I

As Flavius and Quintus hurried into the courtyard of the headquarters building, Flavius's eye was caught by a light flickering above the board carrying the monthly information bulletin circulated from Rome. He stopped abruptly and reached out an arm to hold back Quintus.

'Are you quite sure this courier is who he says he is?'

'Yes, sir.'

Flavius pointed to the bulletin board. 'That tells us the emperor is in Egypt.'

'Correct, sir.'

'Quintus, has it not occurred to you that this could be a hoax?' It had crossed Flavius's mind that it was not impossible this was some birthday surprise devised by his grandfather, who had the time, the means and the mischievous urge to play unwelcome practical jokes. Yet as soon as he had thought of this, he dismissed it as a mark of his own jangled state of mind. It was most probably nothing to do with his grandfather, but it could still be a trick of a more sinister kind. 'We don't,' he added, 'want to find ourselves the victims of a modern version of the Trojan horse.'

Quintus thought this was meant to be amusing. He grinned. 'No hoax, sir, I've seen this man very close to the emperor.'

A few minutes later, Flavius came face to face with the messenger who had commanded his presence. He was dressed for hunting, in the style favoured by Romans when they followed the chase through the outlandish forests of northern Europe: a thick, full, knee-length, hooded woollen cloak to guard against the unfamiliar cold and, rejecting as barbaric the trousers worn by local hunters, puttees wound round the legs from ankle to knee as protection from the undergrowth.

'You are the prefect Flavius Valerius Paulus?' he enquired.

'I am.'

'Sir.' The man acknowledged Flavius with a quick, sharp bow of his head.

Flavius recognised in his brisk, disciplined movements the bearing of a highly trained soldier; when one edge of his cloak was caught by Flavius's desk and pulled aside, he saw that the folds of the courier's tunic were secured by a soldier's leather belt, and that he carried not only a hunting knife but also an army short-sword. He was exceptionally tall, with powerful shoulders. When he spoke Flavius's name it was in a Germanic accent.

Flavius understood now the remark made by Quintus about him being 'very close to the emperor'. This man was clearly one of the elite corps of the twenty-four Praetorian Guards who ensured the emperor's personal safety.

'Your business here?' asked Flavius.

'I am charged, sir, by the emperor to inform you that he will spend tomorrow night in this fort. He will arrive at dusk.'

There was a trace of contempt in his gaze, Flavius thought, as if he were waiting to see a raw, untrained commandant throw himself about the room in ecstasy or perhaps terror at this announcement. Although he did, in fact, feel as if the roof had fallen in, Flavius said coldly, 'I assume, then, that the emperor is already in Britain.'

'He is hunting bear in the far north.'

'North of the wall?'

'Yes.'

'That is dangerous ground.'

'The emperor is never afraid to face danger.'

'He is courting danger, not facing it,' said Flavius. 'Why?'

The emperor's guard frowned. 'That is not a question that need concern either you or me, sir.'

'Then perhaps you can answer this one. Rome told us that the emperor and the imperial court, together with the empress and his heir, the future emperor, were travelling through Egypt. But the emperor is in Britain. The bulletin lied, which is not its custom. Why?'

The man hesitated. 'When the bulletin was despatched, it was true. For an explanation of the emperor's reasons for changing his plans, I refer you to him.'

'Then can you at least explain to me why he chooses to spend the night at Alauna when there are a dozen or so wall forts thirty miles nearer?'

'I had no instruction from the emperor to discuss the matter with you.'

The man's dismissive tone roused the combative lawyer in Flavius. 'The emperor should be aware, as you ought to be, that with such short notice I cannot offer him the reception I consider appropriate.'

'The emperor does not come as emperor, but as a member of a small hunting party. I imagine you have experience of encountering other such parties, taken unawares by the early nightfall in these parts?'

'Of course. I understand. He wishes to be treated as any other benighted traveller.'

'Yes. And that none of the activities of the cohort or of your household should differ from normal.'

That, thought Flavius, would be laughable if it were not so ridiculous, but he merely said again, 'I understand. A private visit.'

'More than that, a secret one.'

'Secret? How can it be secret?' snapped Flavius. 'There are five hundred men in this cohort, most of whom saw the emperor every day when he used this fort as his base ten years ago.'

'They will remember him addressing them in a gilded breastplate, with a purple cloak, and probably at times a gilded laurel wreath on his head. They won't recognise him muffled *in a hunting cloak with the hood down to hide his face. I trust that satisfies the prefect's objection?*

'Now, your villa is the first building inside the north gate. He will enter the fort from that direction ...'

'He cannot enter by the north gate,' said Flavius.

The courier stared at him in outrage. 'The emperor has decided on the north gate!'

'No,' said Flavius. 'The road to the north gate leads past the harbour and through the settlement. As you said yourself, dusk falls very early here. Work in the harbour and around the stalls often has to go on into the dark under torchlight. You never know who might be about, and the emperor has enemies everywhere. You think he won't be recognised. I can't be sure of that. The west gate is on the bluff overlooking the sea, and the south gate faces the parade ground before the land slopes away. At dusk I can't watch the approaches to those gates. It is only possible from the east gate, and that is the gate the emperor must use.'

'He is not a man to be dissuaded.'

Flavius gave a sigh of impatience. 'If the emperor neglects his safety in uncharted territory, that is his choice. When he enters an area which has been placed by him under my authority, then his safety is my responsibility. If he were assassinated on his way to the north gate, I dread to think of the consequences for the cohort here. That is an argument I would have thought he would respect. We must remember, too, that he likes at times to declare himself "a Spaniard among Spaniards", and the men here are mostly Spaniards.'

Flavius smiled, but the courier was not amused by what he evidently took to be a flippant reference to his master.

The emperor's courier regarded the commandants of auxiliary units as little better than ignorant civilians. With his impressive stature, and the hectoring manner which the Praetorian Guard chose to cultivate, he took it for granted that he could intimidate anyone he chose. He was unprepared for this alert and lucid military confrontation and found himself at a loss, angry with Flavius for outflanking him.

Nevertheless, the commandant was the senior in rank. The courier said warningly, 'I will, sir, present your suggestion to the emperor, though it will not please him.'

'It is not a suggestion, it is a condition,' said Flavius, unmoved.

He crossed the room to his desk, sat down, and reached for a wax tablet and his stylus. 'I need some more information. How many are there in this hunting party?'

The courier moved a few steps closer to the desk, making a clumsy effort to appear less ungracious. 'Seven in all, including the emperor, all mounted, together with four pack-horses.'

'Who are the other six?'

'His two secretaries, two grooms and –

'And two members of the Praetorian Guard, of whom you are one?' interrupted Flavius.

'Yes.' The man looked at him with something like awe. 'Yes, sir, that is correct.' He hesitated. 'If I might add—'

'Go on.'

'The emperor will be – would like to be – accommodated.'

Flavius nodded, giving a brief smile to acknowledge his companion's more conciliatory attitude. 'And?'

'We two guards will stand duty outside his door, alternating two-hour watches.'

'I understand. A mattress will be arranged for your off-duty hours,' murmured Flavius.

The guard looked at him in surprise. 'Thank you, sir.' He paused. 'The emperor would wish to keep his horse in the stables attached to your villa.'

'Of course.'

'He remembers that when half of the original Spanish cohort was deployed to Judea, the cavalry stables were left empty. One of them would be suitable for the remaining ten horses and the grooms.'

Flavius agreed and made another note on his wax pad.

'The grooms, together with the pack-horses, will arrive first, about half an hour before the main party.'

'Good,' said Flavius. 'That will give us warning of the emperor's approach.' And, he added to himself, tell me whether or not he has consented to use the east gate. He waited, but the other man seemed to be preoccupied with settling his cloak to cover the sword in his belt. 'Is that all?' Flavius enquired.

'That is the end of the instructions given to me by the emperor, sir.'

Flavius rose from his chair. 'You will convey my loyal respects to his majesty. I wish you a safe journey back to wherever you may be encamped for this night.'

When Quintus had escorted the visitor from the fort, he returned to find the commandant bent over his desk, writing rapidly. Flavius glanced up at him and rubbed one hand over his face.

'Quintus,' he said, 'without asking any questions for the moment, will you act as my orderly and fetch these men for me?' He pushed a wax tablet towards him. 'Can you read this?'

Quintus held the list under the lamp on the desk. 'The senior centurion, the six centurions, the chief clerk, the doctor, your house steward.' He looked slightly startled by the curious nature of the list, but all he said was, 'Yes, sir, at once.'

'Get it done as quickly as you can, but discreetly. If anyone asks why, say you don't know why they are summoned – which is true. Tell them it's something that's upset the commandant, him with his legal way of looking at things.'

Quintus nodded. As he made his way to the door, Flavius called out, 'Go to the doctor first. Tell him to come straight here. Let me know as soon as all the others have arrived. No need for military dress.'

Flavius was still working on his notes when the doctor made a breathless entry. He was a lively young Greek, a graduate of the medical school in Athens, with experience in camps in North Africa and on the Rhine.

'You need me, sir? Quintus had obviously run all the way with your message, so I thought I'd better run all the way back. I was up anyway, experimenting.'

'You've been very quick. I'm grateful.'

As he sat down, the doctor gave Flavius a searching look. 'I thought you must be ill.'

'No, but I still need your help.'

He began to explain. The doctor quickly interrupted to say, 'But he's in Egypt.'

'Trust me,' said Flavius. 'He is not.'

When Flavius had finished, the desk between them was strewn with heavily scored wax tablets. 'So you think it might work?' he asked.

'Why not?' said the doctor. 'There's always one somewhere in the winter.' He added cheerfully, 'I shall regard the exercise as an extension of those wild Saturnalian theatricals.'

Quintus opened the door and ushered in the group of men he had snatched from their beds and warm fires. They made a motley collection, Flavius thought; he himself was still wearing his fashionable Roman sapphire blue dinner-set, the doctor had forgotten to take off his hospital apron, Lugo had wrapped his cloak like a shawl round his shoulders over his white night tunic, Quintus was still in his armour and Aelius had found time to dress himself in the chestnut brown tunic he reserved for special occasions.

The doctor stood up and placed his chair in front of the desk for the senior centurion. His junior officers ranged themselves around him, not a little offended to find a non-commissioned clerk and a house steward in the room with them. The doctor they were not sure about. He ranked as an officer, but he was, after all, a Greek.

Not unaware of this, Flavius said sharply, 'Gentlemen!' and paused until they had all given him their attention. 'I have to inform you that the emperor will visit Alauna some time in the late afternoon tomorrow.'

He waited for someone to state the obvious, and someone did. 'But we all know the emperor is sailing down the Nile.'

There was an aggrieved murmur of agreement. Lugo glared over his shoulder and struck his knuckles on the desk for silence.

Quintus, who had been standing at the back of the room beside Aelius, spoke out. 'The emperor's emissary, a man known to me, left here not an hour ago.' He walked to the desk and placed himself behind Flavius. His cheeks began to flush as they always did when he found himself the centre of attention.

'We are obliged to you, sir,' said Lugo, casting another glance over his shoulder.

Flavius, continuing as though there had been no interruption, said, 'The emperor is in Britain with six companions. Those six men, together with the eleven of us in this room, are the only people in the empire who know that he is not in Egypt. He wishes this secrecy to be preserved. He will arrive as the member of a hunting party, and that is how he wishes to be treated. Should any of you encounter him by chance, you will behave with the courtesy that I hope you would show to any stranger in the camp, but with the same lack of interest. Whatever you happen to be doing, you will go on doing. Only inside my villa may we relax the pretence.'

Anticipating the questions that he knew would arise, he said, 'I was not told why the emperor is in Britain, or why the visit is a secret one. All I can do is request that you obey these instructions so as to preserve his safety.'

Flavius looked slowly round the now silent room. 'I will allow no risk. I will therefore close the gates of this fort from now until two days after the emperor's departure, by which time he will safely have left these shores.'

After some hesitation, the senior centurion said, 'Is such a drastic plan necessary, sir? The emperor is much loved here. We are all Hadrian's men, and believe that we are special to him because –

'Because you are Spaniards. Yes, I understand.' Hadrian was probably clever enough, thought Flavius, to leave an impression of feeling a special bond wherever he chose to make the effort. 'Are you saying, senior centurion, that the whole camp can be trusted to keep the emperor's visit a secret? This was his decision, not mine. We all know that there are deep pockets of hatred for Hadrian, from the Senate downwards. There could be disaffected men here just as there could be in the settlement, though we all seem to rub along contentedly enough. I repeat, I will allow no risk. Even well-intentioned men can unwittingly betray secrets.'

'But the prefect must realise that if five hundred men find themselves locked in the fort for the first time in their ten years here, it will raise extraordinary suspicions in their minds and they will talk about nothing else,' a centurion objected.

Flavius smiled. 'Yes, I had realised. That is why the doctor has joined us here. He will post notices that a virulent form of the winter sickness is spreading rapidly from the north. The death rate is high. The gates will be closed as a precautionary measure, and any visitors to Alauna will be thoroughly inspected before they are allowed admission.'

There was a small frisson of movement as men turned to gauge their neighbour's reaction.

The doctor added, 'I shall prepare the hospital as though for an epidemic, and shall myself be at the east gate when our visitors arrive. If anyone wonders why we have admitted seven strangers when our gates are closed to everyone else, I shall be able to explain that they come from the south, which of course they don't, where there is no sickness, and that it would be inhospitable to refuse them help, but I am nevertheless taking the precaution of examining them first.'

Lugo shifted in his chair. His officers watched him, waiting for a contradictory opinion, but he merely grunted as if confused.

The doctor gave him one of his bright smiles. 'When the three days have passed, I shall inform the commandant that the sickness has not affected this area as I feared it would and we may safely resume our normal way of working.'

'When this meeting is over,' said Flavius, 'I wish the doctor to go down to the post-house in the settlement. As you know, the veteran who manages it is the unofficial leader of the local people. He will be given the same information that you will shortly be giving your men, and be asked to spread it as early as possible in the morning. That should save many people from coming here and being refused admission. But there are always one or two who think they are the exception. There can be no exceptions. I realise that this will cause inconvenience, especially to those who make daily deliveries, and I am sorry for the anxiety that will be felt.'

He thought about men like Noricus, who relied on being able to move freely from the fort to the settlement.

'There will be men in the unit who have formed links with local people who will also be worried. They might even try to get out to them. But this mustn't happen. I am not happy about asking you to practise this deception, but with the very little time we have been given to prepare for this visit, I can offer no alternative. We have no choice but to bear it.'

The senior centurion rose to his feet, wrapping his cloak more tightly around himself. Those of the centurions who had no liking for Flavius, and resented his working so closely with the young Greek doctor, listened hopefully as Lugo cleared his throat and began to speak. 'Deception, sir—' he paused to clear his throat '—is one of the arts of military strategy. Many a conflict would have been lost but for a brilliant piece of deception. I would welcome your company on any battlefield.' With a nod to Flavius, he sat down again.

Flavius felt lost for words momentarily. Then he said with a laugh, 'I think we should all be safer if I kept my battles to the floor of the courts'

The tensions in the room were suddenly eased. The doctor, with a quick wink to Flavius, slipped away on his mission.

'I think I ought to explain,' said Flavius, glancing at his centurions, 'why I have invited the chief clerk and my steward here, although I suspect they will have guessed the reasons.

'We are all aware, I am sure, of this emperor's respect for informative and up-to-date records. He may well be curious about the standards we maintain in this frontier fort a thousand miles from Rome. chief clerk?'

The man stepped forward briskly, and stood to attention. 'Sir?'

He was comparatively young to be in charge of a fort's records and the coinage stored in the vaults of the headquarters building. He had achieved his present rank because of his aptitude with figures, together with an almost obsessive need for discipline and order in his surroundings. In the offices under his control, the delineated, partitioned shelves were stacked with neat rows of tightly fastened rolls of papyrus in strict time sequence, so that information could be retrieved in a few minutes. A loose scroll, half-unwound and pushed into any odd space, infuriated him. Officers presuming on their rank, rummaging for documents and destroying the sanctity of his shelves, outraged him. He found it incomprehensible that some people could live without order, just as he failed to understand those who stared, intimidated, at a column of figures when they could so easily have run an eye down the page and set a total at the bottom.

He was a difficult man to work with yet Flavius had warmed to him; he respected another perfectionist. There was no need, he knew, to give him any instructions for the emperor's visit. Anything that should be done within the chief clerk's department would already have been done, as a matter of course. He felt, however, obliged to make some comment.

'Chief clerk, I want you to have the tax receipts ready and the last month's shipping deliveries,' he said, picking items at random.

The chief clerk responded, 'All necessary checks will have been completed, should the emperor wish to visit my offices. '

'I hope he will,' said Flavius. 'I want him to see for himself the meticulous way his requirements are followed in our desolate outpost. Steward!' He turned his attention to Aelius, who cast a mocking glance at him as he made one of the low bows he offered on public occasions.

Flavius looked at the wall above Aelius's head. 'You will have responsibility for the emperor's comfort while he is inside the villa.' He gave a small smile. 'There is a chance, I suppose, that he is coming here merely because he has found that sleeping outdoors is more arduous than he thought, and he wants a warm bath, a soft bed, and something more appetising than packed rations. Can the household manage that?'

Lugo stirred in his chair. 'I don't need, surely, to remind the prefect that his majesty is used to campaign life.'

'Not in north Britain,' said Flavius.

'The emperor was here on this very spot when he was planning his wall,' declared the senior centurion, with some heat.

'He came in April and left before July was out,' Flavius replied, beginning to lose his temper.

Aelius said quickly, 'I can assure the prefect that, whatever the emperor's reason for coming, this household will be able to entertain him in suitable style.'

One of the centurions butted in. 'Yes, but this household of yours ... Can you be sure that these slaves won't do more than entertain the emperor?'

Flavius, Lugo and Aelius all turned to look at him in surprise.

The man stabbed a finger at Aelius. 'You, I'm asking you a question. *You!*'

Aelius assumed the quiet, humble manner that meant he was rising to a challenge. 'My name is Aelius.' He paused tellingly. 'Sir.'

'Another of you Greeks, eh?'

'I do not have, sir,' said Aelius, still soft-voiced, 'the good fortune of being a Spaniard, which allows one to rejoice in being the emperor's compatriot – that is, when he remembers his Spanish sympathies. I am Greek, which is a greater good fortune because mine is the race which the emperor most admires and seeks to emulate. He likes to dress in the Greek manner, he enjoys speaking Greek. I don't suppose any of you have ever been to Rome, and probably never will go, but if you had you would find that he has filled it with buildings in the Athenian style ...'

Flavius struck his desk. 'Steward! Wine, if you please, in the adjoining room. Now.'

Aelius, with a slight sigh as if he had more items of interest to impart but there would be another time, withdrew graciously, leaving the door slightly ajar.

Flavius faced the senior centurion. 'It is not acceptable to me to have officers under my command who equate discourtesy with military authority. When they are addressing civilians, like my steward, who have not been disciplined as army recruits, it is not to be tolerated. Such conduct could be a danger to us all in the outside community.'

Lugo found himself caught between a hot-headed junior officer, with whose views on Greeks he was not unsympathetic, and a coldly angry commandant.

He chose to observe rank.

'Allow me to apologise for my colleague's behaviour, sir. This situation has been a shock to us all, and I think he was only trying to find out – in a regrettably clumsy way – if there was any possible threat to the emperor from your slaves as they come into contact with him. He was worried, I am sure the prefect will understand, because they are not governed by army rules.'

Good try, thought Flavius, for a man who was not in the habit of pleading for the defence – but unconvincing. The culprit was still an ill-mannered lout. 'My slaves are governed by my rules. He should have put his question to me, not to my steward.'

'He would perhaps have felt unable to do that,' said Lugo.

'In that, at least, he would have been correct. It is not for him to question me on any matters concerning my household.' Flavius waited a moment and then added, 'However, as you have pointed out, senior centurion, this is an exceptional occasion, and so I will answer the question. My slaves will be instructed to remain inside the villa. If just one of them disobeys me, they know that I have the right to sell them all in punishment. Out here, that would mean working in the lead and silver mines. They may doubt that I would do it, but they can't be sure. Believe me, they will watch each other like hawks. The emperor will be quite safe.'

Flavius pushed his chair back from the desk to indicate that he had nothing further to say on the subject.

He stood up, and consulted one of his wax pads. 'At dawn, tomorrow, when the gates would normally be opened, they will remain shut. I want the guards doubled on the north, south and west gates; on the east gate trebled, to strengthen the look-out duty in the towers, and from noon tomorrow I want a rota of centurions in command.'

'My adjutant is the only person in the fort who has seen the emperor recently and can recognise him. He will act as liaison officer. He will advise us when the advance-party is first sighted. The senior centurion will then take up his position at the east gate, ready to receive the emperor, who will be identified for him by the adjutant. The adjutant will then escort the emperor to this office. Remember that to the men on the gate this is only a stranded hunting group that are being met by the senior centurion and the doctor to ensure that none of them carry infection, and that is how all of us here must be careful to treat them.'

Flavius leaned across the desk to confirm the arrangements with the senior centurion. 'You will draw up the rotas for me to see?'

The senior centurion looked up at him. 'You do realise, sir, that if the south gate is closed, no-one will be able to get out onto the parade ground? There will be no afternoon weapon drill.'

'Weapons drill will be suspended for three days, yes.'

'What are the men supposed to do without their drill to occupy them? One soldier left idle can be a nuisance. What about five hundred of them?'

'They won't be idle,' said Flavius. 'Believe me.'

He looked at each of the centurions in turn. 'Gentlemen, once your own duties have been agreed with the senior centurion, you will immediately convene a meeting with your section leaders, where you will explain why, on the doctor's advice, I have isolated the fort. You will make it clear that for the moment no-one can predict how long the isolation will have to last, and you will assure them that I will treat as cause for dishonourable discharge any attempts to defy my orders.'

Flavius noticed as he was speaking that the crack in the door had widened slightly. Aelius had plainly returned, as instructed, with the wine and had now resumed what he considered to be his primary duty: knowing what was going on.

'I then need you to pass on the revised work programme for tomorrow. There will be a new one every morning. We, of course, know that there will be only three, but the men will not. So, tomorrow: in place of the afternoon weapons drill, the men will carry out the occupational work they usually do in the morning—'

'But why do that?' interrupted Lugo in dismay.

'Because,' said Flavius sharply, 'I want every section in this fort dusted, swept, scrubbed and in an immaculate state of cleanliness before the emperor is anywhere near our gates. You can tell the men that I prefer not to wait until the next Friday inspection to clear out what's left of the Saturnalia detritus – and that, by the way, includes a larger-than-life wall sketch that resembles one of the virgin water-goddesses worshipped by some of the local people round here, except that her posture is hardly virginal, and the messages scribbled round her are not of a devotional character. It is not something which I think the emperor would appreciate.'

Lugo glanced quickly at Flavius, and then away again. 'No, true,' he grunted, and stirred himself.

'Well, which block is it in?' he shouted, glaring at his flock. Heads were shaken; no-one appeared to know.

'Block E,' said Flavius. The centurion in charge of Block E looked amazed and then slightly outraged when his senior officer told him irritably to get the white-wash organised immediately.

At any moment, thought Flavius, he is going to complain that procuring white-wash is not in his remit as centurion.

The senior centurion appeared to share Flavius's thinking. 'We're all having to do things we never expected to do,' he snapped. 'If you don't know how to find the white-wash, get the quartermaster up. He can issue it.'

'Gentlemen,' Flavius said, calling the room to order, 'I think we have covered as much as we can for the moment. There is wine if you would care for refreshment before a long night's work begins.'

On cue, as Flavius knew he would be, Aelius swung open the door into the adjoining room. There were murmurs of appreciation.

'Just before you go,' Flavius called out, 'might I ask the centurions to suggest to their section leaders that they look at the dust on any stones?'

'Stones?' Lugo paused as he was about to pull himself out of his chair. 'What stones would they be? The pavements are washed every day.'

'I have always been impressed by the number of gaming boards that I see around the fort,' said Flavius. 'You assure me that the men never play for money.'

'Well, of course not, sir,' said the senior centurion. 'Gambling is forbidden by the emperor except during Saturnalia.' He gave an awkward little laugh. 'Instead of coins, they play for pebbles.' He hesitated. 'Oh, *those* stones, sir. Yes, there's usually a bowl or basket of them somewhere in every section.'

'I find it curious,' said Flavius pleasantly, 'that the boards are never dusty, but the stones are thick with it.'

Lugo began to breathe heavily. 'I have never seen men gaming for money, and none of my officers has ever reported seeing it.'

'Then I have to deduce that you all chose, at times, to look in a different direction.'

Lugo drew himself up stiffly. 'Does the prefect wish to pursue this matter further?'

'No,' said Flavius, 'how can I? I too have never seen the men playing for money. I also think the wisest officers are those who know when to look in the other direction.' He glanced at the chief clerk. 'That's the way the world runs, yes? All I'm saying is, get the stones dusted before the emperor sees them.'

The senior centurion murmured his thanks. 'But you don't really think, sir, that he'll want to walk round the barracks?'

'I don't know what he'll want to do,' said Flavius. 'I don't know why he's coming here.'

'You can be sure that if there's something you don't want him to see, that's where he'll go,' sighed Lugo.

'Wine, gentlemen,' said Flavius, pointing the way.

He remained at his desk, smoothing out his notes on the wax tablets with his stylus. Aelius crossed the room to stand beside him. 'Any wine for you?'

Flavius didn't lift his head. 'No.'

'You stopped me speaking.I was enjoying myself, watching that despicable man's face grow more and more flushed.'

'I'd forgotten,' said Flavius, working away, 'that they weren't, like me, used to hearing your Greek eulogies every day of the week.'

'Every day of the week! That's not fair.'

'No, it isn't,' admitted Flavius. 'Every other day then.' He began stacking the tablets. Aelius bent over him and Flavius slowly turned his head towards him. He was smiling.

'I enjoyed it too,' he whispered. 'That was the man who caused me so much trouble when we first arrived here, but when he started turning lobster colour, I thought you ought to stop. It wasn't quite the time for a gladiatorial blood-letting all over my office floor. '

'Well, let's get on with it, then,' said Aelius.

'With what? I've nothing else to say.'

Aelius sighed. 'No, but there's still the small matter of the hole in the emperor's wall.'

Flavius cried out and leaped up from his chair. 'Quintus!' he shouted. The adjutant appeared in the doorway, a beaker of wine in his hand.

'Quintus, find section leader Noricus for me. I need him in the villa.'

Aelius obligingly stretched out a hand and took the adjutant's beaker away from him. 'Noricus? Who's he?'

'His section does plastering and painting,' said Flavius.

Aelius looked at him in surprise. 'How do you know that?'

'Didn't you?'

'No.' Aelius sounded indignant.

'Oh, well, you can't learn everything sitting in the men's bathhouse,' said Flavius complacently.

Aelius gave him a searching look. 'Have you changed your mind?'

'What about?'

'Staying.'

'Staying where? In Britain?'

'No,' said Aelius irritably. 'In the army.'

'Where on earth did you get that idea from? Of course not.'

'Flavius, you know the names of the section leaders, and what their sections do.'

Flavius, given Aelius's concern, decided he would have to be honest. 'Actually only one, and that was by chance.'

Aelius was not convinced. With an almost grudging respect, he went on, 'You were at home with that lot. You knew what you thought had to be done, and you told them how they were going to do it. You had no trouble controlling them.'

'That wasn't soldiery,' said Flavius. 'That was administration. That's no different for me whether I'm mounting a case in court, persuading a local council to do what's best for them, or instructing army officers on how to behave when an emperor surprises them. You define the problem, assess the available resources, devise the best possible solution – oh, and one last thing. Once you know what has to be done, you let no-one change your mind for you. Happy now, Aelius?'

He grinned sheepishly. 'I did just wonder if the emperor was coming to move you to a legionary commission.'

'Aelius, remember, I don't even know how to balance a lance, let alone throw it. Not quite material for the emperor, eh?'

'Who knows?' said Aelius, but he said it to himself.

'Talking of the emperor ...'

'Yes.' Aelius started to move. 'The plastering!'

II

They stood together in front of the damaged mural. The room had been cleared of the Colchester pottery and also, Aelius was pleased to find, of Lucilla.

'Aelius, the patch is getting worse ... larger!'

'No, it isn't. You're just tired.'

Flavius stared at the empty patch, unconvinced. He was still staring at it when Quintus hurried into the room, followed by a bewildered Noricus. He paused for a moment inside the doorway, overwhelmed by the beauty of the decoration which he had never thought he would see for himself. Then, as he looked about him, his eye lighted on the headless heron, which seemed to be causing the commandant such concern.

'Ah,' he said, and being faced with something that required his professional skill, he strode briskly across the tessellated floor to assess the problem.

Flavius acknowledged his arrival with a grateful nod. 'Aren't the edges crumbling away?'

Noricus pressed his fingers against the wall. 'No, sir. It's a neat, clean cut. Not a problem.'

Flavius was aware of Aelius's smug expression. 'Will it take long?' he asked Noricus.

'Not for a small area like this, but then we have to wait for the plaster to dry a little before the paint can be added.'

'Can you be mixing your colours in here while you're waiting?'

Noricus glanced at Flavius. 'Not me, sir. I can't paint.'

'But your section does plastering and painting.'

'Yes, sir – walls and panels and doors, not figures in pictures.'

Quintus cleared his throat. 'Sir, if you would allow me,' he said in his diffident way, 'I think I could suggest someone who should be able to paint a bird's head for you.'

'Not someone back in Rome, I trust,' said Flavius bitterly.

'That, indeed, would be of no help,' agreed Quintus. 'No, he is here in Alauna. At this moment, he is preparing to white-wash his section wall.'

'Of course,' cried Noricus, 'Lupus! He painted ...' He hesitated, remembering he was in the presence of the commandant.

'... an image of a long-haired water-goddess, yes,' said Quintus.

'Lupus? Isn't that the name of the stone mason working on the new altar?' asked Flavius.

Noricus nodded. 'I can do a fair, straight line for a border, but I can't do a curve like him. Whether he's holding a chisel or a brush, they flow from his fingers, those curves. A bird's head will be no trouble for him.'

Aelius was sorting out the fragments of painted plaster he had saved from the floor. 'But he has to get the right colours as well, Noricus.'

Flavius sighed. 'Yes.' He was beginning to wonder if they couldn't find a large vase or a candelabra to hide the damage, or even sit the emperor with his back to the mural or perhaps feed him somewhere else ... No, that wouldn't do.

If Flavius was despondent, Noricus evidently wasn't.

'We keep all the oddments of paint left over from the jobs we do,' he was explaining to Aelius. 'He'll mix them till he gets what he needs.' He turned back to Flavius. 'If you please, sir, I can bring Lupus back with me when I fetch the plaster. Others from my section can take over the white-washing.'

Flavius motioned to Quintus. 'Go with him. Inform the centurion.'

He sat down on one chair and put his feet up on another. Aelius perched on the table beside him. 'Flavius, while we are alone, a small matter for your attention ...'

He closed his eyes. 'Not now.'

'Yes, now. The bath-house—'

'Small?'

'Flavius, listen: the bath-house and the emperor.'

Flavius opened his eyes and sat up.

'One of the two lads who serve in the bath-house is Greek, he's eighteen, and is what Alis calls personable.'

'Ah,' said Flavius. 'So we move him before—'

'Better to move both of them together. To the kitchens.'

'Good. But who takes their place?'

'I think I do. It is true I am Greek, but I am not young, I am not beautiful and I am married. I should emerge from the bath-house as I went in.'

The both felt the inclination to share a grin, but avoided meeting each other's eyes. They were, after all, speaking about the emperor.

'Do you think,' said Flavius, after a pause, 'that I am forgetting anything else?'

'Not forgetting, avoiding,' said Aelius. 'Do it now.'

Flavius gestured towards the mural. 'I thought I ought to watch ...'

Aelius was in mentor mood. 'The plaster isn't on yet. Now, Flavius.'

With a cross look, he took himself out of the dining-room and round the lamp-lit courtyard to Lucilla's suite.

He could hear women's voices inside. Lucilla was still awake.

He gave his usual tap on the door.

The voices fell silent. There was the sound of movement, then one of Lucilla's angry squeals and the slamming of an inner door. He had raised his hand to knock again when Alis appeared in the doorway.

She faced him uneasily. 'I am sorry, sir, but madam—'

'Madam is not asleep, Alis. Or if she is, she is having a nightmare from which she must be woken.'

Flavius gently moved Alis out of his way and walked towards the inner door that had been slammed.

Alis ran after him. 'Forgive me, sir, but madam does not wish to speak to you tonight.'

'Believe me, Alis, I have no wish to disturb her, but in this world we can't always have what we want.'

He had opened the door as he spoke so that Lucilla could hear what he said. She was perched on her bed, eating one of her favourite honey cakes. She struggled to swallow a mouthful, dragged herself back across the bed, gave another of her squeals of alarm and clutched at one of the draperies round her bed.

Flavius folded his arms and sighed loudly. 'That's enough, Lucilla. Alis, come in here. Put her into a chair. Lucilla, sit still and listen to me.'

He then announced bluntly, 'The emperor will be here tomorrow afternoon.'

Curiously, this had the desired effect. His wife's mouth fell open; she was speechless.

But not for long. 'Why should you think I would believe that?' she cried. 'Are you mad, or sick? It's silly ... cruel. Go away!'

'Very well,' said Flavius. 'If you can't believe me, there's no point in saying any more to you.' He turned back towards the door.

'Madam,' murmured Alis, 'the prefect would never take the emperor's name in vain. You must hear what he has to say.'

'Must I?'

Alis nodded. She reached for the plate of cakes and set it on Lucilla's lap. 'Sir, if you please?'

Flavius walked slowly back to stand in front of his wife. 'I need you to attend carefully. The emperor's visit is a private and secret one. Only a very small handful of people in this fort know that he will be here. I am now trusting you with the secret. You must never, never speak of it to anyone in this villa, in this fort, outside in the settlement, to your friends or your family. Betray the emperor, and I can promise you that if our punishment is merely exile we shall be fortunate. Have you listened me?'

'Yes,' whispered Lucilla, white-faced. 'Will I meet him?'

'Since you are one of the small group here who knows he is the emperor and not a passing stranger, yes, it might be possible for you to dine with him; but, as you must know, he prefers men and women to eat separately. If he refuses, that will be the end of it. You will stay in your own rooms until he leaves, though I promise I will try to arrange a meeting.'

'You will tell him I am of senatorial rank?' Her butterfly mind had restored the colour to her cheeks. 'Alis, can you do my hair in the way the empress does hers?'

'Lucilla,' warned Flavius, 'remember that the emperor prefers women to dress simply.'

'I am aware,' she said, 'of the correct dress for a woman of my rank in the presence of the emperor.'

Flavius flinched. 'Lucilla, please, not too much glistening and tinkling.'

Alis looked at him as if he ought by now to know not to ask for the impossible.

As he stepped back into the courtyard, Flavius could hear behind him noises that could only be cupboard doors being pulled open and chest lids being thrown up against the wall.

He returned with feelings of apprehension to the dining-room, and was relieved to find that work on the mural was progressing. A neat, smooth patch of new plaster was already in place. A newcomer, wrapped in a work-apron splashed with white-wash, was standing in front of it, gently testing the plaster with the fingers of his left hand. In his right he was holding a slender rod of wood, rather like an elongated stylus, with a pointed tip at one end and a smooth surface at the other. Over his shoulder he was giving instructions to Noricus, who was blending colours from a cluster of bowls and jars on the table. Aelius, frowning, was making sure that they were all standing on the pieces of clean rag that he had spread across the table to protect its surface.

At the sound of Flavius's footsteps, the man turned and stood to attention. 'Lupus, sir,' he announced.

'I gathered that,' said Flavius, glancing at the streaks of white-wash. 'Is the plaster ready for the paint yet?'

'Just about right, sir.' With his wooden tool. Lupus lightly pricked a curved line of dots into the damp plaster. He stepped back to look at the outline, and nodded. 'The head, sir.'

Flavius stared at it. 'No,' he said slowly, 'no, it was flatter.'

Lupus obligingly smoothed out the line of dots and made a slightly shallower curve.

Flavius sighed. He put his head on one side, and then the other. Lupus waited patiently for him to admit his mistake.

Then he gave Lupus a wry smile. 'It was right the first time. I'm sorry.'

'As the prefect pleases,' murmured Lupus, and changed the line again. Then he picked up a brush and placed a thread of milky-green colour behind the heron's head to restore the fragment of a leaf that had been damaged. 'You can see the outline of the head more easily now,' he said to Flavius.

'Yes, I can. It's good, Lupus.'

'From where I'm standing,' said Aelius, 'the colour looks too dark.'

'Yes, but as the plaster dries, the colour gets lighter,' snapped Noricus, who was not happy to have Aelius peering over them all the time.

'You haven't got enough black paint here,' said Aelius. 'White, yes, but not enough black.'

'Lupus knows what he wants,' grunted Noricus.

'Are you sure?' persisted Aelius. 'That bird's feathers are a sort of greyish colour. Can't you see? You need to mix up black and white for that.'

'No, Aelius,' Lupus called out, 'blue and brown.' He gave Flavius a meaningful look.

'Blue and brown!' Aelius seemed about to begin an argument.

'Lupus, you will excuse us. We have things to attend to,' said Flavius. 'Aelius, now.'

134

'What is it you want to do now?' demanded the steward as they walked out of the dining-room.

'Nothing,' said Flavius crossly, 'but they need to be left alone to get on with their work, which they know how to do and we don't.'

'Ah.' Aelius nodded. 'Yes, you were being a bit difficult.'

Outside in the courtyard, Flavius felt like expressing himself with one of Lucilla's shrill squeals of annoyance, but he merely let out a deep sigh.

Aelius gave him a look of kindly concern. 'You're tired. I understand. Why not take a few hours' sleep while you can?'

'How could I sleep now?' cried Flavius.

'You could at least rest for a while.' Aelius urged him towards his own room. Flavius sat down grumpily on the edge of his bed and shook his head when Aelius unfolded a fur rug. 'I can't sleep,' he protested.

But he did, as soon as he was left alone. He slept until Aelius shook him awake so that his bed could be dismantled and set up again in the room appointed for the emperor's quarters.

III

It was almost dusk, and the lamps were already burning in the headquarters building. Flavius had been waiting in his office for nearly an hour. Sometimes he was pacing up and down between his desk and the window; sometimes he was sitting at his desk, fiddling to no purpose with his stylus and a wax pad.

His first coherent thought that morning had been for the mural. When he reached the door of the emperor's dining-room, he had found himself hesitating with his hand on the latch, reluctant to see what Lupus had achieved in case it disappointed him, or worse; but when he did push the door open, his feeling of relief was so great that he wanted to cry out with joy.

His lost heron was home again, its proud head poised against the green leaves of the garden. Its delicate ivory and pale grey feathers blended with the heavier feathers of its wings, and a black, beady eye once more surveyed its world.

There was something slightly, very slightly, different about the bird, but Flavius was unable to define what it was. The room was empty, and he moved about, looking at the heron from different angles, still unable to detect any change.

Then, as he was closing the door behind him, he knew what it was. Wherever he stood in the room, the heron's eye had followed him, and that had not, he was sure, happened before.

Whether it was due to some trick of Lupus's brush, or some fancy of Flavius's own mind and lack of sleep, he didn't know. He didn't really care. It pleased him.

Flavius set out to find Lupus to thank him. This was not, he was convinced, considered necessary, or even acceptable, in military practice. A commandant, in particular, would expect to give his orders, have them carried out, and carried out well; end of matter. But that was not his way. He served justice, and courtesy always seemed to him to be a just response to a service well rendered.

He eventually discovered the man in an area against the north wall where the baking ovens were kept, one for each of the barracks. They were still warm from the early-morning bread-making. Close by, under an improvised canopy made from a torn leather tent, Lupus was working on the stone altar which in a few days Flavius would use for the unit's annual sacrifice to its god, Jupiter.

Flavius was appalled. 'Lupus!'

He turned round, straightened up, and said cheerfully, 'I have been excused from cleaning duties, sir, to work on the altar.'

'Here? Your centurion sent you here? I think not.'

'No, sir, but it was the senior centurion who had me moved out of my workshop,' said Lupus. He added delicately, 'Apparently on your orders, sir. I use the old cavalry officers' empty stables and he said visitors on horseback were expected.'

Flavius felt a spurt of exasperation. Lugo had, yes, obeyed his instructions with commendable promptness and the blinkered army drive that allowed no pause for simple common sense. It was the wretched baker's door all over again. There were other empty stables, most of them unused.

Lupus seemed to read his thoughts. 'My stables are the best ones for visitors to use, I suppose,' he said, amiably defending the senior centurion. 'They're smaller and better appointed. They were for the officers.'

Flavius was not amused. He could think only, with horror, of the emperor coming across his cherished Spanish cohort's altar among the bread ovens.

'I'll have you moved as soon as possible, Lupus. You can go back to your workshop tomorrow evening.'

'It's not so bad here, sir,' he assured Flavius in his good-natured, unconcerned way. 'It's warm, out of the way, and there are the odd comforts.' He held up a half-eaten bread roll made from the darkish-coloured flour used throughout the fort. He laughed. 'And there's a delicious smell, too, if anyone's using that fine, light flour you have on your own table, sir.'

Despite everything else spinning round in his mind, Flavius remembered the bread rolls that Aelius served him in the morning and which, although he never said so in as many words, he contrived to suggest owed much to his own skills; but that was something for Flavius to concern himself with at another time.

'Lupus,' he said, 'the reason I came to find you was to thank you for the work you did on the mural. I am very pleased with it, and grateful to you for doing it so quickly.'

He looked surprised. 'I was pleased with it, too,' he said, as if that was all that mattered. He added, 'Someone told me you were expecting visitors today and needed it done fast. These are the people the senior centurion is putting in my stable, I suppose?'

He had an innately courteous manner, but seemed indifferent to the rigid army devotion to the hierarchy of rank. He spoke to his commandant in the same pleasant, easy way he would have used in his section.

Flavius answered him in the same manner. 'These people are strangers to me in that I have not met them before. But they will have heard about the mural, and it might have been a disappointment to them to see it in a damaged state.'

Their eyes met. Lupus knew that he was not being told the whole truth, and Flavius knew that Lupus understood he was not free to say more, and would respect this.

'The heron's eye,' Flavius continued, smiling, 'it seems to be alive.'

Lupus smiled back. 'Yes.'

He was standing in front of the altar, unintentionally masking it, but, as they were speaking, Flavius noticed how carefully it had been cradled on a blanket. Another one lay folded on the ground beside it, used presumably to protect it when it was carried from the stable.

It struck Flavius then that, instead of his initial displeasure at finding Lupus working among the bread ovens, he should be grateful for the man's initiative. Having been turned out of his workshop, he had set about finding himself a reasonably quiet spot, out of the way of the cleaning uproar, searched around for the bits and pieces to make a shelter, and then got on with his work: no complaints, no bother to anyone else, not cut from the same cloth as Rufus Lugo.

Flavius had forgotten whether or not it was protocol to see the altar before it was unveiled before him as the priest conducting the sacrifice. 'May I look?' he asked Lupus.

The mason moved away from the altar and Flavius saw the plain, rough stone of the back. Lupus beckoned him to walk round to the other side, and then stood back.

Flavius, with something of a shock, saw his own name carved in the beautiful style of perfect Roman lettering into the smooth white stone. Across the head of the altar, almost completed, was a crisply executed band of decoration, designed by Lupus to complement the dignity of the occasion.

'It is very fine,' said Flavius gravely. It was no wonder to him that, with work like this simmering in his mind, the man should be so unconcerned with the common preoccupations of army life. He wondered briefly about the goddess-like figure, now obscured under a coat of white-wash on a barracks wall.

But at that moment he saw Quintus hurrying towards him from the direction of the hospital and his urgent duties as commandant rushed back on him. 'Nevertheless, we are going to move you.'

He walked briskly towards Quintus, who was out of breath.

'I've been looking for you, sir.'

'No doubt,' said Flavius. He pointed to Lupus, now happily eating what was left of his roll as he scratched out the next part of his design.

Quintus uttered a little cry of dismay.

'Exactly,' said Flavius. 'He can't stay there. Have him moved somewhere he can get on with his work. See that his stable is ready for him by tomorrow evening. Now what else?'

'All is going well, sir,' said Quintus happily. 'As planned. The centurions found no problems when they met the section leaders. On the whole, they seemed grateful they were being protected from possible infection. They wasted no time in getting their sections working on the cleaning. You can see the baskets of rubbish filling up outside all the barracks blocks. I think the men are enjoying the change in routine.'

'Good,' said Flavius, in a preoccupied manner that disappointed Quintus.

'Sir,' he protested. He raised his voice as if perhaps Flavius hadn't heard him. 'All is going well!'

'Yes, I did hear you, Quintus. I am in no doubt that we can keep the secret of his visit here. But do you honestly believe that the emperor can hide his absence from that company of his in Egypt? Someone must have seen him leave, or discovered he's no longer among them.'

'Oh, no, sir,' interrupted Quintus, relieved that this was all that was troubling his commandant. 'You know what he's like in Rome. When he's in a cheerful mood, he walks about the streets, goes into the baths, talks to everyone. But there are times when he wants to be alone; then he travels round in a horse-drawn litter with the curtains drawn and his private guards on both sides of him. No-one is allowed to approach him. No-one would dare. This might go on for a couple of hours, or several days. If he's travelling over long distances, working on something, he can be even more reclusive.'

'So you are telling me,' said Flavius, without conviction, 'that somewhere in Egypt, the twenty-four members of the elite Praetorian Guard are escorting an empty litter—'

'Only twenty-two. Two of them are here.'

'Surely someone will have wondered why two men are missing?'

'It isn't easy to count twenty-odd men jogging along in flashing armour under a blinding sun, especially when you're stupid with drinking too much in the heat.'

'The other guards, of course, have to know.'

'Yes, but if one of them betrayed the emperor, the others would kill him, as well as anyone he had spoken to.'

'What about the empress?' Flavius persisted.

'Everyone at court knows the empress doesn't welcome Hadrian's company, and he certainly doesn't seek hers.' Quintus hesitated. 'It's sad,' he added, as if he felt obliged to say something else after making such a comment.

'There's his heir, too. Isn't he usually with the emperor?'

'Antinous? Yes, that's true. To be honest, sir, that does surprise me. He would be bound to miss Hadrian. Perhaps he knows, or perhaps he's been sent away on some imperial duty or other.'

'Well, yes, perhaps so,' said Flavius, sensing that Quintus had other things on his mind. 'You're busy. You must go.'

'Yes, sir. Thank you, sir,' said Quintus gratefully, and darted off in the direction of the senior centurion's house.

Flavius looked at the activity going on all round him. Having devised and mounted the operation, suddenly he felt superfluous. Aimlessly, he made his way back to the villa.

He wandered round to see what his bed looked like in the emperor's quarters. He found that not only his bed but his favourite painted chest was in there. The most elegant lamps, ornaments, rugs and cushions had been culled from all over the house, and were being carefully arranged.

'Well done,' he said. The slaves in charge hardly noticed him.

He moved on to the dining-room, thinking he might take another look at the mural. The room was not, as he had expected it to be, empty. Aelius was standing at the head of the table, calling out instructions, with much waving of arms and pointing of fingers, to another group of slaves.

At the other end of the table was a cloth, half-unfolded, of heavy ivory silk damask with a deep gold fringe that, when the cloth was fully spread, would brush the ground. The rest of the table was covered with silver dishes, platters, jugs and bowls. Flavius hadn't seen either the cloth or the silver since he left Stresa. He hadn't even known – and certainly Lucilla hadn't – that Aelius had packed them for Alauna. The thought had never occurred to Flavius, as it had to Aelius, that any grand occasions would ever happen in the wilds of north Britain.

Flavius gratefully put out a hand to touch Aelius on the shoulder.

'What?' He was bending over the table, beginning to sort the silver. He turned his head and saw Flavius. For the benefit of the slaves, he added, 'Sir?'

Before Flavius could answer, the porter on duty at the main door hurried into the room, carrying a small basket filled with white winter roses. Aelius beckoned and the basket was slipped on to the table in front of him.

'Oh,' said Flavius with pleasure. 'Flowers here now?'

'From the wife of one of the centurions. She keeps a small garden. Alis went across to her this morning.' Aelius's clipped voice indicated that Flavius was wasting his steward's time.

'That would be Aemilia,' said Flavius.

'What *do* you want?' snapped Aelius.

For the second time that morning, Flavius felt superfluous.

'I thought I'd see what the mural repairs looked like in a morning light,' he said, feeling that he was having to ask permission to stand about in his own house.

Aelius grunted. 'While you are here, do you know the number of places you need for dinner?'

'Of course,' said Flavius. 'Eight; the emperor and his two secretaries, my adjutant, the doctor, the senior centurion and myself.'

'That's only seven.'

'Yes, my wife will be the eighth, if the emperor permits.'

'He won't.'

'She comes from a senatorial family. He chooses to call himself a senator among senators, and so he treats such families as equals, with courtesy.'

'She's still a woman.'

'Aelius, you will set a place for my wife,' said Flavius, taking charge of his own household again, 'and we will have to see what happens.'

He placed a chair on the spot where the emperor would sit. 'The emperor will be here, Aelius, at the head of the table, with the doctor on one side of him and Quintus on the other. He can talk about Athenian architecture to the doctor and senatorial politics to Quintus. I shall sit opposite the emperor at the other end of the table, between the senior centurion and my wife.'

'She won't like that. She'll expect to sit beside the emperor.'

'She is my responsibility, not his. That leaves the two secretaries facing each other in the middle. Clear, Aelius?'

He sat down in the emperor's chair and looked at the mural as the guest of honour would see it. Would he detect the slight difference in the new heron from the one he'd painted himself a decade earlier? A man could always recognise his own handwriting; hadn't Flavius heard that a painter always knew his own brush-strokes?

'Aelius,' he called, 'I want the tall lamps in a circle closer to the table ... close enough to put the mural in shadow.'

'And what,' demanded Aelius, 'do you suppose the emperor will think when he finds himself staring all the evening at a darkened wall?'

Flavius was aware that Aelius was in the mood to argue about anything, but this time he was asking the right question.

Flavius sighed. 'It could arouse his suspicions, couldn't it?' After a moment's thought he added, 'There's only one thing we can do: we'll have to reverse the seating. The emperor must sit with his back to the mural. I will be here, where I'm sitting now, in what would have been his place.'

'You can't take the seat of honour.'

'Why not? I am the master of this villa. Haven't I the right to sit at the head of my own table, with my wife beside me?'

Aelius shrugged his shoulders.

'There's a chance, I know, that he might glance at the mural as he takes his seat, but you must catch his attention – fuss over him, say something in Greek.'

Aelius looked at him.

'Then, with luck, he'll be drinking enough to forget about it.'

Aelius sighed and selected a silver dish for scrutiny.

'Well, he won't be staring at it all the time, will he? He can't keep twisting round in his chair to look at it,' said Flavius impatiently.

'You could tell him the truth. That your wife maliciously damaged it.' Aelius reached for another dish.

'Then the emperor certainly wouldn't let her dine in here. She might throw the next plate at him! He might even banish her to a far-flung island in case she developed a taste for throwing plates. He wouldn't want to risk the life of one of his most promising commandants.'

Flavius stood up. 'I haven't time for all this now,' he said sharply. He realised, as he spoke, that he had nothing at all to occupy his time until the emperor arrived. However, appearances counted. He strode briskly towards the doorway, a man with a pressing commitment. He called out as he went, 'Move the lamps, Aelius. And I shall want wine to offer his majesty as soon as he reaches the headquarters building.'

IV

Flavius took himself into his office in the headquarters building earlier than he need have done. There was still almost an hour left of the weak winter afternoon light.

He was sure there were issues he should, as commandant, be considering, but his mind was blank. He sat looking at the room. He got up and rearranged the chairs. A basket of reports awaiting his signature stood on the desk. He cleared his writing tools and the basket from its surface, but that made the room look unused, so he replaced them. He picked up one of the reports and unfastened its ribbon. Then he put it back unread.

By the time the last pale streaks of daylight had faded, he felt as if the whole camp had fallen silent, holding its breath as it waited for the emperor's arrival. But he was deluding himself; if he stepped outside his office and crossed the floor of the headquarters hall, he would find the streets of the fort filled with the everyday noise and bustle of activity, and no-one would have an inkling of the approaching presence of the man they revered as a god in their gilded shrine.

He was suddenly aware of raised voices in the adjoining room. It was Aelius and the chief clerk engaged, if not in argument, in some kind of animated discussion. Aelius, he presumed, had elected to house the emperor's wine in the chief clerk's room, and the chief clerk was protesting against this intrusion into his meticulously ordered space.

Compromises must have been made; gradually the voices grew fainter until Flavius was left again in silence. The quiet seemed to have its own weight; it bristled around him.

There was a tap on the door.

'Yes?'

Quintus was standing in the doorway, clutching the latch as if he needed its support. The emperor's party, he announced breathlessly, had been seen crossing the causeway below the east gate.

Flavius suspected that his fingers were trembling as much as those of Quintus appeared to be, but as the commandant it was his duty to look relaxed and confident. He grasped the stylus tightly as though he had been at work on the reports.

'The senior centurion?' he asked briskly.

'He has been informed and is on his way to the gate.'

Flavius smiled at him. 'Good. Well done, Quintus. So we shall all have the pleasure of greeting our emperor in the next few minutes. Splendid. Thank you.'

As Quintus, pale-faced, hurried away, Flavius glimpsed through the doorway the backs of Aelius and the chief clerk. Heads together, they were bent over the chief clerk's desk. Flavius thought he saw, although he knew it wasn't possible, a wisp of steam rising between them.

He rubbed a hand over his eyes. 'Aelius,' he called.

The steward came, carefully closing the door behind him. He had, Flavius noticed, changed into his very best, ceremonial-occasion tunic: chestnut-coloured wool with dark stripes running over each shoulder to the hem.

Flavius leaned back in his chair with his eyes closed. 'Aelius, what are you doing in there?'

'What are *you* doing in *here*? Sit up, Flavius.'

'Have you brought the wine?'

'Yes,' said Aelius, as if he hadn't time for stupid questions.

'Did you bring anything to eat with you – little cakes, oysters, something?'

'No. This is not the hour of the day for titbits.'

'It is if you're hungry.'

'You had plenty of time earlier to think about eating.'

Flavius admitted with a wry nod that he couldn't disagree with that.

The chief clerk put his head round the door. 'Sir, the emperor has entered the fort and the east gate has been closed.'

'Then this is certainly not the moment,' declared Aelius, 'for you to be concerning yourself with food.' He made a rising movement with his hands. 'Stand up, Flavius. Put yourself somewhere over here, facing the door.' Aelius selected a spot.

Even if he'd been on the point of starvation, thought Flavius, he could have sorted that out for himself; but he obeyed the instruction.

'Are you ready?' asked Aelius.

They were eight years old again, setting out on one of their daunting, probably forbidden, adventures. It was always Aelius, the elder by a few months, who decided when to go.

'Am I?' Flavius gave a small grimace.

Aelius picked a shred of fluff from Flavius's sleeve. 'You are now.' He gripped Flavius's arms and gave him a little shake. 'Yes?'

'Yes.' The grimace had given way to a smile.

'Stay there. It won't be long.' It might not have been long, probably only a few minutes, but to Flavius, waiting on his mark, it seemed an age before he heard movement behind the door.

Then, as he faced it, the door was swung open.

Lugo stood erect against it, as if, should it suddenly disintegrate, he could protect the emperor from harm. Quintus was escorting, with deference, a man in a thick, hooded cape, a scarf wrapped round his face. He crossed the threshold with brisk, heavy steps.

'Your majesty,' said Quintus, 'I beg to present the commandant, the prefect Flavius Valerius Paulus.'

The emperor was pushing back his hood and tugging impatiently at the knot in his scarf. Flavius, before he fell on one knee and bowed his head, had a glimpse of grey curling hair and of a beard clipped close to the chin.

Hadrian was the fourteenth emperor to govern Rome since the collapse of the Republic. He was the first to ignore the tradition of the clean-shaven imperial face.

It was widely accepted in Rome that he wore a beard because it was favoured by the Athenian men of letters whom he greatly admired. Some, however – including the empress, who loathed him as much as he loathed her – declared that it simply masked a skin blemish.

The cape and scarf had been dropped on the floor. The emperor addressed himself to the top of Flavius's head.

'So this is the Flavius Valerius Paulus who told his emperor which of his own imperial roads he might or might not use. Get up off the floor, Paulus.'

Flavius stood up. The emperor had taken his chair and was stretching out his booted legs with a grunt of relief. Flavius walked over the discarded clothing.

'I've banished men for less offensive behaviour than yours,' Hadrian shouted.

Flavius faced him across the desk. He felt as if he were opening a difficult case for the defence before an unsympathetic judge. All that was lacking was his lawyer's toga.

'Sir,' he said, humbly lowering his eyes, 'I deeply regret that I have caused offence to your majesty, and I am ready to accept any disgrace you choose to impose on me.'

He paused to raise his eyes to meet the emperor's. 'But I beg you, sir, to consider that I had been instructed that your visit must be secret – without being given any reason for the secrecy.' He hesitated, in case the emperor should be disposed to enlighten him, but Hadrian merely went on glaring at him.

'I had, therefore, to assume that it had to do with your safety and that your life could be endangered. With your majesty's life at stake, I could hardly concern myself with my own position.'

Hadrian struck the desk. 'So now you want a medal for your bravery in daring to offend me?'

'No, sir. A military medal would be of no value to me as a lawyer.'

The emperor's expression changed suddenly and he began to laugh, wagging a finger at Flavius. 'If I hadn't recognised you the moment I saw you, I should have known you from that tricksy courtroom way of yours.'

Flavius realised with alarm that the emperor must have mistaken him for someone else. He had never before been in Hadrian's presence, never spoken to him. In fact, he had never heard his voice before, and was surprised to find that he spoke not with a pure Roman accent but with one that held the trace of a dialect. Hadn't he heard that when Hadrian first entered the Senate as a younger man it had caused ribald comments? Flavius doubted if it did any more.

He doubted, too, if he wanted to disturb the emperor's flash of good humour by telling him he had made a mistake, but it seemed there was nothing else to be done. 'Sir,' he said gently, 'I think your majesty is confusing me with someone else. This is the first time I have had the privilege ...'

'So,' snapped the emperor. 'I am not only incapable of choosing the right road, but I've lost my memory as well? Antioch, Paulus. What about Antioch? And while you're deciding which of us is losing his mind, is there anyone in this place who can find a drink for a traveller parched with thirst? I should have thought that here, at least, you might have had the odd flagon around.'

'But there is, of course, sir. At once, sir,' said Flavius, grateful to be able to get something right. He clapped his hands, confident that Aelius would, as usual, have an ear to the door.

The emperor was surprised and gratified, as well he might be, by the alacrity which Aelius showed in attending him. Bowing to him in the graceful Greek manner, he laid a large goblet of green-tinted glass on the desk before him, half-filled it with wine, and then, to Flavius's alarm, produced a steaming jug, from which he added hot water to the goblet.

'Ah,' said the emperor, delighted. He drank deeply, looked up at Aelius, nodded, smiled and murmured to him in Greek. Aelius, with another of his bows, answered him in the same language. He waited at the emperor's side until the goblet was empty, refilled it with wine and hot water, and then, scooping up the clothes from the floor as he went, removed himself with yet another bow.

The emperor savoured another mouthful of wine. 'I had not expected, Paulus,' he said comfortably, 'to find in this bleak outpost of the empire – even in one of my own forts – anyone who understood my dislike of cold water in wine. Your man was honest enough to admit that it was you who had reminded him.'

Flavius, glancing towards the door, said, 'Yes, a good man.' He was relieved to have an explanation for that earlier wisp of steam.

'So, Antioch?'

Flavius, puzzled by the emperor's repeated reference to it, said, 'I know the city, of course. I spent a brief period at the Greek university there.'

'Explain.'

Flavius took an uneasy breath, disconcerted by the emperor's probing. 'It was advised by my father, after I was qualified to practise law in Rome, at the suggestion of his Greek secretary who was also my tutor. It had been anticipated that I would be handling my father's legal affairs, and by then he had a large range of interests in Greek-speaking provinces, which already outnumbered the Latin ones.'

'A wise move,' announced the emperor. 'Were you aware that when you were living in Antioch, I was governor of Syria?'

Flavius had the uncomfortable feeling that Hadrian already knew what he had been talking about. How did the emperor know that he had lived in Antioch? How did he know it coincided with his own governorship of Syria?

'Yes, sir, I did. I saw you once. There was a very fine arcade in the centre of Antioch, and you arranged to have lights decorating its archways. It was beautiful on warm, dark evenings. When you came to look at it, I was at the back of the crowd watching you. I was never any nearer to you than that.'

'Indeed?' said the emperor. 'What was the last exercise you had to complete at the end of your course?'

'Of the course in Antioch?'

'What else are we talking about? Well?'

'It was a public discourse before the whole university. The subject matter was chosen by the university authorities and revealed to candidates only two hours before ...' Flavius hesitated.

'And your task, Paulus,' interrupted the emperor, 'was to consider the possible consequences to Rome had Julius Caeser not been assassinated. Correct?'

Flavius stared at him. 'Yes,' he said faintly.

'I set the subject myself. As governor of Syria I was a patron of the university, and invited to make my contribution. I was present in the chancellor's box ... out of public sight, of course. We agreed to award the golden palm to you.'

'I have it here, in my library,' murmured Flavius.

'So, perhaps, you can now accept that I wasn't confusing you with anyone else,' declared the emperor.

'Yes, sir, but you must also admit that I had no means of knowing that.'

The emperor stared at him. 'It isn't often that both sides of an argument are proved right. This appears to be one of those occasions.'

'It is also, sir, one of those rare occasions when both sides were proved wrong.'

'You have a quick wit, Paulus. It could be annoying.'

Flavius could think of no useful answer to that, so he stood silent while the emperor splashed more wine into his goblet. Flavius guessed from his frown as he added water that it was no longer hot enough for his liking. Flavius continued to stare at the wall above the emperor's head.

Refreshed, Hadrian went on, 'Now that we have agreed that my memory is as good as it is reputed to be, you will not be surprised to know that when the present governor of your province spoke of his admiration for the work of the then chief magistrate of Stresa, one Flavius Valerius Paulus, I had no difficulty in recalling that day in Antioch. It would seem that, instead of entertaining the good people of Stresa with some jolly festival or other, you spent your money on an orphanage, and devised a system for maintaining it after your year in office was over.'

Flavius looked at the emperor in amazement. 'Your majesty's memory is indeed ...' he said, hesitating for a word.

'Phenomenal, yes. Explain this scheme to me.'

'It was not a new idea. It had been used elsewhere. I merely adapted it for the situation in Stresa.'

'Well?' said Hadrian impatiently.

'There was a lot of uncultivated land round Stresa, good land suitable for farming. We had a number of farmers of moderate means who wanted to expand, but couldn't afford to do so without help. I persuaded the council to buy up parcels of land and rent them out at an annual interest of five per cent. The sum obtained is enough to maintain the building and hire staff for the orphanage.'

'Does it work?'

'I thought the governor might have mentioned that to you, sir. Yes.'

'Hmm,' said the emperor. 'A sharp-witted lawyer who knows how to use money, eh? I offered you a prefecture to give you the experience required by Rome for any man who aspires to a position of standing. How old are you?'

'How old, sir?'

'There are times, Paulus, when that sharp brain of yours tends to slow down.' The emperor repeated his question slowly and deliberately. 'How old are you?'

'Thirty-one, sir.'

'Good. Then in one year you will become eligible for election to the Senate.'

Flavius shook his head. 'With respect, sir, that is not what I seek. Besides, my family is not of the senatorial class. What senator would vote for me?'

'Anyone whose tail I chose to tweak. Your wife is of senatorial rank. Why else did you marry her if it wasn't to start making use of her relatives?'

Flavius closed his eyes. The emperor even knew about his marriage. 'You know a lot about me, sir,' he said, almost laughing.

'I know a lot more,' said Hadrian. 'Of necessity. You interest me. I know, for example, that you are popular among the men here – much more popular than your predecessor, which is perhaps surprising, because I gather he was more easy-going than I think you are.'

Flavius, grateful that the subject of Lucilla had been dropped, said crisply, 'I don't seek popularity. I am merely concerned to see that the men receive fair and reasonable treatment within the army code.'

'But you are not so popular, are you, among your officers?'

'Regrettably not.'

'Why?'

'I discovered that some of them were misusing their power over the men they commanded. It had to be stopped.'

'An example?'

'Yes, sir. Your majesty will know that if a man wants to take leave, he applies first to his centurion, who, if he approves the request, passes it on to the commandant. Certain officers demanded payment before handing a request on to me.'

Hadrian folded his arms. 'Are all your complaints as trivial? That one's common practice, I should say.'

'Not in any fort that I command. Trivial or not, it's illegal. And to the men penalised in this way, it certainly isn't trivial. When the money for bedding and clothes and whatever else is taken from their pay, they have very little left.'

The emperor's arms were unfolded and he was gripping the arms of his chair. Flavius ignored the signs of growing anger. 'Your majesty is much admired for his willingness to share the conditions of the men ...'

The emperor relaxed his grip. 'Yes, I do on campaign,' he said, nodding amiably again.

'But when the campaign is over, your majesty can return to a palace the size of a small town. Forgive me, sir, but you have never in your life known what it was like to have to look twice at every little coin before you spent it.'

'Nor have you,' shouted the emperor.

'No, but my work has sometimes taken me among people who do.'

Aelius slipped into the room, carrying another jug of steaming water as his excuse. He hovered around Flavius. 'Might I request the prefect to inform his majesty that the bath-house is prepared for him?' he murmured.

Flavius motioned him away. Hadrian ignored him and spoke again, in anger, to Flavius. 'Was it worth offending your officers in such a way? You have no experience of combat. If this fort were attacked, your life might depend on them.'

'And their lives might depend on the resources I could collect and distribute.' Flavius paused. In a calmer manner he added, 'You, sir, as emperor, are the commander-in-chief of the armies of Rome. Any corrupt behaviour, however slight, insults you personally.'

The emperor was staring at him. Flavius gazed back. He was looking at a face that for well over a decade had been familiar to him on coinage. The curling hair and the crisp beard were similar, but Hadrian was now in his early-fifties and his cheeks no longer had the smoothness of the younger emperor. Yet, Flavius noticed, there was something else – a haggard air that had nothing to do with the lines brought by the passing years. It was as though a darkness had fallen on him. Flavius looked away quickly as he saw tears forming in the emperor's eyes.

He heard Hadrian say in barely more than a whisper, 'You reminded me then of – someone – someone I used to know.'

Flavius glanced up and saw him bury his face in the goblet. Then he pushed back his chair and turned towards the window behind him.

'It's black out there. So early,' he said with an effort. 'And cold by now.'

'Very cold indeed, sir,' responded Flavius.

'So cold,' said the emperor, rubbing his eyes, 'that when you come into a warm room from outside, your eyes water.' He succeeded in giving a brief, hesitant laugh.

Flavius laughed with him. 'Yes, sir, a nuisance. It's always happening to me, too. And your majesty will be especially sensitive to the cold after travelling across Egypt.'

Flavius had hoped the remark would help the emperor, for he was known to love sailing on the Nile, but it was not the right moment. He shook his head slowly. 'I no longer have any liking for the warmth of Egypt.' He was speaking more to himself than to Flavius who stood watching him helplessly, himself shaken by the sight of Hadrian's despair.

A breath of wind stirred the flame of a lamp and it flashed upon the stylus that Flavius had left on his desk. He was suddenly reminded of the story that Hadrian had, in temper, once thrown a stylus at a man whose outspoken words had offended him. He had blinded him in one eye. Flavius put out a hand to push the stylus out of the way behind the lamp.

As he put his fingers on it, the emperor turned away from the window and saw the blade catching the light. He stared at it, as if, by concentrating on its brightness, he might find the strength to recover himself.

Flavius lifted his hand. Hadrian picked up the stylus and gripped it tightly. 'So you've heard the story? Who hasn't?

'It was a bad thing to do. I've never forgiven myself for it.' He was speaking again in his loud, slightly hectoring manner. 'It's a sober fact, Paulus, that if I do one bad thing it's all round the empire in a week and is never forgotten. If I do a dozen good things, nobody notices – and if they did, they'd never give it another thought. Don't worry, Paulus, if I were going to throw this one, I would already have done it.'

He dropped the stylus back on the desk and rubbed his hands together. 'Now, didn't I hear something about a bath?'

Aelius, who had been standing motionless in the shadows of the room, presented himself. 'Yes, sir, that's the best way of dealing with the cold out here.'

He carried the jug away, and came back holding the emperor's cape and scarf. Hadrian waved them away.

'If you wouldn't mind, sir,' said Flavius, 'we have to cross the assembly hall of the building. If my plan is working, most of the men will be in their workshops, but there might be the odd orderly making deliveries, and there will, of course, be the two guards on duty beside the shrine. They may look as if they are made of stone, but they'll notice everything.'

The emperor pointed to the stylus. 'It's not too late,' he said, but with a grunt of displeasure let Aelius wrap the scarf round his face and arrange the hood of the cape over his head.

'There's one more thing,' said Flavius, ignoring the emperor's glare. 'Crossing the hall, we shall pass the shrine. I shall be on one side of you, my adjutant on the other. We shall both, as usual, acknowledge your statue. It would be advisable for your majesty to do the same. You are, after all, the only man in the empire who would dare to ignore it.'

'Ah,' said Hadrian, 'a good lawyer's point. And I shall probably never have another such opportunity to express my own admiration for myself. Shall we move on?'

With Flavius hastily leading the way, the emperor stepped through the door which opened on to the hall of the headquarters building.

Quintus was waiting to form the other half of the muffled emperor's escort.

The hall was dimly lit at this hour of the day, filling it with shadowed spaces; but this had the effect of making the illuminated red-and-gold shrine shine more brightly, and cast a richer glow across the stone floor that layin front of it.

As the three men walked towards the gilded figure dominating the shrine, the emperor resumed his earlier conversation with Flavius. 'So what happens now with any requests for leave?'

'They come directly to me.'

The emperor gave one of the grunts that indicated the answer was not entirely to his satisfaction. 'I would hardly regard that as a fitting duty for the commandant of one of my military forts – not even for a lawyer. For one of his junior clerks, perhaps?'

Quintus glanced nervously at Flavius, who said, as gently as he could, 'What choice did I have when my officers were doing duty as pick-pockets?'

A sudden heavy fall of rain attracted the emperor's attention as it pattered on the roof and in the courtyard. Quintus, with a sigh of relief, hoped that Hadrian might not have heard Flavius's reply.

He tried to take advantage of the emperor's fleeting interest in the downpour to divert him from answering, and pointed to a window. 'We must be grateful that your majesty reached the fort before this storm broke.'

Hadrian was not pleased by the interruption. 'Boy!' he shouted, clutching at his thick cape. 'Why do you think I'm wearing this hideous thing but to protect me from the rain?'

Quintus swallowed hard, and tried again. His words came out in an awkward rush. 'But, sir, do you know that out here it can rain much more heavily than this? The prefect can confirm how heavy it was when the men had to be moved yesterday. Even with that cape, sir ... I don't think ...' He faltered, his face burning, horrified by the words he had heard himself saying. He saw the wry smile on Flavius's face.

'What men? What move?' demanded Hadrian, looming over Quintus.

Flavius intervened. 'My adjutant is referring to men summoned to yesterday's court-martial. They were lined up, as usual, in the open courtyard. I ordered them to be reassembled at the back of the headquarters hall. I considered it the only reasonable and sensible thing to do, although the senior centurion made his sense of outrage clear.'

'As I would hope,' declared the emperor. 'This is an army camp, Paulus. I am not disposed to approve of enlisted men lolling about in some hallway to escape a few drops of rain.'

'The men stood in a disciplined line in the courtyard, and they held a disciplined line here in this hall. It seemed to me that if they were not drenched and frozen from two hours or more spent standing in a downpour they would be better able to plead their case before the court. I saw no threat to the established ethos of your majesty's military code in that.'

Flavius paused, but before the emperor could reply added, 'His majesty is known to identify himself with his men, and it is understood that he has a particular regard for this first cohort of Spaniards, which he formed himself. I strive only to follow his example.'

The emperor looked hard at him. Then, as though he was chewing the words in his teeth, said, 'Lawyers: tongues like slippery serpents.' And walked on.

They had reached the shrine in the centre of the hall.

Flavius and Quintus bowed their heads. They waited for Hadrian to follow their example, but he was intent on savouring the pleasure the moment was giving him. He advanced towards his own glistening image, bowed deeply and raised his arm with a flourish that imitated the carved outstretched hand above his head.

Flavius stepped up beside him. 'Shall we walk on, sir?'

But Hadrian was now gazing at the gilded standards ranged against the crimson panels at the back of the shrine. 'That,' he declared, 'is a sight that warms my heart – the honours that men will die to protect.' He turned to Flavius. 'Eh, Paulus?'

'No-one could fail to be impressed,' said Flavius, conscious of the lack of passion in his voice, 'by the sight of them carried ceremoniously across the parade ground.'

'Hmm.' Hadrian was not entirely happy with this response. He was now moving along to look at the altar. He bent down to read the inscription. 'In a week's time, Paulus, there will be a new one with your name on it, and you will have sacrificed your bullock to Jupiter. And in every fort across the empire, on that same day, the same ritual will have taken place.' This prospect brought a smile to the emperor's face.

'We sacrifice with grain not flesh here,' said Flavius.

Quintus screwed up his face in alarm, shot a quick glance at the emperor and looked away again. The emperor's mood of high elation had collapsed in an outburst of temper. Aware of the guards on duty before the shrine, he strode angrily away from the altar and watched with mounting fury as Flavius followed him.

The commandant, Quintus observed uneasily, was not moving at anything like the pace that had carried the emperor across the width of the hall. With something of the air of a man leaping to save a comrade from the path of a runaway horse, Quintus stepped in front of Flavius and addressed Hadrian.

'Sir, the practice of using grain in this fort and in others nearby has existed for many years, long before our present prefect was appointed. It would appear, sir, that ...'

The emperor interrupted, 'Who was the commandant then?'

Quintus hesitated. 'I don't think I know that, sir.'

'Well, you should, shouldn't you? You're here to brief him, aren't you, on relevant military matters?' The emperor nodded in Flavius's direction as he spoke. 'Some other interfering lawyer, no doubt.'

He set out at his now preferred brisk step towards the small door that opened on to the lane between the headquarters building and the villa. 'I need to eat.'

Quintus ran ahead of him to open the door, and peered up and down the lane. 'Empty now, sir.' He darted across the lane to rap on the entrance to the villa's kitchen courtyard, which opened to receive the emperor.

Aelius was standing there, with one slave holding a lamp over him and another beside him, carrying a basket of towels. The emperor's mood changed again. He smiled at the sight of Aelius and then nodded his appreciation at the pleasing smell of roasting meat filling the dark courtyard. He fell into exuberant exchanges of Greek with the steward.

Flavius slipped back into the shadows and pulled a despondent-looking Quintus with him.

'What you did,' he whispered, 'was reckless, probably unwise, but splendid. Thank you.'

Quintus was not reassured. 'I didn't know I had to tell you about previous commandants.'

'I wouldn't have been interested if you had. I would have thought it a waste of your time and mine. If I'd cared, I could have found the information in our chief clerk's meticulous records.'

Quintus gave him a shaky smile. 'The emperor was unfair to you.'

'He was unfair to you.'

They listened to Hadrian's voice carrying across the courtyard.

Flavius said irritably, 'Is he always like this? All these sudden violent changes of mood?'

'He's always quick-tempered and changeable, but not in this wild, almost spiteful way he is today. I think he's very disturbed about something. And all this strange secrecy – that's not like him either.'

Emboldened perhaps by the darkness, Quintus laid a hand on Flavius's sleeve. 'Be careful of him, sir.'

'I have more than once this afternoon wondered if the next time I saw Rome I might be chained to the back of his chariot.'

Quintus shook his head at such levity. 'In this state of mind, he frightens me. He's so unpredictable, you can't know what will provoke him.'

As if to prove Quintus's point, the emperor, beginning to move towards the bath-house, turned round. With every appearance of amiability, he called out, 'A few minutes, if you please, gentlemen, and then we will eat.'

V

It was a long few minutes.

The emperor's dinner companions – his two secretaries, the doctor and the senior centurion – were already assembled in the library, and Quintus then escorted them to the dining-room.

Flavius, formally dressed in the white toga with its narrow purple border that designated his equestrian rank, received them and indicated their seats. A line of slaves was setting out cold dishes on one of the serving tables. The emperor would shortly be joining them, Flavius explained.

For a while they made an effort to share in the desultory table conversation of people who are not accustomed to dining with each other.

Time passed. The slaves had gone. The tables designed to carry hot dishes remained empty. Conversation flagged, despite the lively young doctor's efforts to keep it going. He finally left his seat and wandered round the room to look at the mural.

Even Lugo, determined to maintain a stiff, upright posture, began to wilt.

Alis was sent for the fifth time by Lucilla to know if the emperor would accept her presence. By this stage, Alis simply put her head round the door and raised her eyebrows; Flavius, for his part, merely shook his head.

Nearly an hour and a half had passed when Aelius appeared to announce in a lofty manner that the emperor would be arriving shortly, and that he required the two members of his staff to attend him in the bath-house.

'Shortly?' cried Flavius. 'What does that mean?'

Aelius was already ushering the two men towards the doorway.

'Aelius!' Flavius got up from his chair. In his hurry, he caught his foot in the hem of the toga and tripped. He reached Aelius as he was stepping through the doorway.

The steward turned round. His eyes rested on the disarranged folds of the toga. He said nothing, but Flavius could read only too well from his expression the thoughts in his mind: Look at you! You need my help, a pity I have more elevated tasks to engage me.

Flavius was conscious of being tired, hungry and worried; and now, on top of everything else, Hadrian's liking for Aelius seemed to have gone to the steward's head.

'What,' Flavius demanded in exasperation, 'does "shortly" mean when those two have been sent for? What does he want them for?'

Aelius, still in lofty mood, shrugged his shoulders.

'Where are the rest of the dishes that were planned? What is everyone doing?'

Aelius suddenly became his old self again, ready for one of their boyhood-type quarrels. 'Can't you imagine, Flavius,' he snapped, 'what it's like in the kitchen, waiting over an hour to serve food they've been preparing all day? At least all you've got to do up here is sit.'

Flavius felt slightly ashamed that he hadn't considered what must be a scene of turmoil in the kitchen, but he wasn't yet prepared to admit it.

Aelius added, in the laboured tone of one addressing a child of limited understanding, 'The hot dishes will be served as soon as the emperor leaves the bath-house. What else could we do?' He sighed. 'Perhaps if he drinks enough, and he probably will, the emperor won't notice some dishes might not be as perfect as they should be.'

Flavius brooded on the rebuke in silence.

Aelius, enjoying his advantage, returned to his cool appraisal of Flavius's dress.

'Are you, by the way, wearing sandals?'

Flavius stretched out a foot and displayed the closed shoe traditionally worn with the toga. He felt that he was now being treated by Aelius like a sixteen-year-old again, struggling with his first purple-trimmed white toga of manhood. He had hated wearing the closed shoe instead of his sandals and discarded them whenever he could avoid Aelius. Even now he occasionally used sandals in hot weather if he could get away with it.

With a touch of sixteen-year-old insolence, he displayed his second foot for inspection. He was sure he detected a flicker of disappointment on Aelius's face.

But Aelius was not an easy man to beat. He raised his eyebrows. 'You must be growing old, Flavius – doing what everybody else does.'

He stalked away before Flavius could make a reply.

Quintus was hovering attentively. 'May I, sir?' He removed the bunched-up cloth from Flavius's hand, and rearranged it in folds to hang from his left shoulder.

'Explain something to me if you can, Quintus,' said Flavius. 'When a man goes bear hunting in the desolate winter forests of north Britain, why does he need to take two clerks with him? Two? Even one seems to me somewhat out of place.'

'The emperor had two secretaries because one handles his Latin correspondence and the other his Greek,' Quintus explained patiently. 'They are here with him because – well, sir, because they are always with him. Whether the emperor is tracking bears, sailing down the Nile or presiding over the Senate, it makes no difference. He needs them. His mind never rests. He's always solving problems, asking questions or throwing out ideas. He dictates letters everywhere. Walking in the street ...'

'Not, surely,' Flavius interrupted, 'sitting in his bath, in the middle of nowhere, at this hour of the day?'

Quintus appeared to find this amusing. He began to smile until he saw the look on Flavius's face. 'Well, he won't be idle, sir.'

And, apparently, idle the emperor was not, for the following twenty minutes.

Flavius was almost verging on the mutinous act of handing round the cold dishes when the door opened to admit a servant carrying an unlit brazier.

After that, events happened at such a speed that Flavius, with a delicious surge of relief, realised that there was no further need to consider the option of mutiny.

The servant set down his brazier, which Flavius presumed was for the emperor's boiled water, and devoted himself to the task of lighting it.

The two secretaries slipped into the room to take their places again at the table, having murmured to Flavius that the emperor would like the adjutant to escort him from the bath-house.

'Why?' whispered Quintus in alarm.

'You are the only person here that he really knows,' said Flavius. 'Going into a dining-room full of strangers, isn't it agreeable to have an acquaintance for company?'

Quintus looked at him. 'The emperor would enter a den of savages alone without turning a hair.'

The enticing smell of cooking was already drifting into the room. 'Hurry!' said Flavius.

In the doorway, Quintus brushed into the first of the procession of slaves bearing heated dishes. After the last of them came Aelius.

He approached Flavius. 'The prefect would wish to know that the emperor is approaching.'

Flavius rose to his feet and glanced round the room. The tall bronze lamps arranged round the table were casting a pool of light across its surface. The silver shone and there was a glint of gold from the fringe of the table-cloth. Aemilia's flowers, in a bowl decorated with blue enamel, stood in front of the emperor's place.

A number of slaves detached themselves from the serving benches and positioned themselves round the table, one behind each chair.

The room fell silent. The emperor's voice could be heard outside. Flavius moved closer to the door.

Hadrian walked into his dining-room, one hand resting on Quintus's shoulder.

He was dressed in a loose tunic and mantle cut in the Greek style. It was purple in colour, not the deep purple of imperial robes but a paler shade known in the fashion houses of Rome as amethyst. Waves of thick grey hair fell across his forehead.

He held out his hands. 'Gentlemen, you must forgive this unseemly delay, but the prefect's bath was more seductive than I had expected.' He turned to Flavius, with a nod of approval for his formal robe. 'Paulus, I ask you to excuse me for sitting at your table improperly clothed, but the weight of a senatorial toga seemed to me too much of an added load for a pack-horse on rough ground. Your Aelius has done wonders with this old rag of mine – brushed it up, hung it in the steam room, wrapped it round me – and now look at me!'

He was impressive: expansive, gracious, smiling and sparkling with the charm he could exert when he chose. Lugo looked as if he would have died for him, if required, on the spot. Quintus seemed bemused, unable to understand how this captivatingly agreeable man at his side could be the one who had so alarmed him earlier in the day.

The doctor, Flavius observed, was greeting the performance with one of his courteous smiles, being aware, as Flavius was himself, that the old rag was cut from cloth that few people outside the imperial family could afford to buy.

The emperor glanced round the room. 'Oh, a table? We eat at a table?'

Flavius reminded him of his suggestion that, while he was staying at Alauna, life should continue as normal. 'Here in the north,' Flavius explained, 'a number of us prefer to use a table. It is a practice encouraged by the legate in York.'

The emperor turned to Quintus. 'Ah, well, if that is what your revered uncle wants, who are we to refuse?' As Flavius conducted him to his chair, he added amiably, 'For myself, I have always thought it more comfortable to be drunk on a couch than a chair. Does that tell us something about the legate?'

'Perhaps something about north Britain, sir.'

'Ah, always the quick return, Paulus.' As Flavius pulled out his chair, Hadrian paused to look at the mural that would hang behind him as he ate. The white flowers showed up in the shadows. 'Ah, yes. Yes,' he murmured. Then, turning his back on it, he sat down.

'Please, gentlemen, sit.'

As the others settled themselves, the emperor noticed the empty chair with the slave standing idle behind it. 'Is another guest expected?'

'It is another custom now in this house,' said Flavius, venturing carefully on to the subject, 'for my wife, sir, to dine with me in this room. In this household there are no other ladies from my family, and I do not think it proper to leave her to eat alone. I should be grateful if your majesty would allow her to take her usual place.'

Dining with ladies was not something Hadrian enjoyed. In his own world, they occupied a separate sphere, but he was not in the mood to appear ungracious.

He raised a hand to Aelius. 'We will wait until the prefect's wife joins us.' He nodded at Flavius, and then fell into lively conversation in Greek with the doctor sitting beside him.

Flavius went himself to fetch Lucilla. He was hardly surprised to find that she had ignored his advice to dress in the simple manner the emperor preferred.

She was at least not intending to brave the winter night in one of her diaphanous shawls, but a sweeping pale blue cloak of military cut was hardly likely to please Hadrian's taste for the unobtrusive. Lucilla was still under the illusion, devised by Aelius at his most dangerously inventive, that this was a fashion created by Hadrian's empress. What her dressmaker had made of her extraordinary order no-one knew, but Lucilla had been delighted with the result.

Alis removed the cloak as Lucilla entered the dining-room. When she made a deep curtsey to the emperor, glittering little points of light flashed from the gold embroidery on her hem to the jewelled pins in her hair.

Flavius groaned to himself, as well the emperor might have done. Hadrian, however, always chose to treat members of the senatorial class with courtesy, whatever his personal feelings might be.

He rose from his chair and raised Lucilla to her feet. The front of her hair was arranged in curls round her face. The rest, thickened by a false plait, was coiled on the top of her head. It was the kind of elaborate dressing that the emperor deplored, especially as it was a style favoured by his wife.

'A pleasure, madam,' he said, convincingly enough to delight Lucilla.

She responded with her prettiest smile. 'Might I enquire of your majesty whether the empress will be joining him in Britain?'

'No, madam, she has other duties.'

'I have had the privilege of being presented, sir, to her majesty. May I beg you to convey my loyal duty to her?'

The emperor snapped his fingers at one of his secretaries who made a note on the wax pad laid on the table beside him.

'It will be done, madam,' he said. He sat down again and resumed his conversation with the doctor.

Flavius took Lucilla's arm and urged her towards the seat that Aelius was holding out for her. She snatched her arm away.

'Why,' she hissed, 'is that nuisance of a creature ...'

'My adjutant?'

'... sitting beside the emperor? *I* should be there.'

'He is there,' murmured Flavius, 'because he is the highest-ranking person in the room, apart from the emperor himself.' Lucilla sank reluctantly into her chair, and Aelius gave it a sharp push. 'His aunt, by the way, is married to the legate in York.'

Over her head, Aelius smiled blissfully at Flavius. He had always hoped to break this news personally to Lucilla, but he was well pleased with the situation as it was.

Lucilla was quivering. Flavius slipped into the chair beside her, facing the emperor at the other end of the table. 'Why didn't you tell me? Why didn't *he* tell me?' she spat at him.

Flavius whispered into her ear, 'Because your behaviour didn't encourage him to stay anywhere near you.'

Lucilla pushed away the food that was being offered to her. The angry jingling of her bracelets caused Hadrian to glance down the table, and then look quickly away. He was laughing at something the doctor was saying.

Without looking at Lucilla, Flavius said quietly, 'You wanted to dine with the emperor. To please you, I asked him. He agreed, although it went against his usual practice. You will not, my dear, if you please, offend his majesty or embarrass me.'

Lucilla gasped, but before she could find words to retaliate, he added, 'Be quiet, Lucilla.' He was trying to hear what the emperor was saying. He possessed enough Greek to understand that Hadrian was discussing the plan devised to keep his visit secret.

'Audacious!' Flavius heard him declare, laughing again with the doctor. 'Checking the emperor for a disease!'

'A formidable experience, sir,' the doctor agreed. 'But I can't pretend the idea was mine. I was pleased to help, but the plan was entirely the prefect's.'

Aelius was stretching between them to fill the emperor's glass. They drew him into the conversation. 'Audacious indeed, sir, but masterly, wouldn't your majesty say?' Aelius, it seemed, could do and say no wrong. The emperor nodded and raised his newly filled glass to Flavius.

'The choice of the east gate was, I have to admit, Paulus, a masterly decision.' He was speaking again in Latin so that the whole of the table could understand him.

Flavius bowed his head. 'Thank you, sir, but nothing would have worked if my officers, under the guidance of the senior centurion, had not carried out my orders with impeccable precision.'

The emperor smiled slowly and turned towards the senior centurion. He broke into Spanish. 'That doesn't surprise me. The senior centurion and I are old friends.'

Lugo rose from his chair, his face red with excitement.

The emperor repeated his remark in Latin. 'He is the only Spaniard I know who speaks Spanish with a Gallic accent. I was reminded of it when I heard him at the east gate. He was one of a volunteer detail that worked with me when I was planning the wall here. He was only a junior centurion then. We were all younger ... He may have forgotten.'

'Never, sir,' said Lugo.

'Do you remember how we stamped about, testing the terrain, and got the legionary engineers to lay our lines? The arguments we had?' The emperor dug into his capacious memory. 'Weren't there two children?'

The senior centurion looked down at his plate. 'Not any longer, sir.'

'Ah, I wonder what happened to all those old sketches I made?'

'The chief clerk will know, sir, if anyone does.'

'Do you think so? I doubt it. I'd like to look at them again. Those were good days, eh?'

'The best, sir.'

'Try the roasted pork, senior centurion. Aelius recommends it.'

'As you say, sir.' Lugo sounded as if the breath had been knocked out of him. He sat down in a trance-like state as the slave set a dish of meat in front of him. He cut it carefully into small sections, and then left it untouched.

Flavius, sitting between a sullen Lucilla and a tongue-tied Lugo, gave his attention to the camaraderie at the other end of the table. Hadrian, without ever appearing to stop talking, ate heartily. He seemed indifferent to what he was eating – fish, chicken, hare, pork – so long as it was a large plateful. He soon lost interest in making his own choice from the dishes Aelius offered him, and left the steward to choose for him.

The amount he drank, without its having any outward effect on him, amazed Flavius. Hadrian must have been exhausted, but he behaved like a man who knows sleep will be difficult and drinks not for pleasure but to find oblivion. But how, wondered Flavius, could this be true for the emperor, living at the heart of his glittering, powerful world?

Right at that moment he was showing his concern for the senior centurion, and asking if the pork had disappointed him.

Lugo, alerted by a nudge from Flavius, put one of his neat squares of pork into his mouth. It was, he thanked the emperor, delicious.

With a deceptive cat-like smile, the emperor confessed to a feeling of relief. 'I was beginning to think there might be some aversion to flesh in this fort. I understand, to my alarm, that you sacrifice grain to Jupiter. Everyone else here seems to be too young to explain to me why. I was hoping you might be able to.'

Flavius and Quintus exchanged glances. Quintus mouthed, 'He can never let go.'

Lugo, restored by this fresh demand from his emperor, was on his feet again. 'Yes, indeed so, your majesty.' He hesitated. ' I must apologise if part of what I need to say gives offence.'

'I shall attach no blame to you, senior centurion.'

'Thank you, sir. Some years ago, expected supplies of grain failed to reach us. Stocks ran out both here in Alauna and in other forts that took delivery from our harbour. There was plenty of meat and other foods, but the men wanted grain. There was a near mutiny, sir.' He waited to see how Hadrian would react to this shameful admission, but the emperor was busily swallowing wine. 'No-one had realised until then that in some forts grain was valued more highly than meat. One of the commandants suggested that, since that was the case, grain should be offered to our god rather than flesh. It was also felt among the men that Jupiter was angered because we were not offering to him what was most precious to us, and he had therefore prevented the delivery of our grain. Since then, we have honoured him in our worship with grain, and he has never again deprived us of it.'

The emperor held up his empty wine-glass. He looked as if he didn't know how to cope with what he had been hearing. The charm was beginning to fail. 'You're sure you weren't all being squeamish?'

Seeing the look on Lugo's face, Flavius said in as jovial a voice as possible, 'The emperor and his jokes!'

'Joke, sir?' Lugo was aware that he often failed to see jokes that convulsed other people.

'What else?' said Flavius. 'Half the men who were here during that unrest over grain were chosen by the emperor to fight with him in Judea. I think his majesty knows who is squeamish and who is not.'

'Oh.' The senior centurion, still confused, was nevertheless relieved.

By now the emperor was glowering at Flavius as if this was an audacity too far. At any moment, thought Flavius, he was going to command that Alauna should revert to the sacrificial custom of the rest of the empire, but he seemed suddenly to feel wearily that he was bothering with something that was of such little importance. Other matters were filling his mind.

'And what does our present commandant wish to do? He likes to change things, as you know, senior centurion.' The emperor was beginning to sweat, as though he was unwell.

'No, sir. I am one of the squeamish ones. We are shortly expecting a year's supply of grain. I would not dare to offend Jupiter,' said Flavius.

'We certainly can't do that.' The emperor closed his eyes, beckoning to Aelius. As the steward bent over him, Hadrian whispered in his ear and Aelius, with a reassuring nod, hurried from the room.

'Tell me, Paulus, is your Aelius a slave?'

The question startled him. 'No, sir, he is a freed man, my chief servant.'

'That disappoints me,' said the emperor. 'I had hoped to buy him from you. I would have paid any price you asked.'

Flavius said stiffly, 'Your majesty is free to offer him an appointment on your staff.'

The emperor shook his head with a wry smile. 'No. When he refused, as I'm sure he would have done, in courtesy – at the very least – to you, then I would have felt obliged to command his obedience to his emperor, and he, as a loyal subject, would have had no choice but to accept my offer. He would have hated me for the rest of his life. What good would that have done?'

Aelius had returned with a small potion bottle from a collection which he kept in a locked cupboard in his tiny office off the kitchen. He poured a few drops into a beaker and handed it to Hadrian, saying in his kindly nurse-maidish way, 'This will ease the headache, I promise, sir.'

The emperor looked at Flavius over the rim of the beaker. 'This is the better situation, wouldn't you agree?'

Flavius smiled. 'Thank you, sir. Yes.'

Aelius glanced suspiciously from one to the other, but hid his curiosity as the emperor drank his potion. It was Lucilla who broke the silence that had fallen.

'Your majesty is perceptive. Aelius had been a slave all his life until a few months ago. In my opinion, it is a mark that can never be lost.'

Hadrian gave the beaker back to Aelius. He too, was silent for a moment, then he said, with every appearance of courtesy, 'Madam, I assume you know all the present members of the Senate?'

Lucilla moved her head so that her long ear-rings sparkled invitingly. For the first time that evening, she was hearing the kind of conversation she understood.

'There are, of course, sir, some families of senatorial rank that I know more intimately than others, but I think I can say that at some time or other I have met all the members of the Senate.'

'Would it surprise you to know that one of our senators was born a slave?'

Lucilla stared at him in horror. Then her face changed, and she gave one of her tinkling, silly laughs. 'Of course it would. You would be teasing me. It is another of your majesty's jokes.'

'Lucilla!' murmured Flavius.

She ignored him and continued to smile roguishly at the emperor. Hadrian glanced with something like pity at Flavius.

'You mistake me, madam. It is true. Quintus will bear me out. His father has long enjoyed a friendship with the man.' Quintus nodded his head. 'Think, madam, if Paulus here hadn't snatched you away from us as his bride, you might well have married a former slave. He is very rich. Why not? It was Aelius with his potion who reminded me of him.' He smiled and nodded at the steward.

Lucilla said faintly, 'Potion?'

Weariness seemed to have affected the emperor again. 'Quintus, explain to the prefect's wife, if you will. Let us not mention a name.'

Quintus cleared his throat. 'When this particular senator was a young slave, madam, he developed a skill for curing various ailments with remedies he made himself in his spare time. He became widely known for it in his district and was able to save enough money to buy his freedom and set himself up in a small shop, where he could increase his range of products.'

'Of course,' interrupted the emperor, 'his real skill may not have been in devising potions, but in persuading people to swallow them.'

Quintus, not entirely happy with this view, went on, 'Before long, he was able to move to a larger shop near the forum where he rapidly acquired clients from senatorial families. His bottles became prettier and his prices higher. Within a few years, he had amassed the sum required for entry to the Senate, and his new acquaintances were happy to elect him.'

Quintus glanced at Hadrian. 'I think the emperor, like my father, has never regretted his admission.'

The emperor nodded, and Lucilla looked at both of them with an expression of disbelief.

Hadrian leaned forward on the table, almost as if venturing an apology. 'It always puzzles me that so few men have no head for figures, by which I mean no head for handling money. Your husband, by the way, is one of the rare birds who can.'

This was not the kind of exchange Lucilla had expected to enjoy with the emperor. One of her fans lay on the table beside her. She did not, Flavius was relieved to see, dare to wave it about in front of the emperor, but she dropped it into her lap and proceeded to play with its feathers.

'Madam,' said Hadrian, with the sharpness of a schoolmaster addressing an inattentive pupil, 'I am humbled to discover that I appear to share certain of the qualities of our great Augustus. He, for example, saw the importance of devising a fair and workable tax system, as do I – when so many others of our divine calling have failed to show concern for either the fairness or the workability of their taxation system.'

Lucilla sighed.

'Augustus knew, and I later realised, that among our noble ruling class of senators there were far from enough brains to cope with the financial services of the empire. So we had to find ones that could. You will now perhaps understand and even forgive me for welcoming our self-made senator, who knows how to make and use money.' Hadrian gave a shout of laughter. 'And if that still shocks you, wait till you hear what Augustus did! He put a slave, who was still a slave, in charge of *his* money; and that slave kept fourteen slaves of his own, one of whom he employed simply to clean his silver! Now what do you say to that?'

Lucilla said sullenly, 'Why didn't he, at least, buy his freedom?'

The emperor refreshed himself with a draught of wine. 'Perhaps, madam, he knew there were always perceptive people like yourself who believed a slave would always be a slave, so he saved the money and added instead to his silver collection.' He indicated that the matter was closed by turning to address a remark to Quintus.

Flavius saw on Lucilla's face the look she sometimes gave Aelius when, despite his deferential manner, he seemed to be mocking her. She threw her bedraggled fan to the floor.

The slaves had brought in the dessert table. The emperor indicated a wish for nuts, and Aelius was cracking them for him. Flavius took advantage of the moment to stand up and catch the emperor's eye.

'May I beg your majesty's permission to allow my wife to retire? She has fragile health, and needs rest.'

Hadrian hastily pushed back his chair and rose, a trifle unsteadily. 'Madam, I am pleased to wish you a good night and grateful to you for sharing so much of your time with us.'

Lucilla shook her head. 'No, I don't want ...'

But Flavius was gripping her arm, a slave was pulling back her chair, and Alis was returning with her cloak.

Lucilla faced the emperor and made a brief curtsey before Alis covered the glistening, delicate dress with the thick blue folds of the cloak.

The emperor, striving to maintain his code of gracious behaviour towards those of senatorial rank, said, 'That, madam, should keep you warm this winter night.'

Lucilla's sullen manner softened slightly. She stroked the front of her military-style cloak. 'I am grateful to the empress for her example.'

Flavius glanced uneasily at Aelius, but the remark conveyed nothing to the emperor, and since it involved his wife it was of no interest to him.

'Good, good,' he said vaguely, looking round for his chair.

Aelius gave Flavius a look of relief as they slid away from the topic of the empress's cloak, but then, almost immediately, another cause for alarm threatened. The emperor's eye, as he was about to sit down again, fell on the mural behind him.

He squinted at it. He seemed to be showing, at last, some effects from the evening's heavy drinking. 'Do you know,' he announced, 'that there are times when I think my painting much better than I remembered it?' He sat down heavily in his seat.

Flavius took a deep breath. 'Your majesty's picture always gives me great pleasure.'

Hadrian smiled, almost shyly. 'Of course, I didn't paint it all. Hadn't the time.' He lifted his empty glass. 'Aelius!'

The steward, who had been closing the door behind Lucilla, hurried back with wine in one hand and hot water in the other.

As he bent over the table to fill the emperor's glass, he murmured in honeyed Greek tones, 'Might I ask his majesty which part of that enchanting mural is his?'

The emperor drank deeply. 'Guess,' he said, smiling.

Aelius made a show of studying the wall. 'The thrushes?'

The emperor shook his head.

'No, I didn't think so. Not the delicious clusters of green plants?'

The emperor frowned slightly. 'No.'

'It can't be the blue sky, because anyone could have washed that on. The white flowers?'

The emperor nodded.

'I knew I was right,' said Aelius. 'The white flowers, so delicate and gracious. I have to admit, sir, that it was the prefect who first suggested the white flowers to me. Straight away I could see he was right.'

'If I were not half-drunk, Aelius, would I still believe you?' enquired the emperor.

'But your majesty is not drunk at all,' said Aelius, topping up his glass. 'If you want proof of what I said about the white flowers, look along the table.'

The emperor peered at it. 'What am I looking for?'

'The table is decorated by a bowl of fragile white winter flowers, which were ordered by the prefect as a compliment to those painted by your majesty.' Aelius contrived to sound a trifle surprised that such a courtesy could have been overlooked.

'Ah, yes,' said the emperor, nodding in Flavius's direction. 'Pretty little things. Did your lady grow them?' Then he shook his head and answered his own question. 'No, no. If stalks sprouted pearls, she might have done, not otherwise.'

'They were grown,' Flavius hastened to explain, before Aelius could contribute any more of his fanciful inventions, 'by the wife of one of our centurions who has developed a small garden here.'

'Oh, very nice, yes,' said Hadrian, losing interest. He looked expectantly at Aelius. 'Well, come on. What else? Would this be known as Hadrian's mural if I'd been content to sprinkle a few dabs of white paint across it?'

Aelius hesitated for the fraction of a second, but no longer. In an aggrieved manner, he said, 'The prefect could hardly fill the room with a flight of herons to signal his respect for your majesty's work. Of course you painted the heron. Everyone knows that. Every man in this fort knows about the heron in the emperor's dining-room, although very few of them will ever see it.' With a reproachful look, he shifted the blame on to the emperor. 'I thought your majesty knew we all knew.'

The emperor sat in his chair, bewildered. He stretched out a hand to touch one of the flowers on the table. 'These are very like my petals.' His sleeve caught the dish of nuts and knocked it to the floor. The clatter of silver on the tessellated surface made him wince and he put a hand to his head, as though the noise was hurting him.

A slave was hurrying to clear up the mess and Aelius was filling another dish. The emperor was still nursing his head. Flavius and the doctor exchanged glances. The doctor gave a small nod. Flavius stood up. 'With your majesty's permission, my officers have duties to discharge,' he said gently.

Hadrian lifted his head. With an effort he composed himself. 'Gentlemen,' he murmured, looking towards the doctor and the senior centurion in turn, 'I thank you for your company on this enjoyable evening.'

'If your majesty,' Flavius added, 'has no further use for his own staff tonight, I am sure my senior centurion would be willing to escort them to their quarters, or take them to see the view from one of the towers if it be their wish.'

Lugo shot out of his seat as though a trumpet had sounded. 'My pleasure, sir, if his majesty pleases.'

With a nod of his head, the emperor did indicate his pleasure. Then he turned to Quintus. 'Why not walk with the doctor to the hospital? It will reassure the men to see how much concern there is for their welfare.'

Flavius and the emperor were left facing each other down the length of the table.

'Aelius,' called the emperor, 'the prefect's glass is empty!'

'No more,' muttered Flavius when the steward approached him.

'You must appear to be drinking with him. It's well-watered. His isn't. If he wants to drink himself into oblivion, the sooner he does it the better for all of us.'

'But why should he want to?'

'Aelius, what are you doing?' cried the emperor impatiently.

'Coming, sir. I'm trying to persuade the prefect to dilute his wine more.'

The emperor patted the doctor's empty seat and beckoned Flavius to join him.

'At this time in the evening,' he said, 'I would rather be sitting on a couch than on one of your stiff little chairs.' He took the flagon from Aelius's hand and set it on the table in front of him. 'Talk to me about young Quintus.'

Flavius was growing accustomed to the emperor's disconcerting leaps in conversation. 'He is an excellent adjutant, sir.'

'Then he can be moved on.'

Flavius felt suddenly disturbed at the thought of good-humoured, gentle Quintus being transferred to the rigorous hardships of the junior legionary officer's world. 'Not yet,' he said. 'He is still very young. I rather see him in twenty years' time as the governor of a small, peaceable province than as a military commander.'

The emperor shot him a sour look.

'Your majesty asked me for an opinion.'

'Yes, and, as usual, you gave me one. His father won't like that. He's an old friend of mine. Theirs is an army family of long standing.

173

The two eldest sons are already legionary tribunes. He expects Quintus to follow them.'

'Surely,' said Flavius, 'it's a matter of how Quintus can best serve your majesty – and be happiest.'

'Happiest!' The emperor reached for the wine and splashed drops on the table. 'So now that Flavius Valerius Paulus has sorted out the emperor's military staffing for him, what if he turned his mind to the future of Flavius Valerius Paulus?'

Flavius suppressed a sigh. 'Your majesty is already aware of what I intend to do. I shall return to the practice of law and, when the time comes, take control of my family's wine business. I am grateful for my appointment here, because I have gained experience that will help me in both areas.'

The emperor waved his wine-glass. 'And is that a fitting example of how Flavius Valerius Paulus can best serve my majesty? I didn't offer you this prefecture to help you grow fatter grapes. I thought you understood perfectly well that it was in preparation for entry to the Senate. There are pockets of corruption everywhere. I need a sharp-witted lawyer with an understanding of money, to winkle them out for me. You annoy and offend me sometimes, but you have the kind of spirit that I look for.'

The emperor's speech was becoming slurred. 'If the Senate is good enough for an ex-slave shopkeeper,' he shouted, 'why isn't it good enough for a wine-grower's son?'

Flavius said, slowly and distinctly, 'A senator is not allowed to be engaged in commercial affairs, as I would be.'

'Hah! Half the Senate is engaged in them these days. You use agents, man, agents. A close member of family, perhaps?'

'No. I owe my father too much to treat him like that. Besides it is illegal. I cannot bring corrupt officials to justice if I am breaking the law myself, even though it is common practice around me.'

'Oh,' said the emperor with a sneering laugh, 'we're back again with that trivial business of the wicked centurions and the leave passes. Everyone else overlooks it, but not Flavius Valerius Paulus.'

Hadrian paused, confused, as if he was wondering how the conversation had reached this point. He peered round, like a man who couldn't recognise the room he was in, and poured more wine into his glass.

He squeezed his eyes shut in an effort at concentration. 'It is not only your emperor,' he declared, 'who is minded to see you a senator. You did not, I think, take that disagreeable wife of yours because of her pretty face?'

Flavius, who had rarely in his life been drunk, found it difficult to understand the emperor's apparent satisfaction in his own growing lack of control. Hadrian was leaning towards him, wagging a finger. 'No, I'm right, eh?'

Flavius was staring at the pallid liquid in his own glass. 'My marriage was agreed between my wife's father and mine. My grandfather strongly supported it.'

'Ah, so it was your grandfather who wanted to buy you a senatorial bride ... and being well brought-up Romans, your father obeyed your grandfather's directions, and you obeyed your father's.' The emperor guffawed. 'Have you ever thought how galling it must be for a Roman to have a nonagenarian father?' He was lost in thought for a moment. 'I suppose I must have been lucky to be orphaned as a child. Once I was sixteen, no-one could give me orders, but that didn't stop me from making an even worse marriage than yours.'

He was almost mumbling to himself, and Flavius could hardly hear him. 'I should divorce her. I wish I could. But an empire needs an empress. And if I did—' he sighed wearily '—I would have to look for another. I can't face all that, not all that, again.' He twisted himself round in his seat and touched Flavius's arm.

'But you could divorce yours.' He looked like a child, pleased to offer a toy to another child. 'If I arrange your election to the Senate, you won't need her help any more. Your grandfather will be satisfied. You can all be rid of her.'

'No, sir,' said Flavius gently, 'I have undertaken responsibilities for my wife, and I cannot ...'

The emperor's face was screwed up like a child whose gift is being refused. 'You don't have to give up the law, Paulus. Great cases are argued on the floor of the Senate.'

'Yes, sir, but—'

But the emperor had turned away, and was staring at his fingers outstretched on the table. 'I have a great deal in common with my great predecessor, Augustus,' he said.

'Indeed so,' murmured Flavius, striving to follow the emperor's seemingly confused train of thought. 'As you were saying earlier, sir, you share with him a respect for judicial taxation, and a willingness to employ—'

'No, no,' interrupted Hadrian pettishly. 'Yes, that's true, but I wasn't meaning all that. What we also have in common is that we both married manipulative bitches for wives. His was a clever manipulative bitch and he, the gods know how, loved her and was deluded into thinking she cared for him. Mine is a stupid, spiteful bitch and I hate her!'

He lifted up one of his hands and held it to his head. 'Do you know what they shout after me in Judea? "Hadrian, may your living bones rot in you!" She likes to throw the same words after me. Says I am a monster. Perhaps I am. I don't know. Who wouldn't be, with her for a wife? She won't have my children because she says they would all be monsters like me.' Tears began to form in his eyes. 'I have no son, no heir, Paulus.'

With his free hand, Hadrian was feeling for his glass.

Flavius reached for it and slipped it into his fingers. 'Sir,' he said, as the emperor gulped more wine, 'you are blessed with an adopted heir. Your Antinous is much respected and admired. He is welcomed with you everywhere.'

Hadrian looked blindly in Flavius's direction. Tears were streaming down his cheeks and wine was dribbling from his chin. 'Antinous is not here,' he whispered.

Flavius had little experience of dealing with men whose thoughts were clouded by drink. That was something his slaves were usually left to cope with.

He felt the need to say something. 'No, sir, of course Antinous is not here in Britain. Isn't he still with the court in Egypt? Perhaps he is waiting for you in Rome?'

'He is not here,' repeated the emperor, as if it were Flavius's mind, not his, that was confused. 'He is not here with us any more. He has gone. Antinous is dead.'

Flavius was unable to stop himself from blurting out, 'Antinous dead? No. He's hardly more than twenty. How?'

The emperor laid his hands on the table again, and his head drooped over them. 'My Antinous drowned in the Nile,' he cried out, voice choking on his tears. 'My dearest one, my Antinous, my beautiful boy, my love, where has he gone? I would give my whole empire to hold him in my arms again.'

His body rocked to and fro, but at last he was still and the weeping stopped. He raised his head. Flavius thought he had never before seen a face so haggard with despair. Nothing moved in the room. Flavius realised that Aelius must have quietly emptied it of slaves. Only the steward himself remained, motionless in the shadows beyond the ring of lamps.

The emperor began to speak again. 'I was on the bank, close to him. But there was so much noise around me – music and shouting and singing. He might have called out to me, but I wouldn't have heard him. He was dying, and I couldn't hear him crying out for me.'

'Tell me,' said Flavius, very softly.

'When they found him and lifted him out of the water, slaves were wailing, my own people were crowding round me, forcing their fawning sympathy on me. Others were rushing about, crying out the news so no-one would miss the fresh excitement of the evening. The air was stifling, thick with perfume and the smell of roasting food. They went on eating, some of them.'

Hadrian groaned at the bitter memory. 'I wanted to be away from them all. I needed to find fierce, cold darkness, hardship, danger. I came to this place to risk my life bear-hunting. I would have welcomed a bear's embrace if he could have sent me to follow Antinous, wherever he has gone.' Hadrian uttered a short, harsh laugh. 'But I found no bear. The gods were not with me.'

'The gods were wise,' murmured Flavius.

The emperor gave him a curious glance from beneath heavy, swollen lids. Talking had calmed him. He picked up the flagon of wine. 'So now, Paulus, I sit at your table, trying to drown my wits in this excellent vintage of yours.'

Flavius tried to respond to the lightening of his mood. 'I am relieved, sir, that it pleases you. It happens to be the wine our house is contracted to supply to your majesty's palace at Tivoli.'

With a flash of graciousness, Hadrian said, 'Then that must be one of the reasons I find comfort in this fort, just as I did a decade ago.' He tried to smile. 'Am I perhaps misguided in trying to lure you away from your vineyards just to sit in the Senate?'

The smile was still on his face, but it seemed to Flavius as though it was frozen, forgotten, as a fresh surge of despair swept everything else from his mind.

Absently, he refilled his glass then held the flagon upside-down as though surprised to find it empty. 'Another one gone?' he said. 'Nothing left for you, Paulus.'

Flavius shook his head and pointed to the drop that still remained in his own glass. He took a small sip to appear to keep the emperor company.

After a moment, Hadrian said, 'You were right when you said that Antinous might be waiting for me in Rome.'

He took a breath as though preparing himself to face something that was far from easy for him to admit. 'The people of Rome will expect Antinous, who would have been the next emperor, to be buried with ceremony. They will look to their present head of state to lead them in the solemn rites and speak the funeral oration with feeling, but also authority and dignity. After his death, an emperor is revered as a god; during his life he is already half-divine. He must appear as he stands in your shrine: larger than life, golden, holding out an arm to comfort and protect the vulnerable.

'He must not be, as you see me now, shrunken with grief, crippled by human despair. If my enemies – and I have many in Rome – could witness this weakness in me, they would go out of their way to scorn and shun me in public. Before long, they would be seeking to strip me of power, possibly of life as well. I can meet any death I choose to face, but not one that bundles me out of this world with humiliation and disgrace.'

'But, sir, none of this will ever happen,' urged Flavius. 'When will your enemies, whoever they are, have the chance to see you as anything but the emperor?'

It occurred then to Flavius that he was sitting beside the most powerful man in the world as he knew it, with one of the most brilliant minds that world had ever produced, and talking to him as if he were a bewildered child. But the emperor, staring at the table, seemed to be listening to him.

Flavius decided that he had no choice but to go on. 'Sir,' he said, 'you took refuge here in secret, close to your own protective wall, where you could endure alone the shock of your loss. You endangered your own life. The gods intervened. It would seem to be their wish that you should go back to Rome to bury Antinous with the honour they believe he merits. They will bestow on you the strength to perform the rites with the dignity and majesty that Rome loves and reveres.'

Flavius paused. 'Where will your enemies be then, sir?'

The emperor was lost in thoughts of his own. 'Yes, yes, I want him remembered. Remembered always,' he finally declared and pushed back his chair. 'I'll build a great city, named after him ...' He tried to stand up, but had to grasp the table to support himself.

Flavius caught hold of him. Aelius hurried across the room to help lower Hadrian into his chair. His head fell back, mouth open.

Aelius summoned his guards. They came, two tall, powerful men, moving with amazing quietness. With practised ease, they raised the emperor in their arms.

One of them glanced at Flavius. It was the man who had brought news of the visit. 'He won't remember what he said tomorrow. Nor will you.'

Flavius said quickly, 'I shall remember what I chose to remember. You, like the emperor, will have to rely on my discretion.'

The man gave Flavius a look like the one he had given him on the previous night when the matter of using the east gate had arisen. 'Sir,' he said with the same mixture of deference and hostility.

Aelius moved ahead to open doors for the emperor's bearers.

Flavius found that his toga had slipped out of control when he'd reached out for the emperor. Its heavy folds now lay tangled round his feet. He groaned, sat down again and dropped his own head on to the table.

Aelius returned followed by his string of slaves who set about clearing the debris of the meal. 'If the prefect is tired,' he said in the brusquely polite manner which indicated that he was too busy for any nonsense, 'he will find his room is ready for him.'

'Then get me out of this thing,' retorted Flavius.

Aelius, with an impatient sigh, put down the spoons that he was collecting. 'Stand up, then.' He snapped his fingers for a slave. Together they unwound the lengthy fabric of the toga and, spreading it out between them, folded it into a neat, smooth square, which was laid on the slave's outstretched arms to be carried away.

'There we are, then, sir.' Aelius waited for Flavius to follow the slave.

He sat down again, feeling too exhausted to move anywhere.

'Sir!' muttered Aelius.

'I don't want to sleep on that narrow bed you've put up for me.'

Aelius had gathered up his spoons again, and balanced in the crook of his arm was the jug that had been filled and re-filled with the emperor's boiling water.

'It is not narrow and, anyway you've only got to use it for one night. If you don't want to sleep on it, just go and sit on it. I need to clear this table.'

Flavius looked at the jug, pleased for an excuse to stay where he was. 'How did you know the emperor liked hot water in his wine?'

Aelius handed over the jug and spoons, and reached out for knives. 'I listen,' he said, being as short as possible.

'That's not something you could pick up in the bath-house here.'

'It isn't the only one I've frequented in my life.' Aelius moved swiftly away along the table. 'Sir, now, if you would.'

'You could have told me,' muttered Flavius.

Aelius was curt. 'I can't recall that we ever had a conversation about the emperor's wine-drinking habits.'

Flavius groaned. 'How long will it be before he wakes up?'

'People vary.'

Flavius got reluctantly to his feet. At the door he turned back. 'If he wakes before me, fetch me,' he said, as Aelius began to extinguish the lamps.

VI

When Flavius opened his eyes, he saw bright daylight and smelled midday cooking. He shouted for Aelius, and then winced at the pain in his head.

'Is he awake yet?' he asked, shading his eyes from the light, as Aelius appeared.

'The emperor has been awake for two hours.'

'I told you to tell me!' cried Flavius.

'His majesty suggested I let you sleep. You were not, he said, as accustomed to life in field camps as he was.'

Flavius wondered how precisely he was expected to interpret that. Aelius read his mind. 'Kindly meant, I think, judging by his mood.'

Flavius grunted and addressed himself to the matter of standing up. 'Where is he now?'

'Your adjutant left word for you that he is now in the vault under the shrine,' said Aelius. Seeing Flavius's look of alarm, he added, 'He is not alone in there, counting your coin reserves. He sent for the senior centurion this morning while he was eating ...'

'Eating? What did he eat?'

'He asked for bread and ate it dipped in wine. Then they went across to see if they could find the rough maps the emperor mentioned last night. Don't look so worried, Flavius. He put on the cloak and scarf, and they kept out of sight. The chief clerk took them into the vault. He thought he knew the items the emperor was describing, though he never understood what they were because they looked like bits of rubbish. Luckily, arguing that no-one stores rubbish, he bundled them up and put them in an out of the way corner of the vault, together with all the other oddments he can't put a meaning to. So that's what they're all doing there, looking for the emperor's old sketches.'

'And what sort of mood did you think the emperor was in when he told you to let me sleep?' said Flavius uneasily.

'I told you. Kindly. Cheerful.'

'Cheerful? '

When Flavius, in uniform, without breakfast and stinging from the cold water Aelius had poured over him, entered the headquarters building, he found Quintus pacing the floor of the hall, waiting for him.

'Sir, the emperor's party have now left the vault, and are in the chief clerk's office.'

They both saluted the golden image. 'What sort of mood would you say he is in this morning?' Flavius enquired.

'He is in a very pleasant temper at the moment,' said Quintus happily. 'Gratified by the finds.'

'Would you go so far as to say cheerful?'

'Cheerful? Oh, yes.' And as Quintus opened the door to the chief clerk's office, Flavius saw that, amazingly, this appeared to be true.

The table was covered with torn sheets of what seemed to be the cheap parchment used for wrapping, and broken fragments of army-issue pottery. The emperor was bent over them, smiling – almost gleefully, Flavius observed – as he arranged them in some kind of order. Without looking up, he waved a friendly hand as Flavius presented his duty.

Lugo, pink with excitement at assisting the emperor, straightened briefly to acknowledge the presence of his commandant and then returned to his task of sorting through what did indeed appear to be a heap of old rubbish.

Eventually, the emperor laughed, rubbed dusty hands together and beckoned Flavius to join him. The pieces of parchment and pottery were now spread across the table.

The emperor carefully pointed out a fine line passing from one end to the other, small dots piercing the parchment, scratches made on the pottery.

'That,' said Hadrian, 'was a first tentative outline for the foundation of the wall over a difficult stretch of terrain east of Carlisle. Rising ground. I remember that day well.' He glanced at Lugo, who nodded vigorously. 'It was a bright spring day, the air up there fresh with a wind that took your breath away.

'We'd got ahead of the others. That bit of the land had been troubling me for days. Suddenly, I saw how it could be managed. I had to get it down while I was there. But I had nothing to write with. My secretaries, with their fiddling little wax things, were way behind.

'Then my good friend here had an idea. We were all carrying rations of bread wrapped in this parchment stuff. We threw the bread to the birds, and with this wrapping stretched over a stone I was able to prick out the plan with the tip of my dagger. When that was used up, we found some broken beakers that I suppose legionary engineers had left behind when they were surveying the area. All I needed then was a sharp stone, and there were plenty of them about.' The emperor laughed again. 'And here it still is, the basis of the plan we used. The legion's men weren't pleased, they had other ideas, but I'm a better engineer than any of them. Would they ever have conceived of a wall across the width of Britain?'

His hand rested lightly on Lugo's shoulder. 'I was lucky, Paulus, that your centurion here was detailed for escort duty that day, though, of course, he wasn't of such exalted rank in those days.'

If anyone was ever going to burst with pride, it would be now, thought Flavius, looking at the senior centurion.

The emperor – reluctantly, it seemed to Flavius – motioned the chief clerk to clear the table. Then, always curious to know what was happening around him, began to wander about the room. A man with a passionate, even obsessive, love for precise organisation, he recognised with satisfaction evidence of a kindred spirit. 'I'm impressed,' he announced.

The chief clerk, carefully assembling the emperor's fragile lengths of parchment and broken pottery in a box, looked up at Hadrian.

'Your majesty,' he said, with a gratified expression on his face, 'I like a neat, ordered space. I see no point in keeping records if they cannot be retrieved in minutes. I require all our camp records to be housed in their allotted places. When a fresh piece of information has to be copied, the clerks in the outer office have been trained to complete the work and return the original for shelving within twenty-four hours. I do not like to see frantic bursts of copying two or three days before the monthly collections for York and Rome are due. There is never any need for a scroll to be left lying about where it could be damaged or lost.'

As he finished speaking, the chief clerk lifted the last, largest piece of parchment. Beneath it, hidden until then, was a single tightly rolled scroll.

It was at that moment that Lugo's pink cheeks suddenly turned white. He turned to Flavius with a look of alarm and kept giving little nods towards the table.

The scroll, Flavius then perceived, was the one that had given them so much trouble over the matter of the baker's broken door. Lugo was now looking as though at any second he was about to prostrate himself at the emperor's feet, confess to his crime and await whichever of the army's savage punishments for dereliction of duty the emperor might choose to inflict on him.

Flavius frowned severely at him.

The emperor, having graciously allowed the chief clerk the chance to talk about the work that was his life, was now trying to suppress a smile. 'These scrolls of yours, they're like a bunch of slaves. There's always one that manages to escape.'

This attempt at lightness did not amuse the chief clerk.

With the kind of deference that reminded Flavius of Aelius when he wished to show he was offended, he said, 'Your majesty will appreciate that your welcome but unexpected visit caused disruption throughout the fort. When I learned that you would be entering the prefect's office through this room's outer door on to the corridor from the east gate, I felt it would be unwise not to empty my clerks' main office, which is on the other side of this third door. It could have been locked, but this would have been suspicious since my staff usually come in and out as they please. I arranged to move them to one of the offices in the courtyard across the hall.'

'And you were able to convince them,' asked the emperor, 'that a room on the north wall of the building would keep them safer from infection than one on the east wall a few yards away?'

'Of course not, sir. They are skilled men,' said the chief clerk primly, implying that a neat hand at copying could be equated with intelligence. 'I informed them that if this fort was attacked by the sickness, the doctor might have need of an additional ward, and their room would be large enough for the purpose. So yesterday, when this new entry should have been taken for copying and then the original re-shelved, furniture and writing materials were on the move and I thought it best to keep this in here, especially as the new entry had been signed by the prefect.'

Flavius could hear Lugo's heavy breathing as the emperor picked up the scroll. 'What was it for?' He peered at it. 'Repairs to building fabric? What's that – door locks, plaster?'

'As it happens, sir, it was a door lock, and a door with it, and paint,' put in Flavius.

'Ah,' said the emperor, losing interest. He let the scroll spring back into shape. 'Well done, well done. Need to keep things trim.'

He handed the scroll to the chief clerk. 'An excellent idea, moving your people, excellent.' He paused. 'Would this splendid system of yours work anywhere?'

'Anywhere, sir.'

'In the army archives in Rome?'

'Yes. Obviously, material couldn't be retrieved in minutes, sir, but it should be possible to trace anything within three hours.'

'Three hours? I've waited a week before now.' The emperor looked round again at the neat shelves. 'Young man, have you ever considered applying for a posting to Rome?'

'No, sir, never.'

The emperor looked from the chief clerk to Flavius. 'Is there no-one in this place with any ambition?'

Flavius smiled. 'Your majesty sent us all to Alauna. It seems we have grown enamoured with the bitter winter weather.'

The emperor raised an eyebrow. 'If I were not disposed to thank you for this audacious, ludicrous, brilliant deception you have devised for my benefit, I might not be amused by your impudence.

'However the afternoon is passing. Prefect, I should like to address a few words before I leave to all those who have been engaged in keeping my visit secret.'

Flavius despatched his adjutant to fetch the doctor and Aelius. The senior centurion appeared slightly distracted by the shock of relief. 'Senior centurion,' said Flavius sharply, 'you will relieve your officers from duty and replace them with their senior section leaders. They can be told, if they ask, that it is an exercise in their training for promotion.'

The emperor leaned towards Flavius. 'How is it,' he whispered, 'that a lawyer who in court pleads that all he seeks is the truth, can so adroitly spin a fanciful lie?'

'Ah,' said Flavius, 'does your majesty mean like a general despatching a decoy troop?'

The emperor, with mild displeasure, turned back to the table where the chief clerk was knotting cords round the box, ready to replace it in the safety of the vault.

Lugo, glancing back, saw the emperor's hand reaching across the table. He took a step back in alarm, wondering how Flavius could let the emperor and the scroll get so close together. Then, with Flavius pointing furiously behind the emperor's back to the door, he realised that it was the box, not the scroll, that the emperor had in his hand.

'You will keep it here?' Hadrian asked the chief clerk.

'Of course, sir.'

'I think I would like to walk this stretch again.'

Lugo, half-way through the door, turned round expectantly. 'Sir?'

'But not this time, senior centurion, not this time. It isn't possible. I have – I have matters elsewhere.' His voice was hesitant and Flavius saw in his face a flicker of the anguish that had overwhelmed him on the previous evening. Until that moment Flavius had thought him a different man today from the one who had drunk himself insensible. Now he seemed to Flavius like a great actor performing in a vast arena, except that he lacked an actor's mask to hide his face.

'Paulus, come,' said the emperor, and led the way into Flavius's office. He sat in the chair at the desk, his head turned away.

'You know now why I came here?'

Flavius hesitated, uncertain how to answer him. The emperor raised his head and looked at Flavius. 'I do not, as you were probably told, forget my indiscretions of the night before. I find it convenient, however, to let the story ride.'

'Then, sir, I now understand why your majesty left Egypt, but not why you came to Alauna.'

'You must have shared thoughts about it.'

'Yes, sir, but to no purpose. It was suggested that your majesty had not realised how cold it was here, and sought a warm bed and a hot meal.'

The emperor's expression was such that Flavius wondered how on earth he could have said anything so flippant. 'But we were unable to explain why you would chose Alauna when there are so many other forts close to the best hunting areas,' he added, realising as he spoke that he was not helping matters.

'How did you know, Paulus,' said the emperor grimly, 'that I hadn't been to all those others in turn, and this was the only place left with enough food to satisfy me? I have never in my life been diverted from the battle-field or the hunting field by the prospect of a warm bed and a hot meal! What kind of reputation do I have out here?'

Flavius was stung into replying, 'I am sorry, sir, but we were trying to suggest anything that would save us from admitting we were frightened – frightened because we were all thinking that we must have gravely offended your majesty, and we didn't know how.'

Flavius thought fleetingly of his beloved vineyards in Stresa. 'I accepted, sir, that the ultimate blame would have to be mine.'

The emperor, who had idly picked up the stylus that was still lying on the desk, hurriedly dropped it.

Flavius braced himself for another explosive outburst. But considering the gruff, harsh manner of his normal speech, the emperor's next words, though not gently spoken, were remarkably mild. 'Had I been coming here to disgrace you, I would not have come slinking about in the dark. I would have come with full imperial panoply and trumpeted your misdemeanours throughout Britain.'

'In a calmer moment, I, too, had come to that conclusion,' Flavius admitted. 'I then declared to my staff that the reason for your majesty's visit was of no concern to us; all we should do was prepare for it as we had been instructed.'

'Most proper,' commented the emperor in what Flavius thought was a mocking tone. 'But?'

'But,' said Flavius humbly, 'when your majesty arrived, you seemed to know so much about me, and about my time in Alauna, that I began to wonder if I'd been right in the first place.'

The emperor sighed. 'Yes, Paulus, I do know a lot about you, but I know a lot about many people, and I take a special interest in the conduct of the men I chose to take command of my auxiliary forts.'

The answer bewildered Flavius who stared at the emperor.

Hadrian remained patient. 'The empire is large. How do you think it succeeds?'

Flavius wasn't quite sure what he was expected to say. 'It has a highly trained army.'

'That's how it extends its boundaries. How does it keep them? I'll tell you, Paulus. By communication.'

The emperor glanced round the room to see if, on this occasion, any wine had been set out for him. He gave a nod of satisfaction. 'The good Aelius has remembered,' he announced.

Refreshed, he continued, 'You, as prefect, have responsibility for the good order of the military roads in this area. The men train for marching detail on them. An undamaged surface is also essential for imperial couriers ... riding hard, changing horses at stations ten miles apart ... so if trouble were brewing here a man could be in York in the swiftest possible time to secure help from the legion.'

'Yes, sir,' said Flavius. He was beginning to feel that it was his turn to be addressed like a child – not one bewildered with grief, but an inattentive child who might not have taken in yesterday's lesson.

'I know, Paulus, that there hasn't been unrest here for a decade or so, but overnight you could get some young hothead stirring up a riot that could spread.'

'That, I know, sir, is why your majesty requires weapons practice every day, as if an attack was imminent.'

'Ah, so there are some army regulations that our lawyer approves of.'

'There are many I would enforce as rigorously as my senior centurion.'

'But there are others,' said the emperor, 'that you might – stretch a little?'

Not that baker's broken door again, thought Flavius savagely. Hadrian couldn't possible know about that. But what *didn't* he know about?

'I may have done so, sir, when treating a pointless regulation with common sense prevented the kind of unrest in the settlement that your majesty has been describing.'

'And that was not to the senior centurion's liking, eh?'

'He is intensely loyal to all established army procedures. As that includes his respect for rank, however, he has never failed to carry out my instructions, however much they may have offended him.'

'From the information I have received, that does not surprise me,' said the emperor amiably. 'I do know a lot about you because I use those same fast roads to keep me in touch with what is happening in my forts.'

'Information, sir?' said Flavius, picking up the unwelcome word. 'You have informants here?'

'Correspondents. Yes, everywhere. I need to know what is happening.'

'Communication, sir, I see,' said Flavius with distaste.

'Do you inspect the barracks here?' snapped the emperor.

'Every alternate Friday morning, sir.'

'As prescribed – well done, Paulus. And you walk round with your officers and your clerks. What do you learn at the end of it? Only that everyone has a busy evening on Thursdays.'

'I am aware of that, sir.'

'So, have you any idea of what might really be going on?'

'Of course, sir. I go round the barracks alone when most of the men are on the parade ground.'

'This is a small place. You act as your own spy. It is not so very different from what I have to do. I understand, by the way, that you receive some assistance from Aelius after his excursions to the men's bath-house.' The emperor gave a sudden, unexpected burst of laughter. 'Bath-house!' he shouted. 'Paulus, something amusing once happened to me in a bath-house. It was a public bath-house in Rome. I enjoy those places at times.

'Men were lying around with their slaves rubbing them down, but there was one man on his own, sliding his back up and down a wall. It seemed he couldn't afford a slave. So I gave him one, together with a small income for his keep. The next time I went there, would you believe it, I found six men scraping their backs against the wall! What would you have done then, Paulus?'

Flavius, who had never in his life been inside a public bath-house, hesitated. 'Told them to help each other?'

'Yes,' cried the emperor, 'exactly what I did – put them in pairs and told them to help each other. They weren't pleased with me. I suspect they wanted slaves, so that they could sell them on as soon as I was out of the way. I don't take kindly to being thought a fool. But it was a sight, I can tell you, seeing the six of them, writhing about on that wall!'

Since the emperor was now treating him more like a drinking companion than a reluctant schoolboy, Flavius ventured to ask, 'Does your majesty look for his ...' he took a breath '... scouts in the fort or the settlement or further afield?'

The emperor shot him a sharp glance. 'If one of your men asked you which afternoon next week you would be inspecting his barracks, and you told him, there wouldn't be much point in your going, would there?'

Back to the schoolroom, thought Flavius. 'No, sir,' he said glumly.

Almost as if he were waving an admonitory finger at him, the emperor added, 'You make the common mistake of assuming that my scouts are prowling about looking for unsatisfactory practices, when in fact they are also required to acquaint me with conduct I would applaud.'

He paused. 'It is now understood, I trust, that I did not come to Alauna to comment on your success, or otherwise, as commandant. Nor am I here to judge how young Quintus is performing, if that is your next question, nor to look at disgruntled centurions or your record-keeping.' The emperor's voice was rising wildly. 'I am here because I need to be here for myself.' He struck his chest. 'Myself!'

With another of his sudden changes of mood, he laid his hands over his eyes as if trying to blot out the thoughts that had arisen to torment him.

After a while he began to speak again, in a quieter manner. 'I am not a man who likes to admit weakness, even to myself. It shames me. Last night when I was too drunk to hide them any longer, I betrayed my feelings to you. You were patient with me; showed none of the contempt or distaste you might justifiably have done, seeing your commanding general in such a state. I do not take help easily, but you helped me.'

With his hands still covering his eyes, he sighed. 'I am grateful.' That was something the emperor rarely said, and his sigh seemed to recognise this. 'I think you have the right to know why I find myself here in Alauna.'

Flavius shook his head gently. 'I am honoured, sir, but there is no need to explain.'

The emperor seemed lost in his own thoughts. 'Last night you learned why I fled in secret to this part of my empire. I wanted to submit my body to every hardship I could think of, so that I could quench the grief that was consuming my will to live. I thought I wanted to do it on my own. But I found I couldn't bear it on my own. I wanted to go home – not to that vast, magnificent, gilded palace at Tivoli, where carriages pass along the corridors as if they were streets and hundreds dine with me at once round my great lake. Home to me is Spain, where I grew up as a child among people like the men who inhabit this fort. I recruited the first Spanish cohort in the empire myself. They helped to build this fort around me while I planned my wall with people like your senior centurion shouting out to me in Spanish. My family come from a village on the Tiber, but I was never a child there. I couldn't get back to Spain at this moment, could I? So I had to come to Alauna to find the men I think of as my real family. Although they curse me for bringing them to this cold, bleak place, I believe they still regard me as one of them.'

Hadrian had lifted his head from his hands and was staring ahead of him. Flavius was reproaching himself for ever assuming that when the emperor shouted across the parade ground "I am a Spaniard among Spaniards" it was a cynical ploy to attract popularity. It was far from that; and the men, as they cried out a greeting, understood this.

The emperor said wryly, 'Sadly, my being here had to stay a secret. No good risking certain parties in Rome finding out that I was a thousand miles from the forum while my own people were wandering leaderless – unknowingly, of course – across Egypt. Might have lost an emperor then, eh, Paulus? But at least if I can't spend time with all the men, thanks to you I've been with a handful of them and that has warmed me.'

'It has warmed me too, sir.'

Hadrian turned his face towards Flavius. 'I knew from our brush in Antioch that you were intelligent, and from what I'd heard about your work in Stresa that you were resourceful, so I felt it would be safe to trust myself to you in this fort. I was right. I have been gratified by your arrangements.'

The emperor paused in the way he had done before he was about to embark on voicing his reservations. Flavius watched him uneasily.

'But?' he murmured.

'But,' said the emperor, with a flash of irritation at being prompted, 'there are probably a number of other commandants in this province with enough intelligence and resourcefulness to serve my demands equally well.'

The emperor looked away from him again. 'You, however, have another quality that is rare in military circles – in fact, one that most soldiers would have little time for. You have a capacity for anger, the kind that comes from a sense of pity for those who are badly dealt with.'

He closed his eyes. 'My – my Antinous was also such a man. A fool I used to call him, and even mock him, and yet I loved him for it. He would have felt the same anger you must have felt when you saw children starving in the street and decided to spend your money on an orphanage instead of fancy summer festivals on that lake of yours. If he'd been stationed in this fort, like you he would have taken on those officers who were abusing their power to scratch a few coins from the men in their charge and wouldn't have cared if he was shrugged off for it by everyone else, including me.'

He was torn, Flavius could see, between the comfort and the pain of remembering Antinous. 'And I can tell you, Paulus,' he added, with a tearful laugh, 'if he had been involved in that ridiculous business of getting the men out of the rain, he would have wanted to know why they hadn't been marched straight into the building instead of being left outside until you turned up. He wouldn't have cared any more than you did about the outrage it caused among the regular officers.'

Flavius said, as humbly as he could, 'Those incidents you spoke of were the ones your majesty found most displeasing.'

He waited for another outburst of temper, but the emperor sat very still and then slowly nodded his head. 'I was unfair to you, Paulus. Yes, I attacked in you actions which, though they would not have been mine, were of the kind that delighted me in Antinous. I don't understand why. Was I trying to persuade myself that I could escape from my grief by pretending I didn't remember his ways of thinking? Yet all the time I was craving to speak to someone whom I recognised would share his views.' Hadrian gave a little grunt. 'I had to get myself very drunk before I could struggle through my confusion to reach out to you, Paulus.'

Quintus slipped into the room, carrying the emperor's folded hunting cape and his scarf. He laid them on a chair, and announced that the emperor's horse was on its way to the east gate. The men he had asked to see, he added, were already assembled. He slipped away again.

'I was also unfair to you,' admitted the emperor, as if, even with a little practice, the words did not come easily to him, 'when we were discussing that boy last night.'

'My adjutant?'

'Yes, Paulus, who else has just walked in and out of this room? Quintus, your adjutant. I have known him all his life. I've always been fond enough of him, because of my friendship with his father, but I've never thought of him as anything but another future legionary officer in a family interested in nothing else. I thought he needed hardening up a bit to become more like his elder brothers so I sent him here, where the winter conditions might prepare him for army life. He doesn't look any different to me, but then you tell me he won't make a soldier.'

'I didn't say that, sir. I said he had gifts that would make him valuable to you outside the army rather than having serve you as another adequate but unremarkable legionary officer.'

'Yes? Paulus, I hadn't drunk enough at that point to respect what you were saying,' the emperor said. He became lost in one of his long moments of thought then added, 'As you know, I was the emperor Trajan's cousin, and he was my guardian when my father died. He was a good man in many ways, but on the campaign field he could be ruthless. I grew up in a caste which believed that for any Roman of good birth there was only one ambition to follow: achieving military distinction. Anything else degraded the honour of the family. It never occurred to me that Quintus would think otherwise.'

'He might not know it himself yet.'

'You,' said the emperor with an air of exasperation, 'have known the boy for a few months and yet you think you know a different Quintus from the one I know.'

'Sir, I did not have the advantage of an upbringing with the emperor Trajan,' murmured Flavius.

'Nor,' whispered Hadrian, 'did Antinous, as you probably realise. He would, as you must by now guess, have agreed with you. He made me look at many things differently, even when I had no wish to do so. Antinous was not a soldier by choice or inclination, but one who was to inherit a military-based empire had to display some interest in army concerns. He was a fine horseman, and riding behind me on his favourite black mount, in gilded armour with an imperial purple cloak draped over one shoulder, he made a good appearance. That was about as much as he cared for in soldiering. We argued a lot about it ... heatedly on my part, good-humouredly on his.'

The emperor fell silent again, and Flavius prepared himself for whatever the next change of mood might bring. He was startled when Hadrian addressed him with a voice of surprise.

'Paulus, you have made it possible for me to speak about Antinous again without another shaming display of weakness.'

'Not weakness. Not to me, sir; not grief at such a loss. It shows the strength of what you shared with the lord Antinous. If you had felt nothing at his passing, that to me would have been shameful.'

The emperor looked up at him sharply. 'Have you ever—. No, if you have, it wouldn't have been with that disagreeable wife of yours.'

Flavius bowed his head, realising that the emperor was enquiring if he had ever loved. 'No, sir, I have not. When I encounter it in others, I wish I had. I envy them, as I envy your majesty.'

'You saw last night what the cost can be.'

Flavius shrugged his shoulders. 'I am still envious.'

'Don't search for it, Paulus. If it is meant, it will find you. And surprise you. As it surprised me, and surprised Antinous.'

The emperor cleared his throat, as if suddenly embarrassed by the nature of this conversation. 'Better bring them all in, prefect.'

Flavius admitted his fellow conspirators. The emperor rose from his chair at Flavius's desk and crossed to the centre of the room. To Flavius, watching him, it seemed as though he had assumed an invisible cloak of gracious majesty, just as he had when he'd entered the dining-room on the previous evening.

'No salutes,' he called out, as the senior centurion was about to open his mouth. He charmed away Lugo's disappointment with a smile. 'Not for a benighted hunting man, eh, senior centurion?' Lugo was moved to smile back.

The men moved swiftly into the room to take up positions facing the emperor, but Flavius saw, with amazement, that they were quietly intent on arranging themselves in order of rank. The doctor, whom Flavius had never before thought of as an army officer, appeared to take precedence over the senior centurion's deputy, but not the prefect's adjutant. In the eyes of the centurion group, the impeccable chief clerk seemed to have the lowly status of a section leader and was jostled into standing behind them.

This manoeuvring was not unobserved by the emperor. He beckoned to the chief clerk and pointed to a spot in front of him. With a flinty glance across the room, he laid a hand on the clerk's shoulder.

In a loud voice, he said, 'Chief clerk, I must thank you for the valuable work you have done for me today. May I ask if my documents have been safely lodged?'

'Sir, if this fort were ever attacked, even burned to the ground, they would not fall into the wrong hands.'

'Well done, well done,' said the emperor. He turned to Flavius, who was a few paces behind him, saying under his breath, 'They are my beloved Spaniards, this group, but it doesn't mean they don't need a sharp kick every now and then, as you yourself already know.'

He noticed Aelius, who had crept in after the others and was standing by the door. 'My good Aelius,' Hadrian called out in Greek, 'I feared you were too busy to join us.'

'Your majesty must forgive me but I was taking wine to the east gate, so that your last memory of Alauna should be a pleasing one.'

'Hah!' The emperor clapped his hands together. 'Are you sure, Paulus, that I can't take him with me?'

Flavius bowed his head, 'Your majesty, I'm sure.'

'Ah, well, then.' The emperor paused, and drew himself up. 'Gentlemen,' he said, indicating that he was ready to begin. 'If I were visiting this fort at any other time, I would be making this farewell address to the whole company from the tribune on the parade ground. I would, no doubt, have watched your weapons practice, perhaps joined in some of the exercises with you. I think I can pride myself on still throwing a good lance.'

From what Flavius had heard, the emperor's pride was not misplaced. In his early-fifties, he could still balance the weight of a practice lance – made of wood and twice as heavy as the actual metal lance used in battle – and successfully strike the target post. On the occasions when the lance flew wild, his temper for the rest of the day was known to be blistering.

'Unfortunately,' he was saying, 'it is only possible for me to speak today to those of you who know of my secret visit. Yet what I can say is that even the little I have seen in the last few hours of the working of this fort has impressed me considerably. I would never say this if I didn't mean it.'

He paused, casting his smile over each man in turn. 'You had very short warning of my coming. I would not have liked to have been in such a position myself, yet your response to orders of necessity given in haste was flawless.' He glanced at the group of centurions. 'I wish you could have heard the praise of you uttered by your commandant in my presence last night. Your senior officer will confirm this, and, I'm sure, share it with you on a suitable occasion.

'You yourselves will accept that your exemplary conduct owes much to the leadership of the senior centurion and his disciplinary guidance. In other circumstances, I would now award him a decoration for his service to this cohort, but, sadly, huntsmen travel light. However, I promise you that this will not be forgotten, senior centurion. I have a long memory.'

There was a discreet murmur of appreciation, and Lugo stared at his feet to hide his pleasure.

'I have another award to bestow – in spirit, as it were,' continued the emperor, raising a hand to restore silence. 'It has always been my opinion that a good senior centurion cannot function successfully without a good commandant.'

Eyes which had been flickering in Flavius's direction became fixed on him; some surprised, some resentful. Flavius was relieved to see the doctor and Quintus exchange smiles. He wanted to gaze at his feet, as Lugo had, but forced himself to gaze blandly at the emperor.

Hadrian cast another of his amiable smiles around the room in the manner of a man in the company of friends. 'Among our neighbours,' he declared, 'it is not uncommonly accepted that we display a streak of madness in our Roman practice of placing army auxiliary cohorts in the command of a man with no military experience, but who has merely demonstrated wise judgement in another area.'

He spread his hands. 'So far, our neighbours have not made their case – if the commandant will allow me to use a legal expression.' He glanced with amusement at Flavius, inviting the others to share his little joke.

Then, becoming serious, he said, 'The good government of the empire is based on a military structure. Its power usually lies in the hands of experienced soldiers. It is therefore sensible, if distinguished civilians are to hold high office in the state, that they should acquire some understanding of accepted military procedure. On the other hand, when a man chooses to give twenty-five years of his life to army service, and lives among those who have made the same choice, his outlook on life becomes the selective and rigid one imposed by his training. Some auxiliary cohorts may never see a battlefield, but they will all certainly have to live among conquered peoples, and to do this peaceably they must be able to tolerate and respect attitudes to life quite different from their own. They will begin to learn how to do this when they serve under commandants whose experience has been formed in other closed worlds.'

From one or two of the blank and slightly puzzled faces turned towards the emperor, Flavius suspected that no-one before had ever discussed with them the Roman practice of appointing civilian commandants in quite this way. To the officers it probably meant no more than unwelcome interference, especially as the commandant changed every two or three years.

The emperor seemed to have reached the same conclusion. He said, with one of his sudden bursts of irritation, 'I believe this peculiar practice of ours to be a valuable one, and hope you will come to appreciate it when you give yourselves a chance to consider it. It will, of course, lead to friction. It has to. If it doesn't, then either the commandant is slack or the officers indifferent. If any bad feeling arises, I expect it to be resolved in a short space of time.'

Lugo felt that some response to the emperor was required. The task obviously fell to him; although a gold disc had not actually been fastened to his chain-mail, he had nevertheless been selected for a decoration of honour. He also felt it was proper for him to make reference to his commandant because he was at the half-way stage between deploring some of his actions and feeling a liking for the man.

He took a step forward. 'If your majesty would permit me?' Hadrian nodded. 'We are obliged to you for this counsel, to which we will all give thought.' He waited for his officers to murmur their dutiful support.

'I would like also, in all humility, to say that I agree with it.'

The emperor raised his eyebrows. 'That's gratifying.'

'It was the prefect's quick thinking and his precise instructions that gave us the confidence to prepare for your visit in a fitting manner. I owe the award conferred on me to the prefect, sir.'

The emperor beamed and Lugo stepped back, sweat visible on his forehead.

'The award is justly deserved, I assure you, senior centurion, but I applaud your modesty and fairness. Is a little of the prefect's legal wisdom brushing off on you perhaps? And as for the prefect himself, where has he learned this confidence in his own judgement that every good military commander has to acquire? Because confidence he has, I can tell you, gentlemen.'

The emperor leaned forward, like a man intent on sharing a confidence. 'When I planned my visit here, I was determined to use the north gate. Word came back to me that the prefect required me to enter by the east gate. Of course, I refused. I refused explosively, as is sometimes my wont.'

He straightened up and folded his arms. 'In a few minutes I shall be leaving this fort by the same way I came in – the east gate!'

Hadrian smiled again at the murmur of laughter which arose. Flavius suspected it was less from the tale itself than from the sense that he was reaching out in friendship to them.

His next words confirmed this. 'Alauna and its Spaniards are dear to me, another Spaniard. I feel at home among you, and I thank you.' He glanced about him. 'There are those of you here who are not of Spanish birth. I respect your loyalty to your native provinces, but I hope you will allow me to say, with every courtesy, that I embrace you as my adopted Spaniards.'

Flavius looked at Quintus, the doctor, and less confidently at Aelius. 'We are honoured, sir,' he said.

The emperor nodded, satisfied. He resumed the imperial manner. 'Gentlemen, I will have a last word with your prefect.'

When he was left alone with Flavius, he said, almost in desperation, 'How can I repay you? You have more money than you will ever need. You're not interested in advancement. I can't give you – that other thing. Well?'

Flavius shook his head. 'There is no need for anything, sir.'

But the emperor was still thinking. 'I have the idea that the senior centurion is beginning to see you as possible military material. He's not an easy man to please. Have you heard that your predecessor left to join the legion in Judea?'

'Frequently,' said Flavius curtly.

'He couldn't hold a candle to you. Not that I'd put you in a legion. I could use you as a junior officer on my general staff.' The emperor warmed to his subject. 'You keep your head in a crisis, you can devise a workable stratagem in haste, you're a tactician, you can command – pity to waste all those qualities, eh?'

'They are not wasted, sir. They prove very useful in a vineyard.'

The emperor's good humour wavered. He wagged his finger. 'There are men,' he declared, 'who would give ...' He broke off with one of his grunts. 'Cape!' he roared.

Flavius unfolded the cape and put it on the emperor's shoulders. Then he picked up the scarf.

'I'm not wearing that thing again,' said the emperor.

'Yes, sir, I think so.'

'Are you obstinate in the vineyard as well?'

'Yes, sir, when I am right.'

The emperor swore and wrapped the scarf round his face, hiding his beard.

'Yes, that's wiser, sir.'

'Quintus!' shouted the emperor. 'Ready.'

With his hood pulled over his grey, curling hair, and the scarf across his mouth, Hadrian waited impatiently. The sharp grey eyes peered hard at Flavius.

His voice muffled by the scarf, the emperor said, 'You wouldn't do for me in the army. You sleep too late.'

'I work at night, sir.'

The emperor pulled down his scarf. 'Always that slick lawyer's tongue of yours.' As they stared at each other, Flavius suddenly saw the hard eyes softening. 'Paulus, is that what goads me so often to be unfair to you?'

Quintus had joined them and stood watching. The emperor spoke carefully. 'And we both know I have been. However, nothing can change the fact that I owe you much. If there is ever something you want, I will find it for you.'

'Your majesty is generous.'

'Don't make that mistake. I am not generous. I am at the moment in your debt. But if I find what you ask, you will then be in my debt, and I might call it in at any time. Think of those six disappointed men in the bath-house.'

'I prefer to think of the first one.' Flavius knelt down and brushed his lips against the emperor's hand.

'Hmm,' he said, pulling up his scarf.

Later, from the highest point on one of the towers of the east gate, the prefect and his adjutant watched the emperor's party ride off down the hill. They went at a gentle trot, neither too fast nor too slow, so as not to attract attention.

They crossed the causeway and were moving up again towards the thick forest that lay to either side of the military road to Papcastle.

As they were about to pass under the first straggling line of trees, Flavius saw a raised arm holding a hunting-knife. Attached to its tip, waving like a pennant, he thought he saw a scarf.

But it could have been a trick of the fading afternoon light.

Part Three

MARCELLUS

I

Six weeks later, Flavius himself rode out of Alauna by the east gate, crossed the causeway and took the road for Papcastle.

He was accompanied by Quintus and an escort of four mounted men. At the crossroads in Papcastle, they turned south-west, towards the coast again and the harbour fort of Ravenglass.

Unlike Alauna, which faced the sea from a high bluff, at Ravenglass the fort's main gates stood on the landward side of the fort facing east. To Flavius, familiar only with the plan of Alauna, it seemed as though the place had turned its back on the sea, which at high tide might have splashed its walls.

As the road passed through the settlement that clustered round the fort, Flavius paused and turned round in the saddle to take a last look at the soaring range of mountains behind them.

When he walked on the beach near Alauna, enjoying the sight of the mountains he loved, he was separated from them by a wide stretch of water, their outline often blurred by mist; here, by contrast, the vast peaks, their lofty tips piercing the pale blue of a bright, early-February sky, seemed close enough to touch.

A pass carried a road from the harbour at Ravenglass to the lakeside fort of Ambleside. On a plateau close to the summit stood another fort, as yet unfinished, designed to protect Roman transports using the route.

It was because of recent unwelcome developments at the new Hardknott mountain fort that Flavius had been commanded by the legate in York to assist the commandant at Ravenglass. Close on the legate's instructions, an invitation had arrived, courteously suggesting that the prefect might like to combine work with a stay in Ravenglass for the annual fair, when the commandant and his family would be delighted to entertain him as their guest.

With the letter came a note, attached to a small box, both addressed in a woman's hand to the prefect's lady at Alauna.

Aelius, who had followed the courier as he arrived, stood in the headquarters office and noted the expression of pleasure on Flavius's face as he read his letter. He looked even more pleased as he picked up the little box and shook it gently.

'Why not just open that instead of jerking it about?' Aelius demanded impatiently.

'It isn't addressed to me. It's for my wife.'

'I'll take it to her.' Aelius crossed the room briskly.

Flavius kept hold of the box. 'No, I'll take it.'

Aelius took the opportunity to read Flavius's letter. 'Ravenglass?' he said. 'Do I go?'

'No. It's a military matter. What do you know about defending mountain passes?'

'What do *you* know?'

Flavius made for the door. 'The fair isn't a military matter,' added Aelius.

'No.'

Aelius caught up with Flavius before he was through the door. 'Allow me to carry the prefect's parcel.'

'It will hardly tax my strength.'

'It's a servant's duty to carry for his master. Besides, a man who is about to defend a mountain pass should surely not be seen walking about with a pretty little confection like that.'

Flavius groaned and handed over the box. 'If you want to listen to whatever's going on, do just that: listen. Nothing else.'

Flavius had then marched briskly to the villa to find his wife. It was several weeks since she had smashed the plate against the emperor's mural and Flavius had felt himself released from the torment of continually blaming himself for her state of misery. He was no longer apprehensive of offending or upsetting her; she could no longer provoke in him the bursts of anger that left him with the sense of guilt she knew how to manipulate with her tears and pouts.

He tapped on her door and, without any of his former hesitation, opened it. Aelius followed with a solemn air, which was meant to convey that enforced silence had been unjustly imposed on him.

Lucilla was in the grip of one of the wild moods that from time to time engaged her like a recurrent fever. Somewhere near half the contents of her chests were scattered about the room. Alis was trying to arrange the items in some kind of order before her mistress started tossing them around again.

If Flavius had changed, Lucilla hadn't. She waved him away, saying, 'I'm busy.'

He was inclined to say that unless she gave him her immediate attention he would have the whole lot burned, but he could afford to be reasonable since her less than gracious moods no longer distressed him.

'Lucilla,' he said amiably, 'I think you might find it worth your while to see what I have here.'

She glanced at Aelius. 'Why is he here? I don't *want* him here.'

Aelius, still silent, held up the box.

'He carried this here for you. It came with this letter I'm holding,' Flavius had explained.

'Where are they from?'

'Ravenglass.'

'Who should I know in Ravenglass?' Lucilla started searching through a bundle of fans. 'Alis, I can't find the blue one.'

'Lucilla,' Flavius had said, in the same smiling, patient way, 'I have already explained to you that the legate is sending me to Ravenglass. I can understand if you don't remember, though, because I doubt you were troubling to listen to me at the time.'

Lucilla gave him a sharp look, but he was still smiling at her so she returned to the fans. 'Yes.'

'I think the note and the box probably come from the wife of the commandant at Ravenglass. Do read it. It might be something that pleases you.'

'The wife ... doesn't she have Gallic blood?'

Flavius recalled suppressing a sigh at that remark. 'I don't know. If you think the lady is one of your detested barbarian tribeswomen, I can only say, Lucilla, that I have never known one who could write in such an elegant hand.'

His wife stared obstinately at him.

'Shall I open it for you?'

Lucilla shrugged her shoulders.

Flavius unfastened the note. It was written on a thin piece of lime-bark of the kind often used by ladies for informal little messages, and it had come, as Flavius suspected, from the wife of the commandant at Ravenglass. 'Lucilla, this is very kind: she asks you to consider travelling with me to Ravenglass to enjoy the week of the fair with her. If you'd like to stay longer, she and her friends are sure they could find any number of things to amuse you.'

'What friends?'

Flavius pretended not to notice the hostility in her voice. 'Oh,' he said casually, 'other ladies in the camp. Perhaps from the leading tribal families nearby.'

'Possible former slaves then, and barbarians?'

Without another word, Flavius picked up the note and the box. He beckoned Aelius to follow him. 'Alis, the door, if you please.'

Lucilla stared at his retreating figure. For an instant, a rare flicker of alarm showed on her face. 'Flavius,' she called out, 'you're taking the box. It's mine. I want to see what's in it.'

He turned round. For someone unaccustomed to making apologies, it was, he supposed, an attempt on her behalf, if a feeble one. He said solemnly, like the judge he might one day become, 'Yes Lucilla, you are right. It is your box.'

Then, glancing back at the note, he continued as if Lucilla had not interrupted. 'The lady and her friends believe they can find plenty to amuse you. She sends you a small gift to show you one of the things most of them like doing, and hopes it might please you too.'

Flavius opened the box and drew out a long strand of pink river-pearls.

'Oh, madam, how pretty they are,' said Alis, always an ally of Flavius, but from the look on her face meaning what she said as well.

'Yes they are,' he agreed, shaking them so that the tiny pearls threw off shimmering pin-points of light. 'She says they collect these themselves from the river at Ravenglass.' He laughed. 'Imagine stepping into the water and seeing them lying there.'

He scooped up the pearls and held them up in his hands to slip them over Lucilla's head. She stepped away from him in horror.

'Pearls?' She snatched them from his hands and let them dangle from her fingers at arm's length. 'They look like dirty lumps of grit.'

Her moment of repentance had run its course, thought Flavius, with regret but none of the disquiet he would once have felt.

'They are not oyster pearls,' he said mildly. ' These are river-pearls, and this is how they look. They have a delicate appearance that Alis and I like. The ladies in Ravenglass, too, seem to appreciate them.'

'Pink!' cried Lucilla, becoming spiteful. 'How can they call them pink? They're discoloured, that's all.'

Aelius, apparently deciding that in the present circumstances his vow of silence was rescinded, spoke out. 'Madam, river-pearls of the pink variety are found only in the river at Ravenglass. They are much sought after.'

'Not by me,' she snapped. 'What kind of woman wants to be seen wearing nasty little beads like these, or to stand about in a river – stand in a river! – looking for them? How can she expect me to want to do that?'

'I am sure she doesn't want you to do anything you wouldn't be happy to do,' murmured Flavius. 'There will be all sorts of other things to entertain you at the fair. The days are getting longer now, and the weather is improving. My dear, wouldn't this be an excellent opportunity for you to enjoy a change from Alauna?'

Aelius, watching him closely, had observed that, although Flavius was speaking in an eminently courteous manner to his wife, he seemed to have little interest in what he was saying. It was more as if he was dutifully performing a chore.

Lucilla had perhaps sensed something of this. 'No,' she said hotly, 'I don't want to go. I don't want to meet that Gallic woman. Why did you think I would?'

She was preparing, Aelius realised, to produce the petulant tears that would win back Flavius's attention. She sniffed. 'You are trying to make me go.'

She looked rather pretty, Aelius thought, with her fingers clasped together, her eyes wide, tears beginning to appear. He doubted if Flavius would be able to resist. The image of a gold necklace began to occupy his mind.

It came as something of a surprise to him when Flavius answered her without much concern, 'My dear, of course you don't have to go, if you don't want to.' The gold necklace evaporated from his mind's eye, and Aelius experienced a mild sense of rejoicing.

Flavius glanced back at Lucilla. 'The Ravenglass courier is here until tomorrow morning. That will give you time tonight to write to his commandant's lady to explain why you are not accepting her kind invitation. You'd better use the excuse of fragile health, don't you think?'

Lucilla was staring at him helplessly, two useless tears drying on her cheeks. 'You want me to lie?' She tossed her head. 'No.'

Flavius pointed out that he had been forced on many occasions to lie for her. 'Lies are not to my liking either, but I preferred them to offending people who only meant you well. I have no wish now to be disgraced because of your discourtesy, particularly as the lady is the wife of an officer senior to me. In the military world, Lucilla, she outranks you and requires your respect. You will thank her for the necklace as well.'

Lucilla, with a wail of anger, flung the pearls across the room in Alis's direction. 'If she thinks them so pretty, let *her* compose a letter of thanks.'

Alis's face flushed. Lucilla knew that her maid could barely write her name, although Aelius was trying to teach her to read. She bent down to pick up the necklace.

'Leave it, Alis,' said Flavius. He stooped for it himself. 'My steward's wife, Lucilla, does not need to accept as a gift something you throw away as rubbish.'

He motioned Aelius and Alis to leave them. 'Now you can sit down and think about your letter.'

'No, I won't. I can't.'

'If you mean that you don't know what to write, then you will follow me to the library and I will dictate a letter to you. It has to be in your hand. Now.'

Several sheets of lime-bark lay on the library floor before Flavius was satisfied. Lucilla was tired, bewildered and angry because she didn't understand what was happening.

'Everything seems different since the emperor came,' she muttered, almost to herself. 'Is it because I didn't do as you said when he was here?'

'What about what you did before he came?'

Lucilla scowled. 'What I did?' She was silent for a moment and began to fiddle with the ink-stand. Flavius closed the lid. 'You mean when I made that little hole in his tedious mural? He never knew, did he?'

'Not that you did it, no. But you didn't do it to hurt the emperor, did you, any more than it was really Alis you were throwing the pearls at?'

Lucilla devoted her attention to the ink well again. Flavius kept his finger tight on the lid. Suddenly he laughed quietly, gently.

'Do all military wives put their husbands in such danger?'

If only, in that moment, she could have laughed with him.

If only she had laughed back, he thought now, as he rode beside Quintus towards the gates of the fort at Ravenglass.

But Lucilla had not laughed. Instead she had jumped out of her chair, shouting at him, 'I hate you! And I hate this place. I hate you for making me come here. I don't want to stay ...'

Flavius was shaken by the violence of her outburst. He felt no inclination to comfort her, which he had to admit surprised him. Whether that was what she wanted or not, he didn't know. It no longer mattered.

He remembered hearing himself say in the distant, reasonable manner he had learned to use with her, 'If you want to go home, and you are sure about it, then I will see what can be arranged.'

Then he had taken her by the arm and guided her to her own rooms. In the hours that had passed before his departure for Ravenglass, he had seen nothing more of her.

'Look sir,' said Quintus, returning him to the present.

The main gates of the fort ahead of them had opened, and the commandant was waiting there to greet them.

II

The fort of Ravenglass, like Alauna itself, had been built to house a unit of a thousand men, commanded by an officer with the rank of tribune. When half the unit at Alauna had been deployed to Judea, the rank of the commandant there had reverted to that of prefect.

Flavius, therefore, as he dismounted, found himself in the presence of a superior officer. He acknowledged this with military precision, and then presented himself. 'Flavius Valerius Paulus, at your command, tribune.'

The tribune smiled. 'Marcellus Fabius Gallus. You are welcome, prefect.'

He invited Flavius to enter the gate-house. The Ravenglass commandant was younger than Flavius had anticipated, only a few years older than himself, with lively brown eyes that were watching him closely. The smile was reassuring.

As they walked under the long archway of the gate-house, the tribune suddenly stopped asking polite questions about the journey from Alauna, paused and turned to face Flavius. They looked at each other.

They were both cut from the same cloth; wealthy, well-educated young men, who had demonstrated an administrative skill in civil life that had attracted the emperor's notice.

They were suddenly aware of sharing the same thought and both shrugged off military decorum. The tribune grinned. 'Marcellus.' He held out his hand.

Flavius smiled and grasped it. 'Flavius,' he said. In answer to what he knew the next question would be, he added, 'North Italy.'

Marcellus nodded. 'Rome.'

They stepped out from the shadows of the gate-house into the sunlit main street of the fort which, like Alauna, passed between barracks to the headquarters building.

'Paulus?' said Marcellus. 'Isn't that wine? You run your own ships?'

'Yes, true,' cried Flavius, pleased with this recognition. 'And your family?'

'Guess. I gave myself away then, didn't I?'

'You knew about our ships, so is it something to do with shipping?'

Marcellus nodded. 'Ship-building, with some shipping. We do the India run.'

'The India run?' Flavius looked at him in awe. 'A year to get there and back? Have you ever been on one of the runs?'

'Once,' said Marcellus. 'Never again. Storms, rocks, pirates, heat. When you reach India, the trading isn't difficult. Most of our buying is spices and gem-stones. But then you have to wait for the silk caravans to arrive from China. Could be weeks. They don't seem to have the same sense of time as we do.' He laughed. 'Still, when you see those bolts of beautifully dyed silk rolling off the shelves of our fancy shops near the forum, it does seem worthwhile.'

'At your exorbitant prices, it would,' agreed Flavius.

'Your best wines don't exactly sell for a few copper coins.'

'True.' They struck hands together.

A section of men emerging from one of the barracks looked at them with interest.

'They think,' said Flavius, lowering his voice, 'that we have come to an inter-unit strategic decision.'

'Well, we will,' murmured Marcellus. 'Later.' He nodded briskly at the men in passing.

Flavius suddenly remembered Quintus. He turned round to look for him. 'My adjutant?'

'With mine,' said Marcellus. 'He's probably been carried off to one of those obscure corners that young officers keep private until the right moment comes for sharing it.'

Flavius hesitated. 'Quintus is very young – shy.'

'We'll look after him.'

They were approaching the headquarters building. The doors to the street stood open, and beyond them the doors of the hall. Flavius saw inside a glimmer of gold from the shrine. He bowed his head to the customary image of the emperor. Marcellus, more as a courtesy to Flavius than to Hadrian, gave a perfunctory nod.

They reached the tribune's villa. On entering, Flavius could see that it was almost identical in design to his own house at Alauna. His was more gracious and elegant in style, thanks to the early presence there of Hadrian and the later meticulous care of Aelius; but the atrium in which he now found himself had quite a different air. It was slightly untidy, comfortable, warm ... the sort of place where you might expect to meet small children running about.

Even as the thought crossed his mind, his foot caught on something. He bent down and picked up a toy cart with a splintered wheel.

'Oh,' he said in dismay. 'Does this belong to a child of yours, Marcellus?'

'No.' He took the toy and turned it over in his fingers. 'It could have done, but not now.' He noticed Flavius glance at him curiously, and said almost apologetically, 'We had two boys. They both died before they were five years old.' He added quickly, 'Celia will know someone who can mend this. It must belong to a child from one of her classes. She believes in catching them young. There's not an infant toddling around Ravenglass who can't ask for sweets and toys in Latin. Avoid them – they are voracious. But then, you'll know all about that from your own wife. How young are hers?'

Flavius looked at the floor as if he might be searching for more lost playthings. 'We have no schools in Alauna,' he said, 'as yet.' He knelt down to retrieve a shoe, and while still on his knees went on lamely, 'There's only one child in the fort at the moment and he's too young, you see. And in the settlement, well ...'

Marcellus, sensing a delicate area, said, 'Ah, you've found that shoe. Thank you.' He snapped his fingers at a passing slave. 'One of you go and find my wife. Whatever she's doing, this is urgent.'

He took Flavius by the arm. 'This might be a good moment for you to tell me if my wine is acceptable by your standards, as well as to talk about Hardknott.'

He led his guest into the room which at Alauna served Flavius as a library; from the number of small stools, cushions and painted wooden animals piled in a corner, it seemed to serve as one of Celia's classrooms when required, and for the rest of the time as a family sitting-room.

The wine was waiting for them. Marcellus filled a glass for Flavius and handed it to him. He sipped, then drank more deeply. 'This,' he announced after a moment's thought, 'is very good. It must have come from us.'

'You should be a diplomat when all this is over.'

'No, I'm a lawyer. And if I'm lucky, that's what I will remain. You can always trust a lawyer to give you an honest opinion. So tell me, what is happening at Hardknott?'

Marcellus smiled, nodded and poured himself a glass of wine before he began. 'Our problem is that the legate wants a route kept open between the harbour here and the fort at Ambleside, using Hardknott pass.

'Hardknott fort was planned for just that purpose – to secure the pass. The terrain is very difficult, steep and dangerous; there was only one stretch of plateau large enough to place a fort and a parade ground, and that's not far from the summit on our side.'

Flavius nodded. 'Was it worth it? How often is it covered in thick mist up there?'

Marcellus shrugged his shoulders. 'The legions know best. It's still unfinished, so it's not fully manned, is vulnerable to attack, and the skirmishes are increasing. The attacks are not the work of disaffected tribes, but of the outlaws and robber bands hiding out in the mountains.'

'So?'

'The legate wants us to advise him on whether the Hardknott fort should be closed while the surrounding area is cleared—'

'What, by men from Ravenglass and Alauna?'

'No doubt under direction from a legionary squad from York.'

They looked at each other.

'Or,' Marcellus went on, 'should men from the units at Ravenglass and Alauna mount guard on the pass while repairs to Hardknott are carried out and the building completed?'

Flavius groaned. 'I have another idea to put to the tribune. Why not close Ambleside?'

'I must remind the prefect that he is not asked to put forward ideas. All that is required is an answer to the legate's question. After all, what do we know? You grew up in a vineyard, and I grew up in a ship-builder's yard.'

Marcellus broke off and turned his head towards the door. 'I think from the noises I can hear that my wife is on her way. Forget about Hardknott now. We'll go up there tomorrow, and then you'll be able to understand more clearly what the problems are.'

He moved towards the door, which suddenly burst open. A woman darted in, running towards Marcellus. For a startled second, she seemed to Flavius to resemble one of Lucilla's distorted images of a so-called barbarian.

He noticed the boots first. They were made of thick hide with the fur on the inside. They had recently been very wet and, although they were no longer dripping water, they were leaving footprints in her wake. Her head and shoulders were covered by a big knotted shawl. She had a cord fastened round her waist to keep her skirt out of the way of her wet boots, and she was wearing the clumsy kind of gloves that Flavius had seen his mother use when she pruned her roses.

'Celia,' protested Marcellus, 'those boots! Look at the mess they're making.'

'They said you wanted me urgently. So I came as I was. What's happened?'

Marcellus said gravely, 'Two things.' He held up the shoe that Flavius had discovered. 'Do you think you might find time to teach your pupils to say "I have lost a shoe"?'

'Marcellus? What is it?'

'Secondly, the shoe was found by our guest here, the prefect of Alauna.'

Celia spun round, hurriedly pulling the shawl off her head. A number of tortoiseshell pins fell to the floor and strands of black hair tumbled loose.

Marcellus addressed Flavius. 'This elegant apparition is my wife, Celia.'

'Prefect,' she said ruefully, 'it was never my intention to greet you like this. I told them to let me know as soon as you were seen approaching. Nobody came.'

'They probably couldn't recognise you, looking like that,' said Marcellus.

'Madam,' said Flavius, 'if you will allow me, I think I can guess what you were doing. You were standing in the river, collecting pink pearls for your necklaces.'

Celia laughed delightedly. 'How did you know? Oh, yes. I wrote to your wife about it, and she must have let you read my letter. She wrote me a most gracious one in return. You must thank her for me.'

'Yes, I shall be pleased to.' Feeling unhappy about the deception, Flavius glanced away. This was no barbarian. Celia was rosy-cheeked and bright-eyed, with a smile as pleasing as her husband's. He suspected she laughed a lot.

'Actually,' she was saying, 'the pearls I collected today aren't for me. We're going to sell them at the fair. They sell well, especially to the Irish. The money we make we shall spend on balls and hoops and such like for the children who haven't any toys. Only we have to pretend they win them in little competitions we arrange. We can't give to some children and not others; some of the fathers might be too proud to accept them, and break them up.'

'So you're cheating in these little competitions of yours?' said Marcellus.

'Yes, we are. Then everyone can be happy.'

Marcellus dutifully shook his head, but he was smiling at his wife, Flavius noticed, when her back was turned to him.

'We?' enquired Flavius. 'You are not alone in this, Celia?'

'Alone?' said Marcellus. 'She has a whole band of fellow conspirators. They're into everything, they never stop ...'

'They help me,' cried Celia. 'To keep out of your way, we try to amuse ourselves.' To make her indignation clear, she stamped her foot, but the squelching sound made by her wet boot left her bending over with laughter.

Marcellus picked up a block of slate standing by the door and rapped it with his knuckles. A clear ringing tone filled the room.

'What's that?' said Flavius. 'It's lovely.'

'It's a ringing stone,' Celia explained. 'It comes from one of the mountains near here. My friend Elphin gave it to me. She says if you strike the stone, your lover will come to you.'

'But in this house, if you strike it, and you're lucky, a servant will come, said Marcellus. Addressing Flavius, but looking at Celia, he added with a wry smile, 'I will admit that the fellow conspirators can be both thoughtful and kind. They help Celia with her classes, and they mix with families in the settlement, which creates goodwill. We have no hospital as you do, only a couple of medical orderlies, but the ladies are always ready to work beside them if they can be of any use. But sometimes, Flavius, when a less sane impulse seizes them—'

A head peered round the door. 'Ah, well done,' said Marcellus. He pointed to the damp places on the floor and at Celia's boots. The head nodded and withdrew.

'Most of my ladies come from the fort,' explained Celia. 'We have eight wives, one widowed sister and two daughters.'

'And to them,' said Marcellus, 'we have to add the handful of ladies of, shall we say, some standing in the community outside, including one from the island.'

'Yes, that's Elphin.' Celia sighed. 'I'm so sorry I couldn't persuade your wife to come. I'm sure she would have enjoyed meeting Elphin. We were all looking forward to having your wife here, and talking about what we could do to entertain her.'

'Elphin – that's an unusual name, isn't it?' Flavius asked.

'It's Irish.'

A slave came into the room and started quickly mopping the floor. A young girl followed him, carrying a pair of sandals.

'Oh, madam,' said the girl reproachfully.

'Everybody nags me,' said Celia, sitting down and stretching out her feet.

Marcellus glanced at Flavius. 'Would you allow us? I think Celia should get out of these wet boots.'

'Of course, yes,' said Flavius, wondering what else he could say. He asked himself what kind of noise Aelius would make if he found a slave mopping a floor in a public room where a guest was present; what kind of tantrum Lucilla would throw if he suggested she remove her boots in company. But these were silly questions. When would Lucilla ever wear boots like Celia's, or leave wet footprints across the house?

Yet he was becoming aware of a feeling that what would have been unforgivable in Alauna seemed to be the comfortable way to behave in Ravenglass – and that he was beginning to enjoy it.

Celia now had her sandals on her feet. She pulled off the gloves that resembled the ones Flavius's mother used for pruning. Then she stood up to unfasten the cord that had held the hem of her skirt out of the water, and the folds, slightly damp, fell round her ankles. She tied the cord back round her waist.

The slave girl was busy collecting tortoiseshell pins from the floor. Celia twisted up the loose strands of her hair, retrieved the pins and stuck them in at random.

Flavius watched the slender, nimble fingers that had emerged from her gloves. 'How,' he asked, 'were you able to pick up those tiny pearls when you were wearing those gloves?' He already felt sufficiently at ease with both of them to ask questions that he would normally never dream of putting to strangers. He could hardly believe that when he woke up that morning he had not even met them.

Celia was laughing at him. 'Of course I don't pick them up with my gloves on! I have to use my bare fingers. The gloves are for moving the pebbles and rocks to find the pearls.'

'You weren't on your own?' Flavius felt slightly shocked to hear of her working in this way.

'No, though only a couple of the young girls from the fort were with me. The others were all doing things for the fair. I was very glad they were there. I don't think I could have moved one of the rocks on my own.'

Celia looked at Flavius. 'Why have you got such a disbelieving expression on your face?'

'My love, he doesn't doubt what you are telling him,' said Marcellus. 'He is just struggling to come to terms with something new in his experience: the wife of a senior officer in the Roman Army who stands in a river shifting rocks, and plans to serve on a stall in a local market.'

Celia's eyes twinkled. 'Would you ever guess, Flavius, that I was brought up by a strict Roman mother who taught me how to be modest, obedient, sober and dignified, as an acceptable wife should be? I don't undervalue those qualities – but, you see Flavius, I also had a Celtic grandfather.'

'And that,' said Marcellus good-humouredly, 'is her excuse for being at times wayward, whimsical, perverse, given to exaggeration and illogical fancies.'

'You won't get any sympathy from Flavius!' said Celia. 'Look at that light-coloured hair of his. He must have Celtic blood.'

'A very, very long way back.'

'Well, that might explain something,' said Marcellus. 'The legate has asked him to consider whether or not Hardknott should be closed while we clear the outlaws from the mountains, and he said, "Close Ambleside".'

Celia clapped her hands delightedly. 'That sounds like a lovely piece of Celtic thinking, so it will be a wise solution.'

'It certainly isn't a straightforward, hard army response,' said Marcellus.

'It's merely common sense,' protested Flavius. 'If the solution to a problem appears improbable, one looks for something more practicable.'

Marcellus was trying not to smile. 'If you hadn't already told me, might I have guessed you were a lawyer?'

Flavius began to laugh at himself. 'Yes – not Celtic, not army, just pompous!'

They all looked at each other. It wasn't really a matter for joking, thought Flavius, but they were all laughing.

'I think,' said Marcellus, 'that this is a good moment for me to take Flavius for a disciplined military walk round the harbour. We can benefit from the cooling late-afternoon air.'

'What he means,' explained Celia, 'is that he wants to check on his patrols. By now, the harbour will be filling up with little boats coming in for the fair. You'll probably enjoy seeing them, Flavius.'

'Yes, they'll be unloading on the wharves and that needs to be controlled. They'll be bringing in a fair number of undesirables, too. That means a watch on the storage sheds, and we try to keep an eye out for any stolen stuff that might be shipped in for unloading on the stalls. And then, of course, there's the swarm of pickpockets. We grab any known ones.'

'I think I shall enjoy my breath of fresh air,' said Flavius.

'Good. We'll make ourselves conspicuous. When they see you beside me, they might think I've sent for reinforcements.'

'Think,' said Celia, 'five hundred Spaniards sweeping down from the hills around Alauna.'

'Well, six of us,' said Flavius. 'Celia, do you think, before we go, I could see if your stone would ring for me?'

She nodded, amused, swept up the block of slate and held it out to him. Flavius rapped his knuckles against it.

The ringing sound filled the room. Flavius was enchanted. He struck it a second time. It rang again.

'Are you calling anyone?' asked Celia.

'Anyone,' he murmured.

III

The harbour, as Celia had guessed it might be, was a joy to Flavius. It was crowded with small working craft. They bobbed about on the slightly choppy water, masts swaying, sails flapping, as if they were as excited as the men bringing them in to be gathering for the opening of the fair.

Marcellus had satisfied himself that his patrols were operating as instructed and he and Flavius stood together, watching the unloading along the wharf.

Then Flavius saw, beyond the harbour, faintly but clearly, the outline of the island, a low long shape like a crouched sleeping animal.

'Marcellus,' he said, 'it's our island!'

'Ours as well as yours.'

'In the ten months I've been here, I've seen it only four times.'

'We probably see it more often than you do, but I doubt very much more. You sometimes think you see it, but then it's only a low cloud close to the water, that drifts away.'

'A lot of my men in Alauna think it's Ireland.'

'That's hardly surprising,' said Marcellus. 'When Hadrian was here, he made his friend Agrippa responsible for rebuilding the harbour as you see it now, and he assumed this island was Ireland, the only island of which he'd already heard.

'When your newly founded cohort of Spaniards was settled at Alauna, Agrippa became their first commandant and still described it as Ireland. A lot of your men, like mine, can't be persuaded otherwise. But no, Ireland is very different. Much, much larger, and it's about the same distance again as Ravenglass is from the island. We call it Manavia. The native name is Manannàn – the island that belongs to the god Manannàn.'

Flavius repeated the name. 'Another British god? Should I have heard of him?'

'No, you wouldn't know about him in Alauna. His cult is almost confined to the island. On the south edge of the Irish Sea, I believe there are a few small sites. One or two of the veterans from the camp here who have decided to settle in the area – married to local women – worship him.' Marcellus smiled. 'I notice though, that they still join us for the annual sacrifice to Jupiter.'

Flavius smiled back. 'No point in offending anyone. What kind of outpost do you keep on the island?'

'None.'

'None?'

'It's never been necessary.' Marcellus looked around him. 'We think of ourselves as living on the remote north-west edge of a vast expanse of territory that covers a large part of Europe, the eastern Mediterranean and North Africa. But we are also part of another world – the circle of coastal lands surrounding the Irish Sea. At the centre of that circle lies the island of Manannàn, landfall to all the craft that do business in those waters.'

Flavius looked again at the island. Grey clouds were forming above it, but behind it the sky was streaked with deep pink.

'It offers,' Marcellus was saying, 'a safe harbour in bad weather, shelter to anyone stranded, workshops for repairs, abundant food, water, supplies. The islanders go out to save drowning men. To the dead they give decent burial. There is trust on both sides.'

'Even from the Roman conquerors?'

'We need them as much as anyone else. They welcomed us as they welcome everybody. When Agrippa arrived here, the head man came across to meet him. He brought his small daughter with him, to show he came in peace and with trust. The child, by the way, was

Elphin. He does the same whenever a new commandant arrives. That was how Celia first met her.'

'Head man?' said Flavius, frowning. 'Hasn't he been given some proper sort of title: chief magistrate, first lord, master of Manannàn?'

'Perhaps. I don't know. I suppose if it were part of Ireland with its host of tiny kingdoms, he might be called its king,' said Marcellus. 'But don't kings count their wealth in terms of land? His is judged by the size of his herds. Chief herdsman? No, I don't think it has the right ring about it, do you, Flavius?'

But he had lost interest in possible titles. 'How could he bring a child with him? A little girl? He couldn't have known that first time how Agrippa would behave.'

'As I understand it,' Marcellus explained patiently, 'Agrippa behaved as sensibly as one would hope a close friend of the emperor's would behave. He expressed his thanks for the gracious visit and assured the island's leader that he sought only friendship. He probably already knew, Flavius, that they had nothing that resembled anything like an army; all they could summon was a primitive kind of militia made up of farmers and fishermen. Anyway, Agrippa said that he was gratified to learn that he was under no threat from the islanders, so there was no reason *for* him to impose any form of Roman presence on their land.'

Marcellus gave Flavius a quick smile. 'If Celia were here, she would tell you that Hadrian never had any intention of wasting time on Manannàn because he was sure there were no mineral ores worth mining there.' When Flavius cast a questioning look at him, he shrugged his shoulders. 'All I will say is that I think the shrewdness of Elphin's father tends to be overlooked. Agrippa promised that in view of their declared friendship, although the Roman Empire was bounded by the shores of Ravenglass, the leader of Manannàn and his heir could rely on Roman protection should they ever need it.'

'What heir?' asked Flavius.

'Elphin, the child standing beside her father.'

'How could she be his heir?'

'She's not a child now. She's a woman.'

'Yes, a woman!'

Marcellus was amused by the expression on Flavius's face. He took him by the arm. 'Let's walk along the beach before we go back. Flavius, the islanders are Celts, not Romans. Agrippa may not have known where Ireland was, but he was able to grasp that. Now, look at the beach.'

The tide was out. Flavius found himself looking at a broad, straight sweep of smooth, flawless pale yellow sand. He gave a gasp of pleasure.

Two young men were galloping along the edge of the water. They were some distance away, but the sound of their laughter and shouting was carried on the wind. Flavius stared.

'That's Quintus,' he said in surprise.

'With my adjutant, yes. I told you we'd look after him.' Marcellus gazed with satisfaction at the expanse of firm sand. 'Let's hope this weather lasts for another two days. Then, Flavius, you will have the splendid sight of horses thundering from one end of the beach to the other. It's the main event of the fair, one of the great occasions, actually, of the Ravenglass year.'

'Racing? Who races?'

'Anyone who owns a horse, or can borrow one. They come on anything – ponies, farm horses. Most of them know they don't stand a chance of getting anywhere in the first heats, but they enjoy the excitement of being here. They will do their little bit of racing tomorrow, and then the great race of the twenty or so champions is held on the next day. Work stops, everyone gathers here to watch. They shout for their favourites.'

'Do your men take part?' asked Flavius, wishing there was a beach like this under the bluff of his own fort.

'They are invited to join in. I would prefer them not to do so. My best couriers could out-run all the others in a few seconds. If any man chooses to ride I allow it, but he would be under strict instructions to withdraw after an early heat. It is not our race. It was a festival here long before we arrived. I like to show our support by helping to steward the heats and dealing with any of the brawling that might occur.'

Marcellus laughed. 'In a return of courtesies, I have been awarded the honour of crowning the winner with his wreath of oak leaves.'

'That I would like to have seen,' said Flavius, smiling.

'But you will,' cried Marcellus. 'You will stand right beside me as a distinguished visitor.'

Flavius shook his head. 'No.'

'You mean you can't see us both squashed together on one of those minute podiums they supply on these occasions?'

'No,' said Flavius, beginning to laugh with him. 'I mean I can't stay. I am expected back in Alauna.'

Marcellus stopped laughing.

IV

'You can't stay?' said Celia in amazement. 'Flavius, why not?'

They were sitting down to dine at the fashionable Roman hour of late afternoon. Flavius supposed that somewhere in the villa was a large dining-room like his own at Alauna, but they were eating in a small, prettily painted room that caught the last of the February sunshine. Celia's tumbled hair had been brushed into a smooth coil at the back of her head in a style which Flavius liked, but which Lucilla would probably would have condemned as five years out of date. His hostess wore long silver ear-rings set with tiny amethysts, and on one wrist a gold bracelet.

'Why not?' asked Celia again. 'We were so pleased that you would be here to share the day with us. It's only one extra day. What does that matter?'

Marcellus reproached her gently. 'It probably matters to his wife. She is alone and unwell.'

'Oh!' Celia was contrite. 'You are worried about her, Flavius, of course you are. But think: today, you rode all the way from Alauna; tomorrow you have that dreadful journey to Hardknott and back. Do you want to be riding on to Alauna the day after that? If it were Marcellus, I would be happier if he took a day's rest in between. I know you are both army officers for the moment, but you are neither of you trained cavalrymen. I am sure your wife would feel as I do, Flavius. I could send a message to her, if it made you feel easier.'

Marcellus looked at her. 'The Roman Army would be pleased to send a message, yes, Celia.'

She ignored him. 'And, Flavius, if you stayed another day, you would have time to find her a nice present. Does she like jewellery?'

'Yes.' Flavius was grateful for the chance to say something truthful about Lucilla.

'The island people make beautiful gold ornaments. They'll be selling them at the fair. Your wife would never be able to buy stuff like it in Rome.'

Celia shook her head so that her long, slender ear-rings moved. 'These came from Rome. Romans like straight lines.' Then she held out the wrist on which shone the gold bracelet. Fine strands of gold were twisted round each other in flowing curving forms 'Celts prefer curves,' she said. 'When you arrive home with a piece of Celtic gold for her, she will be delighted that you stayed here for another day.'

'We did,' said Flavius, trying to combine courtesy with a shred of truth, 'once discuss looking at goldsmiths' work while we were here.'

'Well, there we are then,' said Celia happily. 'You must stay.'

'Don't interfere, Celia,' said her husband.

'Someone must.'

'Pick up your knife and eat something.'

Celia picked up her knife. She smiled at Marcellus.

He turned to Flavius. 'Are you worried about the way the members of your household might be treating your wife?'

'No,' said Flavius. It would have been a relief to be able to say that he was worried about the way his wife was treating them. Furnaces could be roaring, Alis might be in tears, cupboards were probably being ransacked as she decided what she wanted to take home, Aelius would inevitably be exploding over everyone else because he had to keep his temper in front of Lucilla.

'No,' he said again. 'No, not at all.'

'Good. In that case,' Marcellus replied, rising from his chair, 'I shall take advantage of my position as your superior officer. I instruct you to remain in Ravenglass to support me during the festivities of race day.'

Flavius stood up. 'And if I refuse the tribune's instructions?'

'Court-martial.'

'I am pleased to accept the tribune's instructions.'

'A wise choice, prefect.' Marcellus gave Flavius a playful box on the shoulder. 'Now pick up your knife and eat.'

Celia clapped her hands together. 'You two are very good at play-acting soldiers, though perhaps you're a little short on the saluting and making a lot of clashing noises.'

'We are not foot-soldiers,' said Marcellus, 'nor will we be playing soldiers when we climb up to Hardknott pass tomorrow and decide the fate of the unfinished fort up there.'

'No, of course not,' she murmured.

Flavius was sitting down again. He couldn't quite understand why, but he was feeling a warm satisfaction about having been manoeuvred into staying for the racing, although it was not a sport he had ever been particularly interested in. As he began to eat with relish, he realised – selfishly, he admitted – that he didn't really care any more about what would be happening in Alauna while he was on the beach at Ravenglass.

Celia was leaning forward to talk to him. 'When you get to Hardknott, Flavius, make sure you take time to enjoy the view. With this kind of weather, it should be amazing.'

'As I thought I had explained to you, Celia, we are going to Hardknott to solve a military problem, not to look at the view.'

'In ten years' time,' she said, smiling enchantingly at Marcellus, 'you won't even remember what it was you were so worried about today, but you will never forget that view.'

'There might not be a view,' Marcellus persisted. 'The island might be hidden in mist, as it usually is. Indeed, the mist might be rolling towards us like a wave across the pass, and we could find ourselves standing waist-high in it as it slides past us. We shouldn't see much of the valley then.'

'All the more reason,' said Celia meekly, 'that you let Flavius enjoy the view if it is there.'

Marcellus conceded this with a smile at Flavius. He held up his glass of wine to his wife. 'My love, I promise you that if there is a view to be seen at Hardknott, we shall stop playing soldiers for as long as Flavius chooses to feast his eyes on it.'

Celia raised her own glass. 'Then may we have a good day tomorrow.'

Flavius lifted his. 'And may no-one offend the god of the island.'

Celia and Marcellus looked at him. Flavius was surprised that they didn't understand what he was talking about. 'When the people living round Alauna can't see the island,' he explained, 'they say the god of the island is angry, and when he is angry he folds up the island and carries it away. Don't they say that here?'

'No,' said Celia. 'I didn't think they knew of Manannàn that far north.'

'Oh, they don't know him by name. They see an island that comes and goes, so there must be a god who can make that happen. I always ask them what happens to the people who live on the island. Are they folded up as well, or do they fall into the sea? Do they drown or swim away to another island?'

'What do they say?' asked Celia.

'They just look at me.'

She laughed. 'You can't treat a piece of Celtic whimsy like an army report.'

'What do you do with it?' enquired Marcellus.

'You ask yourself what it is trying to tell you.'

'And what might that be?'

'In this instance, I think it's warning you never to offend your gods.'

'So, how do we find out what offends them?' said Marcellus, raising an eyebrow.

'Ah, well,' said Celia, 'isn't that for all of us to discover in our own way?'

Marcellus shook his head. From a cupboard, he produced a board drilled with a series of holes, a set of carved pegs and dice. 'Flavius, this is a game devised to exercise logical minds. Will you join me?'

Celia laughed until her ear-rings danced.

V

When the two commandants left early next morning for Hardknott they could see a mist rising from the water beyond the harbour. The island looked as insubstantial as a low-lying grey cloud, but

224

Flavius had the satisfaction of knowing that this time the grey cloud wouldn't drift away into nothing.

They rode alone to cover the steep, coiling road more quickly than a file of men. At times they paused to rest the horses, or to lead them on foot. Flavius had known easier trails in the Alps.

As they approached the fort poised on its spur overlooking the valley, the air was clear and bright, the soaring mountain peaks standing against a pale sky.

Marcellus tapped Flavius on one shoulder and pointed. Flavius glanced behind him and saw a spectacle that took away his breath.

The whole of the valley to the shore beyond lay in sunlight. Far below the outcrops of rock near the summit of the pass, a thick forest of oaks reached as far as the coastal farmlands; and on a shining sea, a long way off, but as clear as though it were lying at his feet, was the Isle of Manannàn.

It looked, Flavius thought, magical and mysterious, like all islands one has never put foot on. What happened in the hollows among those green hills? What sort of people lived there?

Marcellus took him gently by the arm.

They were seated, shortly afterwards, with the harassed commandant of the fort of Hardknott, in his cramped villa that was still only a quarter of its intended size. Marcellus, as senior officer, refreshed their minds by reading aloud the legate's letter.

Flavius, as the newcomer to the area, initially kept a courteous silence, but when the arguments began to grow repetitive, he ventured to take his place in the discussion.

'Gentlemen,' he said, 'I am unfamiliar with this territory that you know well, but I am experienced at living among mountains, which probably you are not.' He paused. 'I am of the considered opinion that whichever of the legate's suggestions you favour, the effect will be the same.'

The Hardknott commandant's expression was rapidly growing less cordial. Marcellus studied his hands.

Flavius went on. 'We are all agreed, I think, that the men lurking in the mountains around us are not looking for armed skirmishes with our men. They're thieves, living off what they steal. If we close the fort they'll be off, searching for somewhere else to rob, long before we can start clearing the area. If we bring up reinforcements to protect the fort while it's being completed, they'll disappear as soon as they catch the first glint of armour in the valley.'

He stretched out his hands. 'I'm sure we can all see that once things had quietened down again – after whichever course of action the legate decided upon – our marauders would creep back. The whole procedure would have to be mounted time and time again until someone finally had the sense to evacuate or dismantle this fort.'

'Sir,' cried the outraged commandant, 'you are clearly ignorant of the vital importance of our work here! We protect the route that carries supplies from Ravenglass harbour to Ambleside fort.'

Flavius glanced at Marcellus. 'I will admit that I once thought Ambleside was causing the problem at Hardnott and was expendable, but ...'

Ambleside, he was tartly informed, had authority over a district rich in iron ore and possibly silver.

'Yes,' Flavius agreed, 'I am now aware of that, and I also accept that its supplies must be safe-guarded, but they are not safe, are they, travelling on this route?'

'But there *is* no other way!'

'There must be,' snapped Flavius. 'This mountain range doesn't run the length of the British western coast.'

'Perhaps,' said Marcellus, applying balm, 'we might consult a map.'

As he had supposed, finding the right map at Hardknott was not as simple as in well-ordered camps like Ravenglass and Alauna. Marcellus and Flavius were left alone temporarily.

'I thought,' muttered Flavius, 'that when the emperor selected his auxiliary commandants—'

'Like us?'

'Yes, like us, he required a reasonable degree of common sense.'

'Flavius, this is a very odd sort of place, however beautiful. With all this space around it, it's enclosed in itself. We have settlements and harbours round us ... fishermen, farmers, stall-holders, inn-keepers ... roads going in all directions. No-one will ever have that up here; and we think *we're* isolated on the far edge of the empire!

The Hardknott commandant can't even bring his family and his household here yet. In winter, when the valley is thick with mist and there's ice on the pass, would you, or I, have much time for common sense?'

'Hmm,' said Flavius. 'Yes, I think I would – and all of it would be devoted to finding another route to Ambleside.'

When Marcellus grinned, he added in a whisper, because he could hear footsteps returning, 'But I will bear your words in mind.'

The commandant reappeared carrying a map from which he was still trying to brush a thin film of dust.

Marcellus rose to his feet graciously. 'That's very good of you. Thank you.' He took the map, spread it across a table and put out his hands to reach anything he could use to weigh down the corners.

'Splendid,' he said. 'Now let's all have a look and see where we are.' He bent over the map.

As they both moved towards the table, Flavius addressed himself to the commandant, who seemed to be avoiding meeting his eye.

'You must feel very honoured to receive the emperor's commission to take command at Hardknott,' Flavius said gravely. 'His majesty must consider it one of the most magnificent of his sites in Britain, perhaps of the empire.'

The word 'honoured' had its intended effect. The commandant turned eagerly towards Flavius. 'It is, isn't it, a remarkable place?' He bobbed his head up and down, and Flavius nodded with him.

'The emperor,' Flavius went on, 'would obviously have filled the post with care, and I do think it would disturb him to know of the unhappy conditions in which you have to live here.'

'It is not always easy.'

'I am inclined, then, to offer the tribune my opinion that the completion of this building should be the legate's priority. I do not believe, as you know, that the army can inflict any lasting damage on these mountain bandits – you can't make a surprise attack on a mountain, or infiltrate an enemy camp that doesn't exist – but the army does have a responsibility to house one of the emperor's chosen officers in acceptable comfort.'

'How useful it is,' said Marcellus, looking hard at Flavius, 'to bring a legal mind to bear on the subject.' In the measured way he could use when he deemed it appropriate, he added, 'This is certainly, gentlemen, a difficult decision to make because neither of the suggestions proposed appears to offer any lasting solution, and that would seem to be what the legate is expecting. In the circumstances, I am disposed to find your reasoning, Paulus, as sensible as anything else we might devise. The final say, however, must rest with you, commandant. Will you put your hand to such a reply to the legate?'

The commandant of Hardknott, looking slightly dazed by the flow of words, expressed his grateful agreement, and suggested food.

Marcellus laid his hand on the open map. 'I think before we finish, we ought to take a look at this map as we have it here in front of us. Here's Ambleside.' He tapped the map. 'Then Hardknott and Ravenglass. Now move south from Ravenglass along the coast. Find the estuary of the River Leven.'

Flavius peered at the map. After a moment, he said, 'Yes, I have it,' and looked up at Marcellus.

'You're interested in Ambleside, remember.'

Flavius hunched himself over the table, muttering to himself, moving a finger to and fro. Marcellus sat back in his chair.

The commandant watched them both uneasily.

Flavius suddenly gave a shout and swung round to laugh with excitement at Marcellus. 'You've followed the river?'

'Only as far as the tide took me. I like to find out what's going on along the coast. I saw a little settlement on the east bank, mostly fishermen. Greenodd was the nearest I could get to the name they used. They had wharves, but no warehousing.'

'How far up the river was that?'

'About four miles from ...'

'... from the southern tip of the lake!' cried Flavius.

Marcellus smiled back at him. 'I would guess about four miles. The thought of Ambleside never occurred to me until you talked about another route just now.'

'What a joy it is,' murmured Flavius slyly, 'to have the benefit of an experienced seaman's knowledge – sir.'

He took another glance at the map. 'So, we could take shipping up the estuary as far as the wharfing?'

'On the top of the tide, yes.'

'Grain?'

'I would say so, but I would have to look at it again. We might need more wharfing space, and certainly warehouses and stables.'

Flavius nodded. 'We unload there onto pack-horses or wagons. If there's a village to the east, there's bound to be a track along the east bank of the river as far as the lake. At its southern point, we reload the supplies and they travel the rest of the way by water to Ambleside.'

The commandant was indignant. 'How big is that lake?'

Marcellus gave him a look that he hoped conveyed surprise at the man's ignorance. 'About ten miles or so from one end to the other.'

'You can't take a heavy cargo over a lake like that.'

'Yes, you can,' said Flavius, determined not to let his irritation show again. 'I know mountains and I know lakes. It's smooth going all the way, less taxing on both men and beasts – and the beasts count, commandant – as well as less dangerous.'

'It won't please the emperor. He commissioned this fort ...'

'My friend,' said Marcellus, at his most reasonable, 'this is only an idea we are opening for discussion. You believed there was no other possible approach to Ambleside. We have discovered that there might be one. Information is always useful. The legate might be grateful for it at some time.'

The commandant regarded him with open disapproval.

'After all,' Marcellus persisted gently, 'isn't this why the emperor wants civilians like us to spend a brief period in his army? He hopes we will bring our different ways of thinking to military problems. He may or may not respond to any of our ideas, but he has a lively and enquiring mind—'

The commandant was driven to interrupt. 'That is not, sir, the way I view my appointment. I think we are brought into the army to be shown the value of the military code.'

'Which is?'

'Unquestioning obedience to orders, and unflinching defence of one's designated territory.'

'That's interesting, you know,' said Flavius. 'My predecessor at Alauna apparently shared your view. He applied for a permanent position in the legion that is now fighting in Judea. Hanging onto this untenable fort on this unnecessary route should qualify you for a similar post.'

They left Hardknott without staying to share a meal.

'I hope,' said Marcellus light-heartedly, as they made their way back to Ravenglass, 'that you never meet the emperor in one of his black moods. That quick wit of yours could be dangerous.' He pulled some squashed bread rolls out of a pouch and handed one of them to Flavius. He laughed. 'More than once, I didn't know how to maintain my dignity as a tribune during that discussion.'

'In that case, if I ever should happen to encounter the emperor, let's hope it's in one of his more jolly days,' said Flavius, 'because I might be tempted to ask him why on earth he put that fort up there!'

He took one long, last look at the walls rising from their foundations of rock against the backdrop of the mountains.

'Yet it is a splendid site.'

'But not for a fort.'

'No,' said Flavius, 'for a delectable villa, full of silks and treasures from one of your father's India runs.'

'Hmm,' murmured Marcellus, his mind running on other things. 'That odd man up there ... he didn't like us, did he?'

'He didn't like me, but why shouldn't he like you? Despite your misgivings, you were the perfectly impartial senior officer.'

Marcellus was amused by this. He shook his head. 'Perhaps Celia was right. We didn't make enough clashing noises. I thought if we went there alone in an informal, friendly way, he might feel more at ease talking about his problems. But perhaps he thought we were belittling him. Perhaps he would have preferred us to arrive with an escort of a dozen men, a trumpet and a standard ...'

'... and you in ceremonial dress.' Flavius grinned.

'Ugh! Climbing up here? Such a weight to carry, eh? Best avoided at any time.'

VI

Nevertheless, the following afternoon, when he arrived on the beach to preside over the Ravenglass annual horse-race, Marcellus was resplendent in a tribune's parade armour. Celia had convinced him that this was not an occasion to forgo ceremony.

Flavius had been detailed to escort her to the canopied platform erected by army carpenters for the officers' ladies and the wives of invited local dignitaries.

There was a wind rising from the water, but the sky was clear and bright. 'There's no sign of rain,' said Celia. 'I'd rather stand with the crowd.'

Flavius took her gently by the elbow. 'No, Celia. You are the judge's wife and you will take the seat in the centre of the platform. Those are my instructions and I intend to see them carried out.'

She lowered her eyes like a demure Roman wife and allowed Flavius to help her mount the platform. They could both see Marcellus at the far end of the beach, moving among the horses that were gathering there and talking to the riders. The sun glinted on polished metal and gilded leather; the wind stirred the red crest on his helmet and caught his cloak.

Celia whispered to Flavius, 'I love to see him dressed like that. I imagine your wife feels the same about you.'

Flavius was taken by surprise. 'I don't think she's ever seen me in ceremonial dress. She's certainly never mentioned it.'

He had answered without thinking. He saw Celia give him a curious glance. Then she said quickly, 'She's probably too shy to mention it.'

Celia sat down. The horses were beginning to form a line. 'Now which one are you going to support, Flavius?'

'Which horse? I don't know anything about them.'

'You've got to choose one,' Celia persisted. 'Everyone does.'

'Are you laying wagers?'

'Of course not. We just shout. Hurry up, Flavius!'

'Who are you supporting?'

'I'm the judge's wife, I have to be impartial. Flavius, which one!'

He gave in. 'Oh, well, I don't know. The chestnut.'

'Why the chestnut?' demanded Celia.

'Because,' said Flavius shortly, 'the rider is wearing a bright green scarf tied round his head and I shall be able to pick him out easily among the others.'

'Oh,' said Celia.

The horses were now positioned along the starting line. Marcellus came striding down the beach towards the judge's podium. Behind him followed his adjutant, and an orderly carrying the wreath of oak leaves that would crown the winner.

Marcellus paused to salute the ladies on the platform.

Celia called out, 'Flavius is shouting for the chestnut.'

'Ah,' said Marcellus. 'Are you ready, Flavius?'

He joined the judge's procession. The line heavily scored in the sand to mark the end of the course was carefully inspected and pronounced in order by the judge, who then mounted his podium.

Marcellus drew his short-sword and raised it in the air. A hush fell over the crowd lining the course. When an arm was waved beside the starting line, the sword fell.

As the horses leaped forward, a great roar broke out. Flavius wondered what he was supposed to do. Did he shout out chestnut or green, or just yell, or even mouth a yell? Possibly, if he eased behind the podium, Marcellus's invisible cloak of impartiality could be assumed to cover him as well.

Thirty or so horses thundered across the sand. Flavius could catch only a brief flash of the green scarf, but the field was beginning to thin. The green scarf was in the first dozen or so. He moved to get a better view.

A sudden gust of wind swept the beach. The ladies on the platform gave little cries of surprise and alarm as their leather canopy flapped above them. Flavius saw the rider on the chestnut horse put up a hand to keep the scarf from the wind, but it was too late to save it. The scarf was whisked away.

Behind it flowed a mass of tawny-coloured hair, with flecks like burnished copper moving in the sunlight.

Flavius stared, then clutched the rail of the podium. 'Marcellus, it can't be, can it? A woman there!'

Marcellus, intent on taking the victor's wreath from his orderly, glanced up. 'What? Oh, that's Elphin. She rides well, doesn't she? She won't win, though she should make a good third or fourth. A sound choice of yours, that chestnut.' He straightened up, assuming a smile of welcome for the winner.

Flavius was shaken with amazement. He couldn't even bring himself to join in the applause and cheering as Marcellus placed the wreath on the winner's head. He was staring with distaste at Elphin.

She had crossed the line in third place, and Flavius had seen her smile and bow her head as Marcellus acknowledged her. She had laid her cheek against the chestnut's neck and then slid to the ground. Now she was standing beside the winner, clapping her hands. She kissed her fingers and touched the oak leaves, laughing as she struggled to stop the wind blowing her hair across her face.

Marcellus had removed his helmet and his cloak, passing them to his orderly. He turned to Flavius with a wry look of relief.

'He wears that now for the rest of the week, King of the Fair, and then they burn it.'

Elphin was moving now among the other riders. Why were none of them offended by her presence? Flavius realised that Marcellus had been talking to him.

'Burn what?'

Marcellus raised his voice. 'The winner's oak wreath.'

'Oh. That's the custom, is it?'

A boy had emerged from the crowd and taken hold of the chestnut's reins. A grey wolfhound followed him and made its way towards Elphin. She turned round and made a motion with her hand. The dog came to her side and pressed its flank against her. Flavius thought that he had never before seen a woman with hair quite that colour.

He suddenly felt angry. Then he was bewildered by his anger, and that made it worse. He wanted to vent his feelings on something.

'What happens to that horse of hers?' he demanded. 'Does it get pushed on to a boat for the island now?'

Marcellus looked at him. 'No,' he said quietly. 'She has stables along the coast here. That boy is employed there. No-one understands horses better than Elphin. She breeds them on the island. That's where the family stables are. Her father taught her to ride as a child. He used to win these races when he was a young man. He was probably in the crowd watching her, though he would have told her he'd come over to the fair to look at cattle.'

Elphin was talking now to Celia, and then she hurried away towards the harbour, the dog beside her.

'Isn't Elphin staying?' Marcellus asked when Celia joined him.

'She wants to catch the tide with her father.' Celia turned with a smile to Flavius. 'Did you enjoy that? Third place!'

'Treat him gently, Celia,' said Marcellus, taking her arm. 'He is feeling the shock of seeing a woman on horseback. Then, when I unwisely mentioned that she breeds horses, he appeared to lose the power of speech.'

'How can a woman be allowed to join in a race like that? It's dangerous. For everyone.'

'Not many women do ride in races like that. But not many women ride like Elphin.' Celia put her head on one side. 'Flavius, would you have been happier if she'd come in last, a long way behind the men?'

She slipped her free arm under his, and they moved, all three together, in the direction of the fort.

Flavius said obstinately, 'What did your party of ladies on the platform think about it?'

'Most of them were from the settlement so they're Celtic, like Elphin. The ladies from the fort know her as a friend, as do I, and understand her. Flavius, I'm sure when your wife goes about in your own settlement, she must have met spirited women like Elphin.'

'No,' he said.

Celia misunderstood the reason for his denial. 'She probably doesn't mention it to you. You must surely have come across some yourself.'

Flavius said after a moment, 'There is one who runs a weaving shed alone. It was her husband's. But my wife hasn't met her.'

'But how ...'

'Celia,' interrupted Marcellus, 'you are forgetting that Flavius's lady has indifferent health. She is not as strong as an ox, like you.'

'Yes, Marcellus. I'm sorry, Flavius.' She paused. ' I have heard that in the London arena they have female gladiators. So, if they are in London, they are probably elsewhere. Of course, I haven't seen any myself.'

'Nor,' said Flavius grimly, 'have I.'

VII

A large dinner party was held at the fort that evening to mark the occasion of the fair. Marcellus entertained the dignitaries of the growing township in the larger dining-room, and Celia received their ladies in the room with the pretty painted walls.

It reminded Flavius uncomfortably of the more modest party which he and Lucilla had hosted soon after their arrival in Alauna, one which he had wrongly assumed would be the first of many similar functions. He remembered Lucilla's shattering outburst of temper that had brought an end to the possibility of future convivial dinners. It had left them eventually with an empty home and an empty marriage.

At Ravenglass, he was seeing something very different.

When the last cheerful and satisfied guests had departed, Marcellus and Flavius joined Celia. She was sitting in one chair with her feet on another; in her lap was a plate of honeyed delicacies.

'I'm starving,' she said. 'Everyone kept talking. It all went so well. I wish you'd invited that poor, sad man at Hardknott to come back with you, though.'

'He isn't poor,' said Marcellus, 'and you've no way of knowing if he's sad or not. I must admit, I did think about it. But when I knew I couldn't trust Flavius here to be civil to him, I decided against it.'

'Flavius uncivil? No.'

'I have to agree, Celia, that I was less than polite to him. Your husband quite rightly reproved me. Didn't I make every effort to make up for it, Marcellus?'

'He gave a florid display of insincerity, Celia,' said Marcellus. 'He'll be a great lawyer. But he couldn't even keep that up, could you, Flavius?'

'The man was such a fool. We were trying to help him with this Ambleside business, but he's a typical military man. Can't allow an original thought into his head unless he has a chit from the legate authorising it. Yes, a good military man – let someone else do the thinking for you.'

'There you are, Celia. What did I say?' Marcellus grinned at his wife.

'Be serious, you two. If this plan of yours for a new route is any good, why can't you take it straight to the legate?'

'He wouldn't understand it,' said Flavius. 'He's never been to Hardknott and wouldn't want the effort.'

'It would finish up in a furnace in York.' Marcellus gave a deep sigh. 'Well, Flavius, there's but one course open to us. One of us must make the sacrifice, and get into the Senate.'

'But no-one,' objected Flavius, 'among all those senators, is going to care about a delivery road on the north-west edge of the empire.'

'No,' agreed Marcellus, 'so they would pass a bill without thinking about it.'

Neither Flavius nor Marcellus had taken enough wine to be drunk, but they had drunk enough to be silly. They both giggled. 'You're the elder, so you must go,' said Flavius. 'You'll carry more dignity.'

'No, you're the younger. You must go. It might take a long time to get a hearing.'

They giggled again.

Celia looked up from her plate. 'Wouldn't it be easier if you just asked my grandfather?'

'What?' asked Flavius.

'Of course!' cried Marcellus.

'He doesn't spend much time in Rome now, but he would go if he were asked.' said Celia. 'He is still a great orator. If he were listed to speak on mud, Flavius, the Senate would be crowded to overflowing.'

'Mud?' murmured Flavius.

'Celia,' said Marcellus, 'wait. My love, it's late. Flavius doesn't know what you're talking about. You told him yesterday that you had a Celtic grandfather, but you didn't mention that he was a member of the Senate.'

'A Gallic Celt in the Senate?' said Flavius, looking at Celia. 'He must have been the first one, perhaps the only one?'

Celia nodded, smiling with pleasure.

'He was brought up in the old Celtic tradition with a vivid spoken language but no written form,' Marcellus explained, 'so a brilliant style of oratory was developed to make what had to be said memorable. When you were training as a lawyer, Flavius, you probably spent a few months in a Celtic university acquiring their skill?'

'Yes,' said Flavius. 'Bordeaux.'

'Oh,' cried Celia, 'that's where one of the emperors heard my grandfather speaking ...'

'Claudius,' murmured Marcellus.

'... and decided he was needed in the Senate.'

'Of course, in those days,' Marcellus went on, 'the sitting members of the Senate were adamant that they would never elect a Gallic farmer, even though he did have the necessary financial qualification; but Claudius persisted, and, by whatever methods emperors employ to get their own way, eventually got Celia's grandfather accepted. His oratory became famous.'

'So you are a senator's grand-daughter,' said Flavius to Celia, forgetting about Ambleside. 'As is my wife.'

'There,' said Celia, clapping her hands, 'I knew we would have a lot in common.'

'Is it possible,' enquired Flavius, 'that you might have met her at one of the empress's receptions?'

'Does she attend them often?'

Flavius hesitated. 'I know she speaks of one occasion when she was pleased to be presented to her majesty.'

'Then she must have a more amiable nature than mine. I avoid going whenever I can find an excuse. I loathe the empress, and I loathe her receptions. Thousands of women ...'

'Two hundred at most,' Marcellus corrected her.

'... crammed round that awful, huge pool of the emperor's, which he built because he saw one somewhere else...'

Marcellus glanced at Flavius. 'Egypt.'

'... and had to have one, only bigger.' Celia sighed.

'The truth is that many of the ladies of the old patrician families – and I know this wouldn't be true of your wife, Flavius – don't accept new senatorial families like my grandfather's as being of the same standing. The empress is the worst of them all. Perhaps she thinks my grandfather still wears woollen trousers under his toga.'

'This would never be Hadrian's view,' said Flavius angrily.

'No, but he doesn't go to the empress's receptions for senatorial ladies. So you can see why I am not anxious to attend them.' Celia laughed suddenly. 'Perhaps when your wife comes, she can persuade me to take a more kindly view of her majesty.'

Flavius was beginning to feel uneasy about the false image of Lucilla that he seemed unwittingly to have helped to create. Celia's next words were of little comfort to him.

'Your wife seems a quiet, reserved sort of lady. I think perhaps it's better that she didn't come with you this time, with all the noise and excitement going on. When you get back, please tell her how much all the ladies here wanted to meet her. And ask her, please, to come when things are quieter.'

Flavius wished he didn't have to say what he had to say next. 'Celia, I doubt if it will be possible for her to come later.'

'Not in the summer? Surely then?'

'No, Celia. She ...'

'Oh, you don't think we will look after her well enough? Flavius, I promise you, we will do only what will please her.'

'No, no, Celia, I don't mean that. Of course, I don't!' cried Flavius. 'She is going back to Rome.'

Celia's hands flew to her face. 'Oh, I didn't realise how ill she was. How upset she must be.'

'Will she be able to travel?' asked Marcellus.

'It is her choice.' said Flavius, able to speak the truth for once, but knowing it would be misunderstood.

He was. 'She is a brave lady,' Celia said solemnly. 'You must be so upset. I am so sorry, Flavius. I must find something to send her from all of us, so she knows we will be thinking of her on that long journey back.'

Celia jumped up, the plate on her lap flying to the ground.

'Oh, dear,' she said, glancing back at the mess on the floor as she disappeared out of the door.

Marcellus led Flavius in a more leisurely manner into the courtyard outside. The night was clear, with bright stars.

'It's a good night,' Marcellus said approvingly, and explained, 'for the people staying overnight. Can you hear that noise coming from the beach?'

'Yes, faintly.' Flavius nodded.

'They light bonfires. They cook on them. They play extraordinary musical instruments and break into wild local dances.'

'And Elphin no doubt rides among them in a chariot?'

Marcellus smiled. 'Elphin doesn't spend all her time on horseback.'

VIII

Flavius left Ravenglass with Quintus and his escort early next morning.

He carried with him a small yellow silk pouch which Celia had given him as he left the villa.

'For your wife,' she told him. 'It came back from one of my father-in-law's voyages to the East. It's a silk shawl, very light but warm. It would be a comfort round her throat if the wind was cold from the sea.' She added, 'Were you able to buy anything at the fair?'

'Yes,' Flavius told her, which was true and also untrue. For his mother he had found a little gold ornament in the shape of a bird, and for Alis a necklace of pretty polished stones to recompense her for the string of pink pearls which he had refused to let her keep when Lucilla had thrown them at her. But he knew that Celia had been thinking of his wife, and for her he had bought nothing. He was not prepared to take back any lovingly crafted piece of native work for which she would show only contempt.

He took Celia's hand and bowed over it as she wished him a safe journey. There were many things he would have liked to say to her, but he said only, 'Thank you.'

She nodded her head and smiled. 'Come back soon, Flavius. I shall rap on my block of slate and it will be ringing for you to come back to us.'

Marcellus had walked Flavius to his horse. 'The wretched stone apart, I should welcome you here again before too long. I find myself intrigued by our possible alternative route to Ambleside. I'd like to explore it further. Are you interested?'

'I am indeed.'

'Good. We'd need to explore the whole length of it. If we found it worthwhile, we might consider having a word with Celia's grandfather about it.'

Flavius was delighted with the idea. 'When do you suggest we meet again?'

'Probably in about a month. I'll arrange a boat and a local guide from here.'

As Flavius mounted his horse and they gripped hands, Marcellus said, 'When things are ready, I won't rap on Celia's stone. I'll send my adjutant.'

Riding north, Flavius turned his mind to the real Lucilla, and what needed to be done to get her back to Rome as safely and comfortably as possible.

Crossing the causeway to begin the slope towards the east gate of Alauna, they saw the guards turn out to receive them. That meant the inhabitants of the villa would have been warned of their approach. Celia would have imagined that at that moment Lucilla would be hurrying towards the gate, even if someone had to carry her; but for Flavius, dismounting to all the clashing noises of salutes, there was – predictably – no sign of his wife.

He went straight to his office in the headquarters building and surprised the chief clerk, who had expected him to go first to the villa. He was engaged in laying out on Flavius's desk all the items that needed his attention.

'Is there anything from London?'

The chief clerk was pleased to lay his hands at once on a scroll of very thick and expensive cream papyrus, which carried the mark of the governor's palace. Flavius tore off the ribbon and, as he read, smiled.

He rolled the scroll carefully and re-tied the ribbon. 'I'll deal with the routine stuff later. Is there anything else of any urgency?'

The chief clerk said, in a grave, almost reverential tone, 'Well, as a matter of fact, sir, there is. It's a matter of the greatest urgency.'

Flavius was struck by the change in the chief clerk's usual crisp, self-confident manner. 'What kind of–'

The door opened and Aelius stepped into the room, interrupting him. 'I was apprised of the prefect's arrival.'

'Yes, good, Aelius. I'm covered in dust and I've swallowed half the road.'

'That can soon be remedied, sir,' said Aelius, indicating the open door.

'But, sir,' protested the chief clerk, with an air of desperation, 'this really is a matter of importance.'

'I won't be long, chief clerk.' Flavius smiled kindly as he followed Aelius.

'What were you doing in there?' demanded Aelius, when the door was closed behind them. 'We were expecting you to come straight to the villa.'

'I wanted to see if this had arrived.' Flavius showed Aelius the scroll he was carrying.

'The lady wasn't pleased, and she was far from happy when you didn't return yesterday as promised, I can tell you.'

'I sent her a message.'

'But you didn't say why you were staying on.'

'You know as well as I do that she doesn't really care whether I am here or not.'

'True, but any excuse will do for making a scene. We certainly had one of those.'

'Why,' asked Aelius a little later when he was drying Flavius's hair in the bath-house, 'did you stay for another day?'

'Pressure from my senior officer. Will that do?'

'It seems as if it will have to,' said Aelius.

'You can tell Lucilla that I require her to eat dinner with me, I have a gift for her and a letter that concerns her. That should make the task of persuasion easy for you. Why not see her now and get the temper performance over?'

'No, I have apparently more important work to do.'

The chief clerk greeted him on his return to the headquarters building with what sounded to Flavius like a deep sigh of relief.

Flavius was amused. 'So what is this matter of such concern?'

The chief clerk was beginning to let a note of excitement creep into his voice. 'It's a leather container, closed with the emperor's seal, and delivered here with the emperor's courier. As you were absent, it was entrusted to my keeping with instructions that its arrival was to be kept secret and the seal was to be broken only by yourself.'

Flavius hoped he was displaying a suitable degree of solemnity. 'I can understand the weight of responsibility this has placed on you. Now where,' he added, trying not to sound hasty, 'is this leather-thing?'

'If you would be so good as to follow me, sir?'

They moved from Flavius's office into the adjoining room. From a small, discreetly placed locked box, a smaller box, also locked, was retrieved. A large key was extracted. While Flavius could have screamed with impatience, the chief clerk insisted on relocking the empty box, then the larger one, and then returning that to its designated place.

They proceeded out of the records office and into the narrow corridor that ran behind the shrine. The chief clerk unlocked the doors that opened on to the vault beneath. He stooped to pick up the lantern that was always kept beside the doors, already lit.

He led the way down the steps into the vault.

We could do with another lantern down here, thought Flavius, as the chief clerk made his way into the depths of the vault. He returned carrying a largish leather pouch, its shape distorted by whatever was packed inside it.

The chief clerk placed the lantern and the pouch on top of one of the coin chests. He offered Flavius a knife to cut the straps and break the seal.

Flavius slid his hand into the open pouch. He could feel two objects: one small and round, the other long and thin. Both were swathed in a thick wrapping of cloth.

Flavius drew out the smaller piece and carefully unfolded the wrapping. He found himself looking at a plump disc of gold, engraved with the emperor's profile. The chief clerk lifted the lantern and the gold glowed in the dimness of the vault.

'It's a military decoration, sir,' he said breathlessly. 'I didn't think he meant it, not like this.'

'Nor did I,' murmured Flavius.

They were both remembering the last minutes of the emperor's brief winter stay in Alauna. Usually on a visit to one of his forts, he'd reminded them, he would be speaking not to a handful of men but to a parade ground filled with the whole cohort, where he would publicly honour officers like the senior centurion.

'He said he wouldn't forget, but I thought he meant in his head, if you understand me, sir.'

'Yes, I do.'

'And there was something else he spoke of, sir. He said a senior centurion could only work well if he had a good commandant. What else do you think is inside that bag?'

'Take it out,' said Flavius.

The chief clerk removed the second object and laid it carefully on the chest. When Flavius nodded, he slowly unwound the layer upon layer of cloth.

As the last piece fell away, a ceremonial short-sword lay between them. The scabbard was of bronze, overlaid with patterns of gold surrounding a golden boar: the badge of the first cohort of Spaniards. The tusk was a piece of polished ivory and the eye a ruby. On the finely chased gold of the hilt, surmounting the emperor's cipher, was a large cabochon emerald.

The chief clerk gasped in wonder. He lifted it up and held it out to Flavius. 'This is for you, sir. The emperor has sent this for you.'

The sword lay across Flavius's outstretched palms. He stared at it. 'What a beautiful thing,' he said almost to himself.

Then he recollected himself. 'Put these back in the pouch and bring it up to my office. I want you to fetch the senior centurion at once, whatever he happens to be doing.'

'He usually takes a rest at this time of day, sir.'

'A good officer is never off duty,' said Flavius sententiously, and then wanted to laugh at himself. 'He must be in full dress uniform.'

'I'm afraid he'll grumble, sir.'

'If people hear him, all the better. They won't think anything unusual is happening.'

Flavius started to climb the steps out of the vault. 'Arrange to keep a second lantern by the door here, if you would, chief clerk.'

The gold disc was hidden from sight when the clerk conducted Lugo into Flavius's office. His expression conveyed his annoyance at being summoned in this way during an afternoon nap, and, what's more, in dress uniform.

'If this is about the posts, sir ...'

'It is not about the posts, senior centurion. I accept your suggestion. We don't want the men's skill at throwing a lance hampered by splintering wood. The work will be put in hand tomorrow.'

Lugo, prepared for an argument, looked bewildered, almost cheated. Flavius then placed himself in the centre of the room and invited the senior centurion to stand in front of him.

Lugo, after casting a questioning glance at the chief clerk, obeyed.

Flavius, now holding the gold disc, smiled. 'Kneel down, senior Centurion,' he said gently. The chief clerk nodded, and Lugo lowered himself grudgingly.

In measured tones, Flavius said, 'I represent Hadrian the emperor. On his behalf I award you this decoration to honour your service to this fort and the army of the empire.'

He leaned forward to slide the two hooks attached to the back of the disc into the senior centurion's chain-mail military tunic. 'You may now stand.'

But Lugo remained on his knees. Flavius and the chief clerk raised him between them.

When he seemed capable of standing on his own, Flavius gripped the officer's forearms. 'Congratulations,' he said warmly. Then he laughed. 'I think you will understand now why I wanted you to wear uniform. Those hooks might not have done you much good stuck into anything else.'

Lugo, pink-faced and no longer dry-eyed, agreed. 'I can't wear it, though, can I, this medal? It would betray the emperor's visit.'

'The emperor would wish you to wear it, so you must. We just have to tell a few small lies. If anyone asks about it, say that he gave it to you on his last visit to the north-west – which is true, isn't it? Then they'll want to know why you haven't worn it before. You could say you felt shy about it because no-one else at Alauna had ever had such an award. Then you can explain that when I learned about it, I insisted on your wearing it. And that also is true.'

Lugo seemed pleased, if a trifle confused. He brushed his eyes with the back of one hand. 'Yes, sir.'

I ought not to let the lawyer in me escape so often, thought Flavius. 'Now go,' he said to the senior centurion, 'and walk through the streets of the fort in your gold medal, and be proud of yourself. You deserve to be.'

As Lugo marched away, the chief clerk enquired if any record should be kept of the courier's mission.

'Did he carry any document?'

'No sir, he made it clear there were none.'

'Then nothing happened here,' said Flavius. 'By the way, what happened to the courier?'

'He left early this morning.'

'From here?'

'No, sir, from the post-house. The imperial couriers always stay there.'

A thought flickered across Flavius's mind, but he had no time to pursue it because it must now be time to return to the villa for his dinner engagement with his wife.

He tucked the emperor's leather pouch under his arm. Before he went into the dining-room, he slipped it into one of his bedroom chests. He made a bet with himself on how long it would be before Aelius found it and satisfied his curiosity about what was inside.

IX

His wife was already seated at the table when Flavius arrived, carrying Celia's gift and the governor's letter.

'I was not sure if you would be here, Lucilla,' he said agreeably. He picked up her hand and brushed his lips against it as he sat down beside her. 'I heard you were resting, and feared you might be unwell. I see you are not.'

She had not been pleased by his summons and that showed in her sullen expression; but, as he had supposed, curiosity and her acquisitive nature proved persuasive.

Her eyes lighted on the yellow silk. 'Is that for me? From the fair? From you?'

Flavius motioned the slaves not to serve food for the moment. He drew out from its pouch a yellow silk shawl embroidered with sprays of silver blossom.

Lucilla said, 'I don't like yellow.'

'I don't see how you can fail to love this. It isn't from the fair and it isn't from me. It is a gift from a lady whom I'm sure you would like because you have so much in common. Like you, she was born and brought up in Rome. Like you, she is the grand-daughter of a senator. She asked me if she might have met you at one of the empress's receptions.'

Lucilla had turned round in her chair and was staring intently at Flavius. She was in the grip of near-ecstatic delight.

'This lady,' she said breathlessly, 'is of senatorial rank like me, and she is staying at the fort in Ravenglass?'

'Not staying, Lucilla. She lives there. She is the wife of the commandant. She was anxious to meet you. Indeed, she wrote you a letter, telling you that, if you remember?'

Lucilla gave a long, wailing cry. 'Why didn't you talk to me about her? Why?' She banged her clenched fists on the table.

'How could I?' said Flavius, grasping her hands to keep them still. 'I knew nothing about her. I thought from her letter that she sounded kind and thoughtful, I said so at the time, but that didn't interest you much. You didn't want the pearls she sent you. You were the one who knew all about her. She was a Gallic ... what did you call her? And where did that come from incidentally? Kitchen gossip?'

Lucilla began to cry.

'The lady does, in fact, have some Celtic blood, of which she is justly proud, as am I of what little I have. Fortunately, she has no idea about the way you behaved, and believes the lie about your fragile health.'

Flavius paused. 'She even asked me to persuade you to visit her in warmer weather, when you might feel stronger.'

Lucilla's tears stopped. 'Yes, yes, I could go ...'

'No, you can't. I explained that you were going back to Rome. That's why she chose the shawl for you. It is very light, she said, but warm, suitable for a sea crossing.'

The shawl lay discarded on the table beside Flavius. He picked it up again. 'Look how light it is. It's a beautiful thing; rare, too. It comes from the East. You won't see many like it even in your favourite Roman shops. Do you really dislike it?'

Lucilla stretched out her hands to take it. She stroked it gently and smiled – not with gratitude for Celia's generosity, thought Flavius, but for the satisfaction of owning something that other women in her circle would envy.

'I don't have to go home,' she said, 'not just yet.'

Flavius unrolled the governor's letter. 'You can't change your mind now. The governor has granted you the privilege of travelling to York on military roads. He has agreed to this because he has been acquainted with the delicacy of your health. It would be most unwise suddenly to deny it now.'

'Oh,' said Lucilla, not displeased at the prospect of special treatment.

'There is a condition, as you will see, if you trouble to read the letter for yourself.'

Lucilla shook her head. 'What condition?'

'You must use a light two-seater carriage – you and one of the girls.'

'I can't travel with only one slave. I won't!'

'That's the way you arrived here.'

'But you were with me too,' said Lucilla. 'Why can't I have my boxes and all my maids?'

'Because you would need an ox-wagon and the weight would damage the surface of a military road, which has to be kept in good condition. If you would rather travel on one of the lower roads in a wagon, of course you may. We might even find you a larger carriage, but it would still be slow and not very comfortable.'

Lucilla sulkily considered this, and grudgingly opted for the military road.

'It's only as far as York. The other staff that you want and all the luggage will be waiting for you there, and then you won't be separated until you get to Stresa.'

Lucilla began to sniff again.

'You won't be alone, if that's what you are worrying about. I will ride as far as Papcastle with you, and Quintus will stay with you for the rest of the journey to York. There will also be an escort of four mounted men. My father's agent will look after you in York and see you safely onto the ship. You met him with his family when we came over, do you remember? You will be comfortable with them.'

Lucilla appeared to doubt this.

Flavius sighed and pressed on. 'One of his men will stay on the ship with you until my father meets you in Bordeaux. Then we can leave things to him.'

'Your father will take me to Stresa?'

'Yes,' said Flavius, envying her.

'But I don't want to go to Stresa. I would rather live in Rome with my own father until you come back.'

The slaves were laying food in front of them. Flavius took a few mouthfuls before he braced himself to answer her.

'When I married you, Lucilla, your father, by law, relinquished his responsibility for your welfare to me. If I am unable to act for you, then liability for your protection falls on the senior member of my family – in this case, my father.

'I am happy for you to see your own father as much as you wish, but if you deliberately choose to live under his roof, I shall accept that as a declaration of divorce. As you know, it will then need only a few words of assent between us to conclude matters.'

There was for a moment a flash of defiance in Lucilla's eyes, but then she glanced down at the Paulus bracelets and rings she was wearing, and lowered her eyelids.

They both ate carefully and slowly, without speaking. Plates were changed, fresh dishes placed on the table, glasses refilled.

Then Flavius, with an effort to dispel the thing that now lay between them, said brightly, 'Now, my dear, have you decided yet who your carriage companion will be?'

Lucilla responded with a small laugh. 'Of course. Alis.'

'Have you spoken to her about it?'

Lucilla dismissed this. 'I'll tell her in good time.'

Flavius said anxiously, 'Lucilla, she is no longer a slave, to be told what to do. She is a free woman, and a married one too. How often do you have to be reminded of that?'

Lucilla shrugged her shoulders.

'I think,' said Flavius, as they left the dining-room, 'that we ought to get this business with Alis settled.'

His wife shrugged her shoulders again.

'And it has to be Alis together with Aelius, I think.'

They sat in Lucilla's room, and sent for them. Alis seemed nervous, Aelius wary. Flavius tried to put them at their ease but it was not easy with Lucilla sitting beside him, flicking one of her fans to and fro.

'Aelius,' said Flavius, 'you are aware, I'm sure, that my wife will shortly be returning to Rome.'

'We are indeed,' Aelius answered, bowing his head in Lucilla's direction. He was at his most deferential, and that, Flavius knew, meant that there was something up his sleeve.

'My wife wishes to select a travelling companion, and Alis would be her first choice. She realises that Alis's decision must be subject to your agreement.'

Aelius, with great courtesy, declared that he was unable to give his wife permission to leave Alauna. 'Madam will understand,' he said, addressing Flavius, 'how much I depend on Alis for her help in managing the prefect's household. That apart, however, I could not allow her to undertake a journey of any length at this time—' he glanced at Alis, who was looking at the ground, her cheeks flushing ' —because she is pregnant.'

Lucilla threw down her fan, as if this had been contrived to cause her the greatest inconvenience. Flavius motioned Aelius to take his wife away.

'Well, my dear, now you know where you stand with Alis, might I suggest you start training a new maid as quickly as possible?'

Lucilla turned her back on him.

Flavius followed Aelius and Alis to their rooms on the upper floor to express his joy for them. He produced the necklace he had bought for Alis at the Ravenglass fair. 'May I have your agreement to offer this to your wife? I've chosen a rather good moment, haven't I?'

'You have,' said Aelius. 'And what's that thing downstairs in your chest? Did you get that at the fair?'

Aelius followed Flavius down the stairs when he left. 'Why has Hadrian sent that useless object to you? It's the sort of thing he might have given to that lad Antinous, but not to you.'

'Perhaps it's a bribe,' said Flavius, 'and in return he's going to ask me again to part with you.'

'Hmm. You couldn't even cut a bunch of grapes with it.'

'He was very drunk and very upset. Perhaps he thought I was of more help to him than I actually was. I don't know.'

'Don't trust him, Flavius. So what are we going to do with it?'

'Keep it in the chest, and every so often we'll lift the lid and admire it. By the way, you've just won me a bet I was having with myself.'

'There are times, Flavius, when I know you are not drunk, but you talk as if you were.'

'It's the Celtic blood, so I've recently learned – every bit as wayward as the Greek.'

The next few days in Alauna were tempestuous. Lucilla refused to speak to Alis, but had no difficulty in upsetting several of the other girls in the household. At one moment she was complaining bitterly about the time she was having to wait while her journey was being arranged, and the next in tears because she was going to live with her mother-in-law. She wanted to take the green-leaf dinner service with her; when Flavius refused, she told him she never wanted to see it again, so he might as well leave it behind in Alauna.

Gradually, however, as Flavius's arrangements fell into place, as the disputes about which members of the staff should travel with Lucilla were settled and the lists of items to be packed finally completed, life in the villa became more tranquil.

A letter from Crispus, Flavius's father, even produced a kind of harmony. He reminded Flavius of the pavilion he had built for him in the gardens at Stresa when he had reached a suitably responsible age. This, he suggested, might be refurbished as a suite of apartments for Lucilla. She started clapping her hands with glee, and Flavius felt grateful to be released from the guilt he was hiding at inflicting Lucilla on his parents' ordered and comfortable life.

Flavius and Lucilla began to behave with each other rather in the manner of cordial acquaintances of long standing. When they made their last farewells at Papcastle, he kissed her politely on both cheeks, and she responded in the same way.

As her carriage drew away, she put out a hand from beneath the edge of the hood and waved.

Part Four

ELPHIN

I

Flavius arrived at the military cemetery in Ravenglass as the burial service was coming to an end.

The newly dug grave lay in a corner beside the wall facing the sea. The mourners were beginning to move away from the graveside in twos and threes. Some were in uniform. The others were dressed Roman-style in dark clothing, some of the men without belts, and a few of the women with unbound hair, as signs of respect.

Marcellus, with a black cloak hanging from his shoulders, stood at the foot of the grave. Flavius approached him slowly. At the sound of footsteps close to him, Marcellus turned his head.

'Flavius?' he murmured, and thrust out a hand.

'Forgive me. I'm late.'

'How could you even be here?' Marcellus's face was drawn and pale, but there was a brief smile for Flavius. 'I didn't think my message could have reached you.'

'No, it hadn't, but I had your earlier one, when you sent your adjutant to tell us Celia was ill. You asked for our doctor's advice, but when I heard what he said ...' Flavius broke off hurriedly. 'I decided to come then. The weather was terrible. I was already on my horse when they told me there were trees blocking the road to Papcastle. I tried to get a boat, but no-one was leaving the harbour. So I took the coast road.'

'Were you *mad*?'

Flavius pulled a wry face. 'I hadn't ridden it before. It might have been better without the wind. So, I was late.'

'You're not the only one held up by the storms. There were no boats to and from the island this morning.'

Flavius, with the grave at his feet, was suddenly overwhelmed.

'I can't believe she's dead!'

'Nor can I,' said Marcellus quietly.

'Oh, I'm sorry. How could I say something like that?'

'At times like this,' said Marcellus, patting him on the shoulder, 'we all find ourselves saying things we wish we hadn't. We can't all stop speaking.'

'Do you mean that?' said Flavius. 'Then let me say now what I longed to say to you, but because I was afraid that ...' He took a deep breath. 'I am over thirty years old. During that time, I spent only a few hours with Celia and with you, yet I knew you were the sort *of* people I had wanted to meet all my life. Celia had the great gift of kindness, she was generous, she had a bright spirit and I'll swear she lifted the hearts of anyone who was privileged enough to know her. I envy you the years you shared with her.'

They were walking towards the cemetery gates. Ahead of them the trail of mourners slowly moved along the quarter-of-a-mile path that led to the fort and the funeral breakfast.

'I'm sorry,' said Flavius, staring at his boots. 'I've delayed you. Your guests will be wanting you.'

'Yes. But first stand with me on the verge here. She loved looking at the sea, and watching the boats going in and out of the harbour.' Marcellus watched the waves for a moment. 'They're not so fierce as they were when you were struggling along that coast road. The wind is dropping.' He paused. 'Flavius, when you spoke to your doctor, he told you there was no time, didn't he?'

'Do you want to talk about this now?'

Marcellus nodded.

'He recognised the sickness when your adjutant was trying to describe it. If he had had the slightest hope of helping Celia, he would have come to her. But he told me that not only would it be too late to save her, but too late to find her – still living.' Flavius looked anxiously at Marcellus.

'Yes, yes, it was so quick ... so quick, Flavius. She fell in the courtyard. I thought she had just twisted her ankle. I picked her up and she laughed about always being clumsy. But then we realised that it wasn't her ankle. Her whole body seemed to be drained of strength. I laid her on her bed. She could hardly speak because her breathing was so uneven. She became very hot, feverish. She asked for Elphin. I sent a boat and she came right away.'

Marcellus pulled the black cloak more closely round his neck as if was feeling the cold. 'But when Elphin spoke to her, Celia didn't recognise her. That was when I sent my adjutant to you.'

He was still gazing at the sea, when he suddenly pointed towards the harbour. 'Look, Flavius, the first boat just coming into land.' He peered at it. 'I'm sure it's Elphin.'

Flavius saw a grey dog leaping on to the wharf. 'Yes,' he said, without enthusiasm.

Marcellus turned towards him. 'She was very good with Celia.'

'Well, they were friends, weren't they?'

'Elphin stayed with her. She got the medical orderlies here to help her keep Celia cool and prop her up. By then her breathing was painful to hear. She was crying out – once, Elphin said, for her mother, she thought, and then for our lost boys. Elphin tried to talk to her as if she was her mother and had the boys with her. It comforted Celia, but only briefly. She clung on to me, and, for that, Flavius, I was grateful. Then she fell quiet. Elphin helped to ease her into my arms and left us alone. I don't know when exactly she left me.'

They were both silent, Marcellus deep in his own thoughts, Flavius respecting the moment. The mourners at the head of the column were about to enter the gate-house when there was a flurry of movement that attracted Flavius's attention. They were giving way to a large, grey dog, intent on moving in the opposite direction.

It was followed by Elphin.

Flavius was not sure he would have recognised her as the woman who had raced across the beach, if he had not caught a glimpse of the rare glowing colour of her hair.

She had shocked him on that February morning. She shocked him even more as she threaded her way among the drably robed company.

Her hair was no longer flying about her face, but braided and coiled at the back of her head in a Roman style. With a circle of gold pins holding it in place, however, it was more like the style a Roman woman would have worn for a reception, not a funeral.

She wore a long green coat with thick fur at the neck and wrists; beneath it, visible as she moved, was red silk, embroidered with gold. There was more gold in a large round brooch fastened on one shoulder.

Flavius was startled when Marcellus stepped forward to greet her, apparently unconcerned by her appearance. She spoke to him in what Flavius assumed was her native dialect. Marcellus replied in the same tongue. As she came closer, Flavius could see the fine workmanship of the beautiful brooch she was wearing: two strands of gold, edged with silver, winding in and out of each other in an endless circle. Some sort of barbaric Celtic charm, he supposed with distaste.

They seemed now to be talking about her journey.

Marcellus, of course, decided Flavius, had to be civil to her because she had nursed his wife, nursed her with compassion. He could hear Elphin's voice. Having no understanding of the words she was using, he could only listen to the sound of it. It was a soft voice, clear and low – a magical voice.

He glanced at her vivid coat. He was very tired, bewildered by the thoughts that were turning and twisting in his mind like the gold strands of her brooch. Her voice was magical, and she was shining and strange and beautiful like her brooch. It was strong and brave of her to have crossed the water that morning, but that, he decided in his confusion, was disruptive and alien to the kind of world he was familiar with.

Marcellus was putting out a hand to draw him into the conversation. In Latin, he said, 'Elphin, this is the prefect from Alauna. He—'

She interrupted him. 'Yes, this is Flavius. Celia spoke of him.'

Caught by surprise, he bowed his head. 'My lady,' he said stiffly.

'He came by the coastal road,' said Marcellus.

Elphin looked at Flavius and nodded her head. 'Both of us have had a long and difficult journey, but for Marcellus this little walk from the fort has been worse.'

'My lady, yes.'

'Elphin. I am Elphin.'

'Elphin.' Flavius found it difficult to look at her.

'I think I displease you, Flavius. You believe I insult Celia's memory, and hurt Marcellus.'

Flavius realised then, stupidly, that she had been speaking to him in his own language.

'You mourn your dead with sombre garments. We prefer to honour them by wearing the most precious things we possess. Your people and mine, we choose to express ourselves in different ways, but it is the same grief, the same loss.' Elphin was speaking gravely, but not unkindly.

She looked at his companion. 'I think Marcellus understands that.'

He nodded. 'Do you wish to see her grave?'

'Let me mourn in my own way first,' said Elphin, 'and then I will respect yours.'

She pointed across the grass towards a line of trees. 'The little mill stream there – she loved that place. Will you walk with me, Marcellus?'

He glanced at Flavius. 'Celia used to like looking for her pink pearls along that bank. That's where she'd been that day you met her and she was talking about moving stones to find them.'

'Yes, I remember. She wanted them for the fair.'

Elphin turned to look again at Flavius, this time with a flash of surprise. 'Oh, you knew about that? Then perhaps, sir, you will come too?'

'If Marcellus wishes it.'

They moved together to the spot that Elphin indicated. The water was shallow and clear there, foaming over the clusters of small rocks.

Flavius was reminded of the necklace of pearls that Celia had sent to an unresponsive Lucilla; as he had read out Celia's letter, he had imagined – rather to his own embarrassment – the pearls lying in just such a stream. Now, Marcellus's Celia would never again step into that water, never walk her damp boots across the villa floor. Wasn't the world cruel enough without taking her away?

He bent down to stroke the dog to hide a dampness in his own eyes. Elphin was kneeling on the verge, tears on her own cheeks.

She slowly unfastened her brooch, fumbling a little as if she couldn't see what she was doing.

Then it was lying in her cupped hands. She leaned over the water, opened her hands and let the brooch fall into the stream.

'My lady, no!' Flavius stretched out a hand to try to reach it.

Marcellus caught his arm. 'Leave it. It is their way.'

Flavius could see a glint of pale gold as the brooch sank through the water.

Marcellus lifted Elphin to her feet. He kissed the palms that had held the brooch.

Then Elphin faced Flavius. 'You burn flesh to placate your gods, whom you believe to live in the sky above you. We think the god of our island, Manannàn, dwells in the regions beneath the waters, and we give to him our most treasured possessions to thank him for the love he gives our lost ones.'

'He will take Celia's spirit back under the water with him, and the water will change into a path of flowers. He will lead her along the path to a summer garden where she will wait at peace for her beloved ones to come to her. Perhaps her dead children are already playing again with her there.'

'You don't believe that,' said Flavius.

'I would like to believe it,' said Elphin. 'Is it any stranger than your beliefs? You make sacrifices to a vast company of gods and, if they are not satisfied with your offerings, they destroy you with malice or spite. Do they ever show any love to you? What comfort will they give Marcellus?'

When Flavius was silent, she added in a quieter voice, 'Perhaps we all look for our own gods. Perhaps the god we find says something about ourselves.' She reached for Marcellus's arm. 'I will go to visit her grave now.'

Flavius allowed himself to be delivered into the hands of Marcellus's body-servant, to suffer whatever remedy could be applied to his wind-tossed appearance.

'The buffeting I got on the coast road was nothing compared to the one I got from Elphin this morning,' he grumbled to Marcellus. 'Can you sort that out?'

'No, you will,' said Marcellus.

Half-an-hour later, when he was escorted to the room where the male members of the mourning party were assembled, Flavius found the solemnity of the occasion already wearing thin as food and wine were being circulated. He sipped some wine, exchanged trivial remarks with people he didn't know, even heard inane jokes. He noticed Celia's block of ringing slate lying in a corner. It wasn't the place for him.

He slipped out of the room into the garden courtyard outside.

He sat down on a bench sheltered by flowering shrubs. It was quiet there, the noise from the room he had just left muted by closed doors.

He shut his eyes, as if that might relieve him of his disquieted thoughts. He felt that he was wandering in a land that was unfamiliar to him, without direction, bruised – bruised by what, by her contempt? But why should the opinion of a local woman like Elphin, whom he was never likely to see again, matter to him? In his imagination he saw her again, with the folds of her beautiful coat around her as she knelt down on the ground, tawny head bent over the water, tears on her cheeks.

Had it been contempt? Wasn't she defending, bravely defending, something that was precious to her, and hadn't he provoked her words by his own ungracious remarks? Why did he do that? How could he have done it?

He was distracted by a brief burst of sound from the opposite side of the courtyard. From the shrillness of some of the voices, it was coming from a room assigned to the ladies. Then he heard a door being quietly closed, shutting out the voices again. Someone else, like him, had apparently made an escape.

Then he saw that the green coat was no longer in his mind's eye, but a few yards away from him.

He turned his head away, so that if she did notice him she need not catch his eye and feel obliged to address him; but when he glanced up, Elphin was not disappearing from the courtyard. She was walking towards him, with the grey dog at her side.

She stood in front of him and motioned the dog to sit.

'Flavius,' she said, 'you must forgive me if I am disturbing you.'

How could you not be disturbing me? he found himself wanting to say. Instead he rose to his feet, and murmured, 'My lady? Will you sit?'

'Thank you, no. A boat will be waiting for me. I'm Elphin, do you remember? I wanted to find you before I left. I need to apologise to you.'

'To me? How can that be so?'

'It is. You Romans always speak most generously of our tribal gods. I should have shown the same respect for yours. I am ashamed.'

Flavius gazed at her. Then he began to smile slowly. 'What you said was true. There's no need to apologise for the truth.'

She shook her head. 'There is if it offended you.'

Flavius said gently, 'The only offensive behaviour in need of forgiveness was mine.'

She smiled back, quickly, happily. 'Then all is well between us?'

When he nodded she laughed with pleasure, and her pleasure became his. 'Now I can find Marcellus and tell him I must leave,' Elphin said.

'Shall I fetch him for you?'

Flavius went back into the room he had just left, caught hold of a slave and sent him to warn the tribune that the lady Elphin was waiting to go.

Marcellus appeared, carrying a cloak which looked as if it had been snatched up hurriedly on the way. He swung it over his shoulders.

'Is it the boat, Elphin?' he asked. 'I'll walk with you to the harbour. I'm ready.'

'No, no,' she cried, 'there's no need. 'I don't want you to leave your guests. The dog is protection enough for me.'

'Nonsense, how long will it take? I doubt if they'll even notice I've gone.'

'Why,' suggested Flavius, 'don't I walk to the boat with Elphin – if she would allow it?'

Marcellus looked at him and then at Elphin.

'That would be very kind,' she said primly. 'I would prefer not to take you away from the funeral party, Marcellus.'

She unwrapped his cloak and dropped it on the bench beside them. With a wry smile, Marcellus embraced her.

'Thank you. And thanks to you, Flavius.'

As they left the fort, Elphin said, 'Would you mind if we walked along the beach?'

The early storms had died away, and there was a streak of thin blue behind the clouds.

'No,' said Flavius, 'but it's the longer way, and you're in a hurry.'

'Not that much of a hurry. I didn't want to stay in there any longer. I couldn't bear the way they were talking.'

Flavius grinned. 'That's the very reason I was sitting alone in the courtyard.'

'Oh!' cried Elphin, pleased. 'Then, you don't want to hurry back either. We'll go on the beach.'

They had reached the low stone wall that formed a boundary between an ancient track leading into the settlement and the long stretch of beach. Flavius stepped on to the wall and jumped down on to the sand. Elphin was gathering up her skirts to follow him but, before she could jump, Flavius had raised his hands and lifted her off the wall to stand on the sand beside him.

They stood for a moment, looking at each other, before Flavius released her.

She said breathlessly, 'I don't think Celia would mind us coming here today. She liked to walk by the water's edge.'

'Then let's do the same, shall we?' Flavius smiled at her.

They walked slowly towards the foaming ripples. The dog, at a word from Elphin, ran in and out of the water. She picked up a piece of driftwood and threw it into the shallow waves for the excited animal. 'You hardly knew Celia.'

'I spent only a few days with her last February, but I shall never forget them.'

'She told me how intrigued you were by the block of ringing rock I gave her.'

'She spoke to you about me? Why should she do that?'

'Because I asked her who you were.'

'But, Elphin, we have never met before today.'

'Not to speak, no. You were at the race, though. I saw you here.'

'You *saw* me? There were crowds of people.'

'You were talking to Marcellus, when he was standing with that wreath in his hands. You looked very serious, even angry, so I thought it best to stay out of your way.'

I was angry, thought Flavius, because I saw a woman racing on a horse, and I couldn't understand how it could be allowed. 'Elphin ...' he began.

'Flavius, I thought we were the only two people on the beach, but look at those two boys along there. Flavius, look!'

He saw two boys skimming stones across the water.

'They're quite good. Can you do that?'

'I don't recall that stone-skimming was a required accomplishment for army commandants.'

Elphin turned her head to smile at him. 'Shall I teach you?'

'It's bound to be useful some day.'

'Be serious, Flavius. First, you have to find the right kind of stones – smooth, flattened and about this size.' She bent down to pick up a stone at the edge of the water, and held it up between finger and thumb.

Elphin sighed. 'It wasn't just pearls Celia liked collecting. It was pretty stones as well. You can see all sorts of colours when the stones are wet.'

Flavius knelt down and searched. Then he stood up and showed Elphin the stones lying in his palm.

'Yes,' she said, 'they should do well enough. Put them down there.' She pointed to the pile she had already collected.

'Now you hold it like this.' She positioned a stone and motioned him to copy her.

Flavius put a stone between his fingers.

'No, like this.' She put her hand on his and moved his fingers.

'Now watch. You throw like this.'

The first stone went too high and fell with a single plop. The second was too low to skim properly. The third one satisfied her. 'There now, that's what you need to do. It often takes two or three throws to get the movement right.'

She threw a fourth stone which flew farther than the third. 'There,' she said happily. 'Now you try. It may take a while to find your style, but it will come in the end.'

'You pick a stone for me.'

Elphin bent down again to choose one and placed it in his outstretched hand.

Flavius stepped close to the water, balanced the stone, drew back his arm and threw. With a perfect skimming movement, it went further than Elphin's best throw, further than anything the boys had been able to do. They turned to stare at him in admiration.

Elphin looked at him furiously. 'You've done that before!'

Flavius groaned. 'It was meant to go wrong.'

'Well, explain.'

'Elphin,' said Flavius humbly, 'I was born beside a lake. I've been skimming stones since I was a child. One of our slaves was champion skimmer for our end of the lake. He taught me.'

'You lied to me.'

'No, I didn't actually lie to you but – ' he groaned again ' – yes, I did mean to mislead you.'

'Why,' she said, almost tearfully, 'should you want to make me feel so foolish?'

Flavius took a deep breath. 'Why, Elphin? Because if I had been honest with you, we should have gone on walking along the beach. You would have been in your boat by now, perhaps even leaving the harbour. I have made you angry, but I have had a few more minutes with you. I don't ask you to forgive me, because, if I had the chance, I would do the same thing again.'

Elphin looked down at the remains of their pile of stones. She pushed them about with her toe. 'Not angry,' she murmured, and Flavius saw she was smiling. 'I was the one, if you remember, who suggested we walk the long way to the harbour.'

Flavius gazed at her thoughtfully. 'That stone you gave Celia?'

'Oh, there's nothing special about it. The mountains round here are full of them.'

'When Celia showed me how to make the ringing sound, she told me about ...'

Elphin interrupted again. 'Oh, the old legend. If a lover appeared every time one of those stones was rapped, the world would be overrun with them! It's the sort of nonsense fishermen's wives round here like to believe. If the boats are late back, they rap their stones to bring their men home. Sometimes they come, sometimes they don't.'

Flavius said, 'Elphin, listen to me. Don't you think that perhaps, in very, very rare cases, the legend might work, if deep inside you pray it will? I touched Celia's stone, and two days later you were here on this beach. I didn't recognise you, except perhaps in that very deep place inside me.' He held up a hand to stop her interrupting again. 'All nonsense, of course. Yet on that morning, I'd intended to be on my way back to Alauna. I stayed for the race only because Celia bullied me.'

Elphin said softly, 'That is very strange. I had not intended to be there either. One of my stable lads was going to ride the chestnut, but he damaged a foot just before the race started. I was anxious to know how the chestnut would go in a noisy, excitable atmosphere, so I had to take him myself.'

'Did you know that I had chosen to shout for your chestnut? Not that I wanted to shout at all, but Celia was bullying again. Perhaps after all I might have recognised you that morning if you hadn't disguised yourself in that green scarf.'

'I hadn't disguised myself,' Elphin protested, laughing. 'There was a wind, and I tied my hair back to keep it from blowing in my eyes. You're not suggesting, are you, that we were both under the power of Celia's ringing stone?'

'That would be rubbish,' said Flavius.

'Yes, rubbish,' agreed Elphin.

Flavius took her hand in his. 'But if it were true, he whispered, 'I should never cease to be thankful to it.' He bent his head and kissed her.

After a while, Elphin with her arms still tightly round Flavius under his cloak, sighed and stirred. 'The boat?' said Flavius.

She nodded.

As they slowly released each other, Elphin glanced towards the far end of the beach where Marcellus had occupied the judge's podium for the race. She pointed. 'Yes, that's where you were standing when

I rode across the line. Though it was crowded, I saw you, and then I saw no-one in that mass of people but you. When you seemed so preoccupied, I ran to Celia to find out who you were. She told me you would be leaving next day. I wanted to go back and find you, but by then you and Marcellus had gone. I thought I would never see you again, but today I was given a second chance.' She smiled happily at him.

'Perhaps it was as well you didn't speak to me at the end of the race,' said Flavius, playing with a loose strand of her hair. 'I thought you were brazen and alarming, and in my state of shock I might have told you so. I dread to think what your response might have been.'

'But you did notice me?'

'Oh, yes, I noticed you.' He picked her up and swung her round. 'Do something for me before we go. Choose another stone for me.'

'Have you no stones on the beach at Alauna?'

'Yes, but Alauna is perched on a cliff, and my arms aren't long enough to reach.'

'Hmm. Just one?'

'The prettiest one.'

Elphin searched through the handful of stones they had left on the sand. She picked out one of them, then held it out to catch the tip of a wave as it left a bubble of foam where she was kneeling. 'This one,' she said. 'It was nothing to look at when it was dry; but now that it's wet, you can see strips of silver and white and dark honey colour.'

Flavius took it from her. 'White and silver like the sea-foam, and dark honey like your hair. Yes, that will do me very well.' The stone was drying in the palm of his hand as he spoke.

'Now it looks like another plain grey pebble, but you and I know its secret.' He opened the leather pouch he wore attached to his belt and gave the stone to Elphin to slip inside it.

He held out his hand and she clasped it in hers. They strolled along the beach, hand-in-hand, not caring if anyone was watching them.

Too soon, they were leaving the beach and were surrounded by the noise and movement of the harbour. The secure and private world they had created around themselves on the beach drifted away. When they saw the men readying the boat for departure, they knew they had only a few more minutes left together.

Elphin, in a moment of panic, seized Flavius's arm in both hands. 'Flavius, I—'

'I know, my love, I know.'

'When are you going back?'

'In an hour or two.'

Elphin gave a little cry.

'I must. But I'll come back. We'll find ways of being together. Yes?'

She nodded her head and tried to smile.

He helped her on to the boat. As it left the wharf, he walked and then ran beside it for as long as he could. The stretch of water between them grew wider. Elphin leaned over the side of the boat and threw out her hand towards him.

Flavius stood watching the boat until it slipped into the off-shore mist.

II

One morning, not long after the commandant's return to Alauna, his villa was in a state of considerable upheaval. It was one of the very, very rare occasions when Flavius could be heard raising his voice to one of his slaves.

Aelius, assuming a relaxed and amiable manner designed to dispel anxieties in the kitchen, overheard the sound of his own name as he passed Flavius's room.

'I don't care what Aelius told you to do,' Flavius was shouting, 'I want it back. Find it!'

Aelius wheeled back on his heel and, after a perfunctory tap, for appearance's sake, opened Flavius's door. 'Is there something I can do for the prefect?' he enquired pleasantly.

He motioned the slave out of the door and closed it behind him. 'What's the matter with you, Flavius? I wouldn't be surprised if they could hear you from one end of the settlement to the other.'

'Have you taken my pouch?'

'Which one? You must have half-a-dozen.'

'Which one?' Flavius struck his fist on a bedpost. 'You know which one – the one I was using yesterday.'

'Well, didn't you notice how mis-shapen it was? It was a disgrace. I told the boy to have a look at it. Do you know what the trouble was? There was a pebble in it.'

'Yes, I know there was a pebble in it,' cried Flavius.

'What was a pebble doing in your coin-pouch? How did it get there? If you knew it was there, why didn't you throw it out, instead of leaving someone else to do it?'

'Aelius, be quiet! It was in my pouch because I put it there, and I didn't throw it out because I wanted to keep it there. Where is it now?'

'How should I know? I suppose the boy threw it away.'

'Where? In the furnace?' Flavius looked distraught.

'This household is not in the habit of throwing stones in furnaces.' Aelius was beginning to lose his own temper.

'Then where?'

Aelius shrugged his shoulders. 'It could be in the yard. More likely it's in one of the bundles of rubbish we dump on the shore, if they haven't already gone.'

'They'd better not have, Aelius. I want it found.'

He looked at Flavius. 'A pebble? Do you think your brain's turned? It can happen, you know, even to men of your age. If pebbles are going to be your thing, then I can go and fill a bucket for you.'

'Not a bucketful but one, Aelius. Now. I'll be waiting.'

And he was waiting, still unhappy and on edge, when Aelius returned over an hour later, carrying a dish with a handful of stones lying in the bottom.

Aelius thrust the dish at him. 'We haven't looked on the roof yet. That takes longer.' He relented slightly. 'Most of these came out of the rubbish. The boy remembers dropping a stone in one of the tubs.'

'Thank you,' mumbled Flavius half-heartedly, peering into the dish. 'I need a bowl of water.'

'What do you want water for?' said Aelius in exasperation.

'Do I have to get it myself?'

When the water arrived, Flavius tipped the stones into the bowl and shook them gently. Aelius watched him curiously.

Suddenly, Flavius gave a shout of joy. He held a wet pebble in his fingers. He leaped up, and the bowl scattered water and more wet stones across the floor. Aelius rolled his eyes heavenwards in despair as Flavius seized him.

'That's wonderful, Aelius, wonderful!'

Aelius grunted and pushed him away.

'You would have thought,' he said furiously to Alis, as he joined her upstairs to eat their noonday meal together, 'that he'd lost that gold sword of his, and that's what I'd found.'

'Could it have been something valuable, like a piece of amber?'

'It was a pebble, Alis, a pebble. I told him his brain was turned.'

'Aelius!'

'Well, he made me cross with all that fuss he was making.'

Alis placed food in front of him, and waited until he had swallowed several mouthfuls. She added a glass of wine. 'You are upset because he's keeping something a secret from you.'

Aelius opened his mouth indignantly. Then he murmured, 'Am I?'

He sipped his wine in silence for a moment before he nodded. 'Perhaps you're right, Alis. We've always shared everything, Flavius and I, since we were little.'

Alis touched his hand. 'You haven't quite shared everything with him, Aelius.'

He looked at her and they smiled at each other. 'But it couldn't be something like that,' murmured Aelius. 'Flavius never goes anywhere. There's nowhere *to* go up here.'

Alis was wearing the necklace Flavius had bought her . 'He's been to Ravenglass twice recently.'

Aelius shook his head. 'No. The first time he went to climb a mountain for the legate, and the next time to attend a funeral. And what would a pebble have to do with it?'

Alis fetched her little box of treasures. She took out a very small glass phial with a broken stopper. 'Do you remember this?'

'No, what is it? Oh, wait a minute. It's not—'

'Yes, it is,' said Alis. 'We had just met. We were both slaves. It was always broken, but I love it dearly because you gave it to me.

Flavius treasures a pebble. That's not much use either.'

Aelius was smiling, but shaking his head dubiously.

'What happened when he got his stone back?'

'He was laughing, excited, charming to everyone.' Aelius was thoughtful for an instant. 'Do you know what he said to me as he danced off? He told me I was right – his brain had been turned.'

'Well then,' said Alis. 'We will help him, if we can, won't we?

Aelius descended the stairs in a more subdued manner than he had stormed up them. The prefect had left the villa, he was informed, apparently humming as he went. In the street outside the headquarters building, the senior centurion was anxious to tell him that the prefect was, yet again, taking the air on the bluff.

There Aelius found him. Like a man whose thoughts were far away, Flavius was gazing across the sea at – as far as Aelius could judge – nothing.

'That thick-headed senior centurion of yours is very concerned about the time you spend up here looking out to sea.'

'Is he?' said Flavius, without much interest.

'He also notices your interest in Ravenglass of late.'

'I've been twice,' said Flavius. 'Once at the legate's command, and once for a funeral.'

'And then there's that business of sending your wife home. Putting all this together,' Aelius said impatiently, 'I gather he thinks you're expecting an invasion force to attack the coast between Alauna and Ravenglass.'

'Is that all you came to say?'

'No. I came up here to bring you this.' Aelius offered Flavius a small wrist purse.

'I never use one.'

'You could perhaps,' said Aelius carefully, 'use one now to keep – what should I call it? – your new amulet safe.' He added hurriedly, 'I understand that many soldiers carry amulets for luck. They are more secure on the wrist than in a pouch.'

'Ah, yes,' said Flavius quietly, 'my amulet. Yes, it would be better here.' He took the purse and strapped it on his wrist. 'Thank you, Aelius, it was a kind thought.'

'Actually, it was Alis's suggestion.'

'She is a thoughtful – and perceptive – lady.'

They looked at each other.

Then Aelius said, 'If we can help in any way ...' He spoke slowly, quietly.

Flavius nodded. 'I understand, yes, thank you, Aelius.'

He took one last glance at the sea.

'What are you looking for?'

'The island. It's not there today.'

III

Flavius and Marcellus peered at each other through the steam rising from the scented water in the bath-house of the villa at Alauna.

Marcellus had arrived without warning, accompanied only by his adjutant. Lugo, alerted by the duty detail, had been flustered, but gratified, to turn out for an officer of tribune rank, even though he was without the customary escort.

In a voice loud enough to be heard by everyone in the gate-house, and even by Flavius hurrying to meet him, Marcellus had announced that he had received a message from the legate of such urgency that he had ridden on ahead of his men.

'So what does the legate want now?' asked Flavius, as they lowered themselves into the water a few minutes later.

'Ah,' said Marcellus, giving him a quick smile. 'If I deceived you as well as your senior centurion, then it must have been a better performance than I realised. There is no legate, no message, no escort trotting behind me.'

He dipped under the water and came up, spluttering. 'I needed to talk to someone of like mind.'

Flavius was touched. 'I'll try to help if I can. By the way, what happens about the dilatory escort? My senior centurion will start thinking they've been ambushed by an advance party of marauding seamen bent on invasion.'

'I haven't neglected them. I have sent my adjutant back to Ravenglass. I've told your senior centurion that he has been instructed to turn the escort back. Good enough?'

'I hope it works,' said Flavius, beginning to laugh at the thought of Lugo rousing the cohort to look for bodies.

Marcellus shrugged his shoulders. 'Celia always did complain about the way we played at soldiers. What do you think the punishment for flippancy among commandants is?'

'Something grisly,' said Flavius. He was glad to hear Marcellus speak so comfortably about Celia.

He waited while his friend took two or three strokes across the bath. 'So what is it you're worried about?'

Marcellus became serious. 'Do you remember that I once spoke to you about the India runs my father's fleet undertakes?'

'Yes, you went on one yourself.'

Marcellus nodded. 'Have you heard that in shipping circles there has been some talk about sailing direct to China, instead of waiting for the China caravans in India?'

'No. It's not a wine-producer's route.'

'Apparently, Hadrian is interested in the possibilities.'

'That doesn't make it a realistic plan, does it?'

'Bear with me Flavius. If my father decides he is interested in exploring such a venture, I am thinking of offering to go.'

Flavius was aghast at what he was hearing. 'No, no!' He spoke with more vehemence than he had meant to express. 'It can't be done.'

'Someone has to find that out. Why not me?'

Flavius tried to calm himself. 'How long would such a voyage take?'

'Two years? I don't know. Perhaps five. That doesn't matter. There's no-one waiting for me to come back, is there?'

'You can't imagine Celia would want you to do this?' said Flavius explosively. As soon as he said it, he regretted his haste.

Marcellus was startled to find him so upset.

'Flavius,' he said gently, 'nothing is decided yet. This is what I want to talk to you about. Sometimes I think that might be the best thing for me to do. At other times, I ask myself if I could ever leave Ravenglass.' He paused. 'I chose to bury her in our military cemetery because I thought that, when the time came for me to leave, there would always be people in the fort to tend her grave; but now I wonder how I could ever think of leaving her to the care of strangers. How could I leave her alone in a foreign place, a place

I would probably never see again, once I had left it? She needs me, and I need to be with her.'

Flavius said, as quietly as he could, 'Some day you will have to leave Ravenglass. You will only be leaving a grave. She is not there in that grave.'

'Then where is she Flavius?' His friend gave him a sad, wry look. 'You would not allow that she is in Elphin's summer garden.'

Flavius felt a tremor of excitement at the unexpected mention of Elphin's name. He managed to say gravely, 'I should not have been so dismissive of her words,' and shook his head at the memory of his behaviour. 'It is a beautiful myth. I was perhaps envious that we have nothing like that in our beliefs. I understand now that she was probably sharing with you a thought that gives comfort to her own people in their time of loss. I am ashamed of my actions.'

'I think Elphin sensed that when you offered to walk with her to the harbour.'

'She was generous in allowing me to do so.'

He wanted to be able to go on talking about Elphin. Even to hear her name spoken was magical to him.

'She talked a lot about Celia,' he said.

'Yes, they were great friends, Celia and Elphin. It helped that they shared two languages. Celia knew her grandfather's Gallic dialect, which is not the same as Elphin's but close enough, and Elphin's Latin is fluent.'

'So I discovered. I was speaking to her for some minutes, before I realised that she was using our language, not her own.'

'You know who you have to thank for that friend? Agrippa. He didn't know Ireland from the back of his hand, as you like to point out, but he had the odd bright idea or I don't suppose he would have been building Hadrian's harbour at Ravenglass. Or – ' Marcellus splashed his hand in the water ' – have been the first commandant to wallow in your exquisite bath here.'

'Yes, thank you, Marcellus, I haven't been able to avoid hearing about him.'

Marcellus frowned. 'Agrippa used to say that as conquerors, we had an obligation to teach a subjugated people two things.'

'I hardly call them subjugated in the north-west,' Flavius interrupted.

'Compliant?'

'Indifferent.'

'As you please. The two things still apply. Firstly, they must be taught to read and write – which means in Latin since none of the Celtic dialects has a written form of language – and secondly, they must learn to wear the toga.'

'The toga?' said Flavius scornfully. 'That wasn't one of his bright ideas, was it? Even in Rome, no-one wears a toga unless they can afford a slave to trail round after them, carrying their books and purses and things. Didn't he notice that most of the men in our north-west settlements here are fishermen or labourers? They couldn't afford a slave, apart from the fact that nobody round here uses them the way we do.'

'Perhaps he was thinking of the odd merchant or farmer,' said Marcellus.

'Would any of them give up wearing trousers in favour of a toga in this climate up here?'

'I must admit, I've never seen a toga in Ravenglass,' said Marcellus.

'I didn't see many north of Colchester, and certainly none here except mine, which I've worn once.'

'Celia used to scream with laughter at the idea. Imagine, she used to say, a Ravenglass fisherman in a toga, trying to take down his sail in a storm. He'd strangle himself with it.' Marcellus smiled at the memory.

'I can imagine her laughing,' said Flavius, 'and her amethyst ear-rings dancing.'

Marcellus nodded and looked at him gratefully. 'Yes. I liked to see her wear those.' He was lost in thought for a moment, then he gave a little shake of his head as though bringing himself back to their conversation. He waved a finger at Flavius. 'The thing she didn't laugh at was Agrippa's first idea – teaching a written language. Elphin's father was one of those who wanted to learn. As a young man he'd sailed round the coast of Britain and seen the effect that learning the language had had in the Romanised towns of the south.'

'What about Elphin?' murmured Flavius.

'Her father persuaded Agrippa to find a tutor for her, and he used to sit beside her while she had her lessons, so they learned Latin together, father and daughter. And the practice spread among those who could afford the time to devote to it. Then the commandant's wife of the time was encouraged by Agrippa to hold classes for children in the settlement. The wives who followed carried on her work, and so Celia, when we arrived, did the same. That's how she met Elphin.'

'The lady Elphin, she is well, I hope?'

Flavius trusted this sounded nothing more than a polite, casual enquiry, though he was aware of the slight tremor of excitement in his voice.

Elphin was so much part of his life now that it was a kind of shock to realise how little he knew about the way she passed her days or how he was to reach her. She, at least, knew where he could be found. He spent much of his spare time these days wandering round the harbour. Ships often came there from Ravenglass and even from her island; a seaman could arrive any day carrying a note from her. So far, there had been nothing.

'Elphin?' said Marcellus. 'I would hope so. I haven't seen her for some time.'

'Not seen her?' Flavius felt a throb of alarm.

'She's in Ireland for a family wedding. The whole clan gets involved and I gather it goes on at some length.'

Flavius's relief was short-lived. Marcellus dealt him an even worse blow. 'I gather her father has hopes of arranging a betrothal for her while they're over there.'

Flavius's throat seemed to have dried up. He could only utter a hoarse, 'Oh?'

'She talked to Celia about it. She wasn't interested in the proposed bridegroom and her father won't insist.'

Flavius plunged his head under the water to hide his feelings. He could have shouted for joy. Elphin could hardly have sent a note from Ireland, and she wasn't going meekly into marriage as an obedient Roman daughter would have done.

When he emerged, he hoped it was with a suitably earnest expression. 'I find it curious that Agrippa did nothing about arranging for Latin teaching up here.'

'Perhaps it's less arduous to plan a harbour than it is to establish a new fort. It does depend really on the ladies of the fort. Perhaps his officers were unmarried. Perhaps, their ladies, like yours, suffered from delicate health. Ah!' Marcellus struck a hand against his forehead. 'Flavius, forgive me. I've done nothing but talk about myself. Never once have I asked you about Lucilla. This separation must be painful for you both. Has she recovered from the journey?'

'She is in good health.'

'That's wonderful news.'

Flavius was suddenly revolted by the deception. 'Her recovery was no surprise to me since she was never in poor health.'

Marcellus stared at him, confused.

'She loathed living here, although it was she who had insisted on coming. She was obsessed with her own rank, but that was not the sort of thing I could say to people who had been kind enough to ask for her company. So I lied, to hide what I suppose was my shame. I lied to my officers and their wives, I lied to Celia and you, Marcellus, I even lied to the governor, when I was desperate for her to go home.'

He was aware of Marcellus's look of concern. 'It was an arranged marriage. There was no heartbreak for either of us in parting. Lucilla is now happy in Rome, spending money; I am happy here, relieved of the guilt I felt for bringing her here.'

He added uncomfortably, 'Marcellus, I owe you and Celia a great deal, and have repaid you in this shoddy way. I would understand if you felt unable to excuse it.'

'My dear Flavius, it was a courtesy to your wife, a necessary exercise in discretion. I am so sorry this is how it is for you.'

Flavius was touched by his generosity of spirit. He would have liked to tell Marcellus how much more he owed to him and Celia. Through them had come Elphin, and a soaring, shimmering enchantment in his life that he had thought would never exist for him. Some day, perhaps, it might be possible to tell him.

Aelius chose this moment to make his presence in the bath-house obvious. Flavius suspected that, as he padded about beyond the steam, re-folding perfectly arranged towels, moving phials of oil and perfume from one place to another, he had, true to form, shared most of the conversation with them.

Aelius was now intent on suggesting with deference that this might be a suitable moment for them to leave the bath, as the table was being set for dinner.

Marcellus fell silent as they sat down to eat.

Flavius was never sure what dictated Aelius's liking for some of his acquaintances and his dislike of others. However, from the concern he was showing for their guest, Marcellus had fortunately passed some kind of Greek approval rating.

'A helping of fish, sir?' Aelius was murmuring.

Marcellus was hesitating, but Aelius gave him an encouraging nod. Marcellus weakened, and nodded back.

It must be, thought Flavius, one of the worst periods in the day for him. The dinner hour was probably a time he and Celia had always spent together, sharing the experiences of the day.

He decided to behave as if he was unaware of this. 'By the way, Marcellus, when you were talking earlier about China, you said your plans might have some relevance for me. I warn you, I have no taste for danger. I have been referred to, by a man of the highest authority, as squeamish, and he was right.'

'I have to admit,' said Marcellus, seeming not unwilling to have his mind diverted, 'that it does involve exploration by water, but not Chinese water, and you'll be back after a couple of days, not five years.'

'Ambleside?' asked Flavius.

'Yes,' said Marcellus, pleased at Flavius's enthusiasm, 'our suggested route to Ambleside, using the River Leven instead of Hardknott pass. We decided we ought to try it, but that was some time ago. Are you still interested?'

Flavius nodded.

'Good. Now, if I choose to go back to Rome, I shall have to leave Britain in August ...'

'This August?' said Flavius in dismay.

'My father will divert his Spanish run to collect me,' explained Marcellus. 'So I want to fit in the Ambleside trip as soon as possible in case I do decide to leave. Even if I don't, it would be a good time of year to visit the lake; very long days, the best chance of warm, dry weather. You'll come then?'

'As soon as you wish,' agreed Flavius. The sooner he had an excuse to visit Ravenglass, the sooner he could find Elphin again, and they could decide how they would send word to each other.

'I'm inclined,' Marcellus was saying, 'to think the best time for the tides would be ten days from now. Would you agree?'

Ten days? It seemed a lifetime to Flavius. 'Could the good weather we're having now last that long?' he enquired.

'It could. What do you think, Aelius?'

Aelius, pleased to be consulted by a tribune, considered the matter. 'I think it possible, but I would be wary of assuming it is certain, sir.'

Marcellus nodded his thanks. 'But you can promise me fine weather for tomorrow?'

'I can indeed promise you a pleasant ride back to Ravenglass tomorrow.'

'I wasn't actually thinking about my own journey along the coast here, Aelius. I was concerned about the lady Elphin sailing from Ireland.'

'No difficulty at all, sir,' said Aelius, smiling confidently as if he had control of the sea lanes.

Hearing Elphin's name so unexpectedly startled Flavius. He spilled wine from his glass.

'Allow me, sir!' Aelius stepped forward to soak up the wine on the table. So that, he thought, hiding a smile as he offered Flavius a towel for his fingers, was the answer to the question that had been occupying his mind in recent days.

As he refilled the glass, his glance met that of Marcellus before they both looked away.

IV

Flavius took the direct coastal route south to Ravenglass.

The last time he had used it, the weather had been dangerous, and he had been fighting time to reach Celia's funeral.

Now he had a sea of blue silk for company all the way, and the brightness of the day seemed to be inside as well as around him.

When the road reached its highest and most westerly point, Flavius paused. He was at the head of the massive red cliff that dominated that part of the Solway coast, and could clearly see Elphin's island ahead of him.

On that earlier journey, the name Elphin had signified for him a woman he had glimpsed only briefly and whose conduct was displeasing to a man of Roman upbringing. Before that same day had ended, it was the name of the woman with whom he had shared the most startling and enchanting hour of his life. As he had seen her stretching out her hand to him before she disappeared into the mist, it had seemed to him as if the whole of his life before that moment now belonged to a distant country. Unprepared, he had been given what he most wanted yet had come to accept would never be his.

The road descended the steep side of the cliff and passed through a terrain of sand dunes and coarse grass. He saw a mill on the way, and the last of the milefortlets that dotted the length of the coast between the emperor's wall and Ravenglass. Any one of them, he knew, would welcome him if he needed rest or food.

He was riding, at last, into the outer lanes of the settlement, intent on taking the one which would lead him towards the harbour; somewhere near there, Elphin kept her stables. She might, with luck, be visiting, or there would be someone, surely, who would know where she was or how to get a message to her.

Yet as he drew nearer the fort, he reluctantly changed his mind. It would be too great a discourtesy to Marcellus not to first let him know of his arrival.

He was escorted at once to the tribune's office in the headquarters building. Marcellus was checking, with an orderly's help, a curious assortment of items piled on his desk. Flavius saw blankets, cushions, warm clothing, lamps, measuring rods, leather wine pouches and food carriers.

'There's just the wax tablets and the stylus, then,' Marcellus was saying. He turned round to smile a greeting at Flavius.

'Here, sir.' The orderly held up a block of wax tablets and a stylus.

'For our notes and diagrams,' said Marcellus, as they were added to the pile.

'This is all for the boat? I didn't know we were going to Ambleside by way of China.'

'Flavius, we're leaving at eleven tonight, and getting back at midnight the day after tomorrow. We shall probably need all this. You'll see.'

Marcellus produced a map and spread it out. 'It will help if I explain the route. Sit down over here, Flavius. The fishing fleet will leave the harbour on the ebb tide, which will be ...'

'... at about eleven,' said Flavius, wondering why he had to hear this now when they would be travelling together all night and have ample time to discuss it.

However, he sat down on the chair Marcellus had pulled out for him.

'We will leave with the fleet and travel with them as far as the night's fishing ground,' Marcellus went on. 'They will anchor there, but we shall go on south, using oars, towards the Isle of Walney, here.' He tapped the map. 'We should be there about five in the morning. We change then from oars to sail.'

Marcellus glanced at Flavius, as if hoping for some comment.

'Ah, yes,' he said. 'Sail?'

Marcellus explained patiently that he had hired a boat built to take six oars, but to carry sail as well. At that size it was large enough for a small cabin, which would save them from sleeping on deck.

Flavius, whose mind had been elsewhere, replied, a shade tartly, that he had assumed sails, but – thinking rapidly to cover himself – wondered why the change was to be made at that point.

Marcellus tapped the map again. 'Look, you can see here that this is a very long, thin island with a little tail that turns east and leads us round to face the Leven estuary, which will then be almost due north.' He was tracing this very carefully with a finger. 'It will be low tide, but we can pick up the usual south-westerly.'

'Ah,' said Flavius, hoping to show affable agreement. 'It's gratifying to know there will be a cabin.'

'There had to be a cabin,' said Marcellus. Then he made the kind of sound people make when they have unwittingly betrayed a secret. Flavius pretended not to have noticed. What on earth could be so important about a cabin on a fishing boat? Perhaps Marcellus's mind, like Flavius's, was sometimes elsewhere.

The door opened, and two more orderlies appeared. Flavius pushed back his chair.

'I can see you're busy, Marcellus. I'll get out of your way. I'm happy to walk round the harbour. We can finish this later. On the boat, perhaps.'

'No, Flavius, thank you, but stay where you are. The men are only here to collect your gear for the boat.'

'Mine? All of that? Then where's yours?'

Marcellus hesitated. 'Oh, that went down earlier.'

His finger was still planted on the map. 'Now, Flavius, this is the River Leven. It's a small, winding river, as you can see, no more than about eight miles in length. Only four of them are navigable. There's a good beach, used by the fishermen, and a scattering of huts beside it.'

He lifted his finger from the map. 'That's all I know. Beyond that it's as much of a mystery to me as it is to you. That's why we're taking a guide who knows the area.'

'To guard us from the hostile natives?'

'I've told you already this isn't China, but neither of us speaks the local dialect. I understand there's a mill nearby that could be very useful to us. Our guide can arrange for us to spend the night there. He understands what we shall be looking for – sites for stabling and storage, suitable tracks ... Things we've already talked about.'

Marcellus rolled up the map. 'On the way back, you'll know what to expect.'

This struck Flavius as a rather odd remark, though he wasn't quite sure why, because it was, of course, true.

He tried again to prepare himself for escape. 'I was wondering, Marcellus ...'

But he was calling out for someone. A slave opened the door and looked in. 'Yes, sir,' he said.

'Food, Flavius,' said Marcellus briskly. 'We've kept them waiting long enough. My fault, but it was important to get this done. Are you ready? Come along now.'

In a mood of near desperation, Flavius followed him. Hadn't he heard of lovers tying messages round stones and tossing them into open windows as they passed? Until now, he had dismissed such tales as fanciful nonsense. Now he wasn't so sure. But which would be the right stable window in Ravenglass? It didn't seem as if he would ever get an opportunity to find out, let alone toss a stone into it.

Marcellus seemed disposed to eat a leisurely dinner. Flavius sensed the loneliness of the villa for him without Celia, though he didn't speak of it.

He referred again and again to the voyage ahead of them. 'We've looked forward to this exploration of ours for so long, ever since that dismal visit to Hardknott, and now, at last, here it is! Think, Flavius, in a few hours we shall step off the wharf at Ravenglass, and twelve hours later our feet will be on that beach on the Leven.'

'Then the hard work begins.'

'Then the adventure begins!'

'And we have how long?'

'A whole day. We arrive on the high tide at eleven o'clock tomorrow morning, and leave at high tide on the next day, which will be an hour later, at noon.'

'A whole day and an hour,' said Flavius. 'A lot can happen in an hour.'

A little later, Marcellus said, 'It seems we shall be lucky enough to have the fine weather you were hoping for. It is a beautiful evening.'

'Yes, it is. Warm and very still.' Flavius paused. 'I think this would be a lovely time to walk along the shore.'

'No!' Marcellus spoke so sharply that *Flavius* was startled. Even his friend seemed disconcerted by his own vehemence.

'What I meant was, I think it would be wiser if you tried to get some sleep now instead of walking. I have a room ready for you, and one of my slaves is waiting to look after you. Shall I show you?'

Flavius allowed himself to be led across the courtyard where Elphin had once come to speak to him.

As they walked, Marcellus said, 'I think we shall enjoy the water tonight. There are so very few hours of real darkness in these northern midsummer nights – it will probably still be a deep blue dusk even when we leave. But when it is dark, with a moon as there is tonight, the water dripping off the oars is a sight worth seeing. Then, before you know it, the sun is rising. It seems a pity to sleep later when we can sleep now.'

Flavius was touched by Marcellus's enthusiasm. They had planned this project together, with a shared passion that had kept it alive. Surely Flavius ought to be able, with good grace, to wait another two days before preoccupying himself with his search for Elphin?

'Marcellus, you're right. We must sleep now – if we can, with all this excitement.' He smiled. 'We will have to try. I can walk along the beach another time.'

In his room, Flavius sat on the edge of the bed. He took Elphin's stone from his purse and held it tightly in his hand. He thought with feeling about Marcellus, now alone in his room, struggling with the emptiness in his life. 'Please understand, Elphin,' he whispered. She cared about Marcellus. She would understand, wouldn't she? Flavius repeated the words again, like a charm.

He awoke with the stone still clutched in his hand, and a clamouring at his door.

He slipped the stone into its purse. 'Marcellus?'

His friend thrust open the door. 'Flavius, forgive me, but I can't come with you tonight.'

'Can't come? What do you mean?' Flavius pushed himself upright.

'Something has happened here. It's nothing you need bother yourself about but I can't possibly leave until it's settled. You'll have to go on your own.'

'I don't want to go on my own. Why can't we wait until tomorrow, and go together?'

'No,' said Marcellus, sounding more and more desperate. 'The boat has been hired, it's already loaded, the guide is here, you are here. We had to choose a day when the tides suited us. I don't know when we could arrange all that again.'

'Surely it couldn't be all that difficult,' protested Flavius.

'We don't know, do we?' said Marcellus, almost shouting. 'I'm disappointed not to be going, of course I am, but I don't know how much time I may have left in Ravenglass. I want the information about the Leven route in time for us to complete our report before I go.'

With his lawyer's ear for contrived defences, Flavius felt there was something not quite right about Marcellus's arguments, although he could fault none of them. Perhaps it was because there were rather too many of them.

Marcellus held out the rolled-up map to him. 'You'd better have this.'

'What a coincidence,' said Flavius, taking it, 'that you took the trouble to explain it so carefully to me this afternoon.'

'Life is full of coincidences, I find.'

'Is it?'

'Flavius, please,' Marcellus was almost pleading with him now, 'you ought to be getting ready.'

He said shortly, 'As the tribune pleases.'

Confused and upset, he prepared to leave the villa. At the doorway, his slave was standing holding a lantern to light his path. In the street outside, Marcellus was waiting. He took the lantern and dismissed the boy.

'If you will allow me, I'll walk with you to the boat. You can hardly do without a lantern.'

'Are you sure the problem won't get worse in your absence?'

'It will wait for me,' said Marcellus gravely. 'When you get back, there will be time to explain it to you, if you still wish to know about it.'

What did that mean? wondered Flavius.

A number of the fishing boats were casting off when they reached the harbour. 'Yours is about ready to go,' said Marcellus, hurrying him along.

They climbed on to the deck, and Flavius was introduced to the captain of the eight-man crew. Marcellus enquired if the guide had arrived, and the man jerked a thumb in the direction of the cabin, where a light was burning.

Flavius felt a moment of alarm. 'Does he speak Latin?

'Yes, of course he does. Do I understand much else? Perhaps you should go and have a quick word with him in there.'

'Yes, I will,' said Flavius, with a marked lack of enthusiasm.

As Marcellus gripped his hand in farewell, Flavius made one last plea. 'Are you sure we can't wait until tomorrow?'

'Sure,' said Marcellus, and left the deck.

As the boat began to move away, he shouted from the wharf, 'Don't forget to collect all the information we need.'

With a spurt of irritation, Flavius shouted back, 'What else am I going for?'

Marcellus waved an arm and Flavius stood on the deck, watching his lantern bobbing away in the darkness.

Then he made his way reluctantly towards the cabin. He saw no reason to knock but pushed the door open.

A figure was bending over the lamp, trimming it. Flavius saw a strand of hair the colour of dark honey with a glint of copper.

The figure stood up. 'Oh, Marcellus, is that ...'

Flavius and Elphin were face to face.

V

'My love,' murmured Flavius as she put her arms round him, her face sparkling with delight.

It took them both some time to disentangle the niceties of Marcellus's plot.

'So Marcellus didn't tell you I was sailing with him?'

Elphin shook her head.

'And you didn't know I would be here?'

'No, he simply talked about a guide.'

'But *I* am the guide. *I* know the country round the Leven well. *I* buy ponies and dogs there. He said he needed someone to talk to the local fishermen and the miller. But it was some time ago that he first asked me about it.'

'And Marcellus and I talked about making this search even before I first saw you at the fair,' added Flavius. 'So he originally assumed all three of us would go together, and all this nonsense about some sudden trouble at the fort must have been made up recently, yesterday even, to give us time alone together.'

They looked at each other. 'How could he have known?' said Elphin. 'You didn't tell him?'

'Of course not. And you didn't?'

She shook her head. 'He couldn't have seen us together because we haven't been together since that day on the beach, and he couldn't have seen us then because he was busy with all his funeral guests.'

'Hell, Elphin, all the time since I arrived here today, I've been trying to get away from the fort to find you, or to learn where you might be, and he kept coming up with reasons to stop me going. I got irritated and upset because I felt he was hiding something from me ... that he didn't trust me. And now this. How can I ever ask him to forgive me?'

'He will know,' said Elphin gently, 'exactly how you must be feeling at this moment. In his heart he will be talking to Celia about it, because he knows how much it would have amused her.'

'Elphin, he wanted so much to come, and he's stayed behind alone, for us.'

'That shows you what a good friend he is to you.'

'I hope he will understand,' said Flavius humbly, 'that there is no-one whose friendship I value more.' Then he gave a little laugh. 'Except, of course, for Aelius.'

'Who is Aelius?'

'Aelius is my house steward. One morning, when I was eight years old, I decided he was my best friend, and would be for ever. I was right.'

'Tell me about him.'

'No, not now, Elphin. It's quite dark now. Marcellus spoke to me this evening about the pleasures of a moonlit summer night in a boat. He could be thinking about them now. Let's at least share them with him in spirit.'

Elphin picked up a shawl. Flavius took it from her, and wrapped it round her shoulders. He was reminded of the time he had seen Aemilia's husband tenderly cover her with his cloak, and of how he had envied them both then.

He lifted Elphin's hair and kissed the back of her neck. Elphin spun round, took his head in both hands and kissed him on the mouth. Then she stepped decorously out of the cabin on to the moonlit deck.

Flavius, copying her serious manner, took her elbow and guided her to the edge of the boat. The air was still warm, the sky cloudless, the moon hanging over the black water. The only sound in the quiet night was the splashing of waves against the oars and the hull.

'Look at the oars,' said Flavius.

As they were lifted from the sea, the dripping blades were running with water alive with luminous flecks of light. When one of the oarsmen heard Elphin's cry of wonder, he bent over the side to scoop water into his palm. Then he held out his hand for Elphin to watch it trickle between his fingers like minute beads of crystal shimmering on an invisible thread.

She laughed and waved to thank him.

'Have you never seen that before?' asked Flavius, surprised.

'When I go on a boat at night, I usually sleep.'

'But not tonight,' said Flavius. 'Tonight you must watch the sunrise. Then whenever you see a sunrise, winter or summer, you will remember our first one together, the one that Marcellus gave us.'

'Yes,' she said, smiling at him, 'that contents me. We will sit inside and wait, and while we do, you can tell me what happened between you and Aelius on that morning when you were eight years old.'

Flavius was dismissive. 'You don't want to hear about that. It's trivial. I don't know why I mentioned it.' He followed her back into the cabin. 'Haven't we other things to talk about?'

'Oh, yes,' she murmured, smoothing back a lock of his hair that was out of place, 'but wait until tomorrow, when we shall have twenty-four hours alone beside the river.'

'Better than that,' whispered Flavius in her ear. 'Twenty-five, actually.'

Elphin started arranging cushions and blankets on the hard cabin bench to make it bearable to sit on. 'Then you can tell me now about Aelius.'

'Elphin, no ...'

She sat down on the now cushioned bench. 'Are you trying to tell me, Flavius, that one morning, when you were eight years old, you and Aelius did something so dreadful that it must never be mentioned?'

'No!' he said, laughing helplessly. 'Sweetheart, I just don't want to bore you.'

Elphin held out her hand to him and pulled him down on to the cushions beside her. 'Flavius, how could you bore me? We know about our feelings, but we know nothing about each other. I want to know what your life is like, what you've done in the past before we met, what happened to that little boy of eight. Please?'

Flavius settled an arm around her. He gave in. 'Well, like all boys in my kind of world, I learned my first lessons at home with a tutor. The tutor was my father's secretary, a slave, a man of scholarship. I shared my lessons with his son ... that was Aelius. He was only a few months older than I was, and we had both been brought up to understand that he would become my personal slave. We did everything together, shared everything.'

Flavius paused. 'Are you asleep yet?'

Elphin, with her head against his shoulder, closed her eyes. 'Almost, thank you.'

'Good. When I was eight, my father decided that it was time for me to go to a formal school where I could mix with other boys. Aelius came with me to carry my school things.'

'Couldn't you carry them yourself?'

'Yes, but he was my slave. That's—'

' —how it was done in your kind of world?'

'Yes. Most of the other boys' slaves played about outside the school, but Aelius came in to sit beside me so that he could understand what I was learning.'

'Who carried his stuff for him?'

'We shared. Elphin, why not go back to sleep?'

'If you wish, but I like a kiss before I go to sleep.'

'That's easily done.'

Flavius made a slight rearrangement of the cushions before he went on. 'After three days, we agreed that we hated the school, we hated the master who was too fond of beating us, and we hated his assistant who was a weasel who spied on us and helped to hold us when the master was punishing us.'

'On the fourth day it grew very hot. We were bored because the master was teaching something we'd already done at home. Aelius was almost asleep.'

'Exhausted by humping all that stuff about for you?'

'Hmm, probably. As I was saying, Aelius was almost asleep and I was playing with a knife and a piece of wood. I wouldn't have been doing that if he had been awake. One of his responsibilities was seeing that I behaved in a seemly manner in public, and though he was only a few months older than me, he was very serious about it.

'I was happy doing my little bit of carving. The master was scribbling on his board, Aelius wasn't watching me, and the weasel was out of sight. Unfortunately, he was hovering at the back of the room, waiting to pounce on me – which he did. He stamped on my carving, which was well on the way to being a small bird, and dragged me by the neck of my tunic to the front of the room where the beatings took place. The master was getting his arm in with a few practice strokes on his desk.

'Then I heard the weasel mention my father's name. He was chief magistrate of Stresa at the time, and they obviously decided it might be better to keep their hands off his son. But they weren't going to be deprived of their pleasure. They would use my slave as a whipping boy. So they let go of me and seized Aelius.'

'And that, Elphin,' said Flavius, 'was the moment when I realised that he was my dearest friend, and I would never let anyone hurt him if I could prevent it.'

Elphin sat up. 'Did you prevent it??'

'Yes,' said Flavius.

'How? Tell me!'

'I butted the master in the stomach with my head. It was part of the street fighting Aelius was teaching me – not an aspect of my education that either my father or my tutor was aware of. Then, while that abominable creature was whining and gasping, I snatched hold of his tawse and shouted to Aelius "RUN!"

'We both ran as hard as we could out of the school, with the weasel screeching behind us. There was uproar in the classroom with other boys fighting to get through the doorway and join in the chase. We darted down any lane or dark alleyway we saw. When we had to stop, breathless and with no idea where we were, we had lost them – or rather, they had lost us. We had a wonderful time, wandering around parts of the town which we realised were the ones we weren't allowed to visit. We came across a bonfire and threw the tawse on it, by which time we decided we were starving. We found our way home, and Aelius looked for a place in the wall that we could climb over, then we crawled on our hands and knees behind a row of bushes and into an old summer-house, where we were sure we wouldn't be seen if we crouched behind the waist-high panels under the windows.

'Aelius crawled round the back of the summer-house and returned with some windfall peaches. They were probably horrible, but they were a treat that day because they were part of our victorious truancy. We sucked the stones clean, and used them as counters on a court that we marked out in the dust of the floor. Then we argued about who had won the most games, and that turned into a fight. After that, we went to sleep. It was a perfect day, Elphin.'

'I love those two little boys,' she said.

'When we woke up, we could hear ominous noises coming from the house. We knelt down and looked out over the edge of the panels. The two senior servants who collected us from school were talking to my mother. They had obviously come back with the news that we were missing. Slaves were running out of the house and she was pointing them in different directions. Then my father, still in a riding cloak, appeared beside her on the terrace.

'Aelius stood up and pulled me to my feet. I thought we were going to run away again, but he said didn't I understand why my father was home so early, and that it was time to go.

'He took out the little comb and brush he always carried with him. He was, as I've already said, only a few months older than me, but he had already taken it upon himself to see that I appeared presentable in front of my father at all times. He started trying to brush the dust and bits of dried leaf from my tunic, but with peach juice dribbled down the front of it, I still looked a mess. After a few tugs at my hair, he gave up.

'We wouldn't wait, he said, to be discovered. He solemnly told me that this was the moment defeated generals fell on their swords. I said we hadn't got any swords.'

Elphin lifted her head. 'In my world, boys of eight are being taught to use weapons and handle horses. Celtic men of birth love to fight.

They set great store by beautifully crafted swords. Goldsmiths are cherished like princes.'

Flavius laughed. 'It so happens that I own a very fine sword decorated with gold and jewels.'

Elphin gasped. 'You have fought with it?'

'No. It's ceremonial. The blade is blunted.'

'But who would sell you such a sword? What use is it?'

'That's what Aelius said. I didn't buy it. It was a gift from the emperor.'

'He is the man you think of as a god? Marcellus bows to his image in the hall of the fort?'

'Well, he is what we call a half-god now. He will be made a god when he dies. Yes, his is the image in the fort.'

Elphin smiled. 'Well, if Aelius dislikes this gift, he will have his reasons. I like Aelius. He cares about how you look. We Celts understand that. We respect a good appearance.'

Flavius gazed at the silver pins in her hair, the colours woven into her dress, the decorated buckle. 'Yes,' he said, 'to my great delight.'

Elphin's cheeks flushed; she smiled and looked away. 'How long do I have to wait to know what happened to the little boys?'

'Ah, yes. My father was sitting at the desk in his library, with Aelius's father standing beside him. At one end of the desk was the hated schoolmaster, huffing and glowering. Perched on a stool beside him was the weasel, smug with nasty satisfaction. Aelius and I were summoned to stand in front of the desk. My father expressed his outrage at the disruption that had been caused at the school. He blamed Aelius for not controlling my behaviour.'

'Aelius was silent, but I didn't intend to be. I interrupted my father to ask for permission to speak, and didn't wait to hear whether or not he would grant it. I told him I refused to allow anyone but myself to use my slave as a whipping boy. I gave the order to run, and as my slave he obeyed me. Had he not done so, he would have incurred punishment; but as it was, he had done nothing to deserve my father's rebuke.

'My father looked at me gravely for a moment and then said he agreed with me. Aelius might step aside. He once told me, years later, that that was the moment when he wondered if he might have a future lawyer on his hands.

'However, as he went on to say, since an outrage had occurred, a punishment had to be imposed. The master, smugly leaning back in his chair, declared that he would be satisfied if I went without my supper and had a good thrashing in front of the whole school.'

'No, my father said, that would not satisfy *him*. That was a form of punishment that seemed to be going on every day in the master's classes. My father had in mind something much more severe. He beckoned Aelius's father to him and they had a lengthy muttered conversation.'

'Then my father stood up. After consultation he had decided, he announced, on the appropriate punishment for his son. He would be forbidden ever to enter the school again. Disobedience would result in removal from Stresa.'

'Oh, wonderful father!' cried Elphin, clapping her hands.

'Yes,' said Flavius, 'that's what Aelius and I wanted to do, but my father shot us a warning look. The master was whining and protesting. My father assured him that he had no intention of keeping his son's alarming behaviour a secret. He would inform all his friends who kept boys at the school of his real reason for withdrawing his son. He was sure the master would care to know that he had persuaded his son's former tutor to continue his education at home.'

Elphin was laughing. 'With that sort of father, it's not surprising you could talk like a lawyer at eight.'

Flavius smiled. 'He was a great civic magistrate.' He had opened the cabin door to see if there were yet any signs of the sun rising. 'I think you should come out now, Elphin.'

'Do you remember whether you had any supper that night?'

'Yes, my father let us have our supper.' Flavius grinned. 'But he told us we had to clean up the mess in the summer-house first. Yet it was a good supper. I think he arranged that, too.'

He held out his hand to her, and she went with him out on to the deck.

'It's still the middle of the night.'

'I know, but it's just beginning. Look.' He turned her to face the rising sun.

Fragile wisps of silvery-grey light were glimmering above the horizon. As they grew stronger, they merged into strands of pale orange, pink and gold. The colours, as they rose higher in the sky, became rich and warm. Then the tip of the sun appeared, splashing its brilliance into the water.

'There,' said Flavius. 'Now you can go to sleep.' Back in the cabin, he rearranged the pillows. When Elphin had curled up on the bench, he covered her with the single blanket that she assured him would keep her warm enough.

Once he had satisfied himself that she was comfortable, he kissed her hand, her cheeks and her mouth. She closed her eyes and sighed contentedly.

He blew out the lamp and closed the cabin door quietly.

He walked down the middle of the boat and settled himself in the bow. The light from the rising sun was spreading along the rim of the sea. As the sky turned gradually blue above him, Flavius himself drifted into sleep, lulled by the motion of the boat and the sound of the water slapping the bow.

Two hours later, they reached the narrow channel between Walney Island and the mainland, and the boat turned northwards into the Leven estuary. Flavius awoke, with a start, to the sound of oars being shipped and the noise of shouting as the square-rigged sail was being raised. The rising tide and the south-westerly wind filling the sail carried them upstream.

Then he smelled fish cooking, and heard the rattle of wooden platters and knives. A hand shook his arm and one of the men, speaking words that Flavius didn't understand, offered him a platter heaped with fish and hunks of coarse bread. Flavius accepted it gratefully. He was offered a knife, but showed that he carried his own in his belt. He expressed his thanks, hoping that if what he said couldn't convey his pleasure, at least his nods and smiles might. A satisfied grunt seemed to suggest they did.

When Flavius had cleared his platter, it was collected; another was handed to him, and a finger pointed towards the cabin. Flavius, with more nods, made his way back to the cabin. Years of sailing on his home lake had taught him how to move on a rolling deck. Among the crew, this did not pass unnoticed.

He tapped on the cabin door. Elphin appeared, her cheeks flushed, her tawny hair pulled away from her face and hanging loose down her back. Flavius felt as if he was falling in love with her all over again. Elphin, aware of the men's watchful eyes on her, gave a little cry of pleasure, broke off a piece of fish with her fingers, swallowed it, smiled and waved at them.

'Ugh,' she said, as Flavius closed the door behind him.

'Don't you like it?'

'I'm not hungry.'

Flavius was concerned. 'You must eat something.' He unpacked the food which Marcellus's kitchen had prepared for them. 'Fruit, cheese, rolls, honey-cakes?'

Elphin shook her head. 'Flavius, I'm very happy. I just don't want anything.'

Flavius looked at the fish and started to eat it himself.

'Haven't they given you any?'

'Yes, but I'm starving. I don't know why. I never eat like this. Do you mind?'

Elphin waited patiently, and then pushed the platter aside.

She wore a demure expression when they emerged together, and led the way to one of the oarsmen's now empty seats. Flavius sat down on the bench facing her. Elphin talked about the land to either side of the winding river. On the eastern bank were grazing pastures for sheep and cattle, and long stretches of sand. On the opposite side the grass became strewn with rocky outcrops.

'Is this,' enquired Flavius, as if it were merely of passing interest to him, 'anything like Ireland?'

'Ireland?' said Elphin, surprised by the question. 'Yes, I suppose so – grass, sheep, hills and rocks, little villages. Why do you ask? There are no forts or Roman towns, if that's what you mean, because there are no Romans there to want to build them.'

'I know that, Elphin. I asked because Marcellus mentioned to me that you had been staying in Ireland for a while, and I just wondered if there was anything out there that especially appealed to you.'

'No,' said Elphin. 'My mother was Irish. As her daughter I am one of her clan. The old clan way of life is still very strong in Ireland. If one person steals, the whole clan is responsible for paying the debt;

if one person has reason to celebrate, the whole clan is expected to share in the occasion. The event I was attending in Ireland was a wedding.'

'Ah,' said Flavius, looking out across the fields, 'Marcellus thought that your father might be hoping for a betrothal for you.'

'Yes,' said Elphin, 'but I was not.'

'Are you not bound by your father's wishes?' asked Flavius, tormenting himself.

'Not any more. I was married at fifteen—'

'Married, Elphin!'

She heard the anguish in his voice and shook her head gently. 'Listen, Flavius. I was going to tell you that I was married then to a man of his choosing. I was widowed at seventeen. It was then agreed between us that if I ever took a second husband, it would be of my own choosing, though I would always listen to any suggestions he might have.'

She smiled at Flavius's look of relief. 'If you are asking me whether or not I enjoyed being in Ireland, the answer, my dear love, is no. I did not enjoy it this time because I was aching all the while to get back home, to get to Ravenglass, to get to Marcellus and hear news of you.'

Flavius looked at her. 'Elphin,' he said softly, 'if we were not sitting in an open boat ...'

'I know,' she said, 'but before very long we shall catch sight of the Leven mill, and there will be no fishermen there tonight.'

'Your husband,' said Flavius, after a while, 'was he one of your islanders?'

'No, his family belonged to the Brigantes.'

'That's the tribe living round Alauna, ' said Flavius, startled.

'They hold land over much of north Britain, especially the north-west. There are tribes within the tribe and they fight more among themselves than they ever did against you Romans.'

'My husband's family had lands among the fells round the village of Caldbeck, so they were mainly sheep-farmers, apart from the hush they worked.'

'Hush?'

'When you live in a place where there is a lot of rain, and there are sloping hillsides with minerals buried in the rock,' said Elphin, as

292

though this was something she thought everyone would know, 'it is an ancient way of getting out the iron and silver, which is what we find around Caldbeck. You cut a narrow trench down the hillside, and at the top dig a deep pit with a sluice-gate for the rain. When the pit is full, you pull out the sluice-gate, and the water pours down the trench, carrying lumps of rock with it.'

'Then,' interrupted Flavius, 'you collect the rock at the bottom and chip out the metal? A surface-mine.'

'Yes, a surface-mine,' said Elphin. 'A hush! That's what your people were looking for. That's why you stayed here. That's why you built your wall, to stop other people getting in.'

'One of the reasons, perhaps,' said Flavius mildly. 'Did we take the hush belonging to your husband's family away from them?'

'No. I own it now – that is, I keep the income my agreement with Rome allows me.'

Flavius stared at her. 'You mean, you own a mine which, if it lies near Caldbeck, probably comes within the jurisdiction of Alauna?'

'Does it?' Elphin laughed. 'Yes, I think, in fact, it does.'

'Didn't your husband's family hate us foreign invaders?'

'Because of my father-in-law's good judgement, we never had any cause to do so, any more than the people round Ravenglass did. He didn't delude himself. He knew what had happened to other tribes who thought they could rout a Roman legion, even some of his own people, further east. If they had initial successes, they couldn't sustain them. The reprisals were savage: slaughter, land wasted, deprivation, even slavery.

'He persuaded his neighbours, if not to welcome then to accept the Romans. As a result, they were allowed to keep their own land and farm it as they had always done, provided they paid their taxes. My father-in-law had to pay a tenth of his annual yield in wool and hides, which was not crippling.'

Flavius was gazing at her. 'I don't think I have ever before had a woman talk to me about taxation,' he murmured.

'Your Roman ladies probably don't know that taxation exists,' said Elphin, 'but when I was widowed I had to understand it all. I still need to, especially with my rights in the hush to protect. You see, Flavius, although your people let us go on farming in our old way, they took charge of securing the minerals.'

Flavius was not sure he cared about the hush, or the activities of his countrymen in earlier years, but he was happy to drift along the river in the bright morning sunlight, watching the changing expressions on Elphin's face as she talked.

'So they made the trench wider and deeper,' she was saying. 'They dug a larger pit, and replaced the old wooden sluice-gate with a metal one. They kept our serfs to do the work, but under Roman supervision. The smelted ore was taken away by cart to the forges and metal workshops behind your harbour at Alauna They even built special roads over the fells for the carts.'

Flavius's attention was caught by this. 'Does your silver and lead still come down to my workshops?' He smiled when she nodded.

'Half the value of the ore comes to me, the other half goes to Rome. That's the agreement my father-in-law made. He was content with it because the amount collected had almost doubled since the Romans reorganised the hush.'

'What was your husband like?' asked Flavius gently 'Don't speak of him if you'd rather not, though.'

Elphin looked down at her hands, lying in her lap. 'I don't mind.' She was quiet for a moment. 'He loved his fells and he loved the sheep he cared for. He gave me a chestnut-and-white pony, and I used to ride out on it to sit with him for a while when he was watching the flock. He was easy to be with. We liked each other.'

She hesitated. 'When I think about it now, I realise how little time we actually spent together. Most of the day I was with his mother.'

Life with Lucilla had introduced Flavius to something that had barely attracted his notice before marriage: that the relationship between wives and daughters-in-law was not always a tranquil one. 'That was difficult for you?' he said, trying to be understanding.

'No, she was very pleasant to me. We had something in common: neither of us was born of Brigantes stock. She came from the Silures tribe to the south. A lot of them are not well disposed towards Rome, but she was not one of those. She had been born and grew up in Caerleon, and she was always talking about this vast, wonderful city that the Romans had built up round their legionary fort. Is it vast and wonderful, Flavius? I have never seen it. I have never seen any Roman city, but from her I learned what they must be like. She would tell me about the rows of shops and what was inside them, about the pleasure of walking on paved streets, about the beautiful public bath that was open only for women on a Tuesday, about the huge waterfront with great ships docking there every day. Is Rome like Caerleon?'

'Larger.'

'Celia came from Rome. When I met her, I would see her using the sort of things that my mother-in-law had described, and when she mentioned her home, I understood the kind of place she was talking about. I could picture the size of the ships that Marcellus's father was building. It helped to make our friendship.'

Elphin smiled at Flavius. 'It was also partly due to my mother-in-law that I could speak your language so easily to Celia, and now to you. She loved to use Latin, and I think she was content to have me as her son's wife because I could understand it. She taught me the words my military tutor would have ignored. I learned to cook Roman dishes – in Latin; to do my hair the Roman way – in Latin; and how to—'

'And how to rebuke an ill-tempered Roman commandant who was falling in love with you without realising what was happening to him – in Latin?'

'Oh, I did that all on my own, without instruction,' said Elphin.

Flavius was struck by a sudden thought. 'What would have happened to us if you couldn't have spoken to me in my own language?'

'Nothing would have happened. How could it?'

'I have always,' he said, 'been critical of general Agrippa, because he didn't know where Ireland was. But if he had known, he would surely never have come to Ravenglass to consider invading the wrong island. Then he would never have met your father and persuaded him of the advantages of acquiring Latin. I shall never in future fail to appreciate Agrippa for his ignorance.'

'Yes, wonderful Agrippa,' said Elphin, laughing.

'Come to think of it, I should be eternally grateful as well to my grandfather for what I thought was his ridiculous obsession with seeing me in the Senate, and forcing me to come here because that's what had to be done.'

'Wonderful grandfather,' agreed Elphin.

Flavius started laughing with her. 'And we mustn't forget the governor of my province, who mentioned my name to the emperor just at the moment when Hadrian needed a man to replace the commandant at Alauna, who had left for Judea.'

'Then,' said Elphin, 'we have to thank the man who went to Judea!'

'Indeed, yes, otherwise I could have been sent in the emperor's good time to a camp in Egypt or Germany or wherever.'

Flavius was suddenly serious again. 'Darling Elphin, what a lot of things have had to happen to bring us to this day.'

She nodded her head vigorously. 'Tell me about your grandfather, and explain the Senate to me? Celia's family were something to do with it, I think.'

'Later. Tell me first what happened to you in Caldbeck.'

'About eighteen months after I was married, my father-in-law died. My husband was his only child, so the whole estate became his. There were always border disputes going on among the different sets within the tribe. Once it was seen that our lands were being managed by a young owner and two women, raids on our stock began. Then they set fire to our grain stores. That roused the Roman soldiers who were guarding the hush. They beat the marauders off and helped to quench the fire, but somehow in all the skirmishing my husband was badly hurt. He died the next morning.'

Elphin sighed. 'You can see why I told you just now that my husband's family never had any cause to hate you. It was only their own kin they needed to fear. The next day, a detachment of cavalry arrived from the fort. They rounded up everyone they could find, and held them until they found out who the leader was; he was accused of causing my husband's death. They didn't put him to death, but they sent him to one of the convict gangs that work the mines – not the hush mines, but the underground ones. They offered us protection, but there was never any need for it after that.

'So all the land, including the hush, became, by law, mine. My mother-in-law had much more right to it than I did, and I wanted her to use it as if it were hers. But she couldn't bear to stay there any longer. Roman justice gave her some grain of comfort, but the only place she felt she might eventually find some help with her despair was among her own family in Caerleon. She offered me a home there with her.'

'That was kind of her,' said Flavius.

'Yes, it was. Perhaps I was selfish, but I couldn't see myself sharing the kind of life she would lead in her big city. I didn't love my husband to anything like the extent that she did, but I had been fond of him and wanted to grieve for him in my own way. I wanted to come home.

'So I sold off a part of the land to give her the kind of sum she would have brought with her as a dowry. I rented the rest to tenants, and entrusted the care of my rights in the hush to someone who controls your army in York.'

'The legate.' Flavius watched the sunlight on her hair. 'You did all this at seventeen? I'm not sure that doesn't shock me more than seeing you riding in a horse race.'

'Why?' asked Elphin.

On the east bank of the river, the slopes of thickly wooded hills were rising behind the fields. On the other side, steep rocks edged the water. The boat rounded one of the river bends, and Elphin pointed excitedly.

'Look. We're nearly there.'

Flavius saw a group of huts and small fishing craft drawn up on the sand. Just before eleven o'clock, on the top of the tide, their boat beached beside them.

'Beyond this point, I presume,' said Flavius, as he lifted Elphin on to the shore, 'there are rocks and shallow water.'

She nodded, and showed him the track that would lead them to the Leven mill, and then on to the lake. 'We can borrow horses at the mill, but for this first part we have to walk.'

Flavius was testing the ground with his foot. 'What do they use this for?'

'Walking. With small carts and the mill horses occasionally, perhaps.'

'Don't they keep any animals here?'

'No. That's why we're walking. If you're wondering about pack-horses, or ox-wagons for the heavier loads, you must tell Marcellus he'll have to put in a road like the one they built to my hush.'

Having sorted out this part of his task for Flavius, Elphin started humming to herself and feeling in the bag she carried on the belt round her waist.

'What have you got there?'

'Honey-cakes. I brought some from the boat. I'm starving.'

'That doesn't surprise me,' said Flavius reprovingly. He bit into one of the cakes she had offered him. 'It's a bit stale.'

'Mine isn't. It's delicious.'

'That's because you're hungry.'

'No,' said Elphin. She suddenly looked shy. 'It's because you're here with me. Everything is different when we share it.'

Flavius took another bite of his cake. 'Of course, you're right. I've never tasted one that I shall remember so well.'

They walked on together, holding hands, while Elphin ate the rest of the cakes. Then she said, surprising him, 'Why did you marry your wife?'

Still keeping hold of her hand, Flavius said, 'It wasn't so much a marriage as a kind of exchange. Lucilla came from an impoverished old patrician family and mine had wealth. Mine was of lower status, but wanted – at least, my grandfather wanted – entry into court circles. So a marriage was agreed.

'I'd never met her until I put the betrothal ring on her finger, and the next time was on our wedding day.'

'But why did you let that happen?' cried Elphin.

'In my Roman world, a father's wishes are paramount until the day he dies. Lucilla and I both accepted without question the agreement our fathers had made.'

'But you were a man then.'

'Yes, I was twenty-six, and practising law. That has nothing to do with it.'

'Supposing someone had a father who was stupid or senile? You should have changed the law!'

'It isn't a law, Elphin. It's a tradition. They are not easy to change. Anyway, didn't your father choose your husband?'

'Not like that,' she said hotly. 'He knew my husband's family. When the cattle were slaughtered for the winter, he would have a large collection of hides for sale. He would take the best of them to Caerleon. It was a long journey, but there he could get a much better price for them than in the local markets. He dealt with a man who was making a fortune supplying in bulk materials needed by the army, and chief among those was hide. In conversation, they discovered that one of them had a grandson in need of a bride and the other a marriageable daughter. So a wedding was arranged; but we were allowed to meet earlier, and we had to give our consent. I think there might have been trouble if we had refused, but who else did either of us know?'

A memory made Elphin laugh. 'There was the hint of a difficulty when my father told my mother-in-law-to-be that, yes, her Caerleon might be considered a fine city, but he found it noisy, full of people pushing other people about, and blighted with strange smells, most of them unpleasant. However, he assured her, he would raise no objection to the match as I would not be spending my married life inside its walls, but in the good air of the fells.'

'He was teasing her,' said Flavius, who liked what he had heard about Elphin's father.

'I think she knew, but pretended not to have heard him. Yes, Flavius, my father chose my husband, but only to assure himself that he had found the right kind of person for me. Your family didn't give that a thought.' She tossed her hair. 'That's wrong.'

'Not all our arranged marriages are the disaster that mine was, Elphin. People come to understand each other, and then affection grows. I think I believed at one time that's what might happen with us, and that I could be satisfied with it.' He stopped walking and put his arms round Elphin. 'When Lucilla and I came to Alauna, and were spending much more time alone together, I realised how fragile was the goodwill I'd thought we were building between us. At home, my wealth could give her the luxury and excitement she loved. I had taken that away from her, and she couldn't forgive me for it. And I couldn't forgive her, I suppose, for the fact that I had to accept she would never want to offer me what I was beginning to realise I longed to find in life more than anything else – and what I found in you when I had lost any hope of it.'

'Elphin, if you are afraid that what I share with you is something Lucilla wants, there is no need. If Marcellus thought that, I don't believe he would have made this time together possible for us. He is a good man, a man of conscience.'

Elphin nodded and bowed her head. Flavius saw a tear on her lashes. He lifted her chin and kissed the tear away.

'Do you realise,' she said, sniffing, 'that some of the fishermen are watching us?'

'If they have any sense,' said Flavius, 'they will realise you have a grain of sand in your eye, and I am using the best way possible to get rid of it for you.'

Ahead of them, the bank bordered a wide arc in the river, which here curved back on itself. On the rim of the curve, Flavius could see a distant cluster of buildings.

'Is that the mill?'

Elphin sniffed again and brushed another tear from her cheek. 'Yes.' She was smiling again. 'There's something special I want you to see.'

'Yes. The mill!'

'Something else.'

How, thought Flavius, could there be any sight more delectable to them at that moment than the mill? Elphin had quickened her step, dancing ahead of him. She turned back, caught hold of his hand and pulled him along.

The course of the twisting river beyond the mill was now hidden by a towering spur of rock extending across the water.

'Close your eyes,' said Elphin, tightening her grip on his hand.

'How much longer?' Flavius cried out, as his foot caught on a stone.

'Now!' she said, with a little shriek of pleasure.

Flavius opened his eyes. They were past the protruding spur of rock and could see what lay beyond the bend in the river.

As though they had been tossed, sometime, by a giant hand from the top of the spur, tumbled rocks filled the narrow gap between the base of the spur and the bank beyond the mill. Water, glistening white in the sunlight, frothed and foamed in a shallow waterfall.

'Listen,' said Elphin. 'We can just hear the sound of it from here. The nearer we get to the mill, the more delicious it sounds. Are you pleased we shall stay there tonight?'

'It must have been waiting for us. Perhaps we should rest there for a while.'

'Now?' said Elphin. 'No, no. First, we must find out for Marcellus whether there is a way to the lake. We will stop now just to borrow the horses, and I can arrange with the woman there to be ready for us later. Flavius, if we stay longer ...'

He nodded reluctantly. 'Yes. We might never reach the lake.'

In the warm air of the late afternoon, they caught their first glimpse of Windermere. They were riding through the dappled sunlight that filtered through a canopy of translucent green leaves above their heads.

When they emerged from the trees, the vast shining surface of the lake, from which the Leven took its waters, lay before them.

'So we can now tell Marcellus,' said Flavius with delighted satisfaction as he gazed around him, 'that there is an open trail for pack-horses from the mill, and I doubt if there would be any problem building wharfing to moor our barges.'

Elphin was enchanted by the view. 'I would love to go out in a little boat and run my fingers through the water, wouldn't you?'

'Yes, but not now. Let's go back, Elphin.'

'Ah, yes. You have to look for a space for the stables for Marcellus.'

'Tomorrow,' said Flavius.

VI

They made love in the mill to the sound of the waterfall. For the rest of his life, whenever he heard a similar sound, Flavius remembered that first time with Elphin. When he awoke, there was a bar of moonlight across the room. He turned over and saw her watching him.

'Love, couldn't you sleep?'

'I didn't want to sleep. I couldn't bear to waste any of the time we have together sleeping.'

Flavius laughed softly and reached out for her; and later, with her head on his shoulder and his arm round her, she did sleep.

They were roused in the early morning by movement around the mill.

'Elphin?' he whispered.

She stirred, and turned her head towards him, smiling sleepily. 'Yes.'

It was the beginning of another bright, clear morning. They were given a beaker of goat's milk, and gruel ladled into a bowl from a cauldron hanging over a fire.

Flavius thought wistfully of the wine, cheese and fruit left behind in the boat. Elphin sipped her gruel as though she hardly knew what she was eating, looking across at Flavius from time to time with a slow smile.

They wandered along the riverbank to enjoy the waterfall. Upstream, the water flowing from the lake was shallow enough for them to see, in the strong sunlight, the tiny stones on the riverbed.

Breaking the surface of the water was a scattering of small rocks, greenish-grey in colour; but when it reached the top of the fall where the heavy slabs of rock had fallen, the leaping, dancing, shimmering cascade of white water pouring over them turned them a shining jet black.

Elphin gave a long sigh of delight, and closed her eyes to listen to the sound of the rushing water. Flavius found himself as much entranced by her pleasure as by his own.

'When I thought I would be coming here with Marcellus,' he said, 'I decided I would bring you back a stone from the River Leven, so that we both had one to keep.'

Elphin clapped her hands together. 'Oh, yes. I'd like that one.' She pointed to the largest rock in the centre of the river.

'Hmm. A good choice,' said Flavius, 'but rather difficult, wouldn't you say, to carry around with you, as I like to do with mine?'

Elphin nodded sadly. 'Wet, too.'

'There is an alternative stone,' said Flavius. He felt inside the pouch hanging from his belt. 'This one.'

Lying on his palm was a heavy gold ring, set with a single smooth polished amethyst.

'Elphin, this was given by my grandfather to my grandmother when they married. She gave it to my father when he was about to marry. My mother passed it to me when a bride had been found for me.'

'Then why didn't you—'

'Give it to my wife? It wasn't a betrothal ring. It was a love token. When my grandfather married, and even my father, we were a humbler family. They were free to choose their own wives, as I was not. I couldn't pass this ring on. I kept it for a woman I loved, which is who it was intended for.'

Elphin shook her head. 'I can't take it, Flavius. It must go to your son.'

'Lucilla and I will never have a son,' said Flavius quietly. 'All its life, this ring has been cherished. Don't leave it to be neglected now.'

Elphin held out her hand and he slid it on to her finger. 'Thank you,' she murmured, eyes shining as she looked up at him. He laughed with the sheer joy of the moment.

They sat down on the rough grass of the bank. For a while they were secure in a world where nothing existed but themselves and their waterfall.

The sun mounted higher in the sky. 'We should go now, Flavius.'

'Not yet.'

'Yes,' said Elphin. 'Marcellus is waiting to know if you could put stabling near the mill. Yesterday you said we would look today.'

'That was yesterday. Anyway, I forgot to bring the measuring rods.'

'I understand stables,' said Elphin, standing up. 'I don't need any.'

Flavius caught hold of her hand. 'When we leave this riverbank, we shall be on our way back. I don't want to begin doing that just yet.'

Elphin knelt down beside him. She held his face in her hands. 'Do you think I want to go? But we owe Marcellus more than we can ever repay.'

Flavius smiled. 'Oh, yes,' he said softly.

They walked round the mill to the empty ground behind where chickens scattered out of their way. Elphin began pacing, one foot in front of the other.

'How many horses would you want to keep here?'

Flavius hesitated. It was not a matter that had ever been of any consequence to him before. 'Twenty?' he hazarded.

'Yes, a good number,' she said. 'There would be room here, and a place for fodder.'

'Fodder?' Flavius realised he would never have thought of that. 'Ah, yes.'

Elphin was rubbing her forehead, as if committing the figures to memory. He had also forgotten to bring Marcellus's wax tablets and stylus from the boat.

She shrugged her shoulders, unconcerned. With their tasks accomplished, and farewells exchanged at the mill, they set off along the path back to the boat. As they reached the bend in the river that would finally hide their view of the waterfall, they stopped for one last glimpse of it.

'Marcellus has never seen that, has he?' said Flavius. 'If he had, I wonder if he would want to stop this plan of ours, as perhaps I think I do.'

'Flavius?'

'I don't want this place to change. How can I be helping to change it?'

Elphin, staring at him, saw the distress that had suddenly overtaken him. She said gently, 'Nothing can change the waterfall. No boats, even the smallest ones, will ever be able to use those waters. If your people can arrange to have your grain milled here instead of at Ambleside, then the existing road will take pack-horses. This road we're on now might need adapting for ox-carts, but this isn't the part you're worried about, is it? The mill will have to be enlarged, but it needs improving anyway, so that will probably make the bank more pleasing to look at. Best of all, Flavius, with more work there, families who might face starvation if there was a hard winter will be saved.'

Flavius pulled her behind a clump of bushes and kissed her passionately. 'For a wild-spirited and head-in-the-clouds Celt, you can be alarmingly sensible at times.'

'And,' retorted Elphin, 'for a stern, disciplined Roman officer, you can be amazingly soft-hearted.' She straightened her hair. Setting a brisk pace, she said. 'Now, hurry, Flavius.'

By high tide at noon they were on the boat, when, with the help of fishermen working on the beach, it was refloated on the river.

Flavius led Elphin to the cabin. Inside, under the warm morning sun, it had become uncomfortably hot. Flavius propped open the door, and unwrapped what was left of the food prepared for them in Marcellus's kitchen. Elphin arranged fruit on one of the pottery platters that had been packed in the basket. Flavius tried the cheese and the bread. The cheese was soft in the heat and the fine white-flour bread not at its best, but washed down with warmish red wine, he found it infinitely preferable to the early-morning gruel.

As he cut with satisfaction another wedge of cheese, Elphin's words came back to him. 'Starvation?' he said, glancing at the lush green fields drifting past the open doorway of the cabin.

'Have you ever passed a hard winter here? Those open fields can be covered with snow and ice, perhaps for weeks. You get so weak from cold that you can't even chop wood or scavenge for scraps.'

Flavius put down his knife. 'I've only been here for one winter. I didn't like it. It was dark and wet and there were gales from the sea, but not snow like that – and I had a heated villa and stores of food.'

'Yes. So you must build your stables and your bigger mill.' She smiled at him. 'No-one can take our waterfall away from us.'

'No, they can't.' Flavius smiled back at her, but Elphin could see that he was still disturbed by what he had heard.

She laid a hand on his. 'Is this,' she asked gently, 'how you looked when you saw the orphans in your streets?'

'How did you know about that?' he asked in surprise.

'I don't know. I suppose Celia or Marcellus must have mentioned it.' She hesitated. 'No, that isn't true. I used to ask them questions about you. I know you built an orphanage near your home.'

'I had to, Elphin. Stresa is a prosperous town. Yet there were little children with nowhere to go but the streets, some of them starving. There were some, too small to walk, just left like bundles of rubbish. I still pay the salaries of the people who work there, which gives me the right to choose who they are.'

'If only others were as practical and compassionate,' said Elphin. She picked up the knife with the cheese still on its point. 'Now eat this. We have another long journey ahead of us. Are you going to tell me more stories about Aelius and your father?'

'Certainly not. One's quite enough.'

'They both care for you, so I enjoy hearing about them. Your father is, I think, a wise man.' She paused. 'Why do you smile to yourself when I say that?'

'I was thinking of something he said before I left to come here. I had no idea then how wise it was,' Flavius admitted. 'He was commiserating with me for being sent to a bleak, lonely outpost of the empire.' He looked at Elphin. 'Then he said that, in whatever kind of place one found oneself, one must always be alert to experiences that one would never encounter anywhere else. I am glad he warned me to grasp the treasure that was waiting for me here, before it slipped away unrecognised.'

In the early evening, they reached the open sea and turned north towards Ravenglass. Sail replaced oars, and there was again the smell of fish cooking on deck. Flavius took Elphin once more to sit in the prow of the boat, to watch the changing colours in the sky. As the long summer evening wore on, clouds began to form high above them, promising a beautiful sunset.

At one point, she said, 'I wish I could know your father, and your mother, too.'

'I doubt if that will ever be possible. We come from different worlds. We are lucky that they touched for a moment.' Flavius wound a strand of her hair round his finger.

'Oh, why,' cried Elphin suddenly, 'couldn't we have been born in the same world – in the same valley, in the same town?' Her voice softened. 'Perhaps we will be, in another life. Perhaps we were together some time in the past, and that's why we're so strongly drawn together now, without understanding why.'

'Elphin, I do understand why I was drawn to you. You are beautiful and brave and challenging ...' She was shaking her head. 'Then explain to me what you are saying.'

'Have you not heard some of our Celtic beliefs? We do not believe in death – that is to say, yes, death happens, but we do not think it is an end to living but the entrance to another life. That is why our ancient Celtic warriors were said to have risked their lives so willingly and recklessly in fighting. That is why our dead are buried with the things they most treasured in life, so that they will have them close in the next time of living.'

Elphin looked at the amethyst on her finger. 'Then you will be able to recognise me by your ring.'

The stone caught the light from the sky. The sun was already out of sight, but, in the darkening sky, the clouds were still aflame with a glowing colour that was reflected in the water along the horizon.

'I believe,' said Flavius, 'that we have only one life, and we should not waste a single moment of it, because that is all we shall have.'

Elphin was near to tears. 'But I don't want to believe what you believe! I think I can see in the distance the fishing boats from Ravenglass, and when we can see them properly we are nearing the end of our journey. Then I won't know when I shall see you again, and I don't want to leave you ... not today, not ever! I don't want to die and never be with you again.'

Flavius put an arm around her. 'Let's go inside and light the lamp and finish up the wine. It's getting colder.'

'Yes, the wind is getting stronger,' said Elphin miserably, 'so we shall get in all the earlier.'

When the cabin door was closed, and the lamp burning, and Elphin had been persuaded to sip some wine, Flavius said, 'What about your god Manannàn and his path of flowers?'

'He is our local god. I like him. I want to believe in him.'

'Yes, I rather like him, too. He seems to care about people who have lost dear ones. That's what you taught me.' Flavius waited a moment. 'There is an advantage to believing in only one life.'

'Yes?'

'Hmm. It means I am aware of how short a time we have, so I have already thought of a way we can meet again.'

'Flavius!' Elphin flung her arms round him. The tears that had been hovering fell on her cheeks, but now they were tears of joy. 'How? Soon?'

'Think. There is one place where our two worlds overlap: you own land that comes under my supervision. Do you ever visit your farm and the hush in the fells?'

'Of course I do. I have things to settle with my tenants. I like to know what is happening with the hush. The seam is running out, and there is talk of opening a drift mine nearby. I always go every year in the autumn, when the seasons are changing, and at other times, too.'

Flavius was delighted. 'Now explain to me how your visit is arranged.'

'One of my father's boats brings me to the harbour at Alauna. I usually have a maid and a groom with me. My chief tenant meets me there with horses. They have the farmhouse ready for me. It's an unusual house for the area. My father-in-law built it to please his wife when they married. It's a smaller version of the Roman style of house she was familiar with in Caerleon – with rooms round a central courtyard. But it has no Roman system of heating, so the courtyard is narrow with a thatched roof, and instead of plants it has an open fire in the centre.'

'Like us,' said Flavius, 'half-Roman, half-Celtic.'

'Warm and comfortable, like us.' Elphin smiled.

'Do the tenants use the house?'

'Not while I'm there. They cook and wait on me, but they live in one of the older houses. The tax collector from your fort spends a day with me whenever I visit.'

'Tax collector?' said Flavius. 'What does he look like?'

'He's small and dark, very neat and precise. He makes very careful lists.'

'Ah,' said Flavius, 'that's my chief clerk, not a tax collector.'

'But I pay my taxes to him,' cried Elphin.

'They couldn't be in safer hands. He will pass them on, with one of his impeccable lists, to the legate's official tax officer.'

'Oh,' said Elphin, bewildered by the curious convolutions of Roman government.

Flavius kissed the bewildered look away. 'I think,' he murmured, 'that since changes will have to be made to the method of mining in an area of imperial property, which you hold as a client-landowner ...'

'Flavius!'

'... I am obliged, as the area commandant, to acquaint myself, on the emperor's behalf, with the probable effects of such changes.'

Elphin burst out laughing.

'Wait! I would, as a courtesy, invite the comments of the said client-landowner, and to that end should expect to be accommodated in the farm villa.'

Elphin stopped laughing. 'No. What about my servants?'

'Listen: I myself, as commandant, will meet you at the harbour. I will provide horses from my stables. I will also bring from my own household a groom, a cook, and a maid to act as your companion. Will your father accept that?'

'I think he may well regard it as an honour. But what difference does it make? They'll all be in the house with us.'

'I promise you, that won't matter.'

'Flavius, how ...?'

'Trust me. Can you?'

He was smiling at her, persuading her.

'Yes,' she said, a trifle uncertainly. Then, as he went on smiling at her, teasing her, she said again, firmly, 'Yes.'

'When we ride away from the harbour, I promise you, you will be pleased.'

'So when will that be, Flavius, when?'

They were aware then of voices calling across the water. Flavius glanced outside. The blackness of the night was now broken by the flares of the fishing fleet on its way back to Ravenglass.

Elphin, at his shoulder, cried, 'There's so little time left. Flavius, please, please, you must tell me when we'll meet!'

Feeling the same distress himself, he turned round to hold her.

'My love, we are drawing closer to Ravenglass, but we're nowhere near the harbour yet.' He stroked her hair. 'We have enough time to decide when we can meet. It matters to me, too.'

She screwed up her nose as if reproaching herself. 'I'm sorry.'

'What about?' asked Flavius fondly. It was still a source of wonder that any woman should feel such alarm at being parted from him. 'Now, let's think; we're at the end of June. In a week's time, my cohort begins summer manoeuvres for six weeks.'

'Then we shall have begun harvesting. Everyone is needed.'

They both sighed, and then laughed. 'Early September?' said Flavius.

'Yes, though it's usually nearer October when I go.'

'I can't wait till then. You will have to tell whoever wants to know that the commandant is anxious to settle your mining problem – because, as everyone knows, that's all Romans care about – and if the client-landowner isn't there, he'll make his decisions without her.'

Elphin was happy again. 'Yes, oh, yes! The earliest possible moment in September.'

'We'll write in the meantime. Perhaps Marcellus will help us. If not, there are couriers and boats. We'll find ways.'

'Write soon.'

'Soon? Is that your favourite word?'

'If it concerns you, of course. There would be something wrong if it weren't.'

Flavius held her at arm's length. 'I love you, Elphin. Now say goodbye to me here, and when we reach the harbour we will both be standing on deck, looking as though we can't wait for the journey to end.'

'Must we?'

'Yes, we must.'

So, when the boat sailed into Ravenglass, Elphin was waiting on the deck, her hood up, a blanket folded neatly over her arm. In the darkness, Flavius thought, no one would notice that her eyes were red.

As the boat moored by the wharf, they saw Marcellus waiting. He had half a dozen slaves with him, two of them carrying lanterns.

He came briskly aboard. 'My lady, prefect, you've had a safe journey, then?'

'Without incident,' said Flavius.

'Good. But you must be tired. My lady, I'm sure you will be relieved to know that one of your father's boats is ready to take you home. If the prefect would be good enough to wait for me here, I'll escort you to the other wharf.'

'No!' said Elphin, looking desperately at Flavius.

He took her hand and kissed it. 'Goodnight, my lady.'

'Perhaps, prefect, you would pay the men while you wait.' Marcellus handed Flavius a purse of money.

'Of course, tribune.' Flavius watched as Marcellus steered Elphin towards the gangplank.

Marcellus motioned one of his slaves to take Elphin's blanket. Another couple he directed on to the boat to clear the cabin. As Marcellus's head was turned, Elphin glanced up at the boat and twisted the amethyst ring on her finger.

Then she walked away with Marcellus and the slave. Flavius, doling out coins, found himself disturbed by the necessary abruptness of their parting. He wanted to throw the money across the deck and run after her, to snatch a single minute and assure her that he was only acting out the role Marcellus had imposed on him. Yet that was unfair to his friend. This was how it would have to be. They were no longer in their own private world, by their waterfall. He went on sorting out the men's pay.

Within a few minutes, Marcellus came hurrying back. From his first words, he seemed to have read Flavius's mind. 'Forgive me for that charade. Elphin's father assumes that she was with me on that trip, and I thought it wise to give that appearance if we could.' He glanced at Flavius. 'I made sure Elphin understood that.'

Flavius smiled wryly at him. 'Thank you. By the way, if you were wondering about the boat, our behaviour was—'

'No, I wasn't,' said Marcellus.

As they walked back to the fort, Flavius, now more cheerful, began to talk about the possible use of the Leven. Marcellus, who at first seemed mildly surprised that he would have anything at all to say about it, grew more and more delighted with what he was hearing.

'So we were right!' he said.

Both too excited now to sleep, they sat in Marcellus's office while Flavius drew sketches and plans, then scribbled out times and rough measurements.

A slave had come into the office, balancing cushions and the measuring rods. Marcellus nodded at the rods. 'So those old things had their use, eh?'

Flavius avoided looking at them. 'Elphin's knowledge was very useful – she understands horses and stables.' He moved on quickly. 'Does this give you enough to make your first appeal to the legate before August?'

'I doubt if he'll show any interest, but we have to start with him. Yes, ample, Flavius, ample. I couldn't be more pleased.' He paused. 'I'm not going back in August.'

Flavius couldn't hide how glad he felt. 'You're staying here?'

Marcellus said apologetically, 'Only postponing the journey. I had a rather curt note from the legate, pointing out the gross inconvenience of a tribune vacating his post during army manoeuvres. To tell the truth, I'd forgotten them. I can't really disagree with the man. I've undertaken to see them out. I still want to go back to Rome in one of our ships, and my father can't divert another until around December. But that won't be bad for our plan. Once the legate gets round to rejecting it, there'll be time to go over his head and submit it to the governor instead.'

'And if he's not interested,' said Flavius, 'we can forget about trying in Britain altogether, and when you get back to Rome you can take it to Celia's grandfather in the Senate.'

They looked at each other. 'Why not?' asked Marcellus. 'That's what she suggested.'

'And, after that, is it still China for you?'

'Ah,' said Marcellus, 'that brought me another reproachful letter, admittedly less curt than the legate's. My father was surprised that he needed to explain to me that, interested as he was in the possibility of trading with China, there would have to be years of planning to design and fit a suitable ship ... well, it went on at length, Flavius. Like the legate, he was right. I seem to have lost my reason for a time.'

'No, you were grieving,' said Flavius. 'That seems to devour a lot of energy and leaves precious little room for common reason.'

'Whatever it was, my father still wants me back. I think he hopes my grandfather-in-law will wangle me into the Senate, to argue against all the shipping laws he hates. You could join me and tie every idea of the emperor's in legal knots?'

'That might be unwise,' murmured Flavius.

'Together we could turn into disagreeable, argumentative old men, filling up places that better men ought to occupy.'

'I like a nice thought to go to sleep on,' said Flavius.

Marcellus laughed. 'I can think of a very nice one for you. Your two-year commission ends in April, doesn't it? I shall certainly be in Rome then. I'll be waiting for you.'

'Yes, slightly better,' agreed Flavius.

Marcellus walked him to his room. It had been midnight when the boat docked, and it was still dark enough for Marcellus to be carrying a lantern. Yet it couldn't be long, Flavius thought, before the brief summer night would be over, and the sun would rise as it had done when he watched it with Elphin.

Marcellus had not mentioned her since they had left the harbour, but when they reached Flavius's door he enquired: 'Was the shared trip a wise idea?'

Flavius looked at him in wonder. 'For the rest of our lives, we shall both be in debt to you.'

Marcellus smiled. 'Good,' he said.

As he turned to go, Flavius asked, 'How did you know?'

Marcellus glanced back at him over one shoulder. 'You both kept asking questions about each other – in such an elaborately casual way. You reminded me of myself when I first fell in love with Celia, before I had permission to court her.'

VII

Flavius rode back through the east gate of the fort at Alauna. He had assumed a severe and disciplined expression, which he hoped would disguise the thoughts dancing in his mind that were neither severe nor disciplined.

He made his way straight into the chief clerk's office. 'I want the records of our mining arrangements with the estate north of Caldbeck.'

The chief clerk shot out of his chair, taken aback by his commandant's precipitate arrival, which was disrupting the orderly calm that he required in his surroundings. He was even more startled by the commandant's request.

'Mining, sir?'

'We do have records?' asked Flavius sharply.

'Yes, of course, sir. I upgrade them once a year. But no other commandant has ever asked for them. Or anyone else. In fact, I can't remember anyone even mentioning them.'

Flavius tried to be patient. 'I suspect, chief clerk, that previous commandants have not asked for them because there has been no need to change the initial agreements with the client-landowners.'

'That is the case, sir.'

'Well, the situation has now changed. Our working of the hush has apparently exhausted the seam. We shall need to open drift mines to reach the lower levels. I feel obliged to visit the site myself and, as a courtesy, discuss matters with the client-landowner. I have no wish to jeopardise the good relations which I gather we have always maintained.'

'Indeed not, sir,' said the chief clerk, a trifle breathlessly.

'I wish,' Flavius continued, 'to spend a few days in the area in early-September, and I would require you to join me there on one of those days.'

'I usually make my visits there in early October.'

'We haven't time to wait. I don't want to arrive and find the legionary engineers are there before us, damaging the goodwill you've helped to build up. I am sure the client-landowner will understand if the position is explained to him.'

The chief clerk said apologetically, 'There is something I think I ought to tell you, sir.' He looked as if he were being forced to utter an obscenity.

'Yes?' said Flavius gently.

'I have to warn you, sir, that the present client-landowner is a woman.'

'Ah,' said Flavius, allowing a solemn moment to pass between them. 'I appreciate your concern. However, it happens that, as a lawyer, I have on occasion taken as clients ladies of means. Most of them have had a sensible grasp of their affairs.'

'Yes, sir, but they would have been Roman ladies, and they would have been accompanied by the male relative designated to oversee their interests, and he would have conducted the discussions with you.'

'Yes, that is so. I do indeed occupy such a position with a great-aunt of mine.'

'But, sir, our client-landowner is a Celtic lady who has no male protector to speak for her.'

At last, thought Flavius, we've reached the point. 'It is not the way in Celtic circles,' he said. 'I understand Celtic women of position can be fiery and outspoken. It this why you are uneasy about dealing with her?'

'No, sir. She is compliant, as all the members of that family have been, with Roman authority.'

'Then where we find compliance, chief clerk, the emperor is anxious we should not interfere with local patterns of behaviour.'

The chief clerk was bewildered. 'I meant no criticism of the emperor, sir. I only wanted to warn you that the owner of the hush is a woman.'

Flavius reproached himself for once again indulging in his lawyer's habit of twisting conversations.

'That was kindly meant, chief clerk. I thank you. I shall now be ready to disguise any unseemly feelings I might experience on meeting our client-landlord.'

The chief clerk nodded, gratified. Then he said, 'I've just remembered. There was somebody once who asked about the mines, though I think it was only a casual enquiry. Nothing of any consequence.'

'Who was it?' Flavius was curious.

'The warden of the post-house, sir.'

Flavius, though not sure why, found this disturbing. 'Whatever would the mines have to do with him?'

The chief clerk shook his head. 'Perhaps before he retired from legionary service, he was an engineer.'

For some time, since the emperor's visit, a small worry had been nagging at the back of Flavius's mind. It was usually provoked by someone's casual remark and, being preoccupied with other matters, he had let it slip away. Now, suddenly, it resurfaced.

Saying over his shoulder as he went, 'Those reports on my desk, if you please,' he left the chief clerk's office as hastily as he'd appeared.

He sought out Aelius. As so often when he needed to talk to him, Flavius found him in his cramped cupboard of a room, engrossed in his accounts.

'Aelius, I want to ask you something.'

He was adding up a long line of figures. 'What now?'

'When the emperor was here, he talked about his network of what he called informants. Did you know about that?'

'Mmm,' said Aelius.

'How did you know?'

'Everyone knows.'

'I didn't,' said Flavius indignantly.

'Then everyone knows about it, except you.' Aelius sighed, and started again on the column of figures.

'I think I know who our spy is,' persisted Flavius.

'Who?'

'The warden of the post-house. It must be him.'

Aelius put down his pen. 'Why must it?'

'Those wardens' appointments are made by the emperor, so Hadrian knows him. He has easy access to the emperor, with all the imperial couriers lodging in the post-house. He's a veteran with twenty-five years' service behind him, so he knows all about the demands of military life. His wife is one of the Brigantes tribe, so he speaks the local dialect. Everyone in the settlement goes to him with their troubles ...'

'He may be the emperor's man, Flavius, but don't forget that if there's trouble between this lot in here and that lot out there, he's the one to smooth it out.'

'So I'm right!' said Flavius. 'You agree with me. *He's* the one that's spying on us.'

'Spying? It's no different from what you do when you make your secret inspections of the men's quarters. Everyone knows you do it, they're just not sure when.'

'That's what the emperor said when I called his informants spies. Which they are,' muttered Flavius.

'What are you so upset about?' demanded Aelius. 'Are you cross with yourself because it's taken you so long to work out who your spy was? Why it never occurred to you before, I can't imagine.'

Flavius shot an angry look at him.

'Don't have one of your huffs with me, Flavius,' snapped Aelius. 'I'm busy.'

'I'm upset,' he said, 'because I liked him. He was easy to talk to, agreeable and gracious.'

'If he'd been disagreeable and ungracious, no-one would have chatted to him, would they? He isn't spying, he's only monitoring what's going on. If things are to be kept in good order, they have to be monitored, as your barracks do. I monitor the work in your household, you monitor my accounts.' Aelius held out a half-completed list.

'I have never in my life demanded to see your accounts,' cried Flavius. 'I only look at them because you make me.' He looked unhappily at his steward. 'I really liked the man. I let him wander freely round this fort ...'

'He has to come in to collect his supplies,' Aelius reminded him.

'... and I see him stopping to chat to the men. What are they saying to him?'

'They're not stupid, Flavius. They grumble to him about the weather, the food, the senior centurion, probably you. But they don't mention that there's illegal gambling every Thursday after midnight in D barracks ...'

'What?' shouted Flavius.

'... just as you wouldn't mention to him what you're doing in Ravenglass these days.'

Flavius stared hard at Aelius. He stared back. 'Trying out the river route to Ambleside, isn't it?' he said blandly.

Flavius got off the stool he was perching on. 'I have work to do.' He took himself off.

Aelius rolled up his accounts and put his writing materials away. He waited, calculating the time it would take Flavius to storm through the villa, and then, with his hand on the door to his library, change his mind and come back.

Aelius pretended to be looking for something when Flavius reappeared.

'I shall be in the library,' he said in a subdued way.

'A few minutes?'

Flavius nodded.

Aelius gave it two minutes and then followed him. Flavius was sitting at his desk, head bowed. Aelius took a chair and sat down, facing him across the desk, saying nothing.

He noticed the sunlight shining on the golden award that came from their days at the University of Antioch, and was wondering if they should hang the emperor's gold sword on one of the walls, when Flavius spoke.

'She's Celtic, Aelius.'

'Flavius, if she's your lady, why should that matter to me?'

He raised his head and smiled. 'Her name is Elphin.' He began to talk about her.

Aelius listened with an attention that was a joy to Flavius.

When he had fallen quiet again, Aelius said: 'Elphin is a very unusual name. Would this then be the lady to whom the tribune referred when he was last here?'

'Yes. She was a friend of his wife.'

Aelius's small nod appeared to be a hint of approval. Flavius was encouraged to ask, 'Would you help me, Aelius?'

'Some time ago, Alis expressed a wish that we should both help you, should you have need of it.'

Flavius smiled broadly at Aelius, who grinned back.

Then Flavius said, 'Some time ago?'

'There were signs, Flavius, but only to anyone who'd known you for thirty years.'

VIII

On a late afternoon at the beginning of September, Flavius stood with Elphin high on the fells north of Caldbeck, looking down on her inherited farmland.

Not far below them was the large pit which marked the top of the hush. It had recently been emptied, and held only the shallow amount of rainwater that had fallen during the previous evening after the sluice had been replaced. The lumps of rock that had been displaced by the torrent of water were still being collected at the base of the long channel that ran down the sloping side of the fell.

Flavius would have enjoyed seeing the hush-water in action, but when it was happening he and Elphin had just reached her farmhouse after their ride from the harbour at Alauna. Aelius and Alis had slipped away to another part of the building, and they were at last alone again after what had been for both of them far too long. At one moment Flavius had murmured drowsily, 'Another sort of waterfall,' but that was as far as his interest in the tumbling foam of the hush took him.

Now, from where they were standing, they could see the farmhouse on the lower slopes of the fell, with Elphin's sheep scattered around it. Smoke was rising above the roof.

'Aelius is busy with our fire,' said Flavius, pleased.

'And Alis will be looking for some pretty pins to put in my hair,' added Elphin, laughing.

Facing them, soaring above the farmhouse, was the flowing, majestic outline of another range of mountains. Those were the ones, Elphin had told him, that would be the first to show a powdering of snow. Those were the ones, Flavius realised, that he had so often seen in the distance, and that made riding east to Papcastle a constant delight to him; now this journey with Elphin had brought him to stand among those very peaks.

He turned eagerly to face her, but she was looking down at the ribbon of the new Roman transport road that ran across the fells down to the army forges behind the harbour at Alauna.

A small group of riders, like black dots on the ribbon, were about to disappear from sight as they began the descent towards the coast.

It was the chief clerk, travelling back to the fort, with an escort to protect the leather bag which held the taxes he had come to collect. He had arrived that morning at a time dictated by Flavius, who by then had left the farmhouse and could be seen in conversation at the hush with the Roman officer in charge.

When Flavius had spoken to Elphin about the chief clerk's alarm at finding a landowner who was a woman, and a Celtic woman at that, she had been amused. 'He's a Spaniard,' she said. 'In some matters, they are more prim than you Romans.' But she had tried not to appear too wild a creature when she received him.

She was not wearing any of her large pieces of Celtic jewellery, and her hair had been twisted into a simple Roman knot. Alis had sat beside her while her taxes were settled and the closing of the hush mine was discussed. When the clerk had gone, with her hair now hanging loose, and her skirt of brightly woven squares caught

319

up over her farmer's boots, she led Flavius along the side of the hush to a smooth ledge just below the summit of the fell.

Now that the men below were no longer visible, she turned her head to stare down at the broad strip of grass running parallel to the road where a line of markers defined a probable site for the first drift mine.

Flavius was concerned to see that she looked upset.

'Elphin,' he said gently, 'it seemed a reasonable suggestion to me. I thought you were happy about it.'

'Yes, yes, I am,' she answered quickly.

'What's worrying you?'

She hesitated. 'It was something your chief clerk said.'

Flavius was surprised. 'I thought he was satisfied with the decisions we had made.'

'It wasn't about that.' Elphin turned to face him. 'He was saying he didn't think the digging would begin until the spring, and he hoped the new commandant wouldn't want to change anything. What did he mean, Flavius?'

He took hold of Elphin's hands that had flown to her face. In that moment, he no longer had any doubts about what he must do.

'Let's go down now and sit by Aelius's warm fire. We'll talk about it there.'

Elphin shook her head. 'No, now.'

'It's beginning to get cold.'

'I don't care. Now, Flavius.'

'Very well. The chief clerk was remembering that I came to Britain a year ago last April. Positions like mine usually last for two years; most auxiliary commandants want to go back to their own lives by then. That's what I expected to do. But it doesn't have to be two years. Some men choose to stay for three years, or even four. Marcellus has been here for more than two years. Celia was happy at Ravenglass.'

'But your wife is not here.'

'Elphin, I have tried to explain to you, our separation is not displeasing to either of us. I shall apply to the legate for another year in office. That is not something I would ever discuss with my chief clerk.'

'Because of me?' she whispered. 'You're staying because of me?'

'Because of you.'

Flavius laughed as she gave a long sigh of relief, and then hung on to him as if her delight had left her without the strength to stand. Then she, too, laughed at herself.

Now that he had put the decision to stay into words, Flavius felt his own spirits lift. How his family would react to his choice was a problem he would have to confront before long, but not now.

'Shall we return to our fire?'

'Please, Flavius, could we go down to the dew pond first?'

'Dew pond? There are so many of them.'

'Yes, little ones, but not like that beautiful one beneath us, there.' She pointed to the pastureland on the other side of the road.

Close to it, in a slight hollow, lay a pool that was almost a perfect oval in shape, except that a bite appeared to have been taken out of one side. In the shadow cast by the sun behind the fells, the surface of the water, set in the dark grass, glimmered like a disc of silver.

They scrambled down the side of the hush, and Elphin ran across the road. 'When I was a child,' she called over her shoulder to Flavius, 'I used to like dancing round dew ponds like this with three or four other little girls.'

'Dancing?' It had a rustic, ritual sound about it that he wasn't sure he liked.

Elphin saw his expression. 'Don't Roman ladies dance together to worship one of your gods?'

Flavius recalled with distaste tales of orgiastic frenzies of dance in certain circles in Rome. 'Nothing of the same sort,' he said briskly.

'We weren't really dancing,' said Elphin, 'though we liked to think we were. We just held hands and ran round the edge of the water. One of the older girls had told us that if you danced round a dew pond three times without stopping and then looked into it, Manannàn would show you the face of your true love.'

'And did he?'

Elphin laughed. 'No.'

'Perhaps running didn't count,' suggested Flavius.

'We didn't think of that. We decided that we weren't yet old enough for Manannàn to decide who would be best for us, so we still kept on running and looking.' She laughed again. 'I suppose we went on until we found some other game to play.'

She knelt down by the pond and dipped a hand in the water. 'Oh, Flavius, you must come and see what's here.'

He stood beside her. Close to, the water was no longer silver but brown. 'See what?'

'I think you'll have to kneel down like me to see it.'

Flavius obediently kneeled.

'If you bent forward a little ...' Elphin gently put a hand on the back of his head. 'There!' she cried. 'I can see the face of my true love in the water of a dew pond. Manannàn brought us here and made it happen for me. '

'He did nothing of the kind,' said Flavius. 'You brought us here and cheated.'

'How can I be cheating? You are my true love.'

'If you were in a court of law, the judge would condemn you for manipulating facts.'

Elphin drew his head towards her and kissed him passionately. 'On that evidence?'

'Hmm. You might stand a chance on appeal.' He kissed her back with the same fervour. 'Yes, I really think you might.'

As they walked across the grass towards her house, he murmured, 'Would you have recognised me if you'd seen my face in a dew pond when you were a child?'

'A horrible little boy's face? I don't think so. But you didn't recognise me a few months ago at the horse race.'

'And what about at Celia's funeral? You treated me with contempt.'

'Well, you were so rude to me. Everyone else was always nice. You were different.'

'You certainly seemed different to me.'

They smiled happily at each other. 'We were slow beginners,' said Flavius.

'But once it began ...' said Elphin.

'Once it began, the world took only a few minutes to turn itself inside out, and it will never go back to the way it was.'

'No, it won't, will it?'

They were disturbed by a voice shouting at them. Aelius was standing at the open door of Elphin's house, a ladle in one hand. From a distance, his expression appeared to suggest displeasure.

'Ouch!' said Flavius.

Aelius had proved in the last couple of days, rather to Flavius's surprise, a more than satisfactory cook; but although working in what he probably regarded as one of the tribal wildernesses of north Britain, he insisted on serving the evening meal at the fashionable Roman time of late afternoon.

Flavius seized Elphin's wrist and they set off at a running walk.

The little villa was clearly a house which met with Aelius's approval. The roofed courtyard with its open fire was precisely the arrangement which he was constantly urging would improve the commandant's accommodation at Alauna.

It was in the glowing warmth of Elphin's courtyard that Aelius had chosen to set a small table. Its probably rustic construction was disguised by a dark covering that he must have raked out from somewhere. The silver knives and spoons had been brought, Flavius suspected, from Alauna. Alis was laying small bowls of hot water on the table together with towels for the diners' fingers.

'Aelius,' observed Flavius, ' has a remarkable gift for—'

Aelius, entering the courtyard with a laden tray, smiled expectantly as he proudly set out the dishes.

'—producing boiling water as required.'

'Hmm,' said Aelius.

Flavius dipped a finger into one of the bowls. 'Yes, perfect temperature, Aelius. Good.'

'Hmm,' he said again.

When the food was eaten, the table cleared, and Aelius with Alis had slipped away to their own corner of the house, Elphin knelt down in front of the fire. Flavius watched the light from the flames playing with the colours in her hair.

Still staring into the fire, she said, 'Flavius, have you ever wondered what it might be like to—'

'Yes,' he said.

Elphin turned round to look up at him. 'Would it please you to—'

'Yes.' Flavius smiled at her.

'But ... Aelius?'

Flavius nodded. He went to a door at the back of the courtyard, opened it and called out, 'Aelius, I'll watch over the fire. Goodnight.'

Elphin heard a muffled reply, and saw Flavius smile as he came back to her.

'What did he say?'

'He said he had assumed that he could leave that to me.'

IX

They walked again next day among the high fells, out of sight of the work going on around the hush.

It was very still and quiet. They could see a long green valley ending in a narrow strip of blue. 'The sea,' said Elphin. 'Tomorrow I shall be on that, going away from you.'

'But not yet,' said Flavius.

'No, not yet.' She looked back in the direction of her house, which was now hidden from them. 'Do you know what I would like to do this evening? I would like to cook a meal for all four of us to eat together, in the Celtic way.'

Before Flavius could reply, she went on, 'Do you remember when we were coming back from the River Leven?'

'I remember very well everything we did on or around the Leven,' murmured Flavius.

'You spoke about us coming here. I couldn't see how we could be alone together, but you told me you would arrange everything. I would have to trust you, but you were sure I would be pleased with what you planned to do.'

'Did I say all that?'

Elphin nodded. 'I want you to know you were right and I am very pleased. I couldn't be happier than I am here. I love being with Aelius, because he cares so much for you, and Alis behaves so sweetly to me. I want them to know how much I value their company. It is our custom, especially on festive occasions, for family and household to share food round their fire. I would like to make something for them to enjoy.'

'I heard Alis laughing with you yesterday,' said Flavius, smiling at Elphin. 'I have often known her to smile in her patient, uncomplaining way, but never to laugh like that. Not that she has ever had much cause to do so. You won't know this, Elphin, but when Alis was a small child, she was bought as a slave by my wife's family. She was never treated badly in that house, but she never had any kindness either. Whatever you do, I think she will enjoy it.'

'But she is not a slave now because she is married to Aelius. Isn't that your law?'

'Yes. I bought Aelius his freedom, and then I discovered he was saving up to buy hers so that he could marry her. He had loved her since she came to my house as my wife's maid. I bought her freedom as a wedding gift for him.'

Elphin threw her arms round him. 'Flavius, you deserve me!'

He kissed her. 'I will never deserve you, but I will never let you go.'

She laughed. 'I'm glad of that.'

As they walked back towards her villa, Flavius said, 'Let me tell Aelius about this evening.'

He was only too aware of how his steward could prickle with displeasure if he felt his work was not appreciated. This, as Flavius had anticipated, was such an occasion.

Aelius assumed his mood of hurt dignity. 'The lady Elphin will cook?'

'Yes,' said Flavius irritably. 'Kindly get it out of your head that this is intended as criticism. She is doing it to thank you.'

'Oh?'

'Yes. More important, it is meant to give Alis pleasure.' He handed Aelius a small box. 'Elphin wants you to give this to your wife.'

'What is it?'

'It's nothing to do with you, Aelius, but if you must know it holds the silver ornaments that Elphin sometimes wears in her hair. Alis has said how pretty she thinks they are. So while Elphin is cooking, she says Alis will have time to pin them in her own hair.'

'Oh,' said Aelius again.

'Is that all you can say?'

'No. It's very kind of your lady, but it still isn't proper, is it? She's a kind of princess in that little island of hers. It's not her place to cook for us. I've never even known your mother to cook – plan menus, perhaps, but never cook in a kitchen – and your wife would be ashamed to admit she knew what a kitchen was. This is not proper, Flavius.'

'For all that sensitive Greek blood of yours, Aelius, no-one is more Roman than you are when it comes to declaring what is, or is not, proper conduct. Elphin's world is not our world. This is her house, on her land. The people around us belong to a tribe very similar to her own. She is offering us the courtesy of sharing her way of life with us. Try to behave as if you understand this, even if you don't like doing it.'

'Actually,' said Aelius, 'I would do anything for your lady.'

'Even that? Good. Well, there's something you could do for her now. She wants you to help me look for cushions to spread round the fire.'

'Cushions?' said Aelius with dismay.

'Is that so different from lounging on Roman couches?' asked Flavius.

'Hardly to my Greek taste,' grunted Aelius. He nevertheless heaped up cushions with a will, saying when they had been arranged to his satisfaction, 'At least we shall have wine and be warm, and that's the same everywhere.'

When they were all four gathered together, it took a while for Alis to overcome her shyness and Aelius his diffidence at trying dishes that had been prepared in ways unfamiliar to him; but by the time they had all tasted Elphin's spiced wine, which she had mulled by using a poker heated in the fire, they were beginning to enjoy talking together. Aelius, encouraged by Elphin, recalled, between mouthfuls of delicious food, youthful exploits shared with Flavius. Most had been long forgotten by him, and were vigorously denied. They fell into amiable arguments, which amused Alis.

Elphin moved to sit beside her. 'Just like eight year old boys again?' she whispered.

'Yes, they are,' agreed Alis.

Then Flavius, turning his head to listen to them, heard Elphin ask if Alis was comfortable.

'It's lovely here,' she said, shifting herself gently and looking into the flames. 'I'm warm and comfortable –' she laughed ' – and so sleepy.'

'And the baby?'

'He's sleepy, too.'

'He?'

'Aelius says it is a boy.'

He glanced across at them. 'Yes. Our son will be given my father's name.'

'Oh?' said Elphin.

'In parts of Greece, it is the custom.'

'So when this son of yours has a son, he too will be called Aelius? Couldn't that become confusing if you have a long-lived family?'

Aelius shot a look at Flavius. 'They have no experience of Greek sensibility on her island,' Flavius murmured to him. He had stretched out his hands to the fire as a flame spurted upward. 'You are right, Alis. This is lovely.'

Elphin said, 'You ought to see the fires we have in my father's house for the winter festivals. There can be fifty or sixty people sitting or wandering about at any one time: eating, exchanging greetings, making music. You have your Roman winter festival in the middle of the winter, just before the solstice, Alis, but we have ours at the beginning, on the first day of November, when the darkness is growing heavier but it is still just warm enough to enjoy bonfires outside.'

'Some people in Alauna,' Alis said, 'believe strange things happen to your island.'

Elphin smiled. 'Are you afraid that if you set foot on the island of Manannàn, you might never be seen again?'

'No, but you can't help feeling there's something strange and magical about it, when one day it's there, and then it disappears for weeks. Yes, I know it's the effect of the mists, Aelius, but I can understand why these stories are told.'

'My island is certainly neither strange nor magical,' said Elphin. 'I love it, but it has nothing like the beauty of the fells round us here. We have hills, but they are low by comparison. It has what I think of as pleasant and comfortable, but unremarkable, country. There is, I suppose, one hill that might pass for a mountain. If you climb to the top of it, on a clear day you can see the shores of Britain and Ireland, and the far coast of the land that lies beyond your emperor's wall.

'When we light our November bonfires across the island, the brightest one burns from that high point. Perhaps, on that one night of the winter festival, when the gold beacons blaze against a black sky, the island might look for a few hours like a magical place for the ships sailing nearby.'

Later, when Aelius had carried a drowsy Alis to bed, and Elphin was roasting apples and the last of the chestnuts in the embers of the fire, Flavius said, 'I'd like to see those bonfires of yours.'

'Then why not come?'

Elphin turned towards him, the glow of the firelight behind her, and repeated with a lilt of excitement in her voice, 'Why not come?'

'Not to your festival?'

'Yes. My father loves to entertain visitors. He always invites the commandant from the fort. Marcellus came with Celia last year. We don't know if he will come alone this year but we hope he will because he will be leaving a month or so later and we shall probably never see him again. If he had you for company, knowing you wanted to come ...'

'If I came with Marcellus, he would have to introduce me to your father. Would that be wise? If your father saw us together, might he not guess what we are to each other?'

Elphin said playfully, 'He might think I have chosen my new husband at last. All over the island they want me to marry again, to find a strong man who will help me protect them when my father leaves them.'

'A Roman soldier? Elphin, be serious. Some of them may trust Marcellus, as your father does, but they know he is leaving. They may think I am using you to take control of their land when he has gone.'

'Flavius, I know we can't be together as we are here. We won't even allow ourselves to be seen together if you say so, but my father will be busy, everyone else will be busy, surely we can find a few moments to be alone in the darkness? And if you won't agree even to that, we can still be in the same place together, we can be near each other, we can see each other. Please, Flavius, isn't that better than nothing?'

He took her face in his hands. 'Yes, of course it is.' He kissed her gently. 'And if we are lucky, we might perhaps find a corner of darkness away from the bonfires.'

When Elphin smiled happily, he added, 'You must find out first if Marcellus is willing to take me. If he is, he must write me one of his brief commandant messages that my chief clerk can copy and put in his files.'

He bit into a chestnut that Elphin had peeled for him. 'It occurs to me that you could repay me with more than a chestnut. If I come to your November festival, you could do me the courtesy of coming to my December one.'

'Your Saturnalia? That's when everybody dresses up as somebody else, and runs about shouting in the streets and gets drunk?'

'Not everyone,' murmured Flavius.

'And in the army forts, officers like you spend the five days of the holiday waiting on the men.'

'When I passed my first Saturnalia in the army last year, that's what I thought happened, but it doesn't. I played the servant for the first day, and then the senior centurion told me I wasn't needed any more. Most of the men were so drunk they didn't know or care what was happening. I was free for four days to do what I liked. I shall be free again for four whole days in the middle of next December, and I know very well what I should like to be doing.'

Elphin laughed with delight. 'Where will I come? Not to Alauna?'

'No, not Alauna, but somewhere close. The shorter my journey, the longer we shall have together. Somewhere like Papcastle.'

'Then why not Papcastle? Lots of roads meet there, don't they? People will be coming and going all the time,' said Elphin happily. 'How far is it from Alauna?'

'About five miles. I could leave Alauna about midnight. They'll be celebrating their own Saturnalia in the Papcastle fort, so someone else wandering the streets at that hour won't be noticed. Elphin, would you be prepared to come all that way? Would it be possible for you to come?'

'It's not our festival. All our markets and fairs go on as normal. There'll be some excuse I can make.'

Flavius felt an uncomfortable twinge of conscience. 'I hate making you lie, especially to someone who loves you, like your father.'

Elphin nodded her head. 'You have to lie, too. Perhaps it is harder for you, because, as a lawyer, you devote your life to searching for truth, but what can we do? We mean no harm, and do no real harm either. We are from different worlds, you and I, Flavius, but we are both bound by constraints that are not of our choosing. Perhaps, if they knew what we are cherishing, they might understand why we deceive them. Perhaps not. Let's hope they never learn of it, and then it is only you and I who need feel disturbed.'

Aelius, who knew from the sound of their voices that they were still up, came into the hall, carrying the small box that held Elphin's silver hair ornaments.

'My lady,' he said, 'Alis ...'

'Elphin,' she corrected him.

'My lady Elphin.'

Elphin gave up. 'Aelius, I would like Alis to keep them. They look much prettier in her dark hair than they do in mine.'

Aelius hesitated.

'Please let her keep them,' said Elphin. 'If she doesn't want them, then, should your baby be a girl, she might enjoy playing with them when she is old enough.'

Aelius shook his head. 'It will be a boy, my lady!'

Flavius waved him away.

X

They rode away from Elphin's villa early the next morning, and at a sedate pace took the Roman-built road that led to the workshops and harbour at Alauna. Elphin waved on the way to the tenants who came out to greet her, and Flavius exchanged crisp salutes with the soldiers working by the hush. As they approached the harbour Aelius rode ahead, seemingly intent on locating Elphin's vessel.

He returned to Flavius. 'There's quite a crowd taking an interest in the ship, among them your spy as you call him. He may, of course, just be wandering about, taking the air. Let's run no risks.'

He turned to Elphin. 'My lady, when we reach the harbour, I will act the groom and help you and Alis to dismount. She and I will walk with you to the ship and see you aboard. Flavius will remain mounted and will not follow, as if he is anxious to get back to the fort as soon as he can. No waving, and no long looks, Flavius.'

Elphin sighed and bit her lip; Flavius swore. Yet both of them accepted his advice.

Flavius remained in the saddle. He watched Elphin walk towards the water, Alis beside her. Aelius was in front of them, clearing the way. Only when she was on deck did Elphin turn her head to look at Flavius and then bow briefly, as if acknowledging Roman authority on British soil.

Flavius responded with a peremptory salute, then wheeled his horse towards the fort without waiting to see the ship depart. As he set off towards the north gate, the warden of the post-house materialised beside him.

'Good day, prefect,' he said in his usual gracious manner. 'From the length of time you have been away, you would seem to have encountered problems perhaps. Nothing too arduous one trusts, sir?'

'More than arduous, warden. I am uneasy at not staying longer in the fells. The failure of a mine up there is a grave business. We can't afford to lose any silver, but prospecting for deeper mining on farming land is not popular. I seriously doubt if the existing serf labour would be practicable ...'

The warden's interest, Flavius happily observed, was not holding up. 'But what might be the effect of using criminal labour? I would welcome your views.'

The warden appeared to be readying himself to follow Flavius into the fort. 'But not now,' he added. 'I have other matters on hand. Good day to you.'

See what you make of that, he thought bitterly as he cantered through the north gate and stopped outside his villa. He dismounted in haste, shouting to the porter to find a groom, then hurried along the streets of the fort and out again through the west gate.

He strode to the top of the bluff. From that point the harbour was hidden from him, but within minutes a boat appeared beyond the cliff, nosing its way into deeper water before it turned south.

Flavius wanted to shout for joy because Elphin had had the same thought as he had. She was standing at the back of the boat, peering up at the fort. He held out the edge of his red cloak to catch the wind and, suddenly seeing it, she pulled the scarf from round her neck and waved it above her head.

Flavius wondered if the rumour about his obsessive fear of a sea invasion was still current around the fort. If someone had seen him waving his cloak in the air, might they not assume he was signalling to the enemy? Now there was a thought to excite their 'spy'. Flavius was delighted with it.

Out of the corner of his eye, he caught a glimpse of a woman's cloak emerging from the gateway.

He spun round. 'Elph—'

He must have been out of his mind. Elphin was at sea, being rowed far too quickly away from him towards an island hidden in mist.

It was Aemilia who was making her way on to the bluff. One hand held the wrist of her toddler; the other rested on the shoulder of a boy aged about eight or nine years old.

'Aemilia,' said Flavius loudly, pulling his red cloak round him. 'It's very windy up here. Should you be out?'

'I was looking for you, sir. I met this young man in the market and he was most insistent that I should take him to the man in charge of the fort.'

She bent down to speak to the boy in the local dialect. He scowled at Flavius and shook his head, then mumbled back at her.

'Oh, sir, I'm so sorry, but he says you aren't the man in charge. You haven't got a stick.'

Flavius put a hand on the hilt of his sword. 'Won't this do?'

'Oh, dear,' sighed Aemilia, 'he says it won't.'

'Who is this child?'

'He's the baker's son, sir.'

'Baker's son?' cried Flavius. 'The baker whose door was broken?'

'I think so,' said Aemilia, bewildered.

The boy was growing impatient. He pulled his shoulder away from under Aemilia's hand and shouted at her.

'Be quiet!' Flavius pointed a finger at him in a way that made translation unnecessary. 'What was he shouting?'

Aemilia hesitated. 'That your sword was no use because it doesn't make a swishing sound.'

'Ah,' said Flavius. 'Follow me.'

He led them back into the fort and to the door of the senior centurion's house. As he raised a hand to rap on the door, Aemilia said, 'The senior centurion likes to take a rest at this time of day, sir.'

'Then I'd better rap hard,' said Flavius, proceeding to do so.

The door was opened by an irate Lugo, dressed in an old off-duty tunic. He stared at the curious assembly gathered on his doorstep.

'Senior centurion,' began Flavius, 'this boy here is looking for the man in charge of the fort.'

Lugo grunted, 'Is he now?' He peered at the boy, and in his own heavily accented version of the local speech, said grimly, 'I know you, don't I? The baker's son. A lot of trouble you caused, especially to me. Well, what is it?'

'I take it that you can produce a stick that makes a swishing noise?' murmured Flavius. 'That is the required proof of authority.'

Lugo put a hand behind his door and held up his cane of office. He brought it down with a sound that made Aemilia jump.

The boy stopped shuffling his boots in the road and beamed at the senior centurion. He showed him a number of small copper coins that had been clutched in his palm.

Lugo grunted again. 'So what's all this about?'

The child began to speak excitedly.

'He is saying,' whispered Aemilia to Flavius, 'that he has brought back the money he took from the soldier during last Saturnalia. These aren't the same coins because he spent them. Then he was sorry, so he saved up the same amount, and now he wants to return it.'

Lugo gazed solemnly at the coins, then carefully picked them up, one by one, and counted them into his own palm.

'Is it the same amount?' muttered Flavius.

'How should I know?' said Lugo. 'I am about to tell him that, pleased as I am to see this money, it is not for me to say that his bad behaviour is forgiven. That is for the man who was robbed to decide, so we will have to find Noricus.'

The boy listened, and looked as if he wanted to run away, but the senior centurion uttered a command. The boy hesitated, then stayed where he was.

'Thank you, sir. Thank you, Aemilia,' said Lugo briskly. 'I'll deal with this once I've dressed.' He beckoned the boy to step into his house.

Flavius watched him obey. 'You seem to have a way with boys, senior centurion,' he said, not without surprise.

'I ought to,' said Lugo, as he closed the door. 'I've had three of them.'

Flavius stared at the closed door. Then he turned to Aemelia, who had bent down to pick up her child. 'Did you hear what he said?'

'No, sir, I'm sorry. What was it?'

'It doesn't matter. Let me walk back with you.'

Moving at Aemelia's slow pace with the child in her arms, they had barely reached her house when the senior centurion appeared again. He was now wearing his chain-mail tunic and had honoured the occasion by displaying on it the emperor's gold disc. The baker's boy was trotting beside him, trying to keep up. They saw him turn the lad in the direction of the steps leading up to the veranda outside Noricus's section quarters.

Once he had left Aemilia, Flavius made for the chief clerk's office. The man seemed to be expecting him. 'Were you wanting my report on the mine visit, sir? I have it ready.'

'No,' said Flavius. 'I want the senior centurion's file.'

As the chief clerk looked along one of his shelves, Flavius asked, 'Were you here when this fort was first opened?'

'Yes, sir, I was newly recruited from Spain.'

'So you knew the senior centurion then?'

The chief clerk laid the retrieved file on his desk. 'Yes, sir, but of course he wasn't the senior centurion in those days.'

'Is it true that he had children?'

'Yes, three sons. The youngest was born here. When he was sent here as a junior centurion, he brought his wife and the two older ones with him.' The chief clerk smiled. 'I remember the pair of them wandering around here. The men made them little tunics out of scraps of leather and painted them silver to look like armour, and they had toy swords and shields.'

The chief clerk paused. 'I believe that, in his heart, the senior centurion has always hoped that when his sons grow up they might join one of the legions. When he takes retirement, he receives Roman citizenship and that means they will acquire it too when they come of age at sixteen ...'

'... and that makes them eligible for legionary recruitment,' interrupted Flavius. 'I still can't quite believe these children ever existed. What happened to them?'

'Long before you arrived here, sir, they were sent home to Gaul.'

'Gaul? But the senior centurion's home is in Spain.'

'He was born in Spain, like most of us here, but he hasn't seen Spain since he was sixteen. Before serving with this First Spanish cohort, he'd spent all his service life in northern Gaul. That's the place he thinks of as home. That's where he'll go when he gets his honourable discharge and his piece of land. He married a local woman there as soon as he achieved centurion rank. His children are with his wife's parents.'

'And his wife?'

'She died, sir. When we first heard talk of a detachment of our cohort going to Judea, I think that the senior centurion would have liked to volunteer, but he couldn't expect to take two small children and a pregnant wife on a journey like that.

'The then senior centurion elected to go, and our present senior centurion was promoted to his office. His third son was born just after the detachment left. In the January after that, we had a bad outbreak of the winter sickness here. That's when his wife died.'

'And then, I suppose,' said Flavius, 'he found he couldn't look after three small boys, one of them a baby, and at the same time carry out his duties as he thought proper?'

The chief clerk nodded. 'We all tried to help, especially the other centurions' wives, but it wasn't right for anyone. So that's how it was the little ones were sent to their grandparents.'

Flavius was silent. The chief clerk pushed Lugo's record towards him. 'It's all here, sir, if you find it difficult to believe.'

'Of course I believe it. I just never thought ...' Flavius shook his head. 'He must wonder at times if she wouldn't have been safer in Judea.'

The chief clerk shrugged his shoulders. 'Who knows, sir? Perhaps he does, sometimes.'

'How long is it since he's seen the children?'

'About six years, sir.'

'Six years, alone every day in that empty, silent house?'

The chief clerk looked at Flavius uneasily. 'It's the army, sir.'

'Yes, of course,' he said crisply. 'It's the army.'

Stepping out of the headquarters building a few moments later, he was disconcerted to encounter Lugo in the street outside. The baker's boy, now in possession of a toy sword, which he was busy lunging at invisible enemies, was still beside him.

'Shouldn't he be back home by now?' said Flavius. 'Won't his family be missing him?'

'If you saw the state of that shop, you'd know that was most unlikely, sir. We've had a busy time. In Noricus's section they were cooking a meal and they let him stay and share it with them, then I walked him round the parade ground and let him stand where you stand, sir, when you review the men. He understands now that, although I am very important here, you are above me because you come from the emperor. Then we went to see the emperor's gold statue, and he learned to bow properly in front of it. He's also mastered half-a-dozen words in Latin, "stop" being one of them. Watch, if you please, sir.'

Lugo turned his head towards the boy. He raised his voice slightly. 'Stop!'

The boy glanced round and then slipped his little sword into a length of rope that someone had tied round his waist to serve as a sword-belt. He came running back.

'I have explained to him,' said Lugo, 'that whenever anyone meets you, and that includes me, you must be saluted, so: I present my duty to you, sir.' The senior centurion produced an immaculate parade salute. He gave the boy a discreet nod. Pink-faced with pleasure, the baker's lad clapped a hand to his head smartly.

Flavius responded with dignity. It was difficult to tell, he thought, which of the two of them was most gratified.

'I congratulate you, senior centurion,' he said. 'The child was rude and truculent before this, but not any longer.'

Lugo motioned the boy to start walking towards the north gate and the settlement. He set off, with a little swaggering step, hand poised on the hilt of his sword.

'Did you give him that?' asked Flavius gently.

Lugo glanced at him. 'Yes,' he said. 'It belonged to my eldest boy. It would be too small for him now, but I liked to keep it around. If it can give some enjoyment to another child, then why not let him have it?'

He stared at the boy. 'If I could have him for a few hours every week, I could work wonders with him.'

'Then why *not* have him for a few hours every week?' said Flavius. Lugo stared at him. 'Think about it. We need a school here. When general Agrippa was commandant, surely he talked about it?'

'I think he did,' said Lugo vaguely. 'There was, presumably, never a suitable time.'

'Well, perhaps that time has now come.'

He saw the not unfamiliar cast of stubbornness appearing on the senior centurion's face. 'Anyway, for the moment, I think you ought to take the boy home. I have a feeling that the baker probably clouts him whenever he turns up, on the grounds that he'll have been causing mischief somewhere.'

Lugo, restored to familiar territory, grunted confidently. 'We're not having that, sir. Don't you worry.' And he set off after the boy.

Flavius went to look for Aelius. He found him in the library of the villa, apparently assuring himself that dusting duties had been maintained in his absence. 'Where have you been?' Aelius said.

'I have been discussing the possible opening of a school here with the senior centurion.'

'With the senior centurion? A productive discussion, was it?'

Flavius ignored this. 'I've also learned something about him that I don't suppose you know.'

'I doubt it. Well, go on.'

'He's a widower, with three young sons.'

Aelius sighed. 'And the talk is that he became a changed man when the children were sent away. The popular joke is that he made army regulations his children instead.' He hesitated. 'I'm sorry, Flavius, I don't think I should have repeated that. It isn't funny.'

'Not when you think of him alone in that house of his, though I might have said the same as you when I first arrived here.'

'He chose the army life,' said Aelius gently.

'Yes, choosing the army life, Aelius. Curiously enough, that's what I need to talk to you about. Could you stop whatever you're fiddling about with and sit down for a moment?'

'Fiddling about with?' Aelius chose to assume his affronted look, but nevertheless sat down, albeit stiffly, on the very edge of a chair.

'You are expecting, I imagine,' Flavius began, 'to be returning sometime next spring to Stresa?'

Aelius looked at him suspiciously. 'Yes,' he said.

'I have to tell you that I have decided to request another year in office here from the legate. There is little doubt that he will grant my request.'

Aelius was silent for a moment. 'Is this because of Elphin?'

Flavius glared at him. 'Yes.'

'Oh, that's all right then. I thought you might be wanting to teach the senior centurion good Roman Ciceronian Latin. Can't have his provincial Spanish accent in your new school.'

'Aelius!' Flavius controlled his temper. 'I need to ask you if you would be willing to stay here with me?'

Aelius shot out of his chair, now genuinely affronted. 'We had all this sort of fuss when you decided you were coming here. I don't know how you can ask me again.'

'Well, how would you like it,' shouted Flavius, 'if I treated you as if you had no feelings and rights of your own? As if I had no respect for you? No affection ...'

Aelius looked back at him. 'Idiot,' he said gently, 'what else would I do but stay with you?'

'Things have changed, Aelius. Before long, you and Alis will be parents. You'll have your son.'

'He'll find it easier to travel the thousand miles back to Stresa when he's over a year old than when he's only a few months.'

'What will Alis want?'

'What I want. We're both glad that you have found Elphin.'

They fell silent. Then Aelius said quietly, 'What happens when the fourth year comes round?'

'I don't know ... I don't know.'

'Wouldn't it be easier if we took her back with us? Have you thought about that?'

Flavius nodded.

'And?'

'I don't know.'

'I think,' said Aelius, 'I will go elsewhere to do more of the fiddling that keeps your villa in such a superb state.'

He paused with his hand on the door. 'I've just had a thought: if we are to spend the next two winters in this indescribable wilderness, wouldn't it be well worth roofing over this courtyard and putting in a hearth? You can't say you didn't enjoy that fire of Elphin's. I have mentioned it before, of course.'

Flavius threw a cushion at him. 'And I have mentioned before that this villa is army property, and not mine to change. The next commandant here will expect to find the kind of villa he would see in any other fort in the empire.'

'And wouldn't he be glad not to find it?' muttered Aelius, slamming the door behind him.

XI

A week later, Flavius was seated at his desk in the headquarters building, trying to compose a letter to his father explaining his reason for seeking a third year in Alauna.

It was proving more difficult even than he had thought it would. He had scribbled one note after another on his wax tablet and had wiped off each of them in turn.

It was a welcome relief when the chief clerk appeared with army correspondence for his attention.

'Two items from York, sir,' he announced. 'One is the monthly bulletin from the legate's office – nothing of any particular interest to us – and the other is a letter from the legate himself addressed to you. There is also a letter for you from the tribune at Ravenglass. Both couriers have been instructed to wait for replies – two at once, if you can believe it, sir.' The chief clerk was gleeful.

Flavius, with a spurt of excitement, snatched up the letter from Ravenglass. 'This can be dealt with at once,' he said, hoping his pleasure was not too evident.

Then he unrolled the scroll from the legate. 'This will take much longer,' he said, after reading it twice. 'I shall need the senior centurion. Send a man to find him. He is to cancel whatever he has arranged for today. No excuses. We have a serious matter here.'

While they waited for Lugo to arrive, Flavius dictated his reply to Marcellus.

'To the tribune Marcellus Fabius Gallus, greetings: Sir, I am honoured that before you leave Britain in December you plan to complete the study we initiated at the legate's request last summer. The period you suggest, between late October and early November, will of course be convenient. I look forward to receiving your final instructions nearer that time.'

Flavius nodded at the chief clerk. 'Get that ready now for my signature, if you please, and attach a copy to my files. Then we can release the courier. He is being looked after, I take it?'

'Both couriers are being made comfortable in the post-house, sir,' said the chief clerk.

'Ah,' said Flavius, 'I'm sure the warden will enjoy their conversation.'

The chief clerk frowned. 'Sir?'

By the time Lugo arrived, red-faced and breathless, the Ravenglass letter had been returned to Flavius for his signature. As he handed it back to the chief clerk, his eye rested briefly, with secret delight, on the word 'November'.

He turned to the uneasy senior centurion. 'I said the matter was serious, not alarming, senior centurion. Do you know anything about the fort of Maia?'

Maia was the most northerly fort on the Solway coast. It stood at the point where the emperor's wall reached the sea. Lugo half rose from the chair in which he had just settled himself. 'Maia!' he almost shouted. 'You've just written to Ravenglass, sir. You think there will be an invasion along the whole coast?'

'No, I do not,' snapped Flavius. 'Sit down. The senior centurion at Maia has completed his twenty-five years' service and will shortly take honourable retirement. That is what the legate has written to me about. He is considering your deputy here as a replacement.'

'My deputy? Isn't there someone at Maia?'

'Not in the legate's view apparently. Naturally, I require your advice.'

Lugo thought for a moment. 'He is good on the parade ground, a good disciplinarian ...'

'... of a disagreeable nature, but that doesn't affect his suitability, I suppose. If he aspires to promotion, which I've no doubt he does, I can think of no valid reason for opposing the legate's suggestion. Do you agree with me?'

Lugo nodded. 'That leaves me without a deputy.'

'Precisely.' Flavius pushed one of his wax tablets towards him together with a stylus. 'Write on there your three preferred candidates, in order of choice. I'll do the same.'

Flavius scribbled on his own tablet, then waited impatiently while the senior centurion wrote with laboured care. When they finally laid their lists side by side, they agreed on the first name, but not the other two. 'Well, that's fine,' said Flavius, underlining the top name on his list. 'That's our man.'

'But we don't agree on the other two names, sir.'

Flavius felt like groaning aloud. 'No, but that doesn't matter, we both agree on your new deputy. We don't want three of them.' He moved on hastily. 'Now, our last decision is probably going to be the most difficult. We shall have a vacancy for a junior centurion. I think I have to leave you to make another list of three. You have selected men for training for possible centurion rank, and you know how they have responded. When you have made your choices, you can discuss them with me.'

As Lugo bent to his task, Flavius willed him to write a certain name. He even wrote it in very large letters on his own wax tablet in the ridiculous hope that it might drift into the senior centurion's mind. He hurriedly concealed it when the officer, with a deep sigh, laid his stylus aside.

Flavius leaned forward. Reading upside down, he saw with relief the name he'd hoped for, but there was also a question mark beside it.

'Why put a question mark? Surely you know whether or not a man is suitable for promotion?' said Flavius severely.

Lugo gave him an unhappy look. 'Sir, I can't decide what I ought to do. He is the man I would choose as far as ability is concerned, but there was that business during last Saturnalia.'

'You don't mean,' said Flavius, exasperated, 'all that trouble about the baker's blue door? I thought we had acquitted the man of blame, agreed there'd be no mark against his record, the baker was more than satisfied with the repairs, and the obnoxious child is now following you about like a pet dog.' He pulled out the wax tablet he had hidden. 'This is the man I would have chosen.'

Lugo blinked at the large letters filling the wax surface. 'Noricus,' he said, looking dazed.

'Yes, exactly what you have written. I wouldn't have shown it to you if we hadn't agreed.' Flavius took the stylus from Lugo's fingers, and with the blunt end removed the question mark. 'There, now we agree completely.'

The senior centurion was staring at him with the bewilderment verging on mild panic that possessed him when the commandant was in one of his brisk moods.

Flavius now understood the man better than he had on first working with him. Lugo disliked change, and, if it had to come, liked a decision to mature in his mind over a period of time.

Flavius said, more slowly, 'I find it amazing that we should have held the same opinions on every matter we had to consider, didn't you? I was prepared for lengthy discussion. It is most gratifying to me to have my judgements confirmed, as I trust it is for you, senior centurion?'

'Yes, sir.'

'Good, good.' Flavius smiled back at him. 'I shall instruct the post-house to prepare the legate's courier immediately for his return journey, and by the time he has eaten our reply will be ready for him. The legate will not, I am sure, be unaware of the promptness of our response.'

Lugo cheered up. 'Yes, sir.'

Flavius nodded and rubbed his hands together. 'We have work ahead of us. senior centurion, I would like you to acquaint your deputy with his proposed promotion. You will make him understand that it must not be mentioned until the legate's formal documentation arrives, but we must hope he acts as quickly as we did.'

'Then once that comes,' said Lugo, now happily on the familiar territory of organised army procedure, 'we arrange his farewell parade.'

'Yes, and we get down to redecorating that house of his for the next occupant. Such a dismal house with all that brown paint. Since Noricus is *section* leader of painters, *I* suspect his men will enjoy doing it for him as a wedding present.' Flavius smiled again, thinking of bright, clean fresh colours being slapped on the dark walls.

The senior centurion was not sharing his pleasure. 'Wedding present? What wedding?'

Flavius, wishing he had kept his imagination in check, said carefully, 'Have I made a mistake? I always understood that, if he ever achieved centurion rank, he would marry.'

'How would you hear that, sir, if I did not know about it?'

'Perhaps my house steward mentioned it. He spends time in the bath-house where he picks up gossip.'

Lugo frowned. He was a man who used the bath-house for washing, not lounging and chattering.

Flavius said quickly, 'I can understand that it might be true. You know how much he admires you. You guessed that during that business last Saturnalia with the baker's child. Noricus is following your wise example, because that is exactly what you did when you became a centurion.'

'Yes, so it was,' said Lugo smugly, with a private little laugh to himself, 'and he didn't want me to know ...'

'... because it might look as though he was currying favour with you,' suggested Flavius, neatly escaping, as he hoped, from a tight corner.

Unfortunately, Lugo was in that moment struck by another offensive thought. 'That's the deputy senior centurion's house you're talking about. Noricus doesn't move into that. That is for my new deputy.'

'I thought,' said Flavius, 'that your new deputy would prefer to stay in the house he now occupies.'

'No, sir. He is the new deputy senior centurion, and he will reside in the deputy senior centurion's house. Why should you choose to deprive him of his rights, sir?'

'Senior centurion, his present house boasts a garden that his wife, Aemilia, has nurtured with care, and he knows how much it means to her. There is no piece of land round the so-called deputy's house which would be suitable for any kind of growing things.'

'With respect, sir, you surely can't believe that a woman's flowers can have anything to do with the privileges of a senior army officer.'

'He has no privileges or rights with regards to any house. There is no designated house for your deputy. Yours is a designated house as is my villa. The remaining centurions' houses are precisely the same in size and design. Wherever your new deputy lives becomes the deputy senior centurion's house.'

Lugo drew in his breath with the hissing noise which marked a state of agitation. 'My deputy has always lived in that same house, close to me. I must have him close to me.'

'To my knowledge,' said Flavius, 'you have only had one deputy, and what you insist on referring to as the deputy's house was only the one he happened to be living in at the time of his appointment.'

Flavius heard another sharp intake of breath and rose from his desk. 'It is my command, senior centurion,' he said sharply, 'that your new deputy should continue to inhabit his present house. His wife's garden, with the herbs grown for our hospital and the flowers which she generously shares, is a valuable asset to this fort which I am not prepared to lose for the sake of an unprecedented army procedure.'

Lugo's stormy expression appeared to freeze for a moment and then change slowly back to one of bewilderment.

Flavius felt ashamed that his contempt for unjustifiable stubbornness had made him speak as he had to a man whose respect for, almost worship of, army procedures and established precedents lay at the core of his existence.

He added quickly, 'Senior centurion, would you, if you please, send an orderly with my instructions to the post-house, and tell the chief clerk to come in here.'

Lugo, as Flavius had hoped he would be, was instantly comforted by the prospect of giving orders to other people instead of suffering them himself from a commandant who, though he was probably a clever lawyer, couldn't grasp the simplest structures of army life. Why couldn't he at least understand that he was wrong about the deputy's house?'

Lugo spied an orderly and yelled ferociously at him.

344

XII

Within a month, the senior centurion's former deputy had left for Maia.

On his final day at Alauna, he was given a ceremonial farewell on the parade ground. Flavius spoke of his regret at losing such a stalwart officer (which was not true) but his satisfaction that he was leaving to enjoy a post of honour in Maia (which was).

'Poor Maia,' muttered Aelius as he watched the officer ride out of the north gate, followed by three carts filled with his worldly possessions and a mounted escort to protect them.

On the next day, the parade ground witnessed a formal greeting from the cohort to its new deputy senior centurion, happily watched by Aemelia.

The last grand occasion on the parade ground came when Noricus, wearing for the first time his centurion dress and carrying his staff of office, mounted the platform to receive his commission from Flavius. The cheers, led by his former section-mates, brought a flush to his cheeks, and he flushed even more when a notice on the bulletin board announcing his forthcoming wedding was received with ribald comments.

When the newly decorated house was ready, Noricus's lady closed her weaving shed in the settlement. As a Roman officer's wife she would be unable to go on trading, and had arranged for one of her former husband's nephews to come from their weaving house in Carlisle to manage her business until her son was of an age to control it. One of her smaller looms was moved to the fort, to the pleasure of the other centurions' wives, who hoped she might teach them to weave.

On the day appointed for the wedding, Noricus, accompanied by Aemilia, walked down to the settlement to escort her back to the fort. In the assembly hall, Flavius joined the bride and groom in marriage again, this time in the Roman manner. Then Noricus's seven former section-mates carried the bride over the threshold of her gleaming new home.

Flavius gave a small wedding dinner in the villa that evening, for the other centurions and their wives to meet Noricus's wife and her son. 'Did anyone,' he whispered as they arrived, 'ever guess about your first wedding?'

'No-one ever mentioned it,' murmured Noricus, 'but I sometimes wondered about my section. Never a hint, though, and they can shout their mouths off at times.'

Noricus's wife said, 'I think, sir, we both owe them a great debt, as we do to you.' She spoke shyly, but then, encouraged by a smile from Flavius, added, 'If it had not been for the way you spoke to Noricus after last Saturnalia, I don't think he would ever have been allowed to occupy his new rank.'

Flavius lifted her hand and looked at her Roman wedding ring. 'And you would not have had this. I, too, am delighted with my work that day.'

They all glanced at the entrance to the villa, where Lugo appeared to be engaged in some kind of dispute.

'What's all this out here?' he demanded as Aelius hurried forward.

Aelius stepped out into the street and came back with one hand gripping the arm of the baker's boy.

'What's he doing here?' asked Lugo. 'This is not the time, boy.'

'As a matter of fact, it is,' said Flavius.

The boy, recognising him as the commandant, wrenched his arm away from Aelius and saluted. Then, with a grin, he turned to the senior centurion for approval.

'Not now,' hissed the officer.

'I invited the boy here and suggested his father should bring him,' explained Flavius, facing Lugo. 'Noricus was concerned about leaving his new stepson alone on his first evening in the camp. Thanks to you, this boy feels at home here and I thought they would be good company for each other. Aelius has found a room for them to play in.'

'Perhaps the senior centurion would come with us to meet our other young guest,' murmured Aelius, leading the way. Lugo moved after him in the ponderous manner of one who could think of better things to be doing with his time.

Flavius quickly put in, 'Senior centurion, Noricus has just been telling his wife how well you understand boys.'

Lugo's disgruntled mood slipped away. He looked for a moment, in front of the bride, engagingly embarrassed, though this was rapidly forgotten in his conviction that the compliment paid him was richly deserved.

The lady was responsive. 'It seems I might benefit from your advice, sir, though I fear you would have very little time to spare for that.'

'Any time, madam. I look forward to meeting your son.'

'Well, here he is then,' said Aelius impatiently, throwing open the door to what had formerly been part of Lucilla's apartments.

'There's enough food in there to last them a week,' grunted Lugo.

'They'll eat it in the first ten minutes,' said Aelius.

The baker's boy and Noricus's stepson meanwhile were busy eyeing each other up.

'There's enough space in here for them to play games, or roll about, or even have a nice little fight if they fancy it,' said Aelius. 'They're of an age, wouldn't you say? Perhaps you could teach them their Latin words together, and with Amelia's boy coming up too, you could find yourself with the beginnings of a proper little Latin class, sir.'

'No,' said Lugo making his way back to the bridal party.

The evening passed well. It was the kind of dinner party that Flavius had imagined he would be hosting every few weeks as commandant, before Lucilla's behaviour had made that impossible.

When his guests had all departed, Flavius sat in one of the basket chairs in his library, his feet resting in another, and stretched himself contentedly. 'What a week!' he said. He held out a glass for Aelius to fill. 'All those parades and speeches and ceremonies – and then a wedding. How many weddings are held in army forts? And if I hadn't been here that wedding would probably never have happened. That is at least one thing I've achieved by being here, Aelius.'

He took the glass from Flavius without filling it.

'Don't forget the retiring veteran from Maia. Nothing would have happened without him, would it?'

Flavius ignored him. 'Now everything will be tranquil again: calm, unremarkable days, restful nights ...'

XIII

He was wrong. He was woken during the night from a deep sleep by noises on the floor above his head, by running steps, by raised voices, and, he was sure, the sound of the heavy door of the villa being pulled open.

He stepped into the courtyard. A girl, running towards the staircase with a basket of linen, nearly knocked him over.

'What's happened? What is it?'

'It is Alis, sir.' She shouted back at him. 'The baby!'

'Oh,' cried Flavius, 'what do I do? Where's Aelius?'

Another woman hurried past him. 'It'll be all right, sir. Look, the lady Aemilia has just arrived.'

Aemilia was removing her cape inside the doorway. Flavius noticed that the door was being closed not by the usual porter, but by yet another woman.

Aemilia took charge of the household. Aelius, with Flavius, was banished from the villa. They spent most of the long night sitting in Flavius's headquarters office. The third trumpet of the morning had sounded before they heard hands pounding on the door.

Aemilia was waiting for them inside the entrance to the villa. She was smiling.

'Alis?'

'Yes, she has survived. She is waiting for you.'

Aelius gave a long sigh of relief, and half-laughed as he looked at Flavius.

'And the child? He is ...'

'Aelius, you have a daughter.'

He stared at Aemilia. 'No?'

Aemilia smiled again. 'Yes. She was born just as we glimpsed the first ray of the sun, so your wife wants to call her Aurelia.'

'That's a Roman name. I want my child to have a Greek name.'

'Aelius,' said Flavius, 'your wife comes from Rome, you have spent your whole life since the day you were born in Roman households. Does it matter if your daughter has a Roman name?'

'To me, yes.'

'Then I'm sure Alis will change it,' said Aemilia.

'So what is this Greek name you want?' asked Flavius.

They waited.

'I don't know. I haven't thought about it yet.'

Flavius and Aemilia exchanged glances. 'It was a very long night,' murmured Flavius. To Aelius he said, 'Well, why don't you put your mind to the problem, and meanwhile the rest of us will make do with calling her Aurelia.'

Half-an-hour later, Flavius was invited to see the baby. Aelius was standing by the window with the child in his arms. He beamed at Flavius. 'This is my daughter, Aurelia.'

Flavius smiled at Alis. 'Do look after him, Alis, he might burst with pride. What a delightful name he's chosen for your daughter. You must be pleased with it.'

Alis, propped up on her pillows, smiled back at him.

Later in the morning, Flavius found a crib standing in the atrium. It had been left by two of Aelius's bath-house companions, who had made it in their spare time from what purported to be scraps of wood left in a store-room. It was beautifully crafted, and made, Flavius observed, from some very choice pieces of wood indeed. He wondered how that had passed through the quartermaster's records.

He sent for Aelius, who regarded the crib without enthusiasm.

'It's very nice,' he said flatly.

'Aelius, it's a very fine piece of work. Alis will love it.'

'Yes, yes, she will,' said Aelius. 'I'm sorry. It's not the crib. I'm very pleased with that.'

'So what's wrong, Aelius? Alis is well, and the baby?'

'Yes. She wants us to go through that recognition ritual. It's not for me.'

'It's a very old tradition. I thought it had rather gone out of fashion.'

'Yes, well, Alis wants it. I don't know why. Would you do it?'

'Not for myself, no. It has implications I don't like. But if my wife wanted it, of course I'd do it. How long does it take? Ten minutes. Do it to please Alis. Tomorrow afternoon?'

So on the following afternoon, a small party met around Alis's bed: Aelius, Aemilia and Flavius, who had parts to play, with Quintus and the doctor as witnesses.

Flavius took charge. 'Shall we begin?' he said, when everyone was in position.

Aemilia took the baby from Alis and laid her on a cushion.

She knelt down in front of Aelius and placed the baby on its cushion at his feet. Aelius then raised Aurelia in his arms, signifying that he accepted the child as his, and would protect and support her. He then handed her to Flavius, who thereby accepted responsibility for her should Aelius no longer be able to do so. Aemilia then returned the baby to her mother.

The ritual was over. Alis was happy. Flavius was curious.

When Aelius disappeared to arrange a tray of delicacies for their guests, Flavius sat beside Alis.

'Will you tell me why this has been so important to you?' he said gently.

'Aelius doesn't understand, does he?' Alis said. 'It is not a Greek practice.'

'I am not Greek, but I don't think I understand either. It seems to me to suggest a lack of trust.'

'Oh, no, not to me, sir.' Alis took a deep breath of contentment. 'When I was a child, as a slave, I thought I could never be anything but a slave. I used to see my ladies with their new babies and envy them so much. I didn't dream that I would one day be free, able to marry and have a child of my own. It is a wonderful moment to share with Aelius.' She smiled. 'You don't look convinced, sir. Aemilia understands.'

'Yes, I do, sir. I was a slave once, too,' the woman said.

Flavius smiled with them both. 'Hmm. Then I am outnumbered.'

XIV

In the last week of October, Flavius was watching a fleet of grain ships enter the harbour at Alauna. When he had walked out along the wharf, he had seen that the senior centurion and the quartermaster were there before him. He felt obliged to join them.

'Splendid sight,' said Lugo.

The quartermaster grunted, 'Work for some.' Flavius, who hadn't left the fort to look at the ships, but to gaze across the water at

Elphin's island – although he knew before he started that in such cloudy weather he wouldn't see it – sighed. 'Poor visibility.'

'Bound to be, this time of the year, with the winter on its way,' said the quartermaster lugubriously.

'It's getting dark very early now,' agreed Lugo, nodding his head.

Flavius smiled to himself. He didn't care if the winter was coming; in fact, he welcomed it, he was waiting for it. In two days he would be leaving for the island, and in the comfortable, safe darkness of the November night he would be with Elphin again, and then there would be the longer, safer darkness of their secret Saturnalia.

He realised that the senior centurion was watching him curiously. Perhaps he wasn't hiding the smile. He said loftily, 'I suppose you get used to these bitter winters after a few years?'

'No,' said Lugo. 'Each one is worse than what you remember of the last.'

'True,' agreed the quartermaster. 'Still, a cold winter in north Britain is better than a warm one in Judea.'

Lugo's glowering look suggested that this sentiment bordered on treachery.

The quartermaster shrugged his shoulders. He looked round the harbour. 'Look, someone else is coming from the fort.' He screwed up his eyes. 'It's your adjutant, sir. He always half runs everywhere, that lad.'

'And always looks as though he's got something to worry about,' added Lugo.

'Always rushing somewhere with bad news,' the quartermaster concluded. 'It seems it's for you this time, sir.'

'Thank you, gentlemen,' said Flavius tartly.

He gave a curt nod and turned to walk back towards the settlement. Quintus smiled with relief when they met.

'I thought I ought to come and find you, sir,' he said breathlessly. 'There's message for you from York.'

Flavius was irritated. 'I have already sent my report about the Maia posting by one of our own couriers. Why does the legate have to send one of his?'

Quintus shook his head. 'This man doesn't look like a courier sir, more like an emissary. That's why I thought I ought to fetch you at once.'

'An emissary?' said Flavius. 'What sort of emissary would the legate send to an auxiliary cohort?'

But when he confronted the man waiting for him in his office, he could understand Quintus's concern. That this was no ordinary courier could be seen from his dress and bearing. He was deferential, yet not lacking an air of authority.

'The legate sends his greetings, Prefect,' he said pleasantly. 'He requests your presence as rapidly as possible in York.'

'This is not something to do with Maia?' Flavius asked.

'Maia? I think not, sir.' The legate's man politely brushed aside Flavius's bewilderment. 'With the day as far advanced as it is, I'm sure the prefect would agree that it is too late to set out for York tonight. We shall take accommodation in the post-house tonight.'

'We?'

'The legate has sent a legionary escort.'

Flavius's temper flared. 'My own cohort provides me with an excellent escort.'

'I have no doubt of that, sir, but you will be aware that legionary business takes precedence on any highway. A legionary escort will ensure that we cover ground in the swiftest time possible. We shall be ready to leave with you at first light.'

'You and the escort may leave at first light, but I shall not.' Flavius tried to speak like a determined but reasonable man, yet he was aware of the chill creeping round his heart. 'It is impossible for me. In view of his approaching departure, my superior officer, the tribune at Ravenglass, requires me to be at his headquarters at the end of this week.'

'The legate's orders supercede any others, sir.'

Flavius could hear the edge of desperation in his own voice. 'I could enter York just four days after you.'

His companion said quietly, 'Sir, my instructions are not to leave Alauna without you, and to leave no later than first light tomorrow.'

'So is this why you've brought a legionary escort? To drag me off by force?' said Flavius bitterly.

'I don't think either of us would let it come to that, sir.' The other man half-smiled.

'So the legate forces me to ignore the tribune, which insults him and puts shame on me. Is that the example of military courtesy he wishes us all to follow?'

'No, it is not, sir. I think you should know that the legate is not acting on his own behalf. He is himself acting on the instructions of the emperor, and his own future could depend on his promptness in meeting them.'

'The emperor!' cried Flavius. 'What have I got to do with all this?'

The legate's man chose not to hear the question. Then, as Flavius flung out of the room, he called out, 'By the way sir, the legate would be obliged if you would travel with your adjutant.'

Flavius hardly ate that evening. Dish after dish he pushed aside after no more than a mouthful. Then suddenly he rose from the table without a word.

Aelius followed him. He found Flavius in the library, a single lamp burning on his desk, scribbling with pen and ink, not on a sheet of parchment but on a scrap of informal lime-bark.

Flavius raised his head. 'Aelius, I don't know what I'm going to do.'

It was his turn, Aelius saw, to be the strong one. 'What's happened?'

Flavius, after thrusting a hand though his hair, told him. 'The disappointment ... it's like a blow, inside me.'

'Flavius, there's nothing you can do about it. You've no choice but to go to York. Unless you desert. And you know what happens to army deserters. What are you trying to do there?'

'Write to Marcellus. But it's no good. How can it reach him in time?'

'One of the couriers, starting out in the morning, should get to him easily.'

'Yes, to tell him I've been summoned to York, but not for him to reach Elphin before the bonfire celebrations begin!' cried Flavius. 'She'll be wandering about, looking for me, and I won't be there. What will she think, Aelius? That I've forgotten her, or didn't want to see her again!'

Aelius put a hand gently on his shoulder. 'If you had had something to eat, you wouldn't have such ridiculous ideas in your head. You are talking about Elphin. Still, I understand. You want to warn her, and we could still do that.'

'How, Aelius, how?'

'Send a courier now ... tonight.'

Flavius looked at him. 'How do you do that? I've been commandant here for a year and a half, and I've no idea.'

'You should spend more time in the men's bath-house,' said Aelius. 'There are men here who would jump at the challenge of a good, hard night ride on a well-disciplined mount. There's not much need for night-couriers here. When does anything urgent happen? But what night-riding we have is discreet, no fuss.'

'Discreet?' said Flavius, alarmed. 'Does that mean there's something underhand about it?'

'I said discreet, not secretive.'

'If there's one thing I've learned in the army,' said Flavius grimly, 'it's how to perfect my lying skills, but I will not break the law.'

'Discreet,' repeated Aelius. 'A few people may notice us, but not many. We don't want to wake up the whole camp. If anyone should question us, you wouldn't even have to lie. In fact, if you think about it, as commandant you're acting in a most responsible way. The legate has heedlessly upset your plans, and you are doing everything you can to let the tribune know as soon as possible. Now, do you want to warn Elphin?'

'Yes.'

'Then finish that letter to Marcellus, and write me an authorisation for the rider. I'll come back for them in about half-an-hour.'

When Aelius returned, Flavius handed him the authorisation and the letter to Marcellus, folded inside a thin leather wallet.

'I've found us a good man,' Aelius said cheerfully. 'I shall use our stables, not the cohort's, and put him on the coastal road.'

Aelius, Flavius could see, was enjoying the excitement. He himself felt exhausted by it. 'Discretion?'

'Thoughtful planning, yes. Riding on the coastal road in the dark, all he has to do is follow the line of coast fences into Ravenglass. Milefortlets protect the way on his other side.'

'Might I enquire,' asked Flavius, 'what incentive this man is being offered?'

'No incentive,' said Aelius primly, 'not to a man in service.'

'But ...'

'But,' Aelius smiled, 'it so happens that he is making me some toys for Aurelia. It is in his own time, and I shall, of course, pay for the materials and his labour. And, as I'm inclined to be careless with money, I will probably pay him much, much more than the toys should cost. You will find the exact sum recorded in your kitchen accounts under the heading of repairs, with the cost of the toys deducted.'

Flavius groaned. 'I suppose, in its tortured way, it is legally defensible.'

'I hope you will think of it, Flavius, as a roundabout way of being fair,' said Aelius, 'which the law, especially military law, doesn't always manage to be.'

A remark like that usually provoked a quick, sharp-witted response from Flavius, but he merely nodded and murmured, 'No, I suppose not.'

Aelius, on his way to the door, turned to look back at him. He felt he could have wrung the legate's neck. 'Flavius, you wouldn't have had very long with her ... only a couple of hours perhaps, and then probably not alone.'

'I would have gone twice the distance to see her for five minutes.'

'What I'm trying to say is that you still have the whole of Saturnalia with her. You haven't lost that. While you're away in York, I'll take a cart up to Papcastle and find something to cheer you up when you get back.'

'And what will you tell everyone in the house here when you ride off in your cart?'

'That I'm going to the market in Papcastle to look for toys for Aurelia.'

That at least made Flavius smile. 'I shall have to build a new villa to house all these toys.'

He wandered out into the streets of the fort before he tried to get some sleep, and met his adjutant coming out of his own quarters, probably for the same reason.

'This won't do, Quintus. We should both be snoring in our beds, ready for the early start. Did you know the legate had specially asked for you to be included on the journey to York?'

'Yes, sir.' Quintus seemed delighted at the prospect.

'I would have taken you anyway. I'm only sorry you have to share my prison escort.'

'Prison escort, sir?'

'Yes, the legionary guard that is here to make sure I leave Alauna when I'm told.'

Quintus burst out laughing, and then broke off as he saw Flavius was far from amused.

'You are joking, sir?'

'No.'

'But, sir, surely you know that when my uncle – when the legate – sends out a legionary escort, it is an escort of honour?'

XV

In the early afternoon of the first day of November, into the fourth day since he'd left Alauna, Flavius reached the legionary fort in York.

When he should have been on the water between Ravenglass and the island of Manannàn, he was entering the headquarters building to announce his presence.

On similar occasions in the past, an orderly had delivered him to a vacant room in the block reserved for unmarried officers. This time, however, it was courteously explained to him that the legate's adjutant had been informed of his arrival and was on his way to greet him.

Within minutes, an exquisite creature in burnished and gilded leather appeared to guide him, with every display of respect, to a room overlooking the private courtyard of the legate's palatial villa. A slave was assigned to him, the position of the bath-house indicated, and he was invited to dine with the legate in an hour's time.

Precisely within the hour, the adjutant returned to escort him to the legate's dining room. While Flavius was in the bath-house, his hair had been washed and dressed, the marks of travel had been removed from his military dress and his boots replaced by sandals.

In the dining-room, the legate, his wife and Quintus were already gathered when Flavius joined them. The legate introduced his wife, and then with a little laugh drew Quintus forward. 'You already know my wife's nephew, I believe.'

They sat down at the table. The walls of the room were painted with views of a sunlit Rome, and they ate off fine antique Roman silver.

The legate's wife enquired of Flavius whether his wife's health had improved since her return home.

Flavius replied that his mother sent encouraging reports on her recovery.

'I am gratified to hear it, prefect.'

'My wife will be touched by your concern, my lady.' For Flavius it was one of the few occasions when he was able to tell the truth about Lucilla.

The legate, sipping a rich red wine from the south, complained that north Britain could only produce a grape that was unfit for harvesting. Quintus asked about the chariot-racing teams in Rome.

The desultory conversation continued around the table. It was becoming evident to Flavius that while the meal was in progress he would learn nothing about the reason for this peremptory summons to York or his extraordinary reception in the legate's villa.

As the afternoon light began to fade, he grieved for what should have been his first step on Elphin's island, for his first glimpse of Elphin on her own land, of Elphin coming towards him as the bonfires were kindled.

He was aware that the legate was making a small signal to his wife as the dishes of fruit and nuts which ended the meal were laid on the table.

She rose from her place. 'Prefect, I beg you to excuse me but I would so like to show my nephew the garden before it is too dark.'

The legate dismissed the servants. He settled himself in his chair with the solemn air of a man who has weighty matters to disclose and took a last sip of wine as if to prime himself.

Flavius waited.

'Paulus,' said the legate, as he set his glass back on the table, 'I speak to you not so much as your commanding officer, but as a representative of the emperor.'

Flavius felt his curiosity and bewilderment touched by a growing uneasiness.

'As a lawyer, you are aware that Hadrian requires the law as practised in Rome to operate throughout the empire.' The legate paused, as if allowing Flavius the opportunity to dispute this if he wished.

'That is so, sir.'

'Good, yes. Now it has recently come to the emperor's notice that in one of the smaller provinces there is still a degree of organised corruption in the courts. He regards legal reform as a matter of the utmost urgency.' The legate shrugged his shoulders. 'I suppose he thinks it could spread.'

'That's possible, sir.'

'So he has decided to appoint a special procurator to put an end to it. As an imperial officer, he will have powers not only to hunt out the sources of the corruption, but to try those concerned by established law and to impose punishment.'

The legate leaned back in his chair and smiled. 'I am sure you can now guess why I sent for you.'

When Flavius, instead of smiling back at him, looked at him with something like alarm, he said impatiently, 'Paulus, don't you understand: the emperor has selected you for the post.'

'Yes, I understand, sir, but it is not what I want at this time.'

The legate stared at him, for a moment angry. Then he laughed, and pushed the flagon of wine towards him. 'It's shock, the emperor's favour coming like this. You can't believe it, eh? Take a sip, it'll restore you.'

Flavius shook his head.

'Come now, Paulus.' The legate poured the wine himself and added affably, 'I will admit, I was shaken myself when I read the emperor's orders. I had always considered you an adequate officer, but I had not appreciated the high regard in which the emperor holds you. I have no doubt that if you carry out this undertaking successfully, as the emperor plainly expects you will, there will be a place in the Senate for you.'

'Senatorial seats are elective, if I may remind you. I am not well known in senatorial circles, sir.'

'Isn't the emperor celebrated for his persuasive powers?' murmured the legate.

'It doesn't happen to be my wish,' Flavius insisted stubbornly.

The legate frowned. 'I find myself failing to understand you, Paulus. You have married into a senatorial family. You have an army commission, which is designed to prepare men of lesser rank to qualify for high office of state ...'

'That was my father's decision and my grandfather's,' said Flavius wearily.

'Then it is also yours,' said the legate with feeling.

'Yes, sir, I accept that, of course, but just for the moment I would like to remain with the army.'

'Ah,' said the legate with surprise. 'Then you will value the emperor's perception of your qualities. He notes your flair for command, and power of rapid and effective judgement. The emperor is a generous man, Paulus. If you are now considering a military career, he would be willing to look elsewhere for a procurator if he can acquire a promising legionary officer.'

'With respect, sir, I have no wish whatever to join a legion. What I want is to stay for another year under your guidance in Alauna.'

The legate regarded him with regret. 'I would have been grateful if you had applied to me, and would certainly have granted such a request. With the tribune leaving Ravenglass next month, I don't welcome another change along the Solway coast.'

'Why then, sir, surely—'

'For you, Paulus,' said the legate, rising from his chair and striking a palm on the table, 'there is no option. Your tenure as commandant of Alauna will shortly cease.'

Flavius looked at him in despair. 'How generous of the emperor to offer me an alternative that would never be acceptable to me.'

The legate walked towards a window from which he could see his wife and Quintus in her garden. 'For your sake, prefect,' he said, with his back to Flavius, 'I shall ignore that remark.'

Flavius stood up. 'May I enquire, sir, when it is intended that my tenure should end?'

The legate turned round. 'The emperor suggests before the end of this month.'

'That's before Saturnalia!'

'Yes. The emperor is graciously mindful that the midwinter weather here makes travelling unpleasant, so it's the sooner the better for you. He himself is now in Athens and expects to return to Rome in the middle of January. He requires you to be waiting for him. Your wife, I'm sure, will be happy to have you back for the holiday.'

'That's impossible,' said Flavius. 'I can't believe the emperor would leave a fort without a commandant for four months. That's about the time it would take to find a new man and get him to Britain.'

'True, but by an amazing piece of good fortune, you yourself provided the solution to that problem. You will remember my asking you, together with the tribune at Ravenglass, to consider the situation at Hardknott. It failed to find me the answer I was looking for, but your report had its uses. You advised me that my prime concern should be to finish the building, to give the resident commandant the accommodation he had a right to expect.'

'So, you see, Paulus, he can take your place at Alauna as a temporary commandant until your successor arrives, and by then his villa at Hardknott will be completed.' The legate smiled complacently at his neat piece of administrative juggling.

Flavius felt like a caged wild animal that finds the door of one wall after another of his cage slammed shut against him.

'What if I refused to leave Alauna?' he cried wildly.

The legate stared at him. 'My dear Paulus! Well, you would be forcibly removed.'

'Supposing I wanted to stay in a place beyond the bounds of the empire, beyond the emperor's power to force me back to Rome?'

The legate glanced uneasily about the room, as if he might be needing help with a madman. He said in a low voice, 'The emperor is a generous man, unless he is thwarted. Then he can be – hard. He would punish you through your family.'

Flavius heard another door slam shut.

'Paulus, I don't understand what we are talking about. I appreciate that you have never wished to follow a military career because you prefer to return to the law. Yet when the emperor himself offers you a legal appointment of distinction – drops it into your lap like a ripe apple – you seem to be doing all in your power to reject it. Do you realise that there are gifted lawyers in Rome who have worked for years to achieve an imperial favour like this?'

'It is a matter of timing,' muttered Flavius.

'How old are you, Paulus?'

'Thirty-two next month, sir.' He was surprised by the question.

'Then I would say the emperor's timing is impeccable. In a month's time you will be eligible for the Senate, and by the time you have completed the emperor's commission, the Senate will be available for you.'

Flavius appeared to be lost in thought. The legate began to think that perhaps he had argued the prefect out of whatever aberration had possessed him; and it seemed that he had.

Flavius said humbly, 'I apologise, sir. I fear the abruptness of your summons and the disruption of my life at Alauna made it difficult to see clearly the honour that the emperor is bestowing on me.'

'Good, good,' said the legate, gratified and relieved. 'Why don't we join my wife in the garden?'

'One moment, sir, if you would be kind enough: I shall still briefly be commandant of Alauna, and I would consider myself to be failing in my duty if I did not warn my colleague at Hardknott that it might be unwise for him to take charge of his new command during Saturnalia. I would be prepared to remain until the festival is over.'

'The emperor's suggested time for your departure is not an invitation, it is a command.'

Flavius, having found a chink in one of the bars of his cage, pressed on amiably. 'You, sir, are accustomed to spending Saturnalia in legionary cities like York, where the Romanised citizens enjoy taking part in our celebrations. Alauna is not like that. The local people lead more primitive, simple lives. They like to keep their old ways. Today they are holding their winter festival. They will not join in our Saturnalia. They will open their shops and taverns because money will be flowing, but otherwise it is not a pleasure to them. There is an amount of resentment simmering not far beneath the surface.'

'There's never been any talk of trouble in Alauna,' protested the legate.

'That is because of the diligence of my officers, and the goodwill, carefully nurtured, of the leaders of the community around the fort.'

'Hmm.'

'Last year, sir, one of our men attacked a shop in the settlement, broke down the door and terrified the women nearby. Two of his section dragged him away. If it hadn't been for them, he could have been injured. With a soldier injured, our force would have had to turn out, and then ...' Flavius shrugged his shoulders and spread his hands.

The legate was showing more interest. 'The man was punished, I hope?'

'Immediate court-martial, attended by involved parties from the settlement. I meted out the punishment which I thought his conduct deserved.' Flavius hoped fervently that the legate would never discover that the man whom he was unjustly maligning was the new junior centurion at Alauna.

'We have to remember, sir, that there is no settlement round the fort at Hardknott. The prefect there has no knowledge of working with a group of local people. It is not fair to impose on him problems which are outside his experience. He is a man with a serious respect for the military code, but no understanding of the value of conciliation because he has never had cause to employ it.'

Flavius paused; the legate was now listening attentively.

'As you will know, sir, an incident like the one I have just described, if unwittingly mishandled, could lead to brawling throughout the settlement. That could spread. There are always disaffected elements looking for a fight. The Solway in flames would not please the emperor, especially if he discovered that, but for a poorly timed appointment it might never have occurred.'

Flavius wondered if he had gone too far, but the exaggerated thrust after a lengthy peroration was often effective in a court of law.

The legate was chewing his lip.

Flavius made his final plea in a gentler tone. 'We must not forget that the emperor has a special regard for Alauna. He recruited the cohort himself, and likes to refer to himself when here as a Spaniard among Spaniards.'

'What are you proposing?'

'That I should remain at Alauna throughout Saturnalia, that's all. I would hold my final parade on the day afterwards, and leave the next morning. My colleague from Hardknott can be received any time after that. He will have ample time to prepare for the two January festivals, and he will do that well because the rituals are familiar to him. The altar for the sacrifice has already been inscribed with my name, but I shall see that it is removed.'

'Then this is the plan you wish me to submit to the emperor?' said the legate. The prospect was clearly not one he relished.

'Is it necessary to disturb him with it? He has allowed me ample time for the journey back. I can travel straight to Rome instead of going first to Stresa.'

'You would be prepared to do this?'

'To spend Saturnalia in Alauna, yes, sir.'

The legate peered at him. 'I give you my promise that I will arrange that. Have I yours that you will leave Alauna immediately after the festival to accept the emperor's command?'

Flavius bowed his head. 'Yes.'

The legate held out his hand, and Flavius grasped it.

XVI

On a November evening, the guard watching from the east gate of Alauna glimpsed what he thought was a riderless horse appearing through the ground mist hovering round the causeway.

Then, as it took the road to the fort, he saw that there was a man sprawled on its back, a hand clutching the horse's mane. He shouted for the duty officer. As the horse galloped into the circle of light cast by the outer lamps of the fort, they both saw the light-coloured hair of the rider.

'Senior centurion, quickly!' said Noricus, rushing down to order the opening of the gates.

Lugo came running as the horse reared inside the gateway. Flavius slid from the saddle into the arms of Noricus and another of the guards. There was a cut on his head, and blood covered his right arm.

They lowered him gently to the ground

'Cloak!' shouted Lugo.

Noricus pulled off his own. Lugo folded it and knelt down to slip it under Flavius's head. 'You're all right now, lad,' he said. 'You're safe now.' He looked up.

'Stretcher, the doctor, move!'

'He's muttering something,' said Noricus. 'Can you hear what it is?'

The senior centurion bent over Flavius, and shook his head. 'Seems to be trying to repeat some word, but I can't tell what it is. Aelius will probably recognise it. Someone go now and warn him that the stretcher is coming. He's Greek, remember. Break the news carefully.'

When Flavius had been lifted on to the stretcher and carried away to the villa, Lugo allowed himself to give way to anger. 'What is going on here? Where's that boy of an adjutant? Where, may I ask, is that spectacular legionary guard ... swallowed up by a crack in the road?'

Noricus had already learned that when the senior centurion was in this kind of mood his questions required no answers.

They had left the east gate and were crossing the assembly hall when the slamming of a door heralded the approach of an irate Aelius. 'I thought this was supposed to be an army designed to protect an empire? Every single afternoon, you play about with lances and swords and you can't even look after your own commandant.' He stalked away as tempestuously as he had arrived.

'Greeks ... I told you,' said Lugo.

He nevertheless followed Aelius back inside the villa and into the room where the doctor was already treating Flavius.

The medical orderlies were bathing the blood from Flavius's wounds. The doctor was bending over his arm. He glanced up with a frown.

'Can you tell me what's been happening here?'

'No,' said Lugo testily, meeting another fierce look from Aelius. 'How is he?'

'The head wound is not serious. There was a lot of blood.'

The doctor paused, conscious of the fact that no-one at Alauna, other than himself, had seen service on a battlefield. 'Even a slight head wound causes an alarming loss of blood. This one was probably made by a stone thrown from close distance. He is only barely conscious, but that should soon pass.'

He picked up a leather strap. 'The other wound is more serious. I need to stop the bleeding.' As he spoke, he fastened the leather strap tightly round Flavius's arm. 'And now I must prevent the wound from putrifying. Seaweed from the shore will be excellent for that.'

Lugo turned to Noricus. 'I want a section on the beach now, each man with a lamp and a basket, placed at regular intervals along the shore, moving in time, to collect seaweed!'

The doctor shook his head. 'Two men, with one lamp and a basket, will be enough. Then I want it pounded into a paste – my own orderlies can do that. I suspect, senior centurion, that this wound was made by a deep, savage thrust from something like a hunting knife. It will be some weeks before he recovers the strength in that arm.'

The senior centurion looked with concern at Flavius. 'Doctor, I think he's trying to say something. When he first came in, he seemed to be repeating the same word, but none of us could understand what it was. We wondered if Aelius might recognise it.'

Aelius, his anger against Lugo slightly placated by the man's apparent anxiety for Flavius, advanced to the bed and knelt down. He listened. Then abruptly stood up.

He shook his head. 'That's no word I know, not in Latin nor in Greek.'

The doctor bent down to listen. 'No, that's not Greek. What is it? El ... elf something?' He looked at Lugo. 'Is it Spanish?'

'The prefect doesn't speak Spanish,' snapped Aelius.

The doctor shrugged his shoulders. 'His mind's confused. It's nothing to worry about. It happens.'

But the centurion couldn't let the matter rest. 'It must mean something to him or why does he keep repeating it? Is it the name of –'

'I've never known him go to a place that sounded like that!' said Aelius stoutly.

It was to his immense relief that the arrival of a distraught Quintus, clutching a red cloak, gave the senior centurion something more pressing to think about.

'Might I enquire, sir –' he paused heavily on the last word '– where you happen to have been? Is it not your duty as our commandant's adjutant to remain at his side?' He pointed to Flavius, lying on the bed. 'It would seem, if you would forgive me, that your dereliction of duty, sir, has had an unfortunate consequence. Do we assume that the escort has accompanied you?'

Quintus looked as if he might be going to cry. He swallowed hard. 'The prefect dismissed the guard when we were about twenty miles out of York. He said they were slowing us down, and he needed to get back to the coast as quickly as possible.'

'You are a professional soldier. He is not. It is your job to stop him making foolish decisions like that,' thundered Lugo.

'That's enough, please,' said the doctor. 'Is that the prefect's cloak you're carrying?'

'Yes, I found it on the Papcastle road, not more than a mile or so from here, on that ridge we can see where the trees are very thick.' Quintus handed the cloak to the doctor. 'There's blood on it.'

'That worried you?'

'Why, yes, especially as I knew he probably wouldn't be wearing his helmet. He'd rather ride without it, if he can.'

'Then I think we can now guess what happened to the prefect,' said the doctor. 'He was riding alone in haste along a road overhung with trees. It was cold and he had his cloak wrapped round him, hiding his military dress. He was bare-headed. Also preoccupied. For a couple of thieves, looking out for prey, he was an attractive target. They aimed a stone at his head to stun him and then seized his bridle. He tried to reach for his sword, and one of them slashed at his right arm. His cloak fell open and they saw he was a Roman officer. In a panic, they rushed off without even trying to rob him. He's still wearing his wrist purse. He managed to get himself back on his mount, and the horse knew where to bring him.'

'Will he be all right?' asked Quintus shakily.

'Yes, with care, so long as we keep an eye on that wound.'

'Sir,' asked Aelius in a quiet voice, 'why was he riding alone?'

'Oh, Aelius, we rode together all the way until we reached Papworth. It was dark when we got there. He asked if I would like a rest and some food. When I said I would, he suggested we stop at the fort where they know us. We went to the officers' quarters, but then he disappeared. I thought he must have gone to speak to the commandant and his wife. When someone asked why he'd ridden away without me, I set out after him.'

'That's so unlike him,' said Aelius. 'Do you know why he was in such a hurry?'

'He did say at one point he needed to send a messenger to Ravenglass. He had to speak to someone from the fort there. At least, I think that's what he said, but I'm not sure. It doesn't make much sense, does it?'

The senior centurion made impatient clicking noises with his tongue. 'Didn't you ask him to explain?'

'No, I didn't like to trouble him,' said Quintus unhappily. 'He was in such a strange mood after we left York, anxious and withdrawn. I'd never seen him like that before. He usually takes an interest in everything that's going on around him, but not after York.'

Aelius and the doctor exchanged glances. Aelius muttered something in Greek and the doctor nodded. Quintus appeared to be swallowing hard again. The doctor put a friendly hand on his shoulder.

'Quintus, do you know what happened in York? We all heard the prefect was summoned there at the emperor's command. Was it good or bad news?'

'I thought it was wonderfully good news, but the prefect was upset by it. The emperor has made him one of his special procurators. The prefect did mention it during our journey, but said he would rather stay at Alauna. I can't understand why. Of course he has to go, it's an imperial command.'

'A profound honour for our commandant and this cohort,' said the senior centurion, drawing himself up to parade stature. 'Does he know yet when he will leave us?'

'The emperor wants him to set out in two weeks' time.'

'The commandant is to leave in two weeks, and this is the first time you mention it?' shouted Lugo.

'Senior centurion, lower your voice! My patient is distressed enough without this further disturbance.'

Aelius smiled to himself. For a twenty-five year old, this was a Greek who knew how to stand his own ground.

'Anyway,' he was saying, 'in this state, the prefect can't leave in two weeks.'

'Well, actually, it's not an issue,' said Quintus. 'The prefect managed to postpone his departure until the end of Saturnalia.'

Aelius looked at Flavius. What clever lawyer's trick had he pulled to bring that off? His golden world had been shattered, but he had at least saved for himself and Elphin their Saturnalia.

'Gentlemen,' he said in a soft tone that he knew would contrast favourably with the senior centurion's raucous voice, 'I'm sure we are all anxious to do anything we can to help the prefect in his recovery. I am concerned that we seem to be neglecting the rather curious, confused utterance of his about messengers and Ravenglass, which did seem to be causing him some distress. I think we ought to do something about it, even though in the end it might all mean nothing. So I would like to suggest that I should go down to Ravenglass and see if there is anything we ought to know. I shall not be taking up any valuable army time, and I don't think I can do much for the prefect while the doctor and his orderlies are looking after him.'

'Yes, that's very good of you, Aelius. If he should mention it again, I'm sure it will calm him if we can say someone has gone,' said the doctor.

The senior centurion made a grunt that might, or might not, signify consent, and Quintus nodded eagerly.

Aelius glanced fondly at Flavius, who seemed to have fallen into a restless sleep. 'You'll note, Flavius,' he said silently, 'you're not the only one in the family with a slippery lawyer's tongue. Rest easy. I'll go to Ravenglass and find your Elphin.'

It was agreed that no mention should be made of the prefect's new appointment until he himself was able to discuss the situation.

As far as his injuries were concerned, a notice written by the doctor was placed on the bulletin board in the headquarters building. The next morning, at dawn, Lugo led a ferocious search of the forest on either side of the Papcastle road.

Aelius travelled with one of the patrols as far as Papcastle and then sped south.

By the late afternoon, when Flavius was no longer feverish, a statement, dictated to the chief clerk, was displayed at various points throughout the camp. The prefect undertook to address the parade as soon as he was allowed up.

XVII

Flavius was sitting up in bed, trying to swallow a rich broth from a spoon held in his left hand. He refused to be fed by someone; having to have his meat cut up for him was humiliation enough.

The door opened and Aelius appeared, carrying a bowl of fruit, peeled and sliced.

Flavius hailed him delightedly, spilling broth on his blanket. 'They've let you back in, at last!'

Aelius mopped up the broth with a towel. 'Yes, we'll soon have your hair trimmed and clean blankets on the bed. How is the arm?'

'Covered in a horrible cold slime, like this broth.'

Aelius took away the broth and put the fruit in its place. 'Try that.' He sat down on the bed. 'To tell the truth, no-one stopped me coming in.'

'But Alis said—'

'Never mind now what Alis said. I wasn't here. I went to Papcastle. Flavius, do you remember? I was going to buy toys.'

Flavius grinned at him. 'Of course I remember. My head was only hit by a small stone. Was your shopping successful?'

'Eminently.'

'Ah.' Flavius laid his head back against his pillow. 'Thank you, Aelius.'

'Actually,' said Aelius, 'I went a bit further than Papcastle, and brought something for you back with me.'

Flavius lifted his head and peered at Aelius as if expecting him to produce a parcel.

'No, I'll have to fetch it. Shall I?'

Flavius nodded and picked a slice of fruit. It was halfway to his mouth when the door opened again. It wasn't Aelius.

'Marcellus!' he cried.

Aelius followed him back into the room. 'Quintus thought he heard you saying you wanted to speak to someone from Ravenglass ...'

'I don't know what I said to Quintus on that terrible ride back from York,' muttered Flavius.

'... so I brought back the best person I could find.'

'And I have brought you something even better than myself,' said Marcellus, 'a letter from Elphin.'

He laid a small packet in front of Flavius.

He touched it gently with the fingers of his left hand, as though it might melt away at a touch. 'Elphin,' he whispered. 'You have seen her?'

'Yesterday Aelius and I saw her together. When you weren't at the festival, she visited her stables in Ravenglass every day, hoping you might come to her on another day instead.'

'Does she understand why I wasn't there that night on her island, and that I wanted to come?'

'Thanks to your intrepid night-rider, I was able to reach her earlier and talk to her about it. I tried to make her realise that you had no choice, but I don't think she really grasps what power our emperors can hold over our lives.'

Flavius was struggling to open the letter with his left hand.

'Then how will she ever understand that he can force me to leave Britain, perhaps for ever, at a few days' notice?'

Marcellus took the letter. 'Let me do that for you.' He removed the fragile piece of lime-bark from its leather wallet and opened it for Flavius.

He picked it up in his left hand and gazed at it. 'I don't think I've ever seen her writing before,' he said, moved by the sight of her flowing script.

Marcellus moved away from the bed to leave Flavius alone with his letter. Aelius took the opportunity to open the chest with the gold sword inside it.

'What a magnificent piece,' said Marcellus. 'It was for some special service, was it?'

'Nothing I know about that would warrant this.' Aelius's face showed his dislike of the treasure. 'I think Hadrian believes he owns Flavius now.'

'I think perhaps he does,' said Marcellus slowly.

Aelius closed the lid of the chest. Flavius was smiling blissfully at his letter. He looked up at them. 'She says, among other things –'

he laughed softly ' – that she is thinking of Saturnalia, and she *will* come.'

'She cried when she heard you'd been hurt,' said Aelius. 'You can probably guess how difficult it was to tell her what happened to you in York. I was grateful that the tribune was with me.'

'But when Aelius was able to tell her how you had managed to stay until after Saturnalia, she was in tears once more, sobbing with relief that she would be able to see you again. That's when she said she must write to you.' Marcellus waited while Flavius re-read his letter. 'After that, Flavius, the three of us began to think of the safest and most discreet way of getting Elphin to Papcastle.'

Flavius wondered if it would ever be possible to show them how grateful he was. 'Did you decide anything?'

'We did,' said Marcellus, exchanging a satisfied look with Aelius. 'Most local markets and fairs are closed during the winter months. In mid-December, many of the small merchants and craftsmen make their way to the towns and settlements based round Roman forts, to make money during Saturnalia. They tend to travel in groups for safety and they'll take the odd wayfarer with them. Elphin knows of a group leaving Ravenglass that goes as far as Papcastle, and she'll be able to lose herself among the women of the party.'

'I have arranged to meet her,' added Aelius, 'by the well in the market-place, which is within sight of the house where you will be staying. That will be some time in the late afternoon of the first day of Saturnalia. I will stay with her there until you arrive. The group starts back at dawn on the day after the festival. That means you will, unfortunately, have to leave earlier if you are to be back inside Alauna for the first trumpet. Elphin understands that. She is worried that you will be riding in the darkness on that road where you were attacked.'

Flavius gave a wry smile. 'That isn't going to stop me.'

'I think I can reassure her about that, having had a word when I arrived with your affable senior centurion. I congratulated him on the speed with which he had scoured the woods, and he tells me he intends to maintain random patrols until the new commandant appears – which I gather is to be that curious creature from Hardknott,' Marcellus put in.

Flavius groaned. 'I don't like that at all. I didn't think I'd mind who followed me, but I do. They're my men, my officers.'

'You'll get over it,' said Marcellus. 'Anyway, he won't be here for long. Now, are you happy with our arrangements for Elphin?'

'If she is happy, I couldn't be more so.'

'Good.' Marcellus picked up a chair, set it by the bed and sat on it. Aelius perched himself on the bottom of the bed.

'While we were riding to Alauna from Ravenglass, we had ample time to consider another matter. We reached a decision, which we hope will be equally pleasing to you. We are not, in fact, prepared to accept a refusal.'

Flavius looked from one solemn face to the other. 'What matter?'

'The matter of your departure from Britain, Flavius. How do you plan to get from Alauna to Rome?'

'Well, what other way is there? Road to York, sea to Bordeaux, road to Rome. What is all this about?'

'I know,' said Marcellus, 'that in a month's time you will be much better, but do you think all that hard riding is advisable for a man who has suffered an injury like yours, especially as your promise to the legate prevents you from travelling in easy stages?'

'That's something I'll have to cope with. I would have made the same bargain even if I'd know what was going to happen to me.'

'Why not go by sea?'

'Like you? My father's ships don't ply round the western coast of Britain. '

'But, by an amazing coincidence, one of my father's ships will be sailing along the very coast near to Alauna during Saturnalia.'

Flavius shook his head at Marcellus. 'Stop playing games, Marcellus. That ship comes for you in the first week of December, and it will be nowhere near Alauna.'

'Flavius, listen, will you?' said Aelius.

Marcellus, like the good-natured man he was, merely smiled. 'Yes, that was the original plan, Flavius, but that was before a thief banged you on the head, and the emperor dealt you a worse blow. To be honest, it would give me great pleasure to share the journey back to Rome with you, and now it becomes possible.'

Flavius smiled back apologetically. 'Does it really?'

'Let me explain. I can delay the ship for a fortnight or so. It could put into Caerleon for a few days and take in black bear pelts and hides for leather. That might interest my father, who doesn't trade yet out here. The ship can then dock in Ravenglass for Saturnalia, and I can't see any of the crew objecting to that. I'll board it the day after Saturnalia and we'll sail up to Alauna, spend the night there and all leave on the early-morning tide for Rome. How does that sound?'

'He's going to a lot of trouble for you, Flavius,' said Aelius severely.

'I can't believe it,' Flavius murmured.

'Not many people get the chance to look after one of the emperor's special procurators,' said Marcellus. 'It would be a much easier journey for you. I know how much you respect your father, and he would certainly be expecting to meet you in Bordeaux if you travel in the customary way. He would inevitably be asking questions about things you would rather not talk about yet, especially while jogging through Gaul on a horse. On board ship you can be quiet if you choose, you can be alone if you choose. At the very least, you can rest and build up your strength. You can't write yet with that arm of yours, so I shall write to your father explaining what's happened to you, and to my own to suggest that he invites your parents to stay in our villa by Rome's harbour and watch for our ship to come in. Finally I shall write to the legate to assure him that, with a very light cargo and a straight run for home, I can deliver you to the steps of the forum at the hour in January required by the emperor and promised by yourself.'

He turned to Aelius. 'I hope you have a good supply of fresh ink to hand?'

XVIII

Flavius rode into Papcastle market-place half-an-hour after midnight on the first night of Saturnalia. He was still wearing the old unbelted tunic that had served as his servant's dress during the eighteen hours he had spent lugging food and wine round the fort. He had waited only to throw on his goatskin coat when Lugo, as presiding general, had given him leave to go.

The market-place, which was usually deserted at this hour, was full of people shouting and singing – mostly soldiers from the Papcastle fort, he suspected, showing the locals how to celebrate the festival. Saturnalian Rome it was not, but there was nevertheless a medley of bizarre costumes and hideous masks.

'Stand by the well,' Aelius had said, 'and look for a cart. We shall be in the house behind it.'

A row of stalls, most of them probably set up by the group which had travelled with Elphin, were still open, their lamps making a chain of light down the centre of the square.

For a moment it blurred his sight. In a panic, he couldn't see a cart anywhere, but then a circle of revellers, swinging in a wild dance to the sound of drums and raucous pipes, broke into a ragged line, and there, directly opposite him, was a cart.

His heart was still thumping when he led his horse across the square. Aelius wasn't the only man out with a cart that night. He knocked on the door. His heart was quiet only when Aelius opened the door and pulled him inside.

Elphin must have been waiting just beside him. She put her arms round Flavius. 'I thought you weren't coming!'

'My love, why?'

'Aelius said you would be coming after midnight. It's been so long since midnight! '

'No longer than on any other day. I did have to ride five miles.' How amazing, he thought, that anyone should wait so anxiously for him. 'I didn't even stop to change my clothes.'

Elphin whispered, 'Aelius expected you might not. He put some fresh ones in the cart.'

'What else did he bring?'

'Some wood for fuel, blankets, dishes, knives, wine, vegetables. He says we can find the rest for ourselves here. You must not be afraid to go out. It is not like Alauna, there your hair is like a beacon among all those dark Spanish heads, but here no-one will know who you are. Or that's what Aelius says.'

'Do you realise: he is trusting us to look after ourselves?'

Aelius, who had stepped out of the front of the house, returned.

'I've hitched up the cart,' he announced. 'I'll take your horse back with me. You won't want to spend time looking after it.' He paused solemnly. 'You understand, sir, that in four days, I shall be back about five in the morning. I'll let you know I'm here by a knock on the door. There'll be a second knock when it's time for you to leave. I will stay with you, my lady, until your group is ready to set off.'

Through a tiny window they watched Aelius ride off in his cart, Flavius's horse attached to it, trotting along behind..

'Is that the horse that probably saved your life?' Elphin asked.

'Yes, that's the one I was riding. I don't really know what happened.'

'Is your arm tender?'

Flavius put both arms round her and held her tightly. 'No. Before many minutes have passed, you will be able to admire my scars. I think when I get back to Rome I shall casually let my sleeve fall back, and they will think I got my scars leading my cohort in a battle that saved the empire.'

Elphin tried to laugh, but Flavius saw her eyes suddenly fill with tears.

'Elphin?'

'I can still just see your horse from the window. The next time I see it, you will be riding away on it and then I shall never see you again.'

The tears were now streaming down her cheeks and she was shaking with sobs.

The fire that Aelius must have lit earlier had burned low. Flavius pulled off his thick coat and wrapped it round her. He saw a bundle of logs, already cut, in a corner of the room.

'We'll make up the fire and drink some of Aelius's wine to get you warm.'

'I'm not shivering from the cold.'

Flavius collected an armful of logs and tossed them on to the fire. Then he put his arms round her and sat her on a chair. He knelt down beside her.

She laid her head against his chest. 'I don't understand,' she said through more tears, 'how that emperor of yours is able to do this to us. Why has he done it?'

'There is work to be done, and he thinks I can do it. It's possible he also thinks I would like to do it.'

'Couldn't anyone else do it?'

'I'm sure they could.'

'Then why did you tell him you would go?'

'I have no choice. I have sworn allegiance to him. In Rome, that gives the emperor the power to command obedience.'

'My father can't make our people do what he wants against their will, unless they have broken our laws, and you have broken none.'

'No, I haven't,' said Flavius, stroking her hair.

'I hate your emperor.'

'I hated him bitterly a few days ago, but that wasn't really fair. He didn't know what his actions were doing to us.'

Elphin lifted her head. 'You were going to stay here for me. Now you are not. Are you pleased to be going? You will see your wife again.'

Tears came into her eyes once more. 'Flavius, I shouldn't have said that, I didn't mean it. I don't know what I'm doing.'

'Nor did I when I left York. I dismissed my escort, my adjutant found me incomprehensible, I charged off on my own, and, because I couldn't think of anything but how to find you, I didn't see the men who attacked me. I could easily have got away from them if I'd been watching the road.'

Elphin gave a shaky smile. 'Roman women don't behave like me, do they? They are always dignified and controlled. They would never shed tears in public. They would keep their more thoughtless outbursts to themselves.'

Flavius said gently, 'I wouldn't know. I've never been loved by a Roman woman. Now I will get that dismal fire burning and some of Aelius's wine.'

When they had sipped the wine and Elphin was no longer shivering, he added, 'You know I must respect my promise to support my wife. If there are public functions or family gatherings to attend, I will escort her, but I shall not live with her under the same roof.'

Elphin nodded, not looking at him, still slightly ashamed of herself.

Flavius understood. He held her close to him. 'Elphin, I love you. I love you more than my family, who are dear to me, more than the practice of law, which was once my life, more than my beloved home by the lake in Stresa. I would give them all up to stay here with you. But we're not free, are we? We've lived in different ways, and I know it's hard for you to accept attitudes that are strange to you. It would be the same for me in your world.'

Elphin nodded again, this time glancing up at him.

Flavius smiled at her. 'But, Elphin,' he whispered, 'at least we managed to cheat my emperor and steal these four days for ourselves.'

'Yes, we did,' she whispered back. 'So we did.'

'Think, just think,' said Flavius, 'four whole days alone together. No-one here knows who we are, or cares what we do.

'We can live as we want. We can eat, we can sleep, we can make love whenever we choose ...'

Firelight glanced off the amethyst in Flavius's ring worn on Elphin's finger.

He laughed softly. 'And we can be like any other married couple in Papcastle behind closed doors. Shall I tell you what we are going to do tomorrow? We will go out, arm-in-arm, and find our way to the nearest farm to see what they can sell us to fill our pot, and on the way back we might wander round the market stalls to search for anything that might tempt us, or perhaps dance round the square to the music. Then we will come home to try to coax some warmth from the logs I clumsily cut before we set off.'

'Do you remember,' asked Elphin, 'when we slept by my fire in the fells?'

'I don't suppose there are any cushions here,' said Flavius.

Elphin clapped her hands. 'Yes, Aelius brought some from Alauna.'

'Ah,' said Flavius. 'One can't fault his memory.'

XIX

Snow fell during the night. It left a smooth, crisp white surface across the square. When Flavius peered out of the window, the stall-holders were brushing it from the tops of their closed booths. He could smell freshly baked bread.

Dressed in his thick coat, he found the baker's, and for the first time in his life had the experience of buying bread in a shop.

Later that morning, after Flavius had hacked at some logs, and Elphin, in her green furred coat, had filled buckets at the well in the square, they walked arm-in-arm, as he had suggested, across snowy fields to fill their basket at a farmhouse kitchen.

Around them, rising against a clear blue sky, they could see, glistening in pale winter sunshine, the tops of the fells they had explored near Caldbeck. They were stepping now across the ground they had seen then far below them.

They were enchanted with everything.

As they crossed the square, the music was already shrill and lively. Elphin had no wish to dance, but she hunted among the stalls to find a little woollen shawl for Aurelia. While she was engaged in a serious discussion on the price, Flavius made a purchase of his own, without any discussion.

Back in the house, they discovered to their satisfaction that the logs, though of oddly assorted sizes, were burning well enough. Elphin spread out her shawl on the table to admire it. 'Did you find something for Aurelia?' she asked.

'No, for you.'

'Oh!' Elphin held out her hands eagerly.

'It's nothing exciting,' said Flavius soberly. 'It's a pen.'

'I have pens.'

'I needed to be sure of that.'

'Why?'

'So that you would be ready to answer the letters I shall write to you.'

Elphin stared at him, and then, with a cry of delight, flung her arms round him. 'You will write to me? I didn't dream you would.'

'My silly love, what will be more important to me?'

Elphin's joy suddenly faded. 'But how can I write to you?'

'You wrote to me when you knew I was hurt.'

'That letter only had to go from Ravenglass to Alauna, and there was Marcellus to bring it to you.'

'Elphin, every day the empire is awash with couriers.'

'Yes, army couriers.'

'No, not only army couriers. My father and I have written regularly to each other. I had a lengthy correspondence with a factory in Gaul.

My wife sent orders to her dressmaker in Rome.'

'But you will have used your army couriers.'

'No, Elphin, that would have been the sort of misuse of army time I wouldn't allow anyone else to get away with, so I could hardly do so myself.' He grinned at her. 'But I did make use of the couriers attached to my family's wine business. We depend on a network of them.'

Elphin was not reassured. 'I shall never know where you are. How can I write to you?'

'It's very simple. My letters will be sent to our agent in York. I will instruct him to arrange for a courier to deliver them ... where? To your stables in Ravenglass?'

Elphin nodded.

'The courier will wait there to collect your reply. Then they go back to York, and from there to our depot in Rome. Wherever I am, they will know.'

'Will that really happen?'

'Yes, I promise.'

Elphin snatched up the pen and kissed it. 'It's the most wonderful present in the world, my darling, darling Flavius.'

Then they laughed together as they unpacked their basket and decided what they would eat first.

XX

The hours they shared together were like a hoard of exquisite and shining gold pieces that they treasured and spent with care, yet they seemed to slip through their fingers like water.

The last morning came too rapidly. Flavius leaned across the table where they were eating their fresh rolls and honey towards a subdued Elphin. 'I think we shall have another beautiful day here. Would you like to walk with me along the riverbank? I've always wanted to do that, and this will be my last chance.'

Elphin brightened, ready to do anything that would give Flavius pleasure. There were few enough hours of daylight in the northern December, but Flavius was right. Before long, a low sun was shining on the snow still lying across the fields.

They walked away from the town towards the nearby river.

The noises of Saturnalia gradually grew fainter. There were very few people close to the river. Elphin stopped for a moment to stare at the deep, smooth-flowing water, brown against the snow.

Flavius said quietly, 'Elphin, what are you thinking?'

She hesitated before she turned towards him. 'Flavius, if you can't stay here, why don't you ask me to come with you? I would come anywhere.'

Flavius took her face in his hands. 'No,' he said.

'Have you ever thought about it?' cried Elphin.

'Since I watched you sailing away from me that first time. I would give my soul to take you with me tomorrow. I have often dreamed of building a house for us in the foothills of the Alps.' He kissed her tenderly. 'But, my love, it isn't possible, is it?'

'Why not?'

'We talk about the obligations that govern me, and which seem so strange to you. I have come to understand that you, too, have obligations. They seem strange to me, but I can't ignore them.'

'No, Flavius ...'

'Your father has brought you up to be able to care for your island as he thinks best for it. If he were a Roman with no sons to follow him, he would look to a cousin or adopt a boy. You live in a world where women are allowed to rule. You have been taught to be brave and strong and clever.'

'I don't care! I'll learn to live like a Roman woman, docile and quiet inside the house.'

'I've been surrounded by Roman women all my life. Not one of them has made the world sing for me. I want my Elphin, as you are.'

He held her arm and urged her to go on walking. 'Think for a moment what would happen if I took you to Rome now. I don't know where I shall be sent, or where I might have to go when I finish this task for the emperor. You might be left alone for long stretches of time. You would find no friends among the other women. Do you know what they would say about you? That you were some barbarian slave I had bought in *an* outlandish place, and that I had brought you home with me to get my money's worth out of you.'

Elphin flinched. 'I wouldn't care.'

'But I would, Elphin.'

They walked on in silence until Flavius stooped to pick up a stone and skim it across the river.

'Elphin,' he said, 'that's an Irish name, isn't it?'

'Yes, my mother's.' She looked at him curiously.

'Is it common in Ireland?'

'No. Why are you asking?'

'Aelius will be relieved.'

'Aelius will?'

'Oh, yes.' Flavius skimmed another stone, and then laughed. 'It seems that when I was only half-conscious, I kept repeating a word that no-one could understand – it was in no language that anyone could recognise. They asked Aelius. He asked how he was expected to know, when all the time he knew exactly what I was trying to say.

'My poor, distraught young adjutant was telling them that I'd talked about the need to get to Ravenglass. My senior centurion has a notion that Marcellus and I are nervous of a joint sea invasion. He has come to that conclusion, Elphin, because he has seen me so often standing on the bluff, trying to catch a glimpse of your island! He wasn't disposed to send one of his own men on what might have been a wild goose chase of the adjutant's making, so Aelius offered to go himself. That's how he came to find you for me. And did you realise that, although Aelius loves trotting about with his cart, he takes no pleasure in using a horse? He rode all the way to Ravenglass and back in misery.'

'Oh!' cried Elphin, wondering what he was going to say next.

Flavius half-smiled. 'Yes, Elphin, and after all that – after Aelius willingly made that nightmare journey, after I cheated the legate, defied the emperor, caused trouble for my undeserving adjutant, got a bang on the head – all so that we could have these four days together, do you remember the first thing you said to me when I arrived?' Elphin looked at him uncertainly.

'My love, I was a few minutes later than you thought I would be. Didn't you say you thought I wasn't coming?'

Elphin nodded slowly. She laid her head against his chest. 'I feared I would never see you again. Every extra minute without you only made me more frightened.'

Flavius held her tight. 'And a few moments ago, when I told you I didn't want you to come to Rome, were you wondering perhaps if I was telling you that I would never see you again because I thought that was best?'

Flavius felt her trembling. 'You made it sound as though it would be impossible for us ever to be together again.'

'Impossible for us now, yes. This has happened so suddenly, but I don't believe, and I won't believe, that we won't find a way back to each other.' He bent his head to kiss her hair. 'Elphin, why did I buy you a pen? Tell me.'

'So that I could answer the letters you write to me,' she murmured.

'Would I have wasted money on a pen if I'd intended to forget about you once I left Alauna?'

Elphin stirred in his arms. 'I never know what you will say next,' she said, beginning to smile. 'I shouldn't have spoken about Rome. Flavius, forgive me.'

'How can I? What is there to forgive? You offered to come with me anywhere I pleased. My dear love, aren't they words I shall always treasure? I think it is you who should forgive me. I was selfish. I don't know what is going to happen to me in the next few months. I need to be sure that you are safe, doing the things you love, surrounded by people who care for you. I think I love you more than you love yourself.'

Elphin shook her head gently. 'I have nothing to forgive either, have I?'

With her hand in his, they walked on.

Ahead of them, rocky ground soared from the centre of the river. Water flowed on either side.

'Look,' said Flavius, 'that's what I wanted to see. That's what I wanted you to see; two rivers coming from different directions, shallow, bubbling rivers, that meet under the rock –'

' – to become one that is broad, tranquil and deep. Yes, it is a beautiful place.' said Elphin. They gazed at each other.

'Is this a place where you might find your Manannàn?' asked Flavius.

'I think he will come wherever he is needed.' Elphin looked at the snow, the pale, clear sky, the water. 'But I am sure he would rejoice in this place.'

Flavius pulled out a pouch from under his coat. 'Hold out your hands, Elphin.' He tipped a number of large gold coins into her outstretched palms.

'Gold?' she said, staring at it.

'Isn't that what you offer Manannàn when you have need of him?' Elphin nodded.

'I know you offer him beautiful objects that you make for him in your own workshops, but this is all I have. They are foreign coins, marked with the images of alien gods. Will he accept them?'

'If it is a gift offered with feeling, I think he would.' She was staring at him with wonder.

'I don't know if I believe in your Manannàn. I don't know if I believe in any god, but if they do exist, Manannàn is the one I would choose to hear my prayers.'

He took the coins back and gathered them in one hand. 'Manannàn,' he said softly, 'keep her safe until you guide me back to her.' He threw out his arm as if he were skimming another stone into the heart of the river. The coins flew from his fingers in a shimmering arc that broke into a shower of spinning golden light before they touched the water and sank from sight.

Elphin gave a gasp of delight and fell on her knees.

XXI

That evening snow fell again, not a heavy fall but soft, light, feathery flakes that drifted on the air. It was no hindrance to the wildness of the revelry that marked the last hours of Saturnalia.

Elphin looked sadly at the bright, pretty stalls that would soon be gone. She wanted to take one last walk in the square that had been part of their life together for the past few days.

Flavius took her arm and they wandered among the clusters of people in their tawdry finery, dancing to pipers in one place, drums in another.

Elphin glanced at the well, the baker's shop and the stalls which they had used, as if thanking them. 'Perhaps,' she said, clasping the hand on her arm, 'we shall never be able to live together again like this.'

Flavius saw she was trying to blink away the tears in her eyes. 'That is possible,' he said gravely, 'but not probable. And, whatever happens, we will both remember this square, and the snow on the fields ...'

'... and our two rivers that became one.' She managed to smile, the tears lost.

'Yes, the rivers.' He smiled back at her. 'What a pity we can't roll all those things up for you to keep – the way in Alauna they say Manannàn does with your island when they can't see it.'

Then his eye caught sight of a necklace of amber beads hanging from a nail on one of the stalls. He laughed softly with pleasure at his find. 'Yet I think there is something you could take away with you from Papcastle. Elphin, I want you to stand here. Don't move.'

He was back in a few minutes. People were swirling round Elphin, shouting at her to join in their fun. He pushed them aside and grabbed her wrist. She was half-alarmed, half-amused. 'They are very drunk. Time is running out.'

Flavius put an arm round her. 'Not quite yet for us. Close your eyes.' He slipped the amber necklace over her head and let it fall down the front of her coat. 'Now you can look.'

She opened her eyes and saw the long strand of polished stones linked by thin bars of silver. She caught her breath. Then she flung her arms round his neck and kissed him. Flavius seized her passionately.

Nobody stared at them. Nobody cared. It was Saturnalia and it was fast slipping away.

Flavius lifted his head. 'I think,' he said breathlessly, 'if we looked at our fire through your amber beads, they would be the very colour of your hair.'

'Then shall we go home?' asked Elphin. 'I would like that.'

As they entered their house together for the last time, they both behaved as if time were of no concern to them. Flavius built up the fire, Elphin lit the lamps and then sat with the necklace in her hands, moving the stones to catch the firelight and then the lamplight.

Flavius turned to look at her. He smiled. 'It had to be yours.'

Elphin held it to her cheek and rocked gently back and fro. 'I love it.'

'Perhaps the silver came from Caldbeck, from your own mine.'

The thought pleased her. 'I suppose it could well have done.'

Flavius sat beside her. 'What do you think would have happened if, that first time I saw you, the wind hadn't blown the green scarf from your hair?'

'But it did blow off,' said Elphin. 'Manannàn raised a sudden gust of wind from the sea, and away it went. After that, I had no choice.'

'Just as I had no choice when the legate in York blew me from Alauna to Ravenglass?'

Elphin pouted, shrugged her shoulders and they smiled at each other. 'So there was no escape for me from finding myself in an extraordinary little place called Papcastle, buying amber beads on a dark winter's night in the snow?'

'How could there be?'

Flavius lifted up one of the amber beads, kissed it and laid the necklace against her hair 'Now I swear it's invisible.'

He settled it carefully round her neck.

Elphin saw a sudden look of despair cross Flavius's face as he took his hands away. She said with great tenderness, 'Dearest love, would it have been better for you if ...'

She fell silent as he took one of her hands between his. He stared into the fire. 'Elphin,' he said, 'I once talked to a man who had just lost someone who was very dear to him. He was almost ashamed of the way his grief had enfeebled him and needed to hide it.'

'Was he a soldier? A Roman soldier?' murmured Elphin.

Flavius half-smiled at her. 'Yes, a great soldier, half-Roman, half-Spanish. Yet one night, very late, when he was very, very drunk and we were alone, he started to talk about it. He wanted someone to listen, and I happened to be there. I remember telling him that, despite the cost he was paying, I envied him an experience that I had sought all my life. And he said to me: never search for it; if it is for you, it will find you.

'He was disgustingly drunk. I was intimidated by his high rank ... didn't like him very much, in fact. I doubt if he recalled anything that passed between us by the next morning, or if he did he would certainly have preferred to forget it – yet those were the truest words anyone ever said to me.

'He was right, wasn't he? One day, sitting in an empty courtyard, sick with myself, a beautiful woman with hair the loveliest colour

I had ever seen came walking towards me, and, quick as a flash of lightning, I had no choice at all.'

Flavius threw some more logs on the fire. 'Were you going to ask me if I ever wished I had ignored that lady and all the enchantment she brought into my life?'

Elphin watched him adjusting logs with his boot. 'You've made a beautiful fire.'

'Yes, I thought so.'

She rose from her chair. 'No more words now?'

Flavius held out his arms to her. 'No.'

They neither of them slept. Elphin said, as she had said once before, that time was too precious for sleeping.

The noise in the square grew more frantic for a while, and then gradually more ragged and distant. The lights began to go out.

They heard the trumpet sound across a now-silent square, announcing the end of Saturnalia. Elphin gave a little whimpering cry and clung more closely to Flavius.

'Shh,' he whispered. 'It's not the end for us, not yet.'

A little later she said, 'Marcellus will have set sail by now for Alauna. Flavius, couldn't I stay to watch you on the parade ground, and then see your ship sail? I wouldn't speak to you, just be near you for a little while longer.'

'No,' he said. 'How would Marcellus and I feel to leave you alone on the harbour at Alauna? You will travel with the Ravenglass group as we arranged.'

'You're treating me like a Roman woman!'

'Yes, my darling, where your safety is concerned, of course I am. I would love to see you there if it were possible, but it isn't.'

Elphin gave a long sigh. 'It seems as if I have to learn to do what you say.'

It sounded to Flavius as if this was not something that displeased her. He cradled her head against his shoulder.

'It doesn't seem to have occurred to us that I might not find favour with the emperor. He might not want to keep me in his service.'

'Yes, but then you would be back in Stresa, and under your father's instructions. I have learned that about Roman families,' said Elphin unhappily.

'True, but my father isn't like my grandfather, obsessed with seeing me in the Senate. He would prefer me to work with him. I think if, for example, I offered to set up an agency in Caerleon to supply wine to the Second Legion there, he would encourage it. Then you could open a small warehouse on that vast quay there and sell your father's hides to the army. We could spend the winter in Caerleon and the summer on your island. I will build you a house on Manannàn instead of in the foothills of the Alps. Aren't there one or two houses there that look like little hillocks with holes in them?'

Elphin laughed. 'On the west coast, where the wind can be fierce, there are one or two houses with roofs of thick turf which come well down over the walls. They rest on poles, so that there is a dry walkway all round the house.'

'Would you like one of those for yourself?'

'No,' said Elphin, 'because none of this is going to happen. You won't lose favour with the emperor. Marcellus tells me your appointment is a very important one and the emperor would have chosen carefully. You were teasing me.'

'No, not teasing you, my love, dreaming for both of us. You can't quite believe we would ever be allowed to find a life together, but I wanted you to see that it would be possible. Trust me, and you know now that when I ask you to trust me ...'

Elphin nodded, '... then I can.' She could no longer manage to stop the tears from flowing. 'But how can I live through these next few days, weeks, months, never being able to see you, never knowing when I shall see you? I need to be with you, to hear your voice, to feel your warmth against me. How can I even drag myself through the next few hours? Flavius, it might be years. I don't know how to bear it.'

He held her close. 'Does it help to know that I shall feel the same? We are one river now.'

She was sobbing so wildly that she seemed hardly able to breathe or to hear what he was saying. Then the fit passed almost as quickly as it had come.

'Please, don't let me go, Flavius.'

'Why should I want to do that?'

'I disgraced you.'

'You made me feel very humble.'

'Why?'

'Because you love me so much. I don't deserve it.'

'If you didn't, I wouldn't. How much time have we left?'

'About two hours.'

'Yes,' said Elphin.

The two hours passed as quickly as all their other hours had passed in Papcastle.

Then they were ready, waiting for the unwelcome sound of a cart.

They sat on either side of their small table, which Elphin had laid with bowls of food that neither of them wanted to eat. Their fingers were linked across the top of it and they were gazing at each other.

Their time had nearly run out. Flavius said, 'Elphin, when we hear the second knock, I shall go at once and ride straight off. You mustn't think I want to do that but I promised Aelius, who is leaving us together for as long as he can before I need to be seen in Alauna. Believe me, with every step I shall be aching to turn back for one last minute with you, one last farewell kiss. Remember that, Elphin.'

She nodded. Their fingers tightened.

It was cold in the house. They both felt it, although they were dressed in thick clothes for their different journeys.

Flavius looked at the almost-dead embers of the fire. 'There will be one somewhat disastrous end to Saturnalia in this house,' he observed.

'This morning's stale bread?' suggested Elphin.

'Worse. I cut too many logs. When Aelius arrives, he will be able to see how badly I did the job. He won't complain to you, but you will have to bear with his pained expression. Aelius is good at pained expressions. As for me, I shall hear about those logs at our next falling out, and the next one, and probably the one after that.'

'Surely what counts,' said Elphin, 'is not the shape of log but the way it burns?' She *smiled* at him and added softly, 'And ours couldn't have burned more beautifully.'

'Will you tell him that?'

'I don't think so.'

They heard then the wheels of a cart crossing the deserted square. Flavius felt Elphin flinch and saw her close her eyes.

The wheels stopped outside the house. They waited for the first knock.

Flavius stood and walked round the table to Elphin. He lifted her to her feet and they slipped their arms round each other. He kissed her passionately, as he had kissed her in the square the night before. Then they heard the second knock.

'Yes,' Flavius called out.

He kissed her again, gently, on her hair, her cheeks, her mouth. Then he let her go, and walked to the door to unlock it.

Aelius stood outside, holding his horse.

Flavius gave Elphin one last look from the doorway, then stepped outside, mounted and rode off towards Alauna.

Elphin ran out of the house.

'Come inside, my lady,' said Aelius.

XXII

It was noticed that, very shortly after the first morning trumpet had sounded, the commandant, in full ceremonial dress, emerged from his villa.

No-one had remarked on the horseman who had ridden out of the darkness into the poorly-lit settlement, tied his horse to a post, and joined the group of tradesmen waiting to get into the fort which had been barred to them during the Saturnalia. Given the cold weather, they were nearly all, like Flavius, fastened into their black goat-skin coats. Once the gates opened, he allowed himself to be pushed with the others into the fort. With his hood pulled over his hair, he slipped down the lane beside the villa and let himself in by the kitchen door. The house was almost empty. Only Alis, the young girl who helped her with the baby and his head groom remained. The rest of the household were on their way to York, together with the last of the ox-wagons carrying his property. Only the basic furniture supplied by the army remained.

He despatched the groom to fetch his horse, and started to change into the military dress that Aelius had carefully laid out on his temporary bed. The groom returned to assist him, he produced – as instructed by Aelius, he explained – the emperor's gold sword. Flavius slipped it under his cloak and departed for the headquarters building.

His early arrival created a flurry of activity.

The chief clerk hurriedly assembled the material that had accumulated during the holiday. As he laid it on Flavius's desk, he saw the ceremonial sword that had been left there.

'Sir, you'll be wearing your gold sword for the parade? I'm so glad.'

Flavius, who was thinking with despair of Elphin in the cold little house in Papcastle as his hands sorted through the documents, said, 'Yes. Fetch me a filing tray, if you would.

'I have signed some of these items,' he explained when the chief clerk hurried back. 'The others I have initialled to show they were promptly handled by your office, but a decision will have to be made by the new commandant.' He placed the second of the piles in the tray.

It was announced that the senior centurion was waiting to see him. Flavius sighed. 'Yes,' he said.

Lugo was wearing his gold disc, and he also glanced with pleasure at the gold sword lying on the desk.

'Nearly a year ago, sir,' he said. 'An unforgettable memory.'

'Indeed, so,' said Flavius. A year ago he hadn't even met Elphin. 'A problem, but we managed it well.'

'You managed it well, sir.'

'Only with remarkable support.' Flavius pointed to the scroll in Lugo's hand. 'Is that for me?'

'Yes, sir, the Saturnalia court-martial charges.'

'I shall not, of course, preside over the court-martial. That will be for the new commandant. He must impose his own judgements. I am nevertheless interested to read your comments. I shall indicate on the charge sheet that, despite unusual circumstances, the list was ready for me this morning. I applaud, senior centurion, your impeccable regard for army regulations.' The remark, which he would once have made flippantly, Flavius now made with grave respect.

The senior centurion carefully laid his charge sheet in front of Flavius. He hesitated and then said in a gruff voice, 'I shall miss you, sir.' Then, with one of his rare displays of emotion, he added, 'I have to admit that when you first came, I never thought I would say that.'

Flavius smiled to himself at this echo of his own change of heart.

'I have learned things from you, sir, for which I am grateful. I realise now that the army way of solving a problem is not always the only one, or even the wisest one. I understand that some rules must never be broken and others can be stretched a little, to reach a more reasonable conclusion. The skill is to know which is which.'

'I think you are getting a good idea of that, senior centurion. I often wondered why certain illegal gambling games on a Thursday evening never attracted any notice.'

Lugo gave one of his grunts, but this time to hide a smile.

'You've taught me a thing or two as well,' said Flavius. 'I used to think living a life of army discipline must be something like living in a prison, but now I know that for some men it means security and purpose, and to be able to work as one in a team is something I had never valued sufficiently until I came here.'

Flavius could see that Lugo was moved and not quite sure how to deal with it. 'Well,' Flavius continued lightly, 'we must hope this wind doesn't bring too much snow with it for the parade.'

Lugo said, 'Sir, will you allow me the honour of fastening your sword belt for you? Your arm is perhaps still troubling you.'

'No. Why do you say that?'

The senior centurion was slightly embarrassed. 'Your face seems a little strained, sir. I thought it must be from pain, and that you might need help with the buckle.'

Flavius smiled at him. 'Preparing to travel a thousand miles is always wearing.' He picked up the sword. 'My arm is well enough, but it would be a pleasure to me if you would fasten it for me.'

As Lugo stepped back to admire his work, Flavius, in his own state of desolation, was reminded of the emptiness of the man's life.

'Senior centurion,' he said, 'I believe you served for many years in north Gaul, south of the Rhine near Bonn?'

Lugo looked startled. 'Yes, sir.'

'That is where your sons are?'

'Yes, on a farm with my wife's parents.'

'Do they ever write to you?'

'They can't read or write. Their grandparents can't, so there is no point in my ever writing.'

'You have no idea what is happening to them?'

'How can I, sir? Had my wife lived longer, it would have been different. I would have had them taught Latin, in case they wanted to be recruited into a legion. That, to be honest, is what I hoped for, sir. Now, they'll be content to be farmers, I've no doubt.'

'Senior centurion, my family owns large vineyards along the south bank of the Rhine. They serve the legion in Bonn. In the larger holdings, my father sets up schools for the children of his workers.' Flavius half-smiled. 'They often make good clerks for our agencies. If you write the name of your father-in-law on this wax tablet here, together with the name of the village nearest his farm, I think one of our agents could find him. If you give me a letter before I leave in the morning, I will see that it gets to Bonn, and from there to your sons. Someone will be sent who can translate for them, and then take down whatever they want to say to you in reply, and then we will get the letter back here. It's just possible it will prove feasible to take them into one of our schools. Then they may grow into wine-maker's agents instead of legionary recruits, eh? But, *at t*he least, we can set up a link between you.'

The senior centurion's mouth had fallen open. He looked for a moment as if he was about to fall on his knees and kiss Flavius's hands as though he were the emperor. Flavius retreated behind the desk.

When he had recovered himself, Lugo asked shakily, 'How can I ever thank you, sir?'

'Easily,' said Flavius. 'Get some kind of Latin school going here. You don't have to do any instruction yourself. Encourage the centurions' wives. Noricus's new wife will know interested people in the settlement, and all the children. This scheme succeeds in other forts. Your first commandant here, the Agrippa whom you admire so much, believed it to be our first duty in the places we occupy.'

Flavius felt suddenly exhausted. He held out his hand.

'Bargain, senior centurion?'

Lugo also looked exhausted. He grasped Flavius's hand. 'Bargain, sir.'

Flavius pointed to the wax tablet and a stylus, and watched the senior centurion inscribe the two names. He handed the tablet to Flavius with a kind of nervous look, as if the commandant might laugh and say it was only a tail-end-of-Saturnalia joke.

But Flavius read the names and repeated them carefully.

He said, 'You see how easy everything is when we have a network of people who can read and write. My father believes that if we have a gift such as this, we ought to share it with as many others as possible.'

'Yes, sir. We'll do it in Alauna. Rest assured.' The senior centurion made his way to the door. With the latch in his hand, he paused as if searching for suitable words. Then, in a rush, he said, 'Thank you, sir,' and rapidly closed the door behind him.

Flavius searched for a scrap of lime-bark and copied the names from the wax tablet in pen and ink. Then he folded the lime-bark and slipped it into the wrist-purse which still carried Elphin's stone. He looked at the stone, and as he put aside the pen saw in his mind's eye another pen, lying in Elphin's hand.

He had a sudden wild impulse to run out of the building, gallop down the coast road and stop her caravan as it trundled towards Ravenglass.

He was brought to his senses by sounds outside his room. They were removing the cohort's standards from the shrine to parade before him. He made his way back to the villa to collect the helmet he so seldom wore.

Aelius had arrived back from Papcastle and was in the atrium, nailing closed the lid on a large wooden crate. Another one, already sealed, stood beside him. A third, still empty, was waiting in a corner.

Aelius straightened his back and looked at Flavius. 'I see you're wearing the emperor's sword.'

'Those were your orders, weren't they?'

Flavius waited for Aelius to tell him about Elphin, but he said nothing. He went on staring at Flavius.

'Aelius, what about Elphin?'

'Yes, she'll be on her way home now. I cleaned the house after that and returned the keys to the owner.'

'Aelius,' said Flavius desperately, 'how was Elphin when she left?'

Aelius gave him a look that was almost hostile. He said harshly, 'You don't Flavius, need me to tell you that, do you?'

Flavius felt the urge to gallop after her again. The anguish on his face moved Aelius slightly. 'Couldn't you have done anything else for her?'

'What? What, Aelius?'

'Taken her home with you. Divorced Lucilla.'

'Do you really think I haven't considered that?'

'There are times when I don't know how your Roman mind works.'

'You don't understand,' said Flavius, helplessly, 'how it has to work.' He sat down on the crate as if he hadn't the strength to stand any more. 'I thought you might have done by now.'

Aelius could never sustain a quarrel with Flavius for long, especially when he was in anything like the state he now was.

'You're right, of course, Flavius. I speak too soon and without thinking. I am too emotional. I am a Greek. Elphin was in distress. Naturally she was in distress. The more she loves you, the more distress she feels. I should have prepared myself for that, and not allowed myself to be so overcome. But she is a lady for whom I have a great liking and respect. As has Alis.

'She was delighted with the shawl Elphin chose for the baby. I had more tears there, I can tell you.'

'We were together when she bought it,' said Flavius, grateful to be at ease again with Aelius.

The steward drove home another nail, and then lifted his head. 'That clattering means they're coming for you,' he said.

'My helmet?' said Flavius.

'On the stairs,' said Aelius. 'Your chest went three days ago. That's why you had to wear the sword. I had to put it somewhere.' As he went to fetch the helmet, he was glad to see he had made Flavius smile. He settled the helmet on Flavius's head and shook out his cloak as he stood up. 'There's a good wind. Don't hold the cloak. Let it fly out. Let them see the sword. Let a northern Italian leave a good impression on all these Spaniards.'

'Aelius!' muttered Flavius.

Quintus and a large escort led Flavius to the tribune on the parade ground. Quite a number of people from the settlement stood round the edges to watch, despite the cold wind. The standards were carried round the ground, the men performed complicated marching procedures, each group, led by its centurion, saluting Flavius in turn. The senior centurion made a speech, Flavius replied, though it was doubtful if either of them was heard against the noise of the wind. It ended with controlled military cheers for the retiring commandant.

Flavius's walk from the parade ground to the villa was a kind of triumphal progress, with men crowding round to thank him and wish him well. Lupus smiled at him and sadly shrugged his shoulders. The baker's son stepped into the middle of the street and gave one of his beaming salutes. The warden from the post-house appeared to say how much he regretted this departure, but was sure that Flavius would serve the emperor with distinction.

'How much do you think he said about me to Hadrian?' said Flavius afterwards, relating all this to Aelius.

'You thought he was criticising you. Perhaps instead he was rather lavish in his praise for you. Unfortunately, as it turned out.'

Flavius looked round the atrium. The two sealed boxes had gone.

'What's happened to the crates?'

'The ship has been sighted. The crates have gone down to the harbour to be loaded when it docks.'

'Why didn't they go off to York with the rest of the stuff?'

'Because I didn't want to let them out of my sight. The larger one holds our most valuable texts, the smaller the green and white dinner service. Two – I beg your pardon – three smashed plates are enough.'

'Do I really want to keep it? Why not leave it behind?'

'What, for the Hardknott man? Flavius!'

He had a sudden idea that pleased him greatly. 'I know, I'll give it to you and Alis as a present on Aurelia's birth.'

' No, Flavius—'

'Please, Aelius. I know that would please Elphin.'

Aelius hesitated. And then he said, 'Well, if that's what you really want, then all the more reason for me to keep an eye on it. We'll have to ask Alis first, though.'

Flavius took off his helmet, his cloak and his sword. Aelius helped him remove the rest of his military dress. He packed them in the empty crate.

'I am now no longer the commandant of Alauna,' said Flavius. 'I have one more thing to do before I leave.'

Later, when it was dark, in civilian dress he walked to the hospital where he knew he would find Quintus with the doctor, playing an intricate board game. He carried a bundle of Greek texts which he hoped the doctor would be happy to add to his meagre library.

They both rose to their feet when Flavius arrived. He shook his head. 'I'm no longer your commandant. I'd like you to regard me as a friend, if you would.' They sat down and the doctor produced wine. He accepted the texts with pleasure, and then insisted on taking a last look at Flavius's arm.

'All is well,' he said, 'but you do look as if a sea voyage might do you good. They are saying in the fort that most commandants look happy to be going home, but you do not.'

'The sudden order to move was a shock, I suppose,' said Flavius, 'and the after-effects of the attack were tiring.'

'Of course,' said the doctor, who knew when he was hearing polite excuses, and was wise enough not to probe further.

Flavius smiled at him gratefully. 'I owe both of you so much for your help and your good humour in this rather solemn place.'

'All I have done,' said Quintus, 'is bring you trouble. I caused problems for you with the emperor, I upset your wife, I don't know how to deal with the senior centurion and it's because I wasn't there that you were injured!'

'Quintus, I've wanted to say something to you for a long time, but as an army officer it wasn't appropriate. Now that's no longer the case. Quintus, I think you would be much happier outside the army. You have qualities that are wasted here, that you don't appreciate in yourself and that your family certainly overlook. Think about a governor's palace rather than a legionary camp.'

Quintus went pink in the face. He looked from Flavius to the doctor.

'How wise Flavius is,' agreed the doctor. 'With the right diplomatic experience, you could one day be an ambassador or a governor.'

'Think about it, Quintus. If you are interested, let me know. For a few months, at least, I shall probably have contact with the emperor. He could be persuaded to deal with your father.'

Flavius stood up and made his farewells. 'Meeting you both has been one of the pleasures of my stay in Alauna.'

Quintus finally found his voice. 'I shall miss you, sir. And I will think about what you say.'

As he walked back to the villa, Flavius found the wind growing stronger and snow in the air. He had finished everything he wanted to do in a Roman fort.

With the prospect of worse weather on the way, Aelius had taken Alis and the baby and her nursemaid down to the ship to settle them there for the night. The groom had followed with the horse. Flavius waited for Aelius to return and then got ready to face a sleepless night on an army bed.

XXIII

The next morning they walked round the villa, lamps in hand, checking that all was in order and nothing of theirs forgotten.

While Aelius was packing the last crate, Flavius went to take his final look at the heron in the emperor's dining-room.

He lifted his lamp to look at the mural. By the flickering light, the heron's black beady eye regarded him dolefully.

'I am glad,' it seemed to say, 'that you remember how once I was your friend, but I am about to become another's friend, so it is time for you to go. I will not remember you.'

Flavius played the lamp over the white flowers, the leaves, the smaller birds, the heron's feathered body. The black eye was impassive. He walked away and closed the door behind him.

Aelius was waiting in the empty atrium, waiting for him to perform the last act before they left.

Flavius knelt down before the alcove which held the shrine for the two household gods of home and the larder, the Lares and Penates. He extinguished the lamp that had burned before them since his household had entered the villa. He handed the small bronze figures to Aelius, who wrapped them carefully and placed them in the last crate. He fastened the lid and opened the door. Two of Marcellus's men from the ship came in to rope the crate and carry it away.

'Ready?' said Aelius.

Flavius nodded.

Aelius picked up a lamp and stepped into the street. Flavius pulled the heavy door shut behind him.

They walked through the north gate, where the guards gave Flavius a final acknowledgement, then through the settlement towards the harbour.

Snow lay thick around them and more was falling fast, driven by so fierce a wind from the north that the flakes were flying level with the ground. The lights of the harbour reached out to them across the darkness.

Marcellus's vessel was moored behind a fleet of grain ships. Their last crate was being loaded. They climbed aboard and the gangplank was drawn up after them.

As soon as first daylight appeared, the ship began to move away from the wharf. Flavius stayed on deck as they approached the bluff. The prow passed the high point where he had so often stood looking for Elphin's island. Two figures were standing there in the pale light, military cloaks flapping in the wind. Two arms sprang up in salute. It was Lugo and Quintus, for once acting in harmony.

Flavius raised an arm in response.

With the strong wind filling their sails, they sped south along the coast. By the time the ship had reached the great projecting red headland, the snow had disappeared. Flavius moved to the other side of the deck to catch whatever glimpse he could of the Island of Manannàn.

Marcellus came to join him. 'I think you should come back to look at Ravenglass.'

'No. I want to watch the island for as long as I possibly can. Elphin is there somewhere. I may never see it again.'

'But she isn't there,' said Marcellus.

'How do you know that?' Flavius wanted to be alone.

'Because,' said Marcellus, 'I have just seen her.' He took Flavius by the arm. 'Come with me quickly.'

They were approaching the long beach where the horses had raced. Marcellus pointed. 'I don't know any other woman who keeps a grey wolfhound and rides a chestnut,' he murmured over his shoulder as he walked away.

She was standing there, a bright green scarf tied round her head. As the ship came closer, she pulled it off and held it up to catch the wind.

He waved both arms frantically. He doubted if she could pick him out, and shouted her name.

Aelius suddenly appeared, pulling off his own long yellow woollen scarf. He thrust it into Flavius's hands. 'She can't hear you, can she? Wave this. She must see it.' He hurried off.

The scarf was heavy, but the wind powerful enough to lift it above Flavius's head where it streamed out like a pennant.

She seemed then to see him, or at least to know it was him. She danced up and down on the sand then bent down to scoop up stones in her hand.

Flavius went on waving the scarf until the ship turned to follow the coastline, and the beach began to slip away from his sight. He saw her hide her face against the horse's mane.

Aelius left him alone for a while and then came back to take the scarf from his hands.

Flavius felt he was drowning in despair, but at the same time the sight of her had given him deep joy.

Aelius told him, 'Even emperors don't live for ever.'

Six years after Flavius left Alauna, the emperor Hadrian died in Rome.

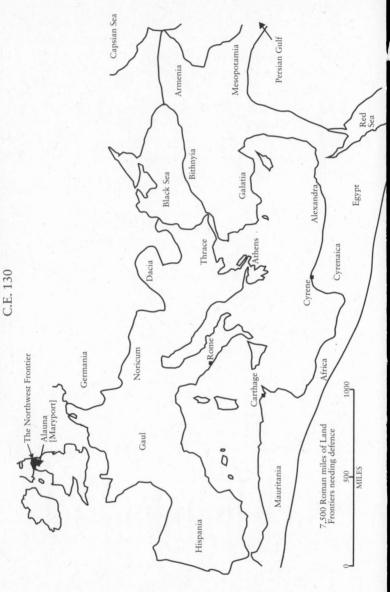

The Roman Empire
[c. 140 C.E] to show Alauna's Position on N.W Frontier
C.E. 130

The Northwest Frontier
Alauna
[Maryport]

Germania

Gaul

Noricum

Hispania

Mauritania

Dacia

Rome

Carthage

Africa

Thrace

Athens

Black Sea

Bithnyia

Galatia

Cyrene

Cyrenaica

Alexandra

Egypt

Armenia

Mesopotamia

Capsian Sea

Persian Gulf

Red Sea

7,500 Roman miles of Land
Frontiers needing defence

0   500   1000
MILES

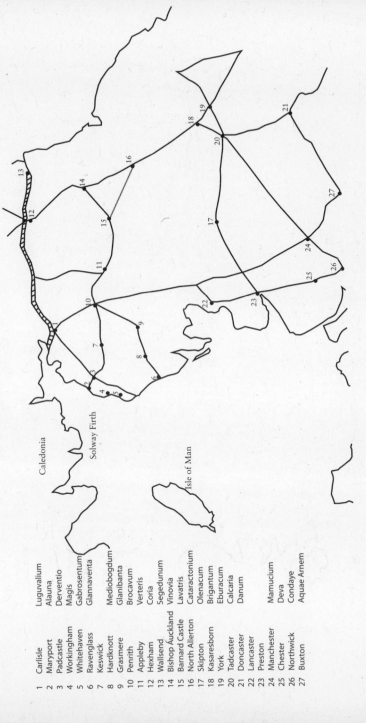

Military Roads and Garrison Towns

1	Carlisle		Luguvalium
2	Maryport		Alauna
3	Padcastle		Derventio
4	Workingham		Magis
5	Whitehaven		Gabrosentum
6	Ravenglass		Glannaventa
7	Keswick		
8	Hardknott		Mediobogdum
9	Grasmere		Glanibanta
10	Penrith		Brocavum
11	Appleby		Verteris
12	Hexham		Coria
13	Wallsend		Segedunum
14	Bishop Auckland		Vinovia
15	Barnard Castle		Lavatris
16	North Allerton		Cataractonium
17	Skipton		Olenacum
18	Kasaresborn		Brigantum
19	York		Eburacum
20	Tadcaster		Calcaria
21	Doncaster		Danum
22	Lancaster		
23	Preston		
24	Manchester		Mamucium
25	Chester		Deva
26	Northwick		Condaye
27	Buxton		Aquae Arnem

Caledonia

Solway Firth

Isle of Man

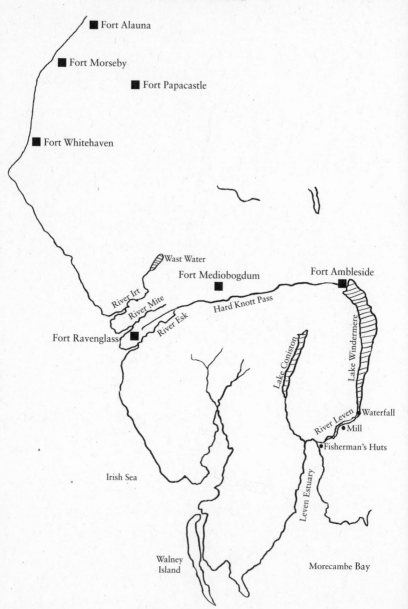

Rome's North-West Frontier c.130 C.E.
Southern Cumbria

Fort Alauna

Fort Morseby

Fort Papacastle

Fort Whitehaven

Wast Water

Fort Mediobogdum

Fort Ambleside

River Irt

River Mite

Hard Knott Pass

River Esk

Fort Ravenglass

Lake Coniston

Lake Windermere

River Leven

Waterfall

Mill

Fisherman's Huts

Irish Sea

Leven Estuary

Walney Island

Morecambe Bay

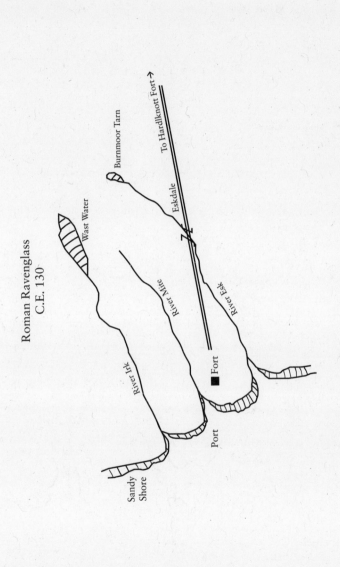

Roman Ravenglass
C.E. 130

Wast Water

Burnmoor Tarn

To Hardknott Fort →

Eskdale

River Irk

River Mite

River Esk

Fort

Port

Sandy
Shore